RAVE REVIEWS FOR

FRANCIS RAY

NOBODY BUT YOU

"A story that tugs at the heartstrings."

—*Romantic Times BOOKreviews*

"Fast and fun and full of emotional thrills and sexy chills. Everything a racing romance should be!"

—Roxanne St. Claire

"Not only does Francis Ray rock in this book but you also see a whole different side of racing that will keep you on the edge of your seat." —*Night Owl Romance*

"A wonderful read." —*Fresh Fiction*

UNTIL THERE WAS YOU

"Ms. Ray has given us a great novel again. Did we expect anything less than the best?"

—*Romantic Times BOOKreviews* (4 stars)

"Crisp style, realistic dialogue, likable characters, and [a] fast pace." —*...rnal*

THE ...

"A romance that w... the next tension-filled ... climax."

—*Fresh Fiction*

"Fans of Ray's Grayson and Falcon families will be thrilled with the first installment in the new Grayson Friends series. And this is done very well . . . told with such grace and affection that this novel is a treat to read." —*Romantic Times BOOKreviews* (4 stars)

"Francis Ray is, without a doubt, one of the Queens of Romance." —*A Romance Review*

ONLY YOU

"Francis Ray's graceful writing style and realistically complex characters give her latest contemporary romance its extraordinary emotional richness and depth." —*Chicago Tribune*

"It's a joy to read this always fresh and exciting saga."
—*Romantic Times BOOKreviews* (4 stars)

"The powerful descriptive powers of Francis Ray allow the reader to step into the story and become an active part of the surrender . . . If you love a great love story, *Only You* should be on your list."
—*Fallen Angel Reviews*

"Riveting emotion and charismatic scenes that made this book captivating . . . a beautiful story of love and romance." —*Night Owl Romance*

"A beautiful love story as only Francis Ray can tell it."
—Singletitles.com

"Readers will find a warm and wonderful contemporary romance with plenty of humor and drama. Adding a fun warmth and reality to these characters and a plot that moves quickly add all the needed incentive to read this fun book." —*Multicultural Romance Writers*

IRRESISTIBLE YOU

"A pleasurable story . . . a well-developed story and continuous plot." —*Romantic Times BOOKreviews*

"Like the previous titles in this series, *Irresistible You* is another winner . . . Witty and charming . . . Author Francis Ray has a true gift for drawing the readers in and never letting them go."
—*Multicultural Romance Writers*

DREAMING OF YOU

"A great read from beginning to end, it's even excellent for an immediate re-read."
—*Romantic Times BOOKreviews*

"An immensely likable heroine, a sexy man with a heart of gold, and touches of glitz and color, [this] is as unapologetically escapist as Cinderella. Lots of fun."
—*BookPage*

YOU AND NO OTHER

"The warmth and sincerity of the Graysons bring another book to life . . . delightfully realistic."

—*Romantic Times*

"Astonishing sequel . . . the best romance of the new year . . . the Graysons are sure to leave a smile on your face and a longing in your heart for their next story."

—ARomanceReview.com

"There are three more [Grayson] children with great love stories in the future." —*Booklist*

SOMEONE TO LOVE ME

"Another great romance novel." —*Booklist*

"The plot moves quickly, and the characters are interesting." —*Romantic Times*

"The characters give as good as they get, and their romance is very believable." —*All About Romance*

BREAK EVERY RULE

"Francis Ray is a literary chanteuse, crooning the most sensual romantic fiction melodies in a compelling performance of skill and talent that culminates in another solid gold hit!" —*Romantic Times*

HEART OF THE FALCON

"[A] well-written, tender story about a man growing into respect and trust." —*Publishers Weekly*

"A new romance you won't want to miss with characters that are so real, you get involved in their lives. Splendid romance by Francis Ray! *Heart of the Falcon* is superb!" —*Literary Times*

"Ray has created another sure-to-be-bestseller sizzler that will singe your mind with the laughter, tenderness, and passion that smolders between the pages."

—*Romantic Times*

TITLES BY FRANCIS RAY

The Falcon Novels

Heart of the Falcon

Break Every Rule

The Taggart Brothers

Forever Yours

Only Hers

The Graysons of New Mexico Series

Until There Was You

You and No Other

Dreaming of You

Irresistible You

Only You

The Grayson Friends Series

The Way You Love Me

Nobody But You

One Night with You

It Had to Be You

A Seductive Kiss

With Just One Kiss

A Dangerous Kiss

~

Trouble Don't Last Always

Someone to Love Me

I Know Who Holds Tomorrow

Rockin' Around That Christmas Tree (with Donna Hill)

Anthologies

Rosie's Curl and Weave

Della's House of Style

Welcome to Leo's

Going to the Chapel

Gettin' Merry

I Know Who Holds Tomorrow

FRANCIS RAY

I KNOW WHO HOLDS TOMORROW

For information address St. Martin's Press, 175 Fifth Avenue, New York, NY 10010.

Library of Congress Catalog Card Number: 2001058903

ISBN: 978-1-250-01637-9

Printed in the United States of America

St. Martin's Griffin trade paperback edition / April 2002
St. Martin's Paperbacks edition / November 2012

St. Martin's Paperbacks are published by St. Martin's Press, 175 Fifth Avenue, New York, NY 10010.

10 9 8 7 6 5 4 3 2 1

This book is dedicated to those who have loved and lost,
and learned to love again.

Acknowledgments

First, I want to thank God. With Him in my life all things are possible.

My gratitude also goes to the following:

Rochelle Brown, executive producer of *Insights*, KDFW–Channel 4/Fox, Dallas, Texas, and Marjorie Ford, producer of *Metro*, WFAA–Channel 8/ABC, Dallas, Texas. Both articulate and awe-inspiring ladies helped immensely during my research into the life of a television talk-show hostess, a life they live. Ladies, I couldn't have written this book without you. I wish you continued success.

Monique Patterson, my editor. Thanks for your guidance and faith in me.

LaRee Bryant and Bette Ford. Good friends who never doubted or faulted.

As always, to the home team, William and Carolyn Michelle Ray, husband and daughter, my biggest fans and supporters. I'm blessed by your love.

Lost

I was lonely today, and you did not listen.
I was reaching out for comfort that never came.
I was hoping that you would see me.
But you ignored me just the same.

—CAROLYN MICHELLE RAY

Chapter 1

"Not again," Madison Reed groaned as she glared at the mocking red numbers of the clock radio on her nightstand. It was 4:33 A.M. Unlike the five previous mornings, she made no attempt to go back to sleep. She knew it would be useless. Instead she stared out the French doors in her bedroom and watched darkness slowly give way to hues of orange and yellow ushering in the coming day.

She didn't have to be a medical doctor or a psychologist to know the reason behind her sleeplessness at night or her headaches during the day. However, knowing the reason and correcting the situation were two entirely different matters. She'd helped so many others find their way, but she just didn't seem to be able to do the same with her own life.

Two doors down the hall was her office. On the walls, on her desk, and in the open bookcase were numerous awards, plaques, and accolades attesting to the success of her professional life. *The Madison Reed Show* had been the top-rated television show in its time period for the past six months, and market shares were increasing with each rating period.

Her dimpled smile was seen by hundreds of thousands in the North Texas region each weekday from four to five P.M. on WFTA Channel 7 in Dallas. The second child of Gladys and Billy Evans had always liked to talk and had put the talent to good use.

The alarm clock shrilled. She punched the off button,

threw back the down comforter and left the bed, pushing her problems firmly to the back of her mind as she did so. Her adoring public and her co-workers could never know that Madison Reed was living a lie.

Crossing the thick oyster-colored carpet, she entered the bathroom. Stripping off her silk pajamas, Madison passed in front of the six-foot-long mirror over the white marble vanity. Not given to conceit, she spared only a cursory glance at her reflection, but it was enough to show there was nothing sagging or protruding where it shouldn't have been.

She'd always been slim rather than voluptuous. Sleek, her mother said, trying to spare the feelings of her youngest child who hadn't matured as her older sister had. Madison had been fifteen before she needed a bra. However, by eighteen her body had come into its own. She had curves instead of angles, and after waiting more than half her life for them, she wasn't in a hurry to see them disappear. Her passion for danishes and chocolates didn't show. Yet.

With a sigh she stepped into the shower and made a half-hearted promise that she'd start exercising before she had to ask Ray, the head cameraman, to put a filter on the lens. Politely she ignored the little voice that said she'd been telling herself that for the past six months. But it was difficult to find the energy when her mind was on other matters.

Adjusting the water, she reached for the floral-scented bath gel. Rubbing her body briskly with a sponge, she realized that, having passed her thirtieth birthday a month before, she wasn't going to be able to shed pounds as easily as before. She only had to look at her mother and her sister, Dianne. Surprisingly it was her mother who, rain or shine, faithfully walked five miles each morning in the neighborhood or in the nearby shopping mall.

On the other hand, Dianne, who had never lacked self-confidence, didn't seem to mind the fifteen pounds she'd added since the birth of her two children. She was always quick to say, if David didn't want her, she could easily find another man who did. On cue, David would always say that after the man got out of the hospital Dianne might not want him. Then, they'd look dopey at each other and grin. Their interchange was the standing joke of the family. They all knew Dianne and David had a good strong marriage.

For a moment Madison's eyes closed with regret before she hurried to finish. She had no time for reflection. They were taping the last show of the season today.

An abrupt knock on the Plexiglas startled her. She jerked around, the sponge falling from her hand. Through the frosted glass she saw the image of a man.

"Madison." The knock came again. Brisker this time and more demanding. "Can I speak with you?"

For a moment longer she hesitated, then cut off the water. Stepping to one side, she slowly cracked the shower door open and stuck her head out. Wes, handsome enough to cause any woman's breathing to stall, stood a few feet away. As always he was impeccably dressed. Today in a dark blue five-thousand-dollar Brioni suit. She had known him almost seven years and had never seen him look less than his best or engage in anything more rigorous than a game of golf.

"I didn't know you were back," she said, then thought how peculiar those words were.

Wes flashed her a smile seen by tens of thousands. If he had his way the number would soon be in the tens of millions. "I got back late last night. I didn't want to disturb you."

Madison nodded, silently acknowledging his reasons and thinking how far they had drifted apart, how effortlessly Wes exuded his boyish charm when he needed something from her.

"I just wanted to make sure that you're still coming with me tonight to the awards ceremony."

Her hand tightened on the door. *Duty called.* "I told you I'd be there."

He opened his mouth as if to say something, then closed it. Soft, manicured hands slipped into the pockets of his tailored slacks. In anyone else Madison might have thought the gesture indicated uneasiness or uncertainty, but Wes had never been either.

"A car is picking us up at seven sharp," he told her.

That was expected. Wes always insisted on a limousine for their public appearances. "I'll be ready."

His gaze narrowed. He crossed the white tile floor until he stood within a foot of her. "This is important to me."

"I know." She brushed the water running from her hair out of her eyes with a hand that wasn't quite steady and wished he had waited until she had gotten out of the shower.

His attention drifted to her lips, moist and trembling. He made a motion as if to step closer, then checked it when she jerked her head back. His mouth thinned. Whirling, he walked away.

Madison closed the door, picked up the sponge, then turned the water back on. There had once been a time when just his nearness would have caused her heart to pound, her body to want. A time when, if he had found her in the shower he would have come inside and come into her. Their cries of passion would have filled the room instead of their stilted, awkward conversation.

Once they'd had so much and had been so sure of themselves, so sure their love would last a lifetime. Once. No more. They were husband and wife, but they only spoke to each other when and if they had to. For a woman who had always dreamed of a loving marriage the cause of her sleeplessness and headaches was all too clear.

Although she worked as a lowly gofer at a TV station in Chicago where Wes was a newly hired roving reporter, the first time they saw each other was at her second job as hostess of an upscale steakhouse. She'd taken the position to help pay off her college loan and help with expenses. Wes had come in with a date, but had called back after leaving and asked to speak with her. She'd thought that tactless and told him so.

A couple of weeks later they'd run into each other at the

station. Wes had redoubled his efforts to get her to have dinner with him. A month later, finally convinced that he and the woman weren't in a relationship, she'd gone out with him. The manager at the steakhouse said he wished Madison had held out longer. Wes, coming in almost every night, was good for business. He always ordered the most expensive item on the menu and the best wine.

Wes had come from money, but he had never been condescending to any of the people working at the restaurant or the station. He was carefree, fun to be with, and attentive. It had been easy to fall in love with him. His parents hadn't felt the same way about Madison.

The first time A.J. and Vanessa Reed had met Madison she'd been working at the restaurant. They'd come from Texas to pay an unexpected visit to Wes, their only child, and he had brought them to see her. His parents' cool reception hadn't bothered Madison. She wasn't naive enough to believe that there wasn't a class and a color system among African-Americans.

Although A.J. Reed was a shade darker than Madison's honeyed-brown complexion, Vanessa Reed was high yellow and so was the obviously wealthy young woman they had with them. It hadn't taken long to realize that she, not Madison, was what the Reeds wanted for their son.

Madison had been taught by her blue-collar parents never to be ashamed of who she was. They might not own their own home or have a college education, but they were honest, hardworking people who loved their children and did without so their kids could have more than they'd had. For Madison to be ashamed of who she was, was to be ashamed of them. She'd shown Wes's dinner party to their seats and come over once at his request, then tried to do the impossible, accept that Wes was lost to her.

Later that night she'd come out of the restaurant to find him waiting with a large bouquet of flowers and a kiss that had made her heart leap and her body ache.

"You're what I want. What I'm going to have."

"But your par—"

He'd kissed her again and she had ceased to think of anything, but being in his arms. The next day they'd met his parents for brunch. The other woman wasn't there. His parents had been pleasant, if not friendly.

Wes had surprised her on her twenty-fourth birthday with a stunning three-carat colorless pear-shaped solitaire engagement ring. Nine months later they'd had the big social wedding that Wes and his parents insisted on, and she had been the happiest woman on earth. By that time they were both in Texas, Wes's home state.

Wes had been hired at a TV station in Fort Worth, and luckily she'd secured a position in nearby Dallas at a rival TV station as assistant to the producer of *Wake Up Dallas*, a morning talk show. They'd spun dreams and plans for a bright future. Wes as head anchor on CNN, and she as the next Oprah Winfrey.

But all that had ended two years ago. Pain and a deep sense of loss hit Madison without warning. Her hand trembled as she cupped her stomach. Tears pricked her eyes. Her baby should have lived, and Wes should have been there for both of them.

Knowing she'd be no good to herself or anyone else if she gave in to the anguish and anger sweeping through her, she firmly pulled her mind back to the present. Shutting off the water, Madison left the shower, grabbed a towel, and quickly dried her body. She had a show to do and an awards ceremony to get through.

Madison wheeled her late-model Mercedes into her assigned parking space a mere thirty minutes before the taping of her show was to begin, Being late irritated the hell out of her. She prided herself on her punctuality. Besides, this was one of the most important shows of the season. But a traffic accident on Central Expressway had virtually shut down the freeway in both directions, and by the time Madison knew what was going on, it had been too late to take an alternate route.

Slamming out of her car, she slung her black Yves St. Laurent duffel bag over her shoulder and sprinted toward the front door, glad she could run in three-inch heels.

She reached for the code box just as she heard the buzzer for admittance. Opening the glass door, she smiled at the receptionist, Frankie. Thomas, the security guard, who everyone knew was trying to hit on Frankie, stood a short distance away. "Good morning, Frankie. Thanks."

"Good morning, Ms. Reed. Good luck today."

"Thanks, Frankie. Please let Sarita know I'm here and I'm ready for her to do my makeup," Madison said on her way past the receptionist.

"Ms. Reed?"

Madison paused in her headlong flight. She glanced around to see a man in his mid-forties with four children in varying ages, from a toddler clutching him around his neck to a gangly teenager staring at her with sullen brown eyes. Impatience radiated through Madison, but she had long since mastered the art of hiding her emotions.

"Yes, but I'm in a hurry now," she told him.

The man visibly swallowed. His hold on the child in his arms tightened. "The—the show you're doing is about breast cancer, isn't it?"

Something like lead settled in Madison's stomach. It had been her idea to end the season with a show that would impact the lives of women and cut across social, economic, and racial lines. "Yes."

"Tell them . . . the women . . . to get checked." He looked at the girls, touched the hair of the oldest. Tears formed in his dark eyes. "Maureen always said she was too busy. We lost her last year, the day after Christmas. She loved me and the girls. I just wish she had loved herself as much." His voice wavered, then steadied.

"After she found out, she wouldn't have the surgery. She

thought it wouldn't make a difference. It wouldn't have, but I couldn't get her to understand. Now I have to raise the girls by myself. She'll never get to do all the things she planned to do with them. A mother should watch her daughters grow up."

A hard lump formed in Madison's throat that no amount of swallowing could move. How many times had she thought the same thing? But fate didn't always cooperate.

"Is everything all right, Ms. Reed?" Thomas asked, stepping beside her. He turned hard, accusing eyes on the man. "He came in with your other guest. His name wasn't on the list so I had him sign in and wait here. He said you were expecting him."

Madison came to a quick decision. "You're perceptive as usual, Thomas." When Thomas reached for the man Madison shook her head. "However, I've decided to add him to the show." She turned to the man. "I think having you and your daughters on the show will speak more eloquently than anything I could say. Are you up for it?"

The man hefted the child in his arms. "None of us have ever been on TV before, but if it will help one family not go through what we're going through, I guess we can do it. A family is too important not to."

Madison agreed. She just wished she knew if she'd ever have one.

The show went well. There hadn't been a dry eye on the set or in the audience by the time the taping was over. More importantly, she hoped women would accept the challenge to schedule their mammogram appointment then notify the station. She wanted the switchboard to be inundated with calls. Then, perhaps, another family wouldn't have to go through Christmas without their mother.

On the second floor of the station where the executives offices were located, she knocked on the door marked GORDON ARMSTRONG, PRODUCER in block letters.

"Come in."

Entering, she smiled across the brightly lit room at her boss, mentor, and friend, for over five years now. The spacious office was a comfortable mix of modern and traditional furniture. Glass and chrome abounded, but Gordon sat behind a beautiful antique cherry desk. The wall to his left had five built-in television screens. He kept up with his station broadcasts as well as with the competition. They were on mute, but Madison had never entered the office when they weren't on.

"Good show."

"Thanks." Her smile broadened.

His approval meant a great deal. She'd arrived at the television station from Chicago eager but still green. Gordon had taken her under his capable wing and given her the benefit of his considerable knowledge. He'd made sure she learned everything required to put a show together in front of the camera and behind it. Because of his encouragement she had tried out for the talk-show hostess job.

"You wanted to see me?" she asked.

Before she finished speaking, the door behind her opened after the briefest knock. Madison glanced over her shoulder, wondering who would be so foolish as to enter Gordon's office without permission. The frown cleared and a certain wariness took its place at the sight of Louis Forbes, her agent. She slanted a quick glance at Gordon. His mouth had flattened into a thin line. She barely kept from sighing.

Louis was a fantastic agent but he had a tendency to rub people the wrong way. One of those people was Gordon.

"Hello, Madison, Gordon," he greeted jovially.

"Hi, Louis," Madison replied. There wasn't so much as a grunt from Gordon. "Did we have an appointment?"

Louis smiled broadened, showing perfectly capped teeth in a dark-chocolate face. "No, but I thought you'd want to hear this from me in person. I just got off the phone with TriStar Communications and they're interested in syndicating *The Madison Reed Show.*"

Madison was stunned, speechless and overjoyed. She'd

hoped, she'd dreamed, but never let herself really believe it might happen. TriStar Communications had the largest distribution of television programs in the country. With their backing she could be seen in outlets across the country.

"Madison is under contract to this station," Gordon stated, coming to his feet. He was two hundred pounds of well-conditioned muscle, wonderfully distributed over a six-foot-frame, with the wide shoulders of a linebacker and the wide-palmed hands to go with it. In his mid-fifties he still had a head of thick, curly black hair with a scattering of gray. He was a good-looking man, but it was his strength of character and his loyalty that attracted people to him. But if you happened to displease him, his laser gaze could slice you to ribbons.

"Which expires in six months at the end of the year. TriStar is willing to wait," Louis put in smoothly, then rocked back on his Italian heels.

Madison could well imagine why he was so elated. Louis was a pit bull when it came to contracts, tough and tenacious. He had the reputation of being one of the best entertainment agents in the business. He not only got the big bucks, he also obtained other perks like maid and car service. Madison's base salary of $400,000 easily went up $40,000 with her extra perks. Although Wes only made a little over $98,000, he had perks as well. Louis played hardball when it came to contract negotiations and he played to win.

Gordon, however, was no pushover himself. "Until the end of the year Madison is under contract with WFTA and I'd like to speak to her privately."

The smile slipped from Louis's face. The trick was to intimidate, not piss off. He knew better than anyone when to retreat. "No problem. I was coming to tell Madison the good news in person; saw her assistant, and she told me where to find her."

"Thank you, Louis. We'll talk later," Madison offered. She might not agree with his in-your-face tactics, but in their cutthroat business you had to be tough. He'd been Wes's agent first. After she'd won the hostess position for the talk show, she'd signed with him as well.

"I have to run now, but I'll see you tonight at the awards ceremony," he said. "Wes will win awards for Broadcaster of the Year and for Top Story of the Year. When he does, the network in Chicago will pay through the nose for him." His smile slid into place, quick and confident as he opened the door. "What a duo you and Wes make. I couldn't have been more on target when I dubbed you two 'the perfect couple,' and you're both under contract to me. Life is good." The door closed behind him.

"How do you stand him?" Gordon asked, sinking back into the cushy comfort of his leather chair.

"He's not so bad and he's done a lot for our careers," Madison said as she settled into a tan leather chair in front of his desk, the top of which, as usual, was strewn with paper. "You know as well as I do that it's just as important to score in public relations as it is with your audience. Louis has done that for us."

Gordon merely lifted a brow at her comment. "That he has, but how long do you think you can go on as if everything is all right?"

Everything in Madison went still. It was only due to years of experience that her expression showed puzzlement instead of alarm. "Gordon, what are you talking about?"

Never taking his gaze from her, Gordon leaned back in his chair. Leather sighed. "It's my job and my inclination to watch people, study them. I don't do it maliciously; I grew up in an area where you had to if you didn't want a knife or a bullet to find you."

Everyone knew Gordon's story, his climb out of poverty from the projects in Los Angeles. He was the youngest of seven children of a single mother. Only two made it to adulthood without a criminal record. Only Gordon and his older sister remained alive. Drugs, bad health, and bad choices had claimed the rest.

"Gordon, you and 'malicious' will never be in the same

sentence," Madison said, meaning it, but also giving herself time to think. "I've probably been a little preoccupied with the show lately. Taking responsibility for the programs of the shows has been exciting and scary."

"If I hadn't thought you could do it, I wouldn't have given you the opportunity."

Smiling, Madison relaxed in her chair. You couldn't have an ego around Gordon. "I know, but in the beginning I didn't have the confidence in me that you had."

"And now?" he questioned, leaning forward in his seat to pick up a gold fountain pen.

"I'm good at what I do and I love doing it," she said, feeling the rightness of her words.

"Exactly, and it shows." He studied her closely. "Your genuine warmth and generosity, your empathy for people, is what gives your show a humanness that others lack. Your feelings, whether you're happy or sad, show."

Madison barely kept the smile on her face, her body from tensing. Gordon had smoothly led her in a circle. He hadn't lost the interview skills he'd honed as a reporter years ago. However, she had no intention of letting him use them on her.

"I worry because my work is important to me." A bright smile on her face, she came to her feet. "If there's nothing else, I have a full schedule before I go home and get ready for the awards ceremony. Wes is having a car pick us up."

Up went his eyebrow again. "Madison, one thing I've learned in living these fifty-seven years is that sooner or later the truth always comes out."

Her smile wavered, then steadied and grew wider. Apparently she hadn't hidden her growing unhappiness with her marriage as well as she had thought. "Gordon, I appreciate your concern, but I assure you I'm fine."

Tossing the pen aside, he stood. "My mistake. Since you're so busy we'll put off discussing the topics you wanted for the next season until tomorrow morning."

Madison felt the sting of his rebuff. Gordon had given her

her first job at the station as his assistant, then supported and encouraged her. Without him she wouldn't be where she was and they both knew it.

He was reaching out to her. But if there was one thing she'd learned in the media it was that if another person knew your secret, it was no longer a secret. That much she and Wes could agree on. "Is nine all right?"

Gordon nodded without glancing at his calendar. "Tell Wes good luck, even if he's going against one of our own."

The heaviness in her heart eased. He had forgiven her. "I will, and thanks."

"Just remember, if you ever want to talk, I'm here."

Her mind in a turmoil, Madison quickly left. If he suspected, perhaps others might also. They had to be more careful. No one could know the image of the perfect couple she and Wes portrayed was a lie.

Chapter 2

"I think Gordon suspects," Madison said as she sat beside Wes in the speeding limousine heading for the Hyatt Hotel in downtown Dallas.

Wes, who had been staring out the window for the past ten minutes, jerked toward her. "Why? What happened?" The words shot out like bullets.

Madison's manicured nails dug into her evening bag. She'd been dreading this conversation ever since she left Gordon's office. "He made a comment that 'sooner or later the truth always comes out.' "

"Are you having an affair?" Wes asked, turning completely in the seat to glare at her.

"Of course not!" she answered, annoyed and angry.

"Then we have nothing to worry about." He relaxed back in his seat. "Gordon is just being introspective in his declining years."

Madison almost rolled her eyes at such an absurd statement. "Fifty-seven is not 'declining.' He's younger than both our parents. He knows something is wrong."

Wes's hand, soft and steady, closed around hers as he stared at her. "Things can change anytime you're ready." The words were a seductive whisper in the enclosed area. "Once we would have made good use of the time together in the back of this limo."

His lingering gaze failed to make need and heat move

through her as it once had. She honestly didn't know how she felt about the loss. She tugged her hand. Immediately she was free.

"I still love you."

She glanced out the window at the passing traffic. He played the loving, dutiful husband so well when it suited him. He'd been out of town for the past five days on assignment and he hadn't once called her. "Wes, please."

His long-suffering sigh drifted between them. "If you ever change your mind, you won't have to say the words. I'll see it in your eyes."

The limo pulled up to the curb. Through the tinted window Madison could see TV cameras. The media had turned out en masse to pay tribute to its own.

Wes's door opened. He flashed a grin just as a camera went off. "Got you working tonight, Jenkins?"

Jenkins, staff photographer for the *Dallas Morning News*, took another shot before lowering the Mamiya. "Yeah, some of us have to work while you big shots play," he commented, then quickly snapped two more shots.

"Save that film because you're about to see beauty in motion." Affable and carefree, Wes stepped out of the car and reached his hand back to help Madison. "Come on, Madison, let's show the world what a lucky guy I am."

Madison hesitated. The light squeeze of his hand on her delicate fingers had her moving again. She stepped out to the brilliant glare of the TV cameras and the flash of cameras. Her smile matched Wes's. As soon as she straightened, his arms curved around her slim waist. Cool lips brushed across her cheek.

And all she could think was, *Keep smiling.*

The Wilshire Ballroom in the Hyatt Hotel was filled with lavishly dressed people, scrumptious food, and breathless anticipation. A hush fell over the room that seated close to five hundred of the top journalists in the country. The biggest award of the night, that of Broadcaster of the Year, was about to be announced by the legendary Walter Cronkite. The nominees' names had already been given. Wes Reed's name was among the four.

Opening the envelope, Cronkite's mouth curved into one of his rare smiles, then he lifted his head and said in that distinctive voice, "For Broadcaster of the Year, the award goes to Wes Reed."

Wes, known just as much for his jubilance as his tenacity, surged to his feet. People from his table and around him, quickly came to offer handshakes and robust pats on the back. He acknowledged them with a flash of the killer smile that had made him a favorite of women viewers. But as the award testified, he was respected by men as well for his hard-hitting commentary.

As applause continued, he turned to Madison sitting beside him, then leaned over and kissed her on the cheek.

"Congratulations, Wes," Madison said, still applauding. She more than most knew how much this award meant to him. Finally he had been validated by his peers, recognized as a great reporter, not just a great black reporter. This award capped off a year when he had won several, including the Ma'At Award from the Regional Association of Black Journalists. He had succeeded in his career, if not in his personal life.

With a final wave of acknowledgment, Wes started toward the stage, then whirled and came back to Madison. His manicured hand extended toward her. Applause erupted again. This time louder. Only Madison, who was watching, saw the almost imperceptible tightening of his mouth, the glint in his hazel eyes. Dutifully, she placed her hand in his. This was his night.

As they made their way toward the stage Madison heard the comments that always made her wince inside.

"Aren't they a beautiful couple?"

"They're so happy."

"They're perfect."

With difficulty Madison kept the smile on her face. Louis's PR had succeeded beyond any of their wildest dreams.

In her mind's eye, she could see Wes, tall and elegant in his tailored tuxedo with a patterned vest, black tie, and snow-white pocket square. Her red Valentino slip gown highlighted her honeyed complexion and chocolate-brown eyes. The gown also picked up the red in Wes's vest and the red in the rose in his lapel. If you didn't look past the surface, they did indeed look good together.

Onstage, Wes accepted the award with one hand and shook Cronkite's hand with the other. Then he reclasped Madison's hand, drawing her with him as he stepped in front of the Plexiglas podium. "Few times in my life words have failed me. This is one of those rare times." As expected, the audience laughed. Wes had earned his reputation as the great "talker."

Finally releasing Madison's hand he ran a long finger over the award. Then his head lifted, his soothing voice was deep and serious. "There are only two occasions that I will treasure more than this one, and since the first is the day Madison agreed to marry me and the second is the day we were married almost five years ago, it is right and fitting that she be with me to share this third occasion." Turning, he stared down into her eyes. "Thank you for putting up with me and my crazy schedule, for letting me follow my dream, and most of all for loving me."

Applause erupted. People stood to their feet. Madison swallowed, unable to say anything. Wes placed a kiss on her forehead that bespoke of tenderness and love. Curving his hand around her waist, he led her from the stage.

It wasn't over.

Backstage more press waited. Microphones were thrust in their faces, cameras flashed, the glaring lights of the television cameras focused on them to catch every nuance.

Well aware of how the media game was played, Wes kept his arm around her waist. Madison's smile never faltered. She also knew the routine, knew the questions that would follow, knew the choreography of tender looks that were expected.

They were the perfect couple and it was showtime. And she wanted to scream.

The next morning Madison woke up with a headache. It was probably the same one that had followed her into sleep. She seldom took medicine and had thought she could sleep off the throbbing pain. She'd been wrong. Wrong in a long list of things.

Standing in front of the wide vanity in her bathroom, she shut her eyes as if to escape the persistent pounding in her temple. That didn't work either. Her lids lifted and she stared at herself in the mirror. The headache was due to emotional problems, not physical ones. But how did she fix her personal life without endangering her career?

Public perception, and more importantly, public confidence, was vital for any person in the media. The public didn't like being deceived or being disappointed, and if they were, they quickly showed their displeasure. More than one person in his professional career had gone under when his image turned out to be less than people thought.

What would happen if people learned that, for the past two years, she and Wes had lived a lie? The answer wasn't comforting.

Sliding her hands into the pockets of her slacks, she headed for the kitchen. The smell of coffee reached her as she turned down the wide hallway.

Wes always started the day off with a cigarette and a cup of coffee. She did neither, but once she would have joined him, laughing, sharing. They used to brag that there was nothing that could come between them, nothing that they couldn't accomplish. They had been so foolish and so very wrong. The first hard knock to their marriage had left them reeling. They had never recovered.

Not wanting to think about that day, Madison lengthened her stride, then faltered when she saw Wes with several newspapers scattered around the high-backed chair he was sitting in at the kitchen table. He was usually gone by the time she was dressed.

He glanced up. "Good morning, Madison."

"Good morning, Wes," she answered, and continued to the refrigerator for her yogurt and a bagel.

"How did you sleep?"

"Fine, thank you. And you?"

"I've slept better." His hand caught hers as she passed.

Surprised, she paused and glanced down at him expectantly. They seldom had physical contact if no one was around. "Yes?"

"I'd like to talk with you."

Her brow inched up higher. Not counting last night, she couldn't remember them having more than a superficial conversation in the past six months. "I have an appointment at nine."

"It's barely eight. You have time," he said. "This won't take long." His thumb grazed the back of her hand. "For two people who make their living talking, we haven't been doing a very good job of it, have we?"

"No," she admitted.

He nodded, still not releasing her hand. "Last night Steinberg offered me the head anchor position at WGHA in Chicago. I accepted."

"Congratulations." Madison wasn't surprised by the announcement. It was what Wes had wanted. What he'd asked Louis to go after once he heard the station was interested in him. The position was with a CNN affiliate, and one step closer to his goal.

He searched her face, then said, "They want you, too."

Madison was already shaking her head. "My contract isn't up until the end of the year."

"Steinberg is willing to buy you out of your contract and work with TriStar," he said with just a hint of annoyance. "Just think, Madison, a nationally syndicated show for you, a head anchor position for me on the most respected station in the country. There'll be no stopping us then. We'll be the most influential couple on television."

It had been a long time since Wes had spoken of them as a team or with such fervency. He was the old Wes once again, ready to challenge the world to get what he wanted. Only this time, she wasn't ready to follow him.

"The station is willing to double your present salary, and with the perks Louis is going to make sure you get, it could easily be worth another couple hundred thousand," he said. "You know as well as I do how fickle the public is. We have to do this now and I know you want this as much as I do."

She had. National syndication had been her dream and she had worked hard to achieve success, but now that it was within reach, she wasn't so sure she was willing to pay the price by living a lie in a loveless marriage. "They want the couple the media sees."

"We can be that way again." Again the whisper of seduction came into his voice. He reached for her hand, but she was already sliding them into her pockets.

"I'm not sure how much longer I can go on this way," she said softly.

Wes's lips firmed. "The public and the TV stations want the perfect couple. That's us. You balk and there's a good chance our popularity, and thus our income, will suffer." His arm waved expansively around the kitchen that had imported Italian tile and hand-blown chandeliers. "Are you willing to throw this all away?"

Instead of answering, Madison glanced around the room. They lived in a custom-built home, purchased mostly with her money. Four thousand square feet of living space in an exclusive gated community with its own golf course and lake, a four-car garage, a professionally landscaped and maintained yard, a miniature practice golf area for Wes, and separate offices for each. But what good was all that luxury when they were living a lie?

"Madison." Wes's voice softened to a croon when she remained silent. "We have a lot more than most of our friends and associates."

And a lot less, she started to say, but didn't. She'd drifted away from her close women friends because friends shared and she hadn't wanted anyone to know about her disintegrating marriage. While her career had skyrocketed, her personal life had taken a nosedive. Her many friends had stopped calling when she kept making excuses not to go out with them. They probably thought she was on an ego trip.

Looking back, she honestly didn't know if their successful careers had been worth the sacrifices they'd made. Once she had known who held her tomorrows. That seemed like such a long time ago. Now, the only thing she was sure of was that she couldn't continue with all the false pretenses. Wes had his dreams and she had hers. They just weren't the same anymore. "Wes—"

"Please, don't say no," he interrupted quickly, as if anticipating her answer. "Just think about it. The station is contacting a realtor about finding us a place. I'd appreciate you flying up with me. The head of the station has invited us to dinner at his house to meet some of the key people."

"And it wouldn't look right if you went without the other half of the perfect couple, would it?" she asked, aware of the biting sarcasm in her voice.

Wes said nothing, merely stared at her. He could rebuke more skillfully with a look than others could with a thousand hurtful words.

"Sorry."

He reached out and ran his hand down her arm. "You've been working hard to finish up the season. I understand. Why don't we forget it for the time being? I'll take you to Oliver's for dinner."

The Italian restaurant was her favorite. "We haven't been there together in over a year."

"I'm sorry for that, but that just points out the importance of us taking the offer. We'll have more time together," he cajoled, and stood. "All I'm asking is that you keep an open mind."

Madison stared up into his handsome face and wished she felt something, anything. Perhaps it was time. Talk was something they hadn't done in what seemed like forever. She couldn't go on with the way things were. The steady pounding in her head told her as much. "I'll be home by five."

Relief swept across his face. "I'll make reservations for six-thirty." He brushed warm lips fleetingly across her cheek. "I promise you won't be sorry."

Madison watched him walk away. He'd promised her the same thing once before and hadn't been able to keep that promise. Madison was painfully aware that he wouldn't be able to keep his promise this time, either.

The last day before hiatus was always hectic and today proved no different. There were the repeat shows to be finalized, the topics and possible locations for future shows to be decided on, and, of course, there were always the ratings to be considered, and the competition.

Madison and Gordon were seated at a small table in her office when the door opened. Frowning, Madison glanced up. She had asked Traci, her secretary/assistant, that she not be disturbed.

Puzzlement turned to concern as Traci, flanked by two uniformed policemen, entered the room. Her young face was parchment-white.

Madison came to her feet, ready to defend the young woman who had been her assistant for the past six months. She'd worked with Traci long enough to know she wasn't the type of person to break the law. "You don't have to be afraid, Traci—I'm sure there has been some misunderstanding, and I'll help fix it."

"Ms. Reed, I'm so sorry," Traci murmured, as tears slid silently down her pale cheeks.

Madison shifted her attention from her trembling assistant to the solemn faces of the policemen. Dread slithered down her spine. Without being aware of it, she reached out for the support of the table.

She had interviewed too many people on her show not to have an idea of what the policemen's serious faces meant. She quickly ruled out their visit having anything to do with her parents or her older sister who lived in Newark. If anything had happened to them, she would have received a phone call.

"It's Wes, isn't it?" she asked, barely able to push the words past the growing constriction in her throat.

The older of the two policemen stepped forward, his brimmed hat in his hands. "I'm sorry, Ms. Reed, to have to tell you this, but your husband has been injured in an accident on the freeway while trying to help a motorist change a tire."

Madison felt arms go around her. In some part of her swirling mind she knew they belonged to Gordon, but she was unable to take her eyes from the policeman. "H-how bad is it?"

"He was airlifted to Parkland. I think it's best you get over there as soon as possible."

Chapter 3

Zachary Holman careened into Parkland Hospital's emergency-room parking lot and braked sharply behind two older-model cars. He didn't see an empty space and had no intention of wasting precious time trying to find one. Jumping out of his truck, he sprinted toward the automatic doors.

"Hey! You can't park there!"

Out of the corner of his eye, Zachary saw a security guard rushing toward him. Zachary kept going.

"You'll be towed!" the rotund guard warned.

Zachary flipped his keys. Startled, eyes wide, the man reflexively caught them in midair. "I'm sorry," Zachary said, and ran faster.

He didn't stop until he stood in front of a glass enclosure labeled ADMISSIONS in block lettering. A woman in an animal-print smock looked up from entering data into a computer. Her eyes rounded on seeing the blood staining his shirt and pants.

"It's not mine," Zachary said, his fists clenching as he fought the tightness in his throat. The Care Flight attendant had thought the same thing. "Wes Reed. Where is he? He was airlifted from an accident on Stemmons."

"Are you a relative?" she asked, peering quizzically up at him.

"I—"

"I heard you admit you're not hurt. You'll have to move

that truck," the security guard interrupted from beside Zachary, his wide-legged stance belligerent.

Zachary ignored the man. He couldn't get the sounds of Wes's painful moans out of his mind. "Please, where is he?"

"Sir—"

"Look, Ms. Johnson," Zachary said, cutting her off after reading her name tag. Intimidation worked best if you had a name. "I know you have a job to do, but in case you aren't aware of it, Wes Reed is a very famous newscaster and he's highly respected and well liked in this city and across the nation. If anything happens to him while you stand there wasting time there'll be hell to pay. I personally guarantee it. So, where is he?" The last words were snapped out. Zachary was used to giving orders and people jumping.

Uncertainty moved in the woman's eyes. She glanced over her shoulder to the two other women in the small cubicle with her. The oldest one, a black woman with shoulder-length braids, stepped forward. "Isn't he Madison Reed's husband?"

Zachary thought Wes would have hated that reference, but right now it might help. "Yes."

"Cubicle six. Down the hall to the right. It's marked on the side of the door."

"Thanks," Zachary said, taking off in that direction, this time going slower because the hallway was crowded with people, hospital beds, and equipment. His hand was shaking when he pushed open the door to cubicle six. He couldn't see Wes because of the number of people surrounding his bed. Then one moved to grab something from a metal tray. Zachary saw Wes and came to an abrupt stop.

His expensive suit had been slashed from his body, a body that was badly bruised and bloody. A large gash ran at least eight inches on his left thigh. But what made Zachary's stomach roll was the blood coating Wes's chest. Blood that also stained the garments of the people working frantically on him. Zachary's unsteady hand brushed across his own bloody shirt. How much blood could Wes lose and survive?

It had happened so quickly. Zachary had been only minutes behind Wes on the freeway. Zachary had been kidding Wes on the cell phone about getting his hands dirty changing a tire. He'd thought Wes's curse had something to do with the tire until Zachary heard the screams and the sickening sound of metal again metal that would haunt him for the rest of his life.

"Blood pressure dropping."

"Dammit. More suction."

"What's the heart rhythm?"

"Sinus tach at one-fifty."

"Blood pressure ninety over fifty and dropping fast."

"He's bleeding into the pericardial sac."

Transfixed, Zachary watched as a long needle plunged into Wes's chest. His stomach rolled again. Wes hated needles. They both did.

"BP ninety-eight over fifty-two. One-oh-two over sixty."

"Let's move it, people, and get him into surgery."

They moved as one unit. Positioned at the foot, head, and side of the gurney, they started toward him. Automatically Zachary moved back. But as they passed he was unable to keep from calling Wes's name.

"Wes." There was no response. Zachary hadn't expected any. There was a tube down his throat and taped to the sides of his mouth. Wes always had energy to spare. Now he was still, and pale. "Wes."

Long, sooty eyelashes flickered in a face so bruised it was almost unrecognizable. Swallowing, Zachary reached for Wes's hand. "You're going to be all right. Hang in there."

"Move!" snapped the middle-aged man who had worked frantically on Wes as he'd shouted orders to the people around him. "We have to get him to surgery," Dr. London bellowed.

Zachary quickly released Wes's hand but, as they moved down the hall, he moved with them.

"I'm sorry, sir, you'll have to wait here or in the surgery waiting room," one of the nurses said.

"I'm not leaving him, and you're wasting your breath

trying to get me to." Zachary's eyes were on Wes; he didn't see the gray-haired doctor shake his head when the nurse lifted her hand toward the watchful security guard.

"From the looks of you, you must be the one trying to help him at the scene of the accident. Are you Zach, the one the attendant said he asked for on the way in?" Dr. London asked, his shrewd blue eyes studying Zachary closely as they moved down the hallway.

Zachary nodded, his worried gaze still fixed on Wes's pale face.

"If you're going to tag along, you might as well try to be useful. Do you know anything about his medical history or family history? Medication he might be on?" Dr. London asked.

Zachary finally lifted his head. "I know everything there is to know about him."

"Good, then start talking," the doctor ordered as they rolled Wes's unconscious body onto the elevator.

Madison and Gordon were met at the entrance of Parkland Hospital by a middle-aged ash-blonde with a trim figure and gentle blue eyes who identified herself as Ann Crane, director of public relations. All Madison wanted to know was Wes's condition.

"He's still in surgery. His doctor will speak with you as soon as he's finished," Ann said, leading them gently but firmly toward the bank of elevators. "If you'll follow me, we have a room ready where you can wait undisturbed."

"Thank you," Gordon said, his arm around Madison's shoulders. He'd never seen her so shaken.

The ride to the fifth floor was completed in silence. Stepping off, the woman led them down the wide hallway. "This is one of our conference rooms." Opening the door, she stepped back for them to enter. "There's coffee, tea, and soft drinks, if you'd care for them."

Madison lifted anguish-filled eyes to Ann. "When they brought him in, was he conscious? In pain?"

"I'm afraid I don't know the answers to your questions, Ms. Reed," Ann Crane offered apologetically. "By the time it was discovered who your husband was, he was already in surgery. I can tell you that Parkland Hospital specializes in trauma, and the best trauma surgeon was on duty when your husband was brought in."

All Madison could think of was that sometimes even the best wasn't good enough. She knew that better than anyone.

"Is there anyone else you'd like me to notify?" Ann asked. She and Gordon traded worried glances when Madison didn't respond.

"Madison, Ms. Crane asked if there was anyone else you'd like her to call," Gordon said gently. "His parents?"

Madison closed her eyes. She hadn't thought of them. They'd be devastated. Wes was more than an only child. They worshiped him, especially his mother. How was Madison going to tell them?

"Madison," Gordon said, "I can call them if you'd like."

Only for a moment did she consider letting him make what was sure to be a painful call. "No, I'll do it."

"There's a phone on the credenza. Just dial nine for an outside line." The spokeswoman pointed to a beautiful carved walnut piece against the back wall. "My card is next to it in case you need to call me. We'll probably be getting quite a few inquiries about Mr. Reed. His condition will be given out as unknown until we have further information. The surgical floor and waiting room are on the floor below us. No one but top-level staff knows where you are. You're welcome to give out this location and the phone's extension to family members and friends."

"Th-thank you." Madison slowly walked over to the phone and stared down at it. Her trembling hand wavered over the beige phone.

"Ms. Reed, is there a problem?" the woman asked.

"I—I can't remember the number." Her voice quivered. "713-555-8888."

Madison whirled toward the deep voice that for a brief moment sounded like Wes's. Seeing the man dashed all hopes that this had been some type of horrible mistake, that Wes was well and not fighting for his life in the operating room.

There was nothing of Wes in the man. Wes was heart-stoppingly handsome and elegant. This man was taller, broader, with a rugged face and wide callused hands with scraped knuckles. This man wore a denim shirt and well-worn jeans, and scuffed workboots. Wes liked to talk. This man seldom spoke unless asked a direct question. She knew all this because he was the contractor Wes had hired to build their house, and while she hadn't gotten to know him well, she knew he was a friend of Wes's.

"Zachary."

He nodded in acknowledgment, but said nothing. His dark face was as grim as she knew hers to be.

"Is—is a member of your family here, too?"

His gaze went briefly beyond her to the other people in the room, before returning to her. He crossed the room and stopped directly in front of her. Midnight-black eyes filled with grief stared down at her. "I'm here because of Wes. We had an appointment. We . . . we were talking on the cell phone when . . ." He swallowed. "I got there before Care Flight touched down on the freeway, and stayed with him. I came on after they lifted off with him."

Madison's eyed widened. She grabbed both of his arms, her nails digging through his shirt into his skin. "Was he conscious? How did he look? What did he say?"

Zachary swallowed again before answering the rapid-fire questions. "He . . . he was conscious for a little while."

"Go on," she urged. "I won't fall apart."

"He was injured pretty bad, but . . . Dr. London seems to know what he's doing. I understand he's the best."

Looking into Zachary's eyes, which kept sliding away from hers, Madison felt a chill. Her fingers uncurled and she turned away. "Wes will come through this. He was offered an anchor position for a national news show last night. He has waited years for this. He has to be all right."

"Wes never let anything keep him down," Zachary said quietly.

Feeling tears prick her eyes again, Madison blinked them away. She felt the gentle pressure of a tissue being shoved into her hand. Dabbing the moisture away, she saw the compassionate face of the spokeswoman. "Thank you."

"Remember, my card is by the phone if you need anything. The hospital won't give out any information other than to confirm that Mr. Reed has been admitted unless you direct us to do otherwise."

Madison knew the calls would be relentless. Wes was well liked in and out of his profession. He made friends easily. She probably wouldn't know most of them because the two of them didn't socialize unless it was on a professional level. "I appreciate what you've done. Thank you."

"You're welcome." The woman touched Madison's arm and smiled gently. "Please call if there is anything you need."

Gordon took Madison's arm and led her to the leather couch on the far side of the room. "Sit down, I'll get you a cup of tea."

Despite the dire situation, Madison's bottom lip curved slightly upward. Gordon might be a hard-nosed newsman, but he firmly believed in the restorative power of tea. He'd often said it was one of the things he had learned from his wife. Madison felt a chill again. Gordon had lost his wife years ago. She hadn't known him then, but how did one survive that? She and Wes were having problems, but she still cared about him.

Madison came unsteadily to her feet. "I should call Wes's parents."

Gordon paused, a tea bag in his hand. "I don't mind calling them."

She took a deep breath. "They deserve to hear it from

me." Walking over, she picked up the phone, very aware that her hand was trembling.

Gordon watched Madison for a brief moment, then turned to the silent man standing across the room. "Zachary, I'm Gordon Armstrong, Madison's friend, and producer. Sorry I didn't get your last name."

"It's Holman." Zachary shook his head when Gordon lifted a cup. His attention was centered on Madison who clutched the phone in one hand and rested her forehead in the palm of the other. The phone call wasn't going to be easy.

Zachary could imagine the reaction of Wes's parents. Wes was everything to them. They loved him unconditionally and exclusively, leaving no room for anyone else.

Madison had planned on being strong, but the instant she heard the East Texas twang in Wes's father's voice, the tears started. She couldn't seem to get them to stop or to get the words to come out.

The phone was gently removed from her hand. Through a sheen of tears she saw Zachary hunkered down in front of her holding up the phone to Gordon who traded the cup of tea for the phone. Just as gently, Zachary folded her trembling hands around the delicate rose-patterned cup.

"Mr. Reed, this is Gordon Armstrong," he said into the receiver. "I'm afraid I have some bad news for you. Wes has been injured in an automobile accident. He's at Parkland Hospital." Gordon laid a comforting hand on Madison's trembling shoulder. "His condition is serious. He's in surgery now. They were kind enough to have Madison wait in a private conference room on the fifth floor. Ask for Ann Crane when you get here and they'll get you to us. All right. Good-bye."

"I'm sor—"

"You're entitled," Gordon said, cutting her off. "Get her to drink that tea. I'll just step outside and make a couple of calls to let the staff know what's going on."

Zachary's large hands closed around hers. "Drink up. You'll feel better."

Madison shook her head. "I don't think so."

"It's almost two. If I recall, from the months of building your house, you didn't eat much for breakfast and tended to call a Danish or a candy bar lunch." He urged the cup back to her mouth. "You're running on nerves now, you need the sugar."

Madison drank the tea she didn't want and couldn't taste. It seemed easier than arguing. Finished, she handed Zachary the cup. Arms folded, she leaned her head back against the chair, closed her eyes, and prayed.

Friends and co-workers came in a steady stream to offer their support. As some left, new arrivals took their place. Refreshments had been replenished twice.

Although Madison appreciated their coming, she wished for a few moments of quiet, for some time when she didn't have to make polite conversation. Because behind the bright chatter she could hear their fear. Wes had been in surgery for more than four hours. For some reason her gaze kept going to Zachary, who remained apart from everyone else. It was almost as if he wanted to be invisible.

Vanessa and A.J. Reed's arrival brought an immediate stop to the hushed conversation in the room. Fear sparkled in the eyes that swept the room for her daughter-in-law. "Madison!" It was half cry, half wail.

Madison felt the tears brim again. Wes's mother had always been so controlled. Now she appeared near her breaking point. Madison's heart went out to the older woman. They had their differences, but there had never been any doubt about Vanessa's love for Wes. Madison left the group and crossed the room to her.

"Have you heard anything else?" Vanessa asked frantically.

"No, he's still in surgery," Madison bit her lower lip. "The doctor is supposed to come up as soon as he finishes."

"I can't wait any longer. The weather was bad at Hobby Airport in Houston and they held up the flight. I almost went crazy waiting. I want to know now. I can't stand this." Vanessa whirled toward her husband, a big, rawboned man with wide shoulders and broad features, her voice demanding, and high-pitched. "Don't you know anyone on the hospital board you can get to intercede on our behalf? They have speakers in the operating room. I want to know how my son is doing."

Madison had never heard Vanessa speak above a polite whisper, but she caught herself looking hopefully at Wes's father. She'd tried to be patient, but . . . "Could you do that?"

A.J. was already reaching inside his coat for his cell phone. "I don't know anyone on the board, but I know someone who probably does." He began to punch in numbers.

"Excuse me, Mr. Reed," Gordon said. "You'll need to use the phone on the credenza. Use of cell phones is prohibited in the hospital."

For a moment A.J. looked as if he might keep on dialing, then he slipped the phone back into the inside pocket of his tailored jacket and went to use the phone Gordon had indicated. "This is A.J. Reed. I need to speak to Mayor Jones. It's an emergency."

In a matter of moments A.J. was speaking again. "Doug, my boy's been in an accident. We're at Parkland Hospital now and can't find out anything. Can you call someone to contact the surgeon in the operating room for us and see what's going on? Yes. The number here is—It's on your caller ID. I see. Thank you." He let the receiver fall back into the cradle. "He'll call us back."

"I can't stand this waiting!" Vanessa wailed again.

"Wes will come though this," Madison said, gently touching the woman's shoulder. "Maybe we'll know something soon."

Sharp eyes lanced back up at Madison. "You're in the media. Why haven't you used your influence to find out what is going on?"

Madison was taken aback by the rebuff, but she had never backed down from Wes's parents. She had no intention of starting now. "I thought of it while I've waited, but I also thought I didn't want to disturb the doctor while he's operating. I want his total concentration on helping Wes."

Vanessa's gaze narrowed as if she couldn't quite make up her mind if she'd been rebuked or not.

"Would you like some tea, Mrs. Reed?" Gordon interjected smoothly as he came to stand by Madison.

Vanessa's expression immediately softened. "Yes, thank you."

"Why don't you have a seat and I'll bring it to you." Gordon turned to Mr. Reed. "Would you like anything? There's also bottled water, coffee, and soft drinks."

"No."

Vanessa started toward the cream-colored velvet sofa in a quiet area of the room, then came to an abrupt halt. Her smooth features tensed.

Madison followed the direction of her mother-in-law's gaze and saw Zachary, arms folded, casually leaning against the wall near the couch. "What's the matter?"

"Nothing," Vanessa said, then turned away. "That love seat over there simply looks more comfortable."

"Of course," Madison said, taking the woman's arm and walking with her to the plump, upholstered love seat on the other side of the room.

Madison looked back at Zachary. She could read nothing in his closed expression. She rubbed her forehead. Everybody was tense and the waiting was making it worse.

Suddenly the phone on the credenza rang. A.J. snatched it up. "Yes?"

Madison and Vanessa both came to their feet.

A.J.'s face became more haggard as the conversation lengthened. Finally he hung up. Madison was almost afraid to hear what he had to say.

"A.J.?" Vanessa asked.

"They're just finishing up. The doctor should be up shortly."

Chapter 4

The door opened and all eyes centered on the tall, lanky man with a long face in a green scrub suit, a white surgical cap, and paper shoe covers. "I'm Dr. London. Is Mr. Reed's wife, here?"

"I'm his wife." Madison's throat felt sandpaper-dry.

"Let's give the family some privacy," Gordon said, holding the door open. One by one they passed by with a word of comfort, a quick hug or a reassuring hand.

Madison barely noticed; all her attention was on the doctor. "Please, how is he?"

"Perhaps you should sit down."

"No. Just tell me."

"Your husband sustained extensive internal injuries when the car pinned him against the guardrail."

Madison heard Vanessa cry out, felt the churning in her own stomach, and fought to hold back her own fear and the nausea clawing at her throat. She swallowed reflexively.

Dr. London's blue eyes watched her closely for a long moment before continuing. "The liver and the left kidney were damaged. We resectioned the liver, but couldn't save the kidney. It was touchy in the operating room. The next twenty-four hours are going to be rough."

"W-will he be all right?" Madison asked.

"We'll just have to take it minute by minute," Dr. London answered.

He gave her no false hope to hang on to. No illusions. All she could think of was that this morning Wes had had such hopes for the future. If she had said yes, maybe she could have prevented this and Wes wouldn't be fighting for his life. "Can I see him?"

"He'll be in the recovery room for at least another hour or longer, then he'll be transferred to ICU," Dr. London explained. "I'll tell his nurse to call up here and let you come in for a few minutes when they get him settled. The waiting area is not as comfortable or as nice as this."

"It doesn't matter. I want to see him as soon as possible." Madison quickly picked up her purse and slung the strap over her shoulder. "Where do I go?"

"Fourth floor. Get off the elevator and turn left," Dr. London answered. "Have the nurse page me if you have questions after you see him."

"I will. Thank you." After Dr. London left the room Madison turned to her in-laws. "Would you like to go with me to wait?"

"If I could see Wes you couldn't keep me away, but you heard the doctor. He won't be in ICU for an hour, perhaps longer. It's pointless to wait there instead of here," Vanessa said, her displeasure with her daughter-in-law abundantly clear.

Madison didn't even look toward A.J. She'd learned when Vanessa made a decision, A.J. followed. "If you need anything while I'm gone, contact Ann Crane." In the hallway, she quickly explained the situation to Gordon and the people who had waited. After handshakes and hugs, everyone left except Gordon.

"You've been here long enough," Madison told him. "You can leave. I'll be fine."

He took her cold hands in his. "I'm going with you to ICU."

Madison loved and appreciated Gordon even more for wanting to be with her, but she knew he'd been working sixteen-hour days for the past week at the station. He had to be exhausted. He was just too stubborn and too good of a friend to leave her. Although she didn't want to go to ICU alone, it wouldn't be as draining for him here as it would be with her. "If you don't mind, I'd rather you stay here to answer the phone and let the people who drop by know what's going on."

"You shouldn't wait alone," Gordon told her.

"Maybe I can help," Zachary said, coming to stand by them. "If Madison doesn't mind, I'll wait with her."

Gordon sent Madison a questioning look. She stared at Zachary. She hadn't realized he had followed her. He was Wes's friend, not hers.

"I just want to help," Zachary said softly, as if he sensed her quandary.

She thought back to when he'd built their house. He'd been hardworking, honest, and dependable. He'd shown that same dependability by staying with Wes after the accident. He was as worried and as concerned as they were. She could see it in his eyes and in the lines of strain around his mouth. "Thank you, Zachary. I'd appreciate the company."

Dr. London had been right, Zachary thought, the ICU waiting room was drab and dreary, matching the tired faces of the people gathered there. The narrow windowless space smelled of stale coffee and fear. The end table, cluttered with magazines, Styrofoam cups, and soda cans, squatted next to a big brown Naugahyde sofa. Each seat was occupied. So were the walls, as people leaned against them.

He glanced at Madison, her arms wrapped around her slim body, the sparkle in her brown eyes dim. She was holding up better than Wes's mother, but then Vanessa had come from a pampered life that had just been turned upside down. Madison's family had struggled for a living. She was made of sterner stuff. In Zachary's opinion, hers was the luckier of the two families.

"If you want to go back up, I'll call," Zachary said. They'd been waiting over an hour. Gordon had been down twice. A.J. and Vanessa once.

"I'm stay—" Madison stopped in midsentence as a loud wail cut off conversation as effectively as if someone had pulled a switch.

"Code blue. ICU. Code blue," came the voice over the loudspeaker. The door behind her swung open and two men and a woman ran through.

Madison started to shake. "God, no! Please."

Zachary's long arm instinctively curved around her shoulder. "Easy, Madison. It's not Wes."

Her gaze lanced up to him, hopeful and terrified. "How do you know?"

"One of my men was in here a couple of months ago," Zachary explained, feeling the erratic beat of her heart. "They have a back elevator, but don't use it very much. All patients come through here."

Madison began to breathe a little easier until she looked around the room at the stark faces. They had family and friends behind the double doors, and one of them was fighting for their life. She idly wondered if they regretted words spoken or unspoken, as she did. But she had time to make it right. Wes *would* survive.

The door to ICU opened again. Face expressionless, the woman who had run in earlier came back out looking neither to the left nor the right. A chill raced down Madison's spine. She was unaware of stepping closer to Zachary, of his arm closing around her shoulder.

"Let's step out for a minute," he said. Not giving Madison a chance to protest, he led her out. They had gone only a few feet when another sound pierced the air. This time, the scream of a woman.

Madison felt the tears clawing at her throat. She opened her mouth to ask Zachary to excuse her. A sob came out instead.

His arms slid around her and pulled her close. "It's all right. Go ahead and cry, but don't give up. Please, don't give up."

Madison heard the thickness in Zachary's voice and let the tears fall. Wes had to live. He had to.

* * *

Zachary was first to see the gurney roll off the elevator. He swiped a hand that wasn't quite steady across his face and swallowed. He'd give anything for this not to have happened. "Madison. I think this may be Wes."

Her head came up. She pushed away from the wall beside him, then followed his gaze down the hall. She started toward the gurney, but Zachary's hand on her arm stopped her.

"If it's Wes, he may look different," Zachary warned, recalling how battered and bruised Wes had been when they wheeled him into the operating room.

Her heart shot up to her throat. On trembling legs, she walked to the gurney. At first she thought Zachary was wrong. This wasn't Wes, this man whose face was swollen and marred. Then his eyelids fluttered open. Light-brown eyes that had once teased and cajoled, were now glazed and unfocused.

"Wes." His name came out in a choked cry.

"Let's get him in his room, then you can come in for just a few minutes," said one of the men pushing the gurney.

Madison bit her lower lip. "His mother can't see him like that."

"This time Vanessa won't have a choice." Zachary took Madison's trembling hand in his and followed the gurney.

In the ICU room machines beeped. Every inch of Wes's body that Madison could see was bruised. An IV line ran from each arm. Another tube ran from the side of his neck. There were wires on his chest connecting him to a heart monitor. A clamp on his fingers monitored his temperature and respiration. A catheter bag dangled near the floor.

Silently, a cold knot in her stomach, her heart thudding erratically, Madison approached the bed. Zachary was close behind her, his presence providing an oasis of calm in the turmoil. Swallowing the lump in her throat, she stopped at the head of the bed.

Trying to stop trembling, Madison leaned to within inches of Wes's face. Her heart clutched at the pitiful sight. Biting her lips, she forced the words out past the constriction in her throat. "Wes. I'm here. You're going to be fine." She swallowed before she was able to continue. "Your parents are here, too. Wes, please wake up."

His eyelids fluttered then opened. She tried to smile and discovered the muscles in her face wouldn't cooperate. "You're going to be fine. When you get out we can go to Chicago just like you wanted."

"Ma—" he gasped. The machine beeped louder.

"Don't try to talk, Wes," she pleaded, positive he was trying to say her name. "I'm here. I'm here."

Wes closed his eyes, then opened them again. Pain and frustration shimmered in his hazel eyes. The machine beeped louder.

"M—an . . ."

"I'm here. Everything will be all right," Madison said, her worried gaze going from Wes to the beeping machines.

The beeping sped up. Wide-eyed, Madison shot a quick look at the climbing numbers that monitored his blood pressure, then anxiously back at Wes, then Zachary. "What's the matter? Can't he see that I'm here?"

"I'm not sure, unless . . ." The frown on Zachary's face cleared. He leaned down and spoke softly to Wes. "She's fine. Don't worry. I'll take care of everything. I promise. Just get well."

Wes's eyelids drifted shut. The machine quieted. The numbers on the blood pressure monitor started to descend.

"What was that all about?" Madison asked, her puzzlement growing.

"I'll tell you on the way back to his parents."

Grasping her arm, he led her away. He didn't speak until they were standing in front of the elevator. "The motorist Wes stopped to help was a woman. There was an infant in the back."

Her stomach clenched. "She's not . . ." She couldn't form the words.

"No. She's fine," Zachary said quickly. "Luckily, she

was properly strapped in a car seat. She's in Children's Medical Center next door. After they took Wes to surgery, I went to see her to make sure she was all right. Her name is Manda."

Madison breathed a sigh of relief that the little girl was unharmed, and was proud of Wes that he had thought of the child. Then another thought struck. "Where's her mother?"

Zachary's silence answered her question. Her head fell forward. Tears brimmed in her eyes. Another child that would grow up without its mother.

Zachary curved his arm around her shoulders. When the elevator door opened, they walked on together. People shifted. Zachary nodded his thanks and kept his arm around Madison. She swiped at the remaining moisture in her eyes as they stepped off the elevator on the fifth floor.

"According to the eyewitness, Wes tried to push her out of the way, but he wasn't fast enough," Zachary said tightly as they continued down the hall.

Rage swamped Madison. She came to an abrupt halt and whirled on him, her small fist clenched. "Don't you dare tell me the driver was on a cell phone."

Zachary's black eyes blazed with equal fury. "The police think he was drunk. He had been arrested twice in the past three months for DWI."

"He probably didn't get a scratch on him," Madison said bitterly.

"Not then, but he tried to leave the scene and struck an abutment. He was pronounced dead at the scene," Zachary said.

"So much misery because he couldn't or wouldn't stop drinking." She lifted troubled eyes to him. "What do you think the odds are that he left a wife and children who loved him?"

"Probably high."

"He's destroyed two families, then—his and that woman's—he won't add a third," she said firmly. "Wes is going to be all right."

"Yes, he is," Zachary agreed.

Madison started down the hall again. "Do you think Manda's family would mind if I went up and saw her?"

"I don't think they'd mind at all," Zachary answered, hoping his voice sounded normal. *Lord, what a mess*—and it could get a whole lot messier if the truth came out.

Friends and associates of both hers and Wes's crowded around them as soon as they entered the conference room, but stepped back for Wes's parents. Madison looked into Vanessa's eyes. During the years she had known Wes's mother, Madison had been the subject of her scrutiny. Those eyes had held everything from disapproval to disgust. Now they pleaded.

Madison thought of two years ago when she had looked into her obstetrician's eyes, begging for reassurance that he hadn't been able to give. Her marriage had died the day her unborn child had. Her fault or Wes's, she didn't know anymore. Nor did it matter.

"He was awake for a little while."

"Thank goodness," Vanessa said, blinking back tears. "Did he ask for me?"

Madison thought the question odd, but her expression didn't change. "He was only awake for a few moments. His concern was for the little girl, Manda. It was her mother that Wes had stopped to help. He was injured when he tried to push the woman out of the way of the car. She didn't survive."

"He's a hero. Wes is one of the most compassionate men I've known," a male voice rumbled.

Madison glanced around to see Louis Forbes. Murmurs of agreement to Louis's statement filtered across the room.

"My son is the best there is," A.J. said proudly. "When can we see him?"

Madison faltered. "I forgot to look at the visiting schedule."

"The next time is a little over an hour and a half from now, at five," Zachary said.

A.J. glanced at Zachary, then centered his attention on Madison. "Would it be all right if Vanessa and I visited first?"

"Of course," Madison agreed, annoyed by Wes's parents' aloofness toward Zachary. They'd been the same way toward her when they'd first met. She hadn't been in their same social circles and they had let her know immediately how they felt. Only their love for Wes had gotten them to bend a bit, but she had always known they didn't think she was good enough for him.

The nouveau riche were permissible, as long as someone else sweated and toiled to do the hard work that earned them the money. Wes's father owned three car dealerships scattered around the Houston area. Madison knew for a fact that not one of his salespeople had even been to his magnificent home by the lake, fished from the pier, ridden in his speedboat. Vanessa, who had never worked, came from a family of bankers and referred to A.J.'s employees as "those people" and considered them "different."

Madison knew nothing of Zachary's background, but his large hands were rough and callused, his speech was neither refined nor cultured, his clothes weren't tailored or expensive. Considering all that, he was completely unacceptable in Wes's parent's snobbish way of thinking.

Wes's parents were who they were, however, and although Madison disapproved of their attitude and behavior, now wasn't the time or place to bring it up. "I'm going to call my family, then I'm going to visit the little girl. Why don't you go downstairs to the cafeteria and get something to eat?"

"Not likely," Vanessa said, her pert nose tilted. "The food here is probably horrid, if one is to judge by the coffee and the mediocre brand of tea. A.J. has already ordered for us from Crown's Deli. We know the owner."

Madison's eyes narrowed; it was all she could do not to mention what other patients' families didn't have or how the hospital had gone out of their way to make this easier for them, but all she said was, "All right," before turning to the people who had come to show their support. Somehow she managed to smile. "Thank you all for coming. I'll tell Wes when I visit him again. I'll keep Gordon posted on Wes's progress."

The room emptied quickly until the only visitor remaining was Louis Forbes, his teeth clamped around an unlit cigar. He strolled over to Madison. "You tell Wes not to worry about KGHA. I spoke with Steinberg. They still want him and will hold the job for as long as it takes him to get well. Doesn't matter that the contract wasn't signed."

The annoyance she had suppressed while speaking to Wes's parents surged forward full force. "How can you think about business now?" she asked, her voice strained and shaky.

He didn't back down. "Because it's my job and it's what Wes wants. We both know that."

He was right. She shoved a hand through her hair. "I'm sorry."

"You have nothing to be sorry about—isn't that right, Forbes?" Gordon asked, his hard stare pinning the smaller man.

"No, not at all." He worked the cigar from one side of his narrow mouth to the other. "I better go. People will want to know how Wes is doing. Good-bye."

"Thanks, Gordon, but you should be going, too," Madison said to her producer. "We've been here since this morning. The station can't run without you."

He studied her closely. "I'd like to think so, but we both know it can."

"Go on. There's nothing to do now but wait."

"I don't want you waiting alone."

"I'll be here," Zachary said.

Madison flicked a glance in his direction. "You should go, too."

"Wes and I go way back. I'm staying." He stuck his hand out toward Gordon. "Wes admires you a lot. I know he'll feel better knowing you were here with Madison."

"Thanks." The handshake was firm. Gordon's attention went back to Madison. "If you need anything, don't think, just call."

On tiptoes, she hugged him. "Thanks." Then he was gone too.

She glanced at Wes's parents, who were sitting at opposite ends on the velvet couch. Madison felt a separation from her in-laws even greater than simply being across the room. Wes wasn't there so they didn't have to feign liking or accepting her. They simply ignored her. A wave of unexpected loneliness hit her.

"You're not alone. I'm here."

Madison's gaze shot up to Zachary. She wouldn't have thought him perceptive, but it appeared she had been wrong. The tension in her shoulders relaxed a little. "Thank you for staying, but you have a business to run."

"My people can work without me standing over them," he told her easily. "Besides, even if I left, my mind would be here and I'd probably mess up anything I touched. Considering I was supposed to help frame today, I better stay here."

She studied him a long time before she said, "I didn't know you two were this close."

Zachary shrugged. "We traveled in different circles and both of us have crazy schedules so we didn't see each other as much as we once did, but we always knew we could count on each other," Zachary explained. "If it was me in ICU and I had a wife, I'd expect Wes to be there with her."

Only if it was convenient for him, Madison thought, then felt ashamed. Wes was fighting for his life. "I'm glad he has you for a friend."

"Call your family, then we'll go see Manda and grab a bite," Zachary said.

Madison went to call. Somehow she knew without asking that Wes's parents hadn't included her or Zachary when they ordered their food.

Chapter 5

Madison heard the crying the instant the elevator door slid open on the third floor of Children's Medical Center. The cries were desolate and desperate. Pity swept through her. No child should ever sound that way. With each step down the brightly colored hallway decorated with rainbows and cartoon characters, the cries increased in volume and distress.

Zachary's fingers flexed on Madison's arm. "I hope that's not Manda."

"If it is, she sounds heartbroken," Madison said, quickening her pace.

Three doors from the nurse's station Zachary pushed open the door to the room the cries were coming from. Madison entered first and saw a nurse in a Disney-print smock trying to soothe the fretful baby in her arms. Madison's heart went out to the inconsolable dark-haired infant.

"Don't cry," Zachary said, arms reaching.

The infant hiccuped and fastened tear-filled eyes on Zachary. He plucked the infant from the arms of the nurse and hugged her to his wide chest. "It's all right. You're all right."

The infant hiccuped again, then quieted.

"You certainly have a way with children," Madison told him as she moved closer.

Zachary gave an offhand shrug, his gaze not quite meeting

hers. "I have a lot of friends with children. They like me, but in this case it's probably more of a familiar face." He spoke to the nurse. "You just come on duty?"

"About an hour ago," she confirmed. "Are you relatives?"

Madison bit her lips before answering. "My husband was injured trying to help her mother. I hope it's all right to be here."

The young nurse's eyes rounded in recognition, her mouth opened, then she shut it abruptly. "Mrs. Reed, I'm sorry to hear about your husband, but Dr. London is the best."

"Thank you." Madison rubbed her hand over the thick, curly black hair of the chubby infant whose cries had dwindled to sniffles, then glanced around the room.

Why wasn't there a relative or two hovering over the child? Wes's family was small, but she'd come from a big family, a close family. Even now, her parents and sister were probably on the phone spreading the word about Wes's accident. She'd tried to convince them not to come, but she'd be surprised if they didn't show up tomorrow.

And when they did they'd find Wes had gotten better. Determined to remain positive, Madison said softly, "Hello, Manda."

The thumb of one hand jammed firmly in her mouth, the infant rubbed her eye with the other. Zachary's large hand continued to sweep up and down the infant's back, much as he had done to Madison.

"How old is she?" Madison asked.

"Nine months according to the information her mother had in her wallet, and as healthy as they come," the nurse announced.

"And not liking it at all that you're by yourself," Madison crooned to the baby. "I don't blame you. But your family should be here soon, sweetie."

The burgeoning smile on the nurse's face died. She crossed her arms. "As far as we've been able to find out, the mother was a single parent. There's no information on Manda's father. The only relative they've found is an elderly aunt of the mother who is in a nursing home in Amarillo. Manda has to have competent care and apparently the great aunt can't give it. If they can't find someone else or if the father can't or won't come forward, Child Protective Services will have to be contacted and she'll probably end up in foster care."

"No!" Zachary snapped, pulling the child closer.

The baby's curly head came up at the brusque sound, her lower lip quivering. Instinctively Madison made a soothing sound. "It's all right, Manda." She turned to the nurse. "Zachary's right. She's lost enough. Surely there has to be some other way. There are some very good foster homes, but we've all heard of stories where that isn't the case. Manda would be helpless to defend or speak for herself if she were placed in an unfit home."

The nurse held up both hands, palms out. "Hey, don't kill the messenger. I wish things were different too."

His expression deeply troubled, Zachary said, "Sorry. It's not your fault."

"Don't sweat it. You're supposed to stay objective, but sometimes the children work their way into your heart. You can tell when they've been loved and hugged like Manda here. It sucks to have all that ripped from her." She smoothed the blanket on the bottom of the crib. "Stay as long as you like. If you have time, could you give her a juice bottle? She hasn't taken enough fluids."

"We have time," Madison said without a moment's hesitation.

"Thanks. I'll be back in a jiffy."

Taking the baby's tiny hand, Madison crouched down to eye level with the infant. "You hav—" Everything inside her froze. Straightening, she turned away from the little girl.

"What is it?" Zachary asked, careful to keep his voice hushed.

When Madison shook her head, he walked around in front of her. Now he was the one leaning down to eye level. "What is it?" he repeated.

Madison brushed the tears away with the back of her fingers. "She has hazel eyes just like Wes."

Zachary stiffened, then said, "She made you think of the child you lost?"

Madison's head lifted. Although it was no secret that she had miscarried, few if any of her close friends at the time ever spoke of it. She had soon realized they were trying to spare her further hurt, but by not talking about the baby she lost, it almost made it seem as if it hadn't mattered. Zachary knew because he'd had to take out the nursery and alter the original floor plans of their house. "Yes," she finally answered.

Zachary withdrew his hand from the infant's back and curved it around Madison's tense shoulders. "There's still time, Madison."

Madison said nothing, simply held her hands out for the child, who, after a long moment, went to her. Cuddling the infant to her, the longing for a child that she had tried to suppress for so long swamped her. Her eyes closed. To have a child of your own to love and spoil, to care for and watch grow up happy and secure, had to be the greatest feeling in the world.

Her eyes opened as she thought that for her, motherhood might never happen. She and Wes hadn't made love in over a year. They had gone their separate ways and communicated only when necessary. Could their marriage be saved? Was there time to find where their marriage had gotten off the track, fix it, and have a family?

She pressed her cheek against Manda's, smelled her baby smells, and lost a piece of her heart to the infant. Her own resolve strengthened. Somehow they'd work through their problems. They had time to start a family of their own. To think of them doing less would be as if she had lost faith that Wes would survive.

Zachary was right. There was time.

When Zachary and Madison arrived at ICU, it was almost five. Not wanting to lose one precious second of visiting time, people were already lined up at the door . . . except A.J. and Vanessa. They stood apart with another well-dressed couple Madison recognized as the mayor and his wife.

Wildly popular and respected, Doug Jones was the first black mayor of Dallas. He'd won his second term by an even bigger margin than his first.

"Madison," the mayor said, taking her hand. "If there is anything I can do, please don't hesitate to let me know."

"Yes, please," Patricia, his wife, added as she reached out for Madison's other hand. She was an attractive, affable woman. It was well reputed that she was the solid rock that kept her husband grounded.

"Thank you." Madison turned toward Zachary. "This is Zachary Holman, a friend of Wes's."

Mayor Jones's shrewd eyes narrowed behind his signature horn-rimmed glasses. "Any relation to the owner of Holman Construction doing the restoration in South Dallas?"

"One and the same."

"I've heard nothing but praise from the councilwoman and constituents in that district on your work in helping to revitalize that area," the mayor said. "Very good work." A nurse opened the door to ICU and people surged inside. The mayor switched his attention to Wes's parents standing a short distance away. "We'll be going, A.J., Vanessa, call if you need us."

"Thank you for coming by." A.J. extended his hand for a brief handshake, then he and Vanessa turned to enter ICU as the mayor and his wife left.

Madison bit her lower lip when the heavy double doors swung shut. "Perhaps I should have warned Vanessa how he looked."

"She'll be all right," Zachary said. "Vanessa may look fragile, but she's tough."

"You know her?" Madison asked, startled by the revelation.

His face closed. "I know of her. I'm going to get a soft drink. You want one?"

Madison knew she was being put off. "No, thanks."

"I should be back by the time they come out." Hands in his pockets, Zachary strolled away.

"Why don't they come out?" Madison questioned, glancing again at the slim gold watch on her wrist. Eight-thirty. Visiting hour for ICU would be over in thirty minutes. She had tried to understand when Wes's parents hadn't come out the first time at five, but this was the last chance she'd get to see Wes for the night.

After visiting him the first time, Vanessa had emerged from ICU tearful and almost prostrate. Ann Crane, the hospital spokeswoman, had been there and immediately obtained a wheelchair to take Vanessa back to the conference room.

While Vanessa reclined on the couch, three of her friends arrived. Instead of helping, their presence caused Vanessa to cry more. A.J. had been totally inept at comforting his wife. Madison couldn't help but think, if only he'd touch her, hold her, perhaps it might help. It flashed through her mind that Wes wasn't much of a toucher himself unless they were making love. The thought made her feel guilty and on edge.

When Ms. Crane asked if she felt up to going with her for a brief news conference, Madison was more than ready. When she stepped on the elevator Zachary was by her side. He'd said he'd stay with her and he had, comforting her, helping her. "If you have trouble, focus on me," he said.

She hadn't thought she would need to take his advice since she made her living being in front of a camera . . . until the reporters began asking questions about the extent of Wes's injuries, and Dr. London began explaining in detail about the surgery. Five minutes into it, she stood, looking blindly for an exit.

Thankfully, Ms. Crane and Zachary were there. They took her to a small enclosed garden. She sat on a stone bench beside a pool of goldfish and cried until her eyes and body ached.

Afterwards, they went back upstairs to the conference room where a chef waited to serve them. A.J. and Vanessa and their guests, who now numbered eight, were already seated around the oblong table, eating. Madison ate because she hadn't eaten earlier when Zachary had taken her to the hospital cafeteria. She now realized she had to, and not just because Zachary kept putting small amounts of food on her plate. She assumed Wes's father had ordered the food until the waiter presented the bill to Zachary. A.J. and Vanessa both stopped eating and pushed their plates away.

As the waiter began to clean up, Zachary said he was going to check on Manda. With an hour before the next visiting time at eight, Madison hurried after him.

In Manda's room they found her fretful, but not crying. She finished off a bottle Madison fed her in nothing flat, then, with her tiny hand clutching Madison's blouse as if to keep her there, she went to sleep.

"She likes you," Zachary said.

Madison, in a rocking chair, glanced down at the peacefully sleeping infant, then looked up at him and smiled. "You're not the only one children like."

"I see," he said, returning her smile.

When they arrived back at ICU five minutes before the last visiting hour was to begin, Vanessa was apologetic for taking up all the last visiting time and pleaded to go in first. After being with Manda, Madison felt sorry for Wes's parents and allowed them go in. The last visiting hour was only forty-five minutes.

Finally, the door opened and Wes's parents came out ten minutes before visiting hour would be over. Vanessa was crying softly. Madison rushed by them. A.J. was finally touching and hovering, as were Vanessa's friends who had followed her to the waiting area.

Aware of Zachary beside her, Madison walked to the bed

and stared down at Wes. His bruises appeared more pronounced. Her finger gently stroked his cold hand. "Everything will be all right. Don't worry. Manda is all right, too. You have to get well so you can see her."

His eyelashes fluttered, then lifted. Her finger stilled. "Wes. I'm here. Everything is going to be okay."

His tongue came out to moisten his dry lips. His mouth worked for several seconds before words emerged, hushed and raspy. "P-promise me."

Madison's heart leaped with joy. He was going to be all right. "I promise. We'll go to Chicago. I'll get a job there and it'll be the way it used to be. You'll see."

With an effort he shook his head. "Something . . . e-else."

Fearing that he would become agitated she rushed to reassure him. "Anything."

"K-keep Manda."

She blinked. She hadn't expected that, but having him talk to her was a good sign he was getting better. She'd promise him anything to get him well. "I promise. Just rest. Don't worry." She blinked back tears.

"Z-Zach?" Wes rasped.

"I'm here." Zachary leaned his face closer to Wes's. "Just rest. Save your strength."

Wes struggled to speak. His gaze clung to Zachary's. "R-remember . . . you promised."

"I remember. Don't worry," Zachary assured, his voice thick, his hand clamped around the bed rail.

Wes seemed to relax, his eyes closing, then suddenly his eyelids shot upward. The alarm sounded on the heart monitor. He gasped, then gasped again. He didn't seem to be able to catch his breath.

"Wes!" Madison cried.

"Nurse!" Zachary yelled, but they were already running into the room.

"What's happening? Please tell me what's happening!" Madison begged.

One nurse began adjusting the bed rail. Another listened to his chest with a stethoscope. "Please leave."

"No, I'm not leaving." She wanted to go to Wes, but Zachary held her back. "I'm not leaving him. Wes!"

He gasped, struggled to speak.

Wrenching away from Zachary, Madison rushed back to the bed. "Wes, what is it?"

"Mine. M-Manda . . . my child."

Madison jerked upward. "Wh-what?"

"M-Manda's mine."

Dr. London came barreling though the door. "Get them out of here!"

The beeping went into a long, eerie wail. "Code blue!"

Someone pushed them outside. People ran past them. The curtains were jerked closed. Madison was unable to make her legs move any farther. Surely she had misunderstood him. He hadn't said what she thought he had. As soon as he was all right, he'd explain.

Zachary kept his eyes on the door of the room. Through the thin partition of glass he could hear Dr. London shouting orders. Zachary's clenched his fists. "Fight, Wes, you can beat this. There's never been anything you couldn't do when you set your mind to it."

He kept that thought for what seemed like an eternity until the door opened and Dr. London came out. Shoulders slumped, his face tired, he approached Madison. "Mrs. Reed, I'm sorry. We did everything we could. We're going to have to call it."

"What?" She blinked, finally drawing her fixed gaze away from the door to Wes's room. "Call what?"

"He's gone," Dr. London said.

"Gone? He can't be gone! We were just talking," she said, as tears slid down her cheeks. "He was trying to tell me something and he got it all mixed up."

"We've done everything we could. His heart is just not responding. There's nothing on the monitor."

Madison wildly shook her head. "No! You have to go back in there and keep trying."

"Perhaps you'd like to lie down," Dr. London suggested, reaching toward her arm.

Madison drew her arm out of his reach and stepped back on wobbly legs. Her chest felt like it was being squeezed by a giant fist. "I don't want to lie down! I want to talk to my husband! Why can't you understand that?"

Zachary heard the hysteria rising in her voice, and clamped down on his own grief. "Dr. London, his parents are outside. Would you please tell them? I'll stay with Madison."

"All right," Dr. London said; his voice sounded as tired as he looked. "I'm sorry. I'm going back inside to call the code as over, then I'll go speak to his parents." He went back into the room, then came back out moments later and walked toward the waiting room. A man pushing a big metal cart with multiple compartments came out directly behind him. So did two other people.

"What are they doing?" Madison cried. "They have to go back in there and help Wes!"

Zachary placed his hand gently on her arm, felt the shivers that raced over her slim body. "Come on, Madison. Let's get out of here."

"No, I'm not leaving." She stared up at him with dazed eyes. "I have to talk with Wes."

His other hand closed around her other forearm. "Wes is gone, Madison. You can't talk with him," he told her, speaking the most difficult words in his life.

She shook her head from side to side. "You're wrong! He has to tell me the truth."

"He already has, Madison. Wes was Manda's father."

Chapter 6

Madison recoiled, Zachary's words were like a punch to the gut. She wanted to deny Wes's confession, but couldn't. No man so gravely injured would claim a child that wasn't his. Her eyes shut tightly. The extent of Wes's betrayal clawed its way through the disbelief and grief. While they were married, Wes had slept with another woman and had a child.

"Madison."

Her eyes snapped open. They blazed with anger. "Let me go!"

Zachary gazed down into her features ravaged with shock and anguish, then slowly uncurled his fingers from around her arms. As soon as she was free, she turned to walk away.

"What about Manda?"

Madison flinched, but kept walking, forcing herself to put one foot in front of the other. She took another step, then swayed as a piercing cry came from beyond the door to the waiting area. *Vanessa.*

Madison shut her eyes, wishing she could shut out the grief pouring from Wes's mother. Shut out Wes's last words to her.

"Manda's mine."

When she opened her eyes, Zachary stood in front of her.

"What about Manda?" he repeated.

She tried to go around him, but he stepped in her path. Rage ripped though her grief. "How can you ask me that?"

"Manda lost, too. She lost a mother and a father."

The reminder almost caused Madison's trembling knees to buckle. "She's not my responsibility."

"What about your promise?" he pushed.

Her hands clenched. "Wes promised something, too," she said referring to their marriage vows. "Now, please let me pass."

Zachary hated that he had to push her, but he didn't have a choice. Somehow he had to get through to her. "I know you're hurting and angry, but you heard the nurse. If you don't take her, she'll go into foster care. You're not that heartless."

His words pricked her, but not in the way he'd intended. "Yes. Good old Madison. She'll take anything." How could Wes have done this to her?

"Mad—"

"No!" she shouted, cutting him off, unaware that the nurses and visitors who had given them privacy were all watching and listening. "I don't want anything to do with her. She's not my responsibility and nothing you can say will change my mind."

She was near the breaking point, Zachary noted. She was hanging by her fingernails. If he pushed any further, she'd crack. "Come on, I'll take you home."

"I—"

"I'm just driving you home," he assured her calmly. "You don't have your car, remember?"

She remembered. Too much. She was tired. So tired.

Gently, his arm curved around her shoulder, drawing her closer to him as he led her out of the room, aware that he was leaving Wes. His throat ached. He wasn't ashamed to cry. There would be time enough for tears later. Now, Madison and Manda needed him. He had made a promise, too.

Zachary located his truck exactly where the security guard, Ronald Jones, had said he parked it. After learning the situation, Ronald had parked the Dakota in the next available parking spot, then brought Zachary the keys and the change of clothes he always kept in the truck. Ronald had waited patiently while Zachary cleaned up, then took the soiled clothes back to the truck. He'd politely refused Zachary's offer of money.

Keeping one hand on Madison's arm, Zachary opened the door with the other. Head down, as it had been since they left ICU, Madison stepped onto the running board but didn't seem to have the strength to pull herself up.

"Let me help you." Placing both hands around her slim waist, he lifted her into the seat, then scooted her legs around. It was on the tip of his tongue to ask if she was all right, then he realized what a stupid question that was. "I'll call Gordon. He'll know how to contact your family."

Her eyes shut tightly, she leaned over farther in the seat. He felt helpless in the face of her grief. Pulling a handkerchief from his back pocket, he pressed it into her loosely clasped hands and closed the door. As long as he could remember, his mother had always insisted he have a handkerchief in his pocket. A gentleman, in her opinion, should always carry one. He might be thirty-five, but he hadn't gotten out of the habit.

Unhooking the cell phone from his belt, he activated it, then using the bright lights from the overhead security lights in the emergency room parking area, he read Gordon's number, then keyed it in. It was picked up on the second ring.

"Yes."

Zachary didn't have to ask if this was Gordon. He recognized his voice, but he was struggling with his own.

"Madison, is that you?" Gordon asked, his tone rising in anxiety.

Zachary sucked in a gulp of air and leaned against the back end of the truck. "It's Zach. Wes . . . Wes didn't make it."

"Oh, God. How's Madi—Never mind. Where is she?"

From the cadence of Gordon's voice Zachary could tell he was moving. "With me in the emergency-room parking lot. I'm taking her home."

"I'll be waiting for you when you get there."

Zachary rubbed his hands across his face. "Do you know how to reach her family?"

"I'll take care of it." The sound of a motor came through the phone. "You just take care of Madison."

"See you." Zachary answered, then flipped the phone closed. He wished he could promise to do that, but if it came down to Madison's well-being or Manda's, there would be no contest. Manda was not going into foster care.

Driving up to the manned guardhouse of the Legacy Estates in far North Dallas, Zachary identified himself, then drove through the ten-foot black iron gates past the splashing thirty-foot waterfall, then followed the curving two-lane road through the exclusive estate where homes ranged in price from a half a million to over five million. There were only twenty-one homes in the development and all were sold. Wes and Madison's sprawling, single-story house sat on a one-third-acre lot in a cul-de-sac.

Zachary saw Gordon pacing by his car the moment he turned into the long driveway lit by four antique gas yard lights Wes had had shipped from England. Zachary's hands clamped on the steering wheel. He could recall it all as if it were yesterday—Wes dragging him out here and telling Zachary his plans to build a showplace. Zachary was to be the builder. He wanted it to be single-story because he had lived in a two-story home growing up and damned if he was going to spend his time running up and down stairs again.

The Legacy Home Association had strict rules and regulations about the houses built there, but Wes had every confidence Zachary would meet and surpass their demands and expectations. He had and they'd celebrated with a beer. Two years. Two lousy years ago.

By the time he braked in front of the house, Gordon was there, opening the door. "Madison. Madison. It's Gordon." Finally she looked at him, then tumbled into his arms. "It's all right. It's all right."

Zachary felt helplessness wash over him again. He

reached out to touch her as he had done with Manda, then jerked his hand back. What a mess.

One of the massive, recessed double doors opened and a diminutive woman came rushing out. Zachary remembered her as Gretchen, the housekeeper.

"I got her bed all ready, Mr. Armstrong. You bring her on in."

Picking up Madison's purse, Zachary followed. The entryway was filled with African art and bronzes Wes had collected in his travels. Knowing the location of the master bedroom suite, Zachary was surprised when Gretchen entered the bedroom next to it. There was no door that connected them.

One look inside the room and he had his answer. Wes liked bold colors, and heavy furniture. The room, light and airy, was completely feminine: a luxurious mix of fabrics and accessories. A canopy bed was outfitted with an array of fluffy pillows, duvet, and adjustable reading lights on either side of the padded headboard. At the foot of the bed was a padded bench in the same fabric as the headboard.

Colors from the deepest rose to the lightest mauve with just a hint of the palest green were repeated throughout the room. The wallpaper was a rose silk he'd put up himself. At the time he'd thought it was to be a guest room. Placing the purse on the small table just inside the door, he went back to the living room to wait.

Gordon joined him less than five minutes later and headed for the built-in bar. "I need a drink. How about you?"

"Scotch."

"Wes's drink of choice." Gordon opened the cabinet and pulled a crystal decanter from beneath. "It's hard anytime, but when it comes out of nowhere . . ."

Zachary walked over and leaned against the oak counter. "You call her parents yet?"

"On the way here." Gordon pulled the stopper and poured a liberal portion in two squat crystal glasses. "I couldn't get them at their home so I called Dianne, Madison's older sister, and spoke with her husband, David. He'd stayed home to keep their two little girls. Dianne and her parents left as soon as they could get a flight out. As it happened he was speaking with her at the time. She'd called from the plane to see if Madison had called back with any more news about Wes. He had to tell her Wes had died. He's flying out in the morning. His parents are coming to take care of the girls."

Gordon's hand fisted on the glass. "I can't imagine how difficult it was for David to tell Dianne or for her to hear such news or worse for her to tell her parents. They're a close family. They must be frantic to get to Madison. Their plane arrives at DFW within the hour." Gordon took a hefty swallow of the amber liquid.

Zachary stared down at his own glass. He knew exactly how Dianne's husband had felt. He'd been the one to tell Wes that Manda's mother hadn't made it. Zachary's chest tight, he glanced up at Gordon's somber face. "I can pick them up if you'd like."

"I'd appreciate it," Gordon said, glancing toward the bedroom. "I don't want to leave Madison alone. Gretchen has been with them for a long time, but I'd feel better staying."

"I'll wait until later to drink this." Zachary pushed the glass away. "Do you have the flight information?"

Reaching into the breast pocket of his sports coat, Gordon drew out a white slip of paper and handed it to Zachary, along with his car keys. "Your truck won't seat them comfortably."

Zachary glanced at the information, then stuffed it into his shirt pocket. "I'd better get going."

"Wait." Gordon picked up a silver picture frame from an end table and removed the picture. "Her parents. It will save you the trouble of having them paged."

Zachary looked down at a good-looking couple on either side of Madison, who wore a wedding gown and a big smile. Zachary remembered the day and how happy she and Wes had been. "Do you think you should call a doctor to give her something?"

"I hope it doesn't come to that," Gordon said, his voice tired. "Sooner or later she'll have to deal with Wes's death. A sedative might knock her out, but when she wakes up, she'll still have to face the problem. Madison is stronger than she looks."

Zachary hoped Madison was as strong as Gordon thought. She'd need to be in order to deal with the loss of her husband, his betrayal, and his child by another woman. "I'll be back as soon as I can."

Opening the door, he stepped out into the night. Overhead, the moon shone; he could hear the faint sound of traffic several streets over. Life went on.

Zachary arrived at DFW International Airport thirty minutes before Madison's family was due to arrive. Finding a quiet corner on the concourse, he pulled out his cell phone and dialed. His mother answered before the second ring.

"Hello."

Her warm voice caused his throat to sting, moisture to form in his eyes. He could picture her sitting at her sewing machine or curled up on the sofa with a book. His father would either be sitting next to her reading the newspaper or at his scrupulously neat desk doing paperwork. They were as much in love as they had been when they married twenty-seven years ago, and, when possible, were never far apart. "Mama."

"Zachary." With a mother's instinct she knew something was wrong. "What is it? Is it Wes?"

Closing his eyes, he rubbed his hand across his face. "He . . . he didn't make it."

"Oh, honey, I'm so sorry," she said, her soft voice filled with love and sympathy. "I've been praying since you called this morning. I know how close you two had grown in the past few years."

"It's hard to believe he's gone," Zachary said, unable to keep the hitch out of his voice.

"Do you want us to come?"

"No." He reached for his handkerchief to wipe his face and remembered giving it to Madison. He used the back of his hand. "I'm all right, Mama. Daddy has to finish the renovations on the Stevenses' house by this weekend so you can go on vacation next week. You've planned too long to miss your cruise."

"There'll be other cruises. You're our only child."

So simple. Yet so profound. The vise squeezing his chest eased. "I'll be home this weekend to see you before you leave. Can I speak to Daddy alone for a minute?" He needed to talk and his father, who, as far as Zachary knew, was the only other person besides him who knew about Manda.

"Should I worry?" she asked.

"No, ma'am."

"I suppose I can find something else to do. Here's your daddy."

"Hello, Zach," his father greeted him. "She's going to worry until she sees you."

"I'm counting on you not to let her," Zachary said, positive his father would do everything within his power to keep his wife happy. Jim Holman had come into their lives when Zachary was eight years old. He had become a father to Zachary, and a husband to his mother six months later. There wasn't a finer man on earth in Zachary's opinion. "Before it happened Wes told his wife about Manda."

"You probably think that was commendable. I don't," his father said, making no attempt to keep the displeasure out of his voice. "It shouldn't have happened and he shouldn't have involved you."

His father was right, but Zachary *was* involved. Inadvertently, he'd entangled his father when Zachary had made the mistake of listening to his messages in his office when they'd returned from inspecting a house he was building. His father had never liked the Reed family, who thought more of money and prestige than they did of people, and after listening to Wes's panicky voice on the answering machine about the woman he'd gotten pregnant and asking for Zach's help, his opinion of Wes went even lower.

"I couldn't turn my back on him. I kept hoping he'd set things right," Zachary said, his voice tired and strained. "He never did."

"He used you," his father accused, his words biting.

"We both know at first I used him," Zachary admitted. He and Wes had gone through so much anger before coming to terms with each other. He'd envied, then hated, the popular, spoiled rich boy with equal intensity while they were growing up in the same small town. But eventually they had gotten past the hurt feelings of their boyhoods and moved on. It hadn't been easy for either of them.

As adults their friendship had grown slowly, cautiously, to deep affection despite their differences. Zachary hadn't approved of some of the things Wes did, tried to talk to him, but Wes always had an answer and an excuse. "He had his faults, but A.J. and Vanessa let him grow up thinking whatever he wanted, he could have."

"Now you have to pick up the pieces." His father's annoyance was clear through the line. "Again."

"If I don't, who will? It's not Madison's or Manda's fault."

"And you'd see that more clearly than anyone," his father said. "You do what you have to. You can count on me."

"Thanks, Daddy, for understanding," Zachary told him, the tension all but gone from his body. "I have to go. Take care of Mama. I'll see you this weekend. 'Bye."

"You know I will. 'Bye."

Zachary disconnected the phone, then started back toward Gate 15 to wait for Madison's family. A short while later the arrival of the plane was announced. He didn't need the picture to identify Madison's parents. Faces lined with worry and grief, arm around the other, the older couple were the first through the disembarking gate. He assumed the attractive woman close behind them was Dianne.

Madison's mother saw the picture in his hand and moved

with surprising quickness to him. "My baby. How's my baby?" she asked, her eyes imploring.

"She'll be better now that you're here," Zachary said, knowing he spoke the truth.

Madison couldn't get it out of her mind. No matter how tightly she closed her eyes, no matter how hard she tried to think of something else, those last seconds with Wes, the image of his face, strained and imploring, kept swimming before her. He had tried so valiantly to say those last words to her and with them he had sliced out her heart.

"Manda's mine."

That betrayal hurt, and she felt worse because she was angry at him for his deceit and for putting her in such a position. She wished he hadn't told her, wished she could have kept the illusion that they had had honesty and trust in their marriage if little else. With his last words he had taken that as well, leaving her nothing.

And he was gone and she almost despised him for that, for telling her, then leaving her to deal with it by herself. It made her angry and ashamed. Wes was dead. How could she be angry with a dead man? Didn't that make her into something unconscionable and vile?

Tired of her own thoughts and realizing she was too wired to fall asleep, Madison tossed back the covers and reached for her robe. After a few steps, she became aware of the pounding in her head. She welcomed the distraction.

She was almost to the bedroom door when it opened. She'd thought she had no more tears, but at the sight of her parents and sister they flooded her eyes.

Eagerly she reached her family, for the solace and the comforting presence she had always been able to find with them. Then she was passed from her mother to her father to her sister, then back to her mother.

"Words don't mean much with all the hurt you're feeling, but just know we love you and we're here," her mother said.

Yes, the words did mean so very much—they meant everything, especially when she was dealing with her husband's betrayal and her own guilt for her anger. How could he have done this to her? There was no answer, only the broken sobs that erupted from her own throat.

Visiting hours were over at Children's Medical Center but that hadn't stopped Zachary from returning after he had dropped off Madison's family at her house, close to midnight. There had been too much death; he needed to feel life and hope.

He had known where to come.

Manda lay on her stomach, her thumb stuck in her mouth, whimpering in her sleep. He didn't hesitate. Picking her up, he took a seat in the rocking chair near the crib. Almost immediately the whimpering stopped, the thumb came out of her tiny mouth. He felt her little body relaxing, curling against him, and his own grief wasn't quite as sharp.

Life did go on. But what kind of life would Manda have? She had lost so much: mother, father . . . and she stood to lose so much more.

With troubled eyes he stared down at the infant asleep in his arms, her cheek pressed against his chest. All he could see was a mass of black curls on top of her head, but he knew the way her light-brown eyes lit up when she was happy, how her lower lip quivered when she was about to cry. If it was within his power, he would do everything he could to make sure her happiness far outweighed her sorrow.

To do that, he had to convince Madison to keep her. It was a great deal to ask of her, but he had no choice. He hated the duplicity, the lies that had to continue. She'd been lied to enough, but Wes's death and that of Manda's mother had left those behind with few options. Even if he hadn't promised, Zachary would have seen to Manda. He knew what it was like not to have a father.

He'd adopt her himself, but his attorney had already

advised Zachary the chances of a bachelor being given custody of a baby girl were slim to none. And if Wes's parents wanted Manda, he didn't stand a chance.

A muscle clenched in Zachary's jaw. There was always that likelihood, but in his opinion they were too hard and cold to want her. Wes was probably the only person they both loved. However, if it became known that Manda was Wes's child, they might be swayed by public opinion. If nothing else, they enjoyed their social position and would go to any lengths to ensure that their status remained secure. The possibility that they might use Manda for their own selfish ends angered him.

He wouldn't allow that to happen. There were things he knew, secrets he'd spill if it came to that. Manda was going to grow up happy and loved. She was not going to go through what he had as a child.

They all repeated the same thing in various ways: their sorrow at her loss, what a wonderful person Wes was, her memories would comfort her. They didn't know that each time they said the words, she recalled Wes telling her that Manda was his, that with his last breath he had proclaimed his unfaithfulness.

All Madison had wanted was sleep, to shut off her brain. But first she had had to get through making the funeral arrangements, the wake, the funeral, and afterwards, when people came back to the house. They'd been everywhere. She hadn't been able to turn around without someone expressing their sympathy.

Occasionally she'd turn and see Zachary watching her, his broad shoulders slumped, his face tired and worn. She had wanted to turn away because he knew her secret and her shame. Yet Zachary's eyes had been so full of grief that she hadn't been able to shun him. That night after laying Wes to rest, Madison had taken off her wedding rings, put them in her jewelry case, then cried herself to sleep, unsure if the tears she cried were for Wes or for herself.

* * *

Long before the dawn broke Sunday morning Madison was awake. The same unanswered questions that had followed her into a fitful sleep were there when she awoke. Who was the other woman? What did she look like? When had they met? Who had approached whom? Had any of their friends known about the affair? Had Wes brought her to their house? Why hadn't Madison suspected? Was that Wes's first affair?

Madison flung her arm over her eyes. So many questions. Questions that she would never have the answer to. Interrogating the woman's aunt in the nursing home about her niece's illicit affair might yield some answers, but Madison wasn't that mean-spirited; besides, she remembered the old saying: Be careful of the rock you turn over . . . you might not like what's underneath. She couldn't take any more at the moment.

Wes's funeral on Friday had been on a clear, beautiful day with just a slight southerly breeze, the kind of day he would have loved to have spent on the golf course, a fact the minister had mentioned. So many people had been there that they had spilled out of the three-thousand-seat church. Although she had asked that in lieu of flowers donations be made to MADD, people still sent them to their home. She'd forwarded them all to Parkland Hospital.

Unable to stay in bed another second, she got up, showered, then used every makeup trick she'd learned in the past five years to hide the grief and strain on her face. She had to convince her parents she was well enough for them to go home today as planned. She couldn't stand seeing the pain and heartache in their eyes any longer. They were grieving for Wes, for her, for the illusion of a happy marriage they'd thought she had.

Happily married men don't have affairs.

Madison smeared her eyeliner. She snatched up a tissue. Her family could never know. At first it had been pride that had kept her silent; then her mother had had a heart attack a year ago. The doctor had warned them against undue stress in the future. She'd retired from her position as a school secretary and now volunteered at the same high school in the library and spoiled her grandchildren every chance she got.

Madison wasn't going to do or say anything that might adversely affect her mother's health. That was another reason they had to leave. It was becoming more and more difficult to mask her anger behind her grief. Finished with her makeup, she dressed in a simple white blouse and slacks, then left her room.

All four were in the kitchen. Her brother-in-law had arrived the day after her family. Her mother was at the stove cooking and Dianne was pouring the men coffee. The moment Madison entered the room her mother left the skillet she had been tending and came to her. "Good morning, Madison," she said, studying her daughter's face with a mother's discerning eyes and seeing beneath the makeup. "Baby, I think I should stay. Your father and I discussed it last night. Neither one of us thinks you should be left alone."

Madison's gaze went to her father, the morning newspaper in his hands forgotten. They were the solid unit she'd dreamed and prayed to have in her own marriage. Tears of regret stung her throat. "I'll be fine." She hugged her mother, then stepped away when she wanted to cling. "Your plane leaves at four and you're going to be on it."

Before either parent could protest, she spoke to Dianne, "April and Summer need their mother and father." She glanced around the room. "I love you all, but you can't stay with me forever."

"Maybe just another couple of days," her father said. Her mother nodded her agreement.

Crossing to him, Madison kissed the top of her father's head where his graying hair was receding, then went to the stove and turned over the bacon. "Today," she said firmly, and picked up the bowl of pancake batter, took a deep breath while her back was to them, and turned. "How many blueberry pancakes, Daddy?"

He and his wife shared a look. Madison's hands clenched on the bowl.

"When you get around to asking me, I want four," David said.

Madison threw him a grateful smile, for loving her sister, and for understanding. "Four it is."

"Better make that three," Dianne said, returning the carafe of coffee. "His pants are getting tight around the waist."

Looking chagrined, David folded his arms. "I've never said anything about the fit of your pants."

Dianne, never at a loss for words, grinned and tossed back, "That's because on me the extra fifteen pounds looks voluptuous."

David grinned. Her parents smiled.

Madison poured batter on the hot griddle. Another unit. Another question.

Had her and Wes's marriage disintegrated because they hadn't loved each other enough, or because they'd loved themselves too much?

Chapter 7

Monday afternoon Madison woke to the ringing of the doorbell. She pulled the covers over her head, trying to tune out the sound. She'd unplugged the phone, but had no idea how to disconnect the doorbell. All she wanted was to be left alone. Visitors usually went away if she didn't answer. This one didn't.

The chime came again and again. Before the sound faded for the seventh time, she was on her feet. She grabbed her long, silk robe, shrugging into it as she stormed down the hallway. With fire in her eyes, she unlocked the door and jerked it open.

"What?" she asked angrily.

"Hello, Madison. Manda and I came to visit," Zachary announced happily.

Madison stared from Zachary to the grinning infant in his arms.

"Thank you. Don't mind if we do." Zachary stepped into the foyer.

Madison came out of her stupor. "What do you think you're doing?" she snapped.

The smile on Manda's face faded. Laying her head on Zachary's shoulder, she stuck her thumb in her mouth.

"I guess you forgot she doesn't like loud noises." Zachary rubbed the baby's back, his voice dropped to a croon. "It's all right."

Madison didn't want to look at the child or think of why she didn't like loud noises. "Please leave." It was said pleasantly, yet her eyes were anything but.

"When I do, Manda is staying," he said just as pleasantly, obviously every bit as determined as Madison.

"If you won't leave, I'm calling the police."

"Maybe you should read this first." He pulled a folded newspaper from the hip pocket of his faded jeans.

She didn't want to take it. Every now and then she'd think of what would happen when people learned about Wes and his mistress—the gossip, the sly looks, the laughs about what a gullible fool she had been. "What does it say?"

"Read it."

She thought of snatching the paper out of his hand, then caught the stare of the baby. Madison wanted to look anywhere but at her. She didn't want to feel anything for her. The baby wasn't her responsibility.

She took the paper. The headline jumped out at her: TV NEWS CORRESPONDENT WES REED DIES A HERO. She quickly read the article. Her hands fisted, her eyes shut. A warm hand and the smell of baby powder had her lids snapping upward and stepping back.

"They think Wes died trying to help a stranded motorist. They don't know she was his mistress," she said, her voice shaky.

"I thought you'd feel better knowing no one else knows."

"You know!"

"It's time for Manda's bottle. Could you put on a pan of water to heat it up?" he said in a conversational tone, then patted the lemon-yellow quilted diaper bag hanging from his broad shoulder. "Her bottle is in here."

"I think I'll call the police instead."

"You could, then they'd ask me why I'm here," he returned.

Color drained from her face.

"And I'd have to say that I came by to visit and overstayed

my welcome, and ask you to keep Manda while they took me to Lew Sterrett Jail."

As easily as he had incensed, he calmed her. He wouldn't blackmail, but he wasn't above badgering.

"You don't know what you're asking." Her stomach knotted.

Black eyes narrowed. "Yes, I do. I'm asking you to keep an innocent child out of foster care."

Manda squealed, drawing Madison's eyes to her again. "After she's fed, you both have to leave." Turning, she went to the kitchen and pointed toward the faucet. "Instant hot water. Wes—" Her voice stopped abruptly. She folded her arms around her waist and glanced out the French doors toward the landscaped backyard.

"Wes didn't like waiting for hot water," Zachary finished. "It'll help to talk about him."

She shook her head and watched the wind play with the leaves of the fruitless mulberry trees in the back. The things she wanted to say wouldn't be healing; they'd be angry and spiteful. She hated that about herself. She heard the water come on and tried to ignore the cheerful babble of the baby.

"Come back here."

Madison turned to see Manda on all fours making her way across the tile floor toward her. Madison took an instinctive step backward. Her panicky gaze went to Zachary, standing with the bottle under the water, then back to the baby who was inches away from her bare feet.

"Come get her," Madison demanded, her distress growing.

"Babies and hot water don't mix," he said casually, not moving.

Babbling, Manda reached for Madison's robe. Since it wasn't tied, when the baby pulled, it gave. Her eyes widened as she went backward and plopped on her bottom. Instinctively Madison swept her up, expecting to see tears. Instead the baby was grinning and waving her hands, her hazel eyes sparkling.

Hazel eyes just like Wes's.

Madison was leaning over to put the baby down when Zachary curved an arm around the infant's waist. "Come here, munchkin. Time for lunch."

As soon as Manda saw the bottle, she lunged for it, grabbing it with both hands and bringing it to her mouth. Loud sucking noises followed. "Did you eat lunch, yet, Madison?"

"I'm not hungry."

His eyes narrowed. "You have to eat."

"I will once you leave." She pointedly looked at the milk in the bottle that was rapidly disappearing.

He'd known it wasn't going to be easy and it wasn't. He'd come too far to back down. "Mind if I sit down?"

Madison smiled sweetly. "As a matter of fact I do."

Zachary shifted from one foot to the other as if trying to adjust Manda's weight. What he was really doing was making sure that when he finished, Manda was staring at Madison. He didn't have to wait long for a reaction.

"Sit down," she ordered impatiently. "I'm going to get dressed."

"Thank you." Instead of taking a seat at the kitchen table, he went into the den and sat in the rattan–and–brown leather side chair. When the baby finished the bottle, he placed a towel on his shoulder and gently but firmly patted her back until she burped.

"That's my girl." Manda grinned up at him. "I think she's softening. But who could resist you?" Zachary said.

She patted his cheeks as if in perfect agreement.

In her bedroom Madison quickly dressed in a pair of black linen slacks and a magenta knit top. She took only a moment to pull a comb through the tangles in her shoulder-length black hair, then she was out the door. They were leaving. Nothing the surprisingly talkative Zachary could say was going to change her mind.

She rounded the corner of the den and saw Zachary holding Manda in one arm, pointing to her body parts and naming them. Manda stared up at him with attentive eyes as if she understood every word.

Madison watched them, her hands stuck in her pockets, and fought to harden her resolve. She wasn't going to be conned or swayed. Manda was not her responsibility. "Shouldn't you be getting her back to wherever you got her from?"

"That would be my house," he said, setting Manda on the floor.

Shocked, Madison whipped her hands out of her pockets. "You're keeping her?"

"Until other arrangements can be made." Unzipping the diaper bag, he took a colorful plastic key ring and handed it to the grasping hands of the child, who immediately stuck it into her mouth.

Madison was already shaking her head at the inference and pointed look. "No. You checked her out of the hospital; she's your responsibility."

"Actually, I checked her out in your name," he told her.

"What!" She stated at him in utter disbelief.

Manda started, turning big hazel eyes toward Madison. Madison in turn glared at Zachary. "See what you made me do," she accused.

Zachary breathed a little easier. She cared. If she didn't, she wouldn't care about frightening Manda. "It's not my intention to upset you, but I made a promise too."

She took two steps toward him. "You knew about this?" Anger shimmered in her voice.

"You were there when I promised to look after her," he reminded her, his gaze steady.

Madison's tense body relaxed. She didn't like to think that she had been duped by Zachary as well. "Then you keep her." She sat in a chair across from him, drawing one bare foot under her.

Zachary glanced at the toenails painted a light pink, then his gaze tracked upward. Even tired, with lines of strain in her face, dark smudges beneath her eyes, she was a beautiful woman. He didn't understand how Wes could have been unfaithful, but Zachary had learned at a young age that a marriage license didn't mean fidelity. And when there were children involved, the fallout was hell.

He switched his attention to Manda, who had abandoned the keys and crawled to the immense glass-and-wood coffee table, then pulled herself up on wobbly legs to study the multicolored prisms of light reflecting in the crystal decanter and glasses in the rattan tray. Zachary pulled it out of harm's way, then retook his seat.

"My lawyer says I wouldn't stand a chance. Besides . . ." He eyed Madison wearily, then leaned over and picked up Manda who had begun making her way to an iron bowl of fruit on the table. "You're not going to like what I'm going to say, but I did it for Manda."

"What did you do?"

"Remember, no shouting?"

Madison simply stared and waited, knowing she wasn't going to like what Zachary had to say.

"A lawyer, acting on your behalf, visited Manda's great-aunt in the nursing home in Amarillo and had her sign papers giving you temporary custody. In view of the circumstance, the lawyer was able to get a judge to quickly grant the request."

Madison's temper spiked, and she held it back with sheer force of will. "You had no right to do that."

"I apologize, but it was the only thing I could think of at the time."

Too angry to sit, she stood, paced, then pinned him with a hard glare. "Wait a minute. Did the aunt know? Is that why she signed the papers?"

Her voice trembled. Zachary didn't know if it was in rage or humiliation. He could handle the outrage; he wasn't so sure about the tears or hurt. "The lawyer simply presented the necessary facts. That despite your husband's injuries he was concerned about the child since it was known that the great-aunt was the only living relative. You consented to care for the child, but due to the circumstances you were unable to check Manda out of the hospital or visit the aunt."

"You think you've trapped me, don't you?" The challenge was back in her voice.

"That was never my intention." He didn't shy away from the anger in her face or in her eyes. She had a right.

"I'll bet. You orchestrated this entire thing." Furious, she shook her head. "Well, it won't work. No matter what papers you have. She can't stay."

"You'd rather send her to a foster home? You said yourself some of them were unfit," he reminded her.

Her hands clenched at her sides. She didn't like him using her own words against her. "Then find someplace else. Ask Wes's parents."

He pulled Manda protectively closer. "Can you honestly imagine A.J. and Vanessa giving her the love and care she needs?"

She couldn't.

"There is no place else," he said, when she didn't answer his question. "When the lawyer visited her great-aunt, she was relieved you wanted to care for Manda. I understand her eyesight is bad, but she's listened to your shows and approved of you caring for Manda. She said Manda's mother didn't have any close friends who might step forward."

"Certainly not married ones," Madison quipped. As soon as the words were out she regretted their snippiness. She dragged her hand through her hair. "I don't want to discuss this. Just leave."

"Please reconsider, Madison. Could you honestly send her someplace where you had no guarantee they wouldn't mistreat her?"

She couldn't, and it angered her that he seemed to know. "If you leave her here you don't have a guarantee, either."

His expression softened. "Yes, I do. I saw you with her in the hospital."

Madison slowly shook her head. "You can't be sure." Her eyes shut. "*I* can't be sure," she mumbled softly to herself.

Zachary heard. "I'm here, aren't I?"

Her eyes snapped open. "You have her, you keep her."

He bounced Manda on his knee. "Told you. My lawyer says I don't have a chance."

Madison rubbed both hands over her face. When had he become so stubborn and so talkative? "Can't you get it through your head that I'm not involved in this? I had nothing to do with her being here."

"Neither did she."

Madison glanced at Manda staring at her and fought hard to rein in her temper. "Why are you pushing this?"

"Remember, I gave my word," he answered simply.

Madison vividly recalled giving her word as well, but she hadn't known the truth then. Much as she tried to close her mind and heart to the baby's happy chattering a few feet away, she couldn't forget how satisfying and good it had felt to have Manda trust her enough to come willingly into her arms, to take a bottle from her, then fall asleep in her arms. "Contact a private adoption agency. You'll be able to check out the applicants personally."

"I know this isn't easy," Zachary said, ignoring her suggestion. "Open your heart, Madison. You both have lost so much."

Madison shoved her hands into her pockets again. "I don't want to discuss it any further. She's been fed, and now you can go."

"You have every right to be angry at Wes, but don't take it out on Manda," Zachary pressed. "Neither of you had any say so in this. You're angry with Wes and no one could blame you, but you're wrong if you take it out on the baby. She's as much a victim in this as you are. More so, because, as hard as it is on you, you know what happened. She doesn't understand why the mother she keeps looking for to walk through the door is never coming back. Her mother is never going to pick her up or sing her a lullaby again. Nothing you're facing can compare to what she's lost."

His words pricked like stinging nettles. The doorbell chimed and she ignored it. "I want you to leave."

"You're better than this. Just open your heart."

She laughed raggedly. "Wes ripped out my heart."

"It may feel like it now, but it's still there, waiting."

"All I want is to be left alone." She paced then stopped and turned. "Can't you understand? I look into her face and see his eyes. I look at her and my stomach knots."

"It's not going to be without some bumps for either of you, but maybe together you can help heal each other."

Madison hung her head, pressing her fingers to her throbbing temple.

The doorbell chimed again. "Why don't you rest and I'll answer it?"

Madison lifted her head, and stared at him incredulously. When he was building the house, he seldom spoke; now it seemed he couldn't shut up.

The chime came again.

"Gather up her things," she told him, her eyes narrowed in determination. "As soon as I get rid of whoever it is, you're next."

Madison walked toward the front door, wondering how she'd get rid of Zachary. She wasn't ready to admit Wes's betrayal to anyone, not even Gordon who, despite his age, could probably toss Zachary out on his ear. She frowned as she unlocked the door. On second thought, that might not be a good idea. The muscles in Zachary's arms were rock-hard, his chest massive. He was probably as strong as an ox. He was certainly as stubborn as one.

Annoyance nipping at her heels, she opened the door. A woman was walking back down the three brick steps toward a car parked in the circular driveway. However, she turned when she heard the door open.

"Ms. Reed?"

Madison frowned. She didn't recognize the attractive young black woman, but there had been many people in the last few days she hadn't known. This one was dressed in a tailored gray blazer, white blouse, and gray trousers. Her straight, shoulder-length black hair grazed her shoulders. The well-worn black leather bag was Louis Vuitton. Whoever the woman was, Madison intended to use her presence to get rid of Zachary. "Yes."

The woman, who looked to be around the same age as Madison, came back up the walkway. As she neared the door she opened the oversized leather bag and pulled out a laminated identification badge. "I'm Camille Jacobs, a social worker with Child Protective Services. I've come to see Manda Taylor."

Chapter 8

Madison barely kept her jaw from dropping as she jerked her gaze back up from the unflattering picture to the woman's face.

Her brow knitting, Camille Jacobs returned the ID badge to her purse. "She was checked out of the hospital three days ago by two men who identified themselves as your lawyer and a family friend, Sam Peters and Zachary Holman. They had temporary custody papers granted by Velma Taylor, Manda's great-aunt, and authorized by a judge. The child is here isn't she?"

"Yes, ma'am, she's here," Zachary said, with a smile from beside Madison. He held Manda in one arm and extended the other one to the social worker. "Good evening, I'm Zachary Holman."

"Pleased to meet you, Mr. Holman." The handshake was brief.

All Madison could do under the watchful eye of the social worker was glare at Zachary. Exposing his duplicity would only create problems. As much as he annoyed her, she agreed with him about the unpredictability of foster care. Manda could be placed in a wonderful home, but what if she wasn't? "As you can see, Ms. Jacobs, she's here. So if you'll excuse us, Mr. Holman and I have a great deal to discuss."

"This won't take very long. I just have a few questions,"

Camille Jacobs said with a smile, but it was obvious she intended to come inside.

Zachary was already opening the door. "Madison always has time to talk about Manda's welfare."

The social worker's expression softened and warmed. "I like hearing that about my clients."

That got Madison's attention. " 'Clients.' You're opening a case file on me?"

"As legal guardian of Manda, it's standard procedure," Camille explained. "The file is confidential and will be closed as soon as it's determined that Manda is being properly cared for."

"Yes, of course," Madison said, leading the woman back into the den. This was definitely getting out of hand. As soon as she got rid of the social worker, Zachary and the baby were next. "Please have a seat."

"Thank you." Camille sat on the supple, brassnail-trimmed leather sofa, then turned toward Manda who was cuddled against Zachary. The social worker smiled. "I see the nurses were right. They said you both did very well with Manda. It's fortunate you were able to help ease her feelings of abandonment."

"I plan to help out any way I can," Zachary said, sitting down across from them on the Barbados chair. "I own my own construction company and, although I'm busy, I have good people working for me so I can take off if Madison needs my help."

I won't need you to take off because I'm not keeping her, Madison thought.

"Then you're a close friend of the family, Mr. Holman?" the social worker asked.

"I built this home for them," he answered.

Camille folded her hands in her lap. "You'll forgive me, but that doesn't answer my question."

Zachary pulled Manda more securely to him. "Wes and I were good friends." His troubled gaze shifted to Madison. "I stayed with Madison at the hospital after Wes was brought in. I never left. Wes would have wanted me to do all I can to help Madison get through this, and that's what I plan to do."

The social worker nodded. "Good friends always help."

"Would you like some tea or coffee, Ms. Jacobs?" Madison asked, adding the social worker's name to the list of people she wanted to get rid of.

"No, thanks." Camille picked up the colorful plastic key ring from the plush cream carpet, then glanced around room. "Your home is immaculate. Quite a feat when caring for an inquisitive nine-month-old."

Once again Zachary jumped in. "She loses interest if she has too many toys so it makes more sense to just give her one."

Camille kept her watchful gaze on Madison. "Do you share the same opinion?"

The woman was no pushover, Madison thought. When dealing with the unknown it was best to answer without explanation. "Yes."

The social worker's head tilted to one side. "You'll forgive me, Ms. Reed, but I was rather surprised to learn that you had decided to seek custody of Manda from the great-aunt. According to my reports you had no prior knowledge of the child before the accident. Do you mind telling me why?"

Madison should have expected the question, should have been prepared for it—perhaps would have been if she had known what Zachary had done. As it was, she was left floundering.

"I—" Again she saw Wes's face, his startling announcement just before . . . Her hand clutched her stomach.

Setting Manda on the floor, Zachary crossed the room and sat beside Madison, covering her hand with his larger one. He hated the thought of putting her through this and wished there was another way. "Ms. Jacobs, could we delay this for a few more days?"

Camille sighed softly. "I'm not heartless, but I have Manda to consider. I don't want you to take this the wrong way, but I don't want Manda to be some type of publicity gimmick."

The hurt vanished as Madison's brown eyes flared. "Another remark like that, and I'll ask you to leave, then call your supervisor."

"I apologize," Camille told her, unfazed by Madison's anger. "But unfortunately people often show their true feelings when caught off guard."

Or when they have no choice, as Wes had when he confessed about Manda. "Accepted."

Manda squealed and they all watched as she pulled herself up using the edge of the glass coffee table. She presented them with a triumphant grin that showed her two front teeth.

"Decided to join us, huh?" Leaning across the table separating them, Camille handed Manda the key ring. After a long moment, the infant took it, rapped it on a magazine a couple of times, then plopped onto her bottom to rap it against the floor. "She doesn't look like the inconsolable baby I heard about in the hospital."

"She's loved and being well cared for," Zachary said, watching the infant with open affection.

"Is that right, Ms. Reed?" Camille asked.

Madison's eyes narrowed. There was something in the woman's tone and in her demeanor that said it wasn't an idle question. Madison had interviewed too many people in the past not to pick up on it. "What exactly is bothering you, Ms. Jacobs?"

The social worker didn't hesitate. "In ICU you were heard to say that Manda was not your responsibility and that you wanted nothing to do with her. After learning of your guardianship, a concerned individual contacted the agency. I won't insult you by saying I know what you must have been going through after losing your husband moments earlier, but I can empathize with you. However, if you are not sure that you are absolutely committed to Manda, I'm here to take her."

"No," Zachary said, his hand closing tightly on Madison.

Manda whimpered. Immediately Zachary got up to sweep the baby into his arms to comfort her. The instant he did, Madison realized his mistake. She should have been the one to offer the child comfort. The social worker was smart enough to pick up on that little point. All Madison had to do was push her gently in that direction and Manda would be out of her life.

"Ms. Reed?" Camille questioned.

Madison didn't look at the social worker. Instead, as if compelled by a will greater than her own, she looked at Manda in Zachary's protective arms, quiet now, her thumb stuck in her mouth, those big hazel eyes fixed on Madison's face. Once again she saw the frightened infant in the hospital, and again remembered how she had slept in her arms. If Madison sent her away, she'd have no idea of what awaited Manda and would have no way of finding out.

While that would keep Madison from the constant reminder of Wes's deceit, it might not be the best course of action for the baby. Whatever decision she made had to be the right one because the consequences would be irreversible and far-reaching.

Madison took a deep breath and hoped she could live with the decision she was about to make. "She's in my home because she needs me. She stays."

"Make sure, Ms. Reed," Camille cautioned. "You live a busy life. Manda is going to require a lot of your time. Your husband died of injuries he received trying to save her mother. That won't be easily forgotten and has the potential of causing problems later on."

"She stays." Madison stood. "If there are no further questions, I have some errands to run."

Camille came to her feet. The women were almost eye level. She handed Madison her business card. "Thank you for seeing me."

Taking the card, Madison went to the front door and opened it. "Goodbye, Ms. Jacobs.

"Good-bye, Ms. Reed. I'll be stopping by on occasion to see how things are progressing."

"I hope you'll call first," Madison said pointedly.

The smile was brief. "I'll try. Good day."

Madison watched the woman walk to a late-model Lexus and get in. Before the car pulled away, Madison closed the door. Zachary stood smiling at her. In his arms, Manda was smiling too.

"I knew you'd change your mind."

"On the contrary. I haven't."

The smile slipped from his ruggedly handsome face. "But you just said you were going to keep her."

Madison brushed by him and headed for the kitchen. "That was to get rid of that too perceptive social worker."

"Then . . . then you don't plan to keep Manda?"

Madison kept walking.

Chapter 9

"Madison," Zachary repeated, his throat dry, trying not to let his fear convey itself to Manda.

Madison opened the refrigerator and rummaged around until she found a container of strawberry-banana yogurt. "She can stay, but only until you can make other arrangements."

"But—"

She whirled. "Don't push it, Zachary." There was just enough snap in her voice to cause Manda and Zachary to start. "It shouldn't be too difficult to find a couple though a private adoption agency who won't mind you checking their references personally, then the great-aunt can sign over custody to them."

Appalled, Zachary pulled Manda closer to him. "You can't pass her around like a sack of potatoes."

"Another family would be best for her." She tore open the carton and discovered she didn't want it after all. She ate some anyway. It was cool and tasted like paste.

"You're forgetting one thing."

She glanced up at him. "What?"

"She has a connection to you she won't have with anyone else. You were married to her father."

Pain widened Madison's eyes. Her hand clenched. Yogurt rose up out of the carton and dripped on the floor.

"I didn't mean to upset you," he said, hating the lost look in her eyes. Snatching a handful of paper towels, he handed her a couple, and deftly, with Manda still in his arms, wiped up the spilled yogurt from the floor. "But I was a teenager before I knew who my father was. It takes a long time to get over that feeling of being unwanted. I know the questions Manda will have when she is older, the self-doubts."

Madison heard the strain in his voice, but wasn't ready to forgive him. "Is that why you're fighting so hard for her?"

"Partly."

She might admire him if he wasn't fighting against her and disrupting her life. "Excuse me." Madison went into her bedroom, combed her hair, and returned with her purse.

Zachary eyed her warily. "You're going out?"

Madison pushed her big-lens sunglasses on top of her head. "I have some shopping to do."

Zachary nodded. "I don't mind keeping her until you get back."

Madison stared at him as he bounced a now-sleeping Manda on his shoulder. "Don't you have a business to run?"

"I can't be at all my sites," he told her. "Like I said, I have men and women working for me that I can trust. If you show me where she's going to sleep, I'll bring in her things."

Possessions means permanence. There was no turning back now. Her stomach felt queasy. "The bedroom across from mine."

He nodded. "I'll just put her down and go get her stuff out of my truck."

She watched him take a light blanket from the diaper bag and try to spread it out on the carpet while not disturbing the child. Madison took the blanket out of his hand. "The floor is too hard."

He looked up at him with dark eyes. "If she wakes up while I'm gone, I don't want her to roll off the chair or sofa and hurt herself."

"You really don't mind staying here, do you?"

"No," he smiled. "If it's all right with you it will give me a chance to see how the house is holding up."

Madison was suddenly tired of the charade. "I was going to the store to buy things for her."

A slow grin spread across Zachary's face. "I think I have everything she'll need in the truck, and what I don't have, if you'll make a list, I'll go get it."

Three hours later, Madison couldn't imagine a single item Manda needed. They'd tried to put the crib, playpen, stroller, car seat, and swing into the bedroom across from her, but it became clear that it wasn't all going to fit. The only other bedroom large enough for all the things Zachary had purchased was Wes's bedroom, but Madison had no intention of going in there. They'd ended up putting the crib in Madison's bedroom for the time being and leaving the rest across the hall.

"She tends to wake up in the night a little fretful, so it may be best that she's in here," Zachary said, aware once again that the bedroom with its soft feminine colors and smells belonged strictly to Madison.

Madison eyed Manda in the swing, "talking" to a butterfly through the French doors in the den. They'd already discussed her care, and the feeding schedule the nurses had helped Zachary work out. Her medical records which, after a special-delivery letter of Madison's temporary guardianship, were being sent from Manda's pediatrician in Amarillo.

Zachary's beeper went off. He glanced at the number and frowned. "Excuse me. I have to take this."

Madison didn't say anything as he moved away a short distance and pulled out his cell phone. She was well aware of the promises men made, but seldom kept. She understood Manda's care would fall to her.

"Is there anything else you think she needs?" Zachary asked, walking back into the room a short while later.

Here it comes, Madison thought. But she wouldn't make it easy for him. She crossed her arms. "No."

Coal-black eyes stared down at her for a long time before

Zachary said, "Why don't I fix you some soup and after you eat, you can lie down? I'll watch Manda."

She snatched her arms to her sides. "What?"

"Don't worry. I know what I'm doing. Between birthday parties, picnics, weddings, and an assortment of other events I've attended, I've taken care of my share of children at a variety of ages." Taking Madison by the arm, he gently led her to the sofa and, with light pressure, urged her down in the seat, then picked up her feet and placed them on the cushions. "You're worn out. Rest, and I'll fix that soup."

Speechless, Madison watched him check on Manda, then head for the kitchen. He wasn't what she expected, and the unexpected often made her suspicious. It wouldn't last, but . . . she hadn't been sleeping well and at the moment she was too tired to worry about the mysterious Zachary Holman. Her eyes flickered close. She'd rest just for a little bit.

In a matter of seconds she was sound asleep.

Madison woke slowly. Before she even opened her eyes, she wanted to shut them again. Instead she sat up, surprised to find herself in her own bed with the duvet thrown over her.

Zachary.

She could either be annoyed or thankful. She decided to let it ride. Annoyance required too much energy. Getting out of bed, she smoothed back the covers. A minute later she discovered she was still standing there, running her hand repeatedly over the same spot.

Once, she never would have avoided a problem, but in the last two years she had evaded issues when she should have faced them. Perhaps if she hadn't, she and Wes could have worked through their problems and he might not have turned to another woman. Was Madison to blame for her husband's adultery? Was there a lack in her that had pushed him into the arms of another woman?

Her eyes closed. How could he have asked her to care for his child by another woman, knowing how devastated she had been when she lost their child?

But if not me, who?

Turning, she saw the four-poster crib, yellow and beautiful with a rainbow and clouds painted on the head and footboard. Despite her best effort, she felt an ache deep in her heart. That should have been her baby's crib. Her head fell forward. There it was, what had been lurking in her subconscious since Wes had told her. Why had his child with another woman lived and not theirs?

She had to get out of there. Rushing to the door, she flung it open and ran straight into Zachary. Manda was asleep in his arms.

"I was coming to check on you." He frowned. "What's wrong?"

She shook her head.

Zachary saw it in her face, the hurt, the grief. Without thought he pulled her against his chest. "It's all right. It's all right."

She smelled aftershave and baby powder. She jerked free. "No, it's not," she hissed. "I hate the thoughts going through my head and I can't stop them." She tried to hold them, but they spilled hot and angry, out of her mouth. "Why couldn't it have been my child that lived and not theirs?"

Zachary's eyes widened.

Before he could answer, she brushed past him. She hadn't known she had that much hate in her.

Placing Manda in her crib, he caught up with Madison as she was going out the French doors in the den. He recalled too well the depth of her pain when she had lost her baby. How much could one woman take?

Furious, she whirled on him with clenched fists. Tears sparkled in her eyes. "Leave me alone!"

"I can't," he said grimly, watching her closely, wishing there was another way. "You're hurting."

Her laugh was ragged. "And that's my excuse for hating her?"

"You don't hate her." His voice was gentle, soothing as he tried to find the right words. "You're dealing with a lot of emotions right now, none of them comforting. It'll take time to work through them. Give yourself that time and don't judge yourself."

"You obviously have come to care about her. How can you stand there and not despise me as much as I despise myself now?" she asked, her voice and body trembling.

"Because I've stood in your place, in a way." His mouth firmed. "My father didn't marry my mother as he promised; instead he married another woman. I was a teenager when I found out who he was. But he had a family and wanted nothing to do with me. There was a time I would have given anything for him to have accepted me."

He gazed down at her with anguished eyes. "In a fit of anger, I spouted off how I felt to my mother, a woman who had always loved me and done her best by me. Until the day I die I'll remember the look on her face—regret, hurt, but so much love. I wanted to hurt her. She understood even while I rebelled and made her life miserable. She never stopped loving me. So you see, I can't judge. If I thought for a moment you'd mistreat Manda in any way, I wouldn't have brought her here in the first place."

Madison took a deep, steadying breath. "You seem to see something in me I don't."

His large, callused hand reached out and gently brushed the hair from her cheek. Her skin beneath his fingers was soft and warm. He had the strangest notion to keep stroking. "I was there when you held and comforted Manda in the hospital. Just follow those same instincts."

"I didn't know who she was then," she pointed out unnecessarily.

"And what do you know now?" he asked quietly, undisturbed by the hard look she sent him. "You know that she's suffered a loss that neither you nor I had to cope with. You know that her birth was not of her doing. You know that she needs a home. You know that when she looks at you it is without judgment. You know she wants to love as much as she needs to be loved. Remember those things when doubts creep into your mind."

She shook her head and stared up at him in amazement. "Why didn't you talk this much when you were building the house?"

He laughed. Even to his ears it sounded forced. *If you only knew.* "Come on. I kept your supper warm."

Thirty minutes later Zachary walked to his truck feeling a lot better than he had when he'd arrived that afternoon. Manda was where she belonged, but he was under no illusions that it would be easy for her to stay. Deep in thought, he opened the truck's door and got inside.

No one had to tell him that another woman would have tossed him and Manda out without a second thought. Others might have kept her out of a sense of duty, but never love. Manda needed and deserved to be loved. Madison, despite all the emotional upheaval she was going through, had put the welfare of Manda before her own. Although she didn't think so, her actions took courage and compassion. She was quite a woman. He hated lying to her, but at the moment he couldn't see that he had a choice.

Zachary eased to a stop at a signal light. Wes had put all of them in a difficult situation, but that was Wes. Zachary had loved Wes, but he hadn't been blind to his faults. He'd give you anything, but he thought what he wanted, needed, was vastly more important than what others wanted or needed.

Zachary pulled off, then hit the Central Expressway going south. Wes had been heartbroken when Madison had lost the baby, but despite Zachary's urging, Wes had never told her how he felt. He'd grown up with the antiquated notion that men didn't share or show their feelings. Instead he had acted as if he wasn't hurting as much as she was. He'd left her alone instead of talking to her about the baby they'd lost.

According to Wes, as time passed, he and Madison had grown further and further apart. Hoping the dream house they'd planned for over a year would bring them back together, he had insisted that Zachary start building. The room Madison now occupied had originally been designated to be a nursery that would accommodate a growing child with an inquisitive mind.

It had fallen to Zachary to ask Madison about the change in wallpaper since the whimsical print she'd picked out would have been a constant reminder of the child she'd lost. She'd chosen the rose silk wallpaper, then asked him to enlarge the room and the bath. He understood why, now. Even then she'd planned to take it for herself.

Not once had she come alone to see the progress of the house, but occasionally Wes would bring her with him to the site. The few times Zachary spoke with her, she'd look at him with such pain in her soft brown eyes that he'd always felt as if he should hug her or speak to her in a hushed tone. He'd thought and worried about her a lot. It had irritated Zachary that Wes never seemed to notice.

But then Wes was gone a great deal and when he was home he was usually out chasing down a story, charming the wheelers and dealers of Dallas which his monied background and status as a celebrity afforded him, or on the golf course. Zachary had tried to talk with him, but Wes always insisted that marriages hit rough patches now and then. He'd use his parents as an example and say they were still together.

Zachary never had the heart or the courage to say that whatever kept them together, it wasn't love. Zachary's mother and stepfather loved each other, and they loved him. The morning after Wes died, they'd arrived at his house just as he was leaving for work. His mother had fussed over him, and made him promise to take care of himself, and that included not making the six-hour round-trip drive to Houston to see them off on their cruise that weekend.

Even if Zachary didn't have a special woman in his life, his parents were a great example of what marriage was supposed to be like. Wes and Madison had it once, but with the loss of their child they'd also lost each other.

Turning into the driveway of his two-story Georgian house in South Dallas, Zachary cut the motor and got out of the truck. He'd saved the house from being bulldozed down ten years ago when he'd barely had enough money to make ends meet. Now, after the revival of South Dallas, the infusion of upscale businesses, the revitalization of Fair Park several blocks away, and the refurbishing he'd done, he found a note in his mailbox almost weekly asking if he wanted to sell. What he'd paid twenty thousand dollars for could now easily go for fifteen times that amount.

The second his booted foot hit the wooden bottom step the motion lights came on. Inserting an old-fashioned iron key, he opened the leaded-glass door and stepped onto the gleaming hardwood floor that his housekeeper repeatedly asked him to carpet. If he did, she'd find something else to complain about. She was only happy if she could fuss, but she hadn't said one word when he'd brought Manda and all the paraphernalia home.

He took the gracefully curved mahogany stairs two at a time. His bedroom was the last one at the end of the hallway done in knot pine. Inside the oversized room with its high ceiling and wide windows, he noticed the quietness first, then the spot where Manda's crib had been. He hadn't expected to miss her so soon, but he did. He glanced at the phone on the bedside by the oak antique bed and almost reached for it.

If he started worrying Madison, she might think he didn't trust her or, just as bad, would tell him to pick Manda up. He had to be patient and trust in his instincts. Uneasiness moved through him.

Those instincts were telling him that the lady wouldn't like being lied to a second time. He just hoped she'd understand when she learned he hadn't been entirely truthful about Manda. He hadn't a doubt that eventually she'd find out. Life had taught him that sooner or later the truth always came out, and when it did, it was seldom pretty or neat.

He just had to be ready.

Chapter 10

Madison was ready, or so she told herself. She'd been up for the past thirty minutes, showered, changed, and had a bottle waiting. Then Manda woke up and fastened those hazel eyes on her, and Madison wasn't so sure anymore. Her stomach took a hard dive. Her hands clenched.

If only she didn't have his eyes. If only . . .

A whimper cut off Madison's thoughts. Manda's lower lip was stuck out and trembling. Soon the tears would follow. Madison studied the pretty, round face of the infant and wondered what features, if any, the baby had of the mother.

Manda whimpered again.

Shutting her mind off, Madison came off the bed and crossed the room. Not giving herself a chance to falter, she reached out and picked the infant up under the arms. Manda's feet dangled in the air. "What I am going to do with you?"

Manda simply stared.

"One of us should have a clue."

Manda flapped her arms and kicked her feet.

"Guess that means you don't know, either." Slowly, Madison gathered the baby in her arms. She was soft and warm. If it had been another child, Madison would have thought nothing of kissing her curly head or blowing kisses on her plump cheeks, as she had done countless times with her two nieces or the babies of acquaintances or associates. But this wasn't just any child.

Battling her anger, wanting to get the baby fed and out of her arms, Madison hurriedly changed Manda's diaper, then headed to the kitchen. Madison was a step away from the stove when Manda suddenly lunged for the waiting bottle in the pan of hot water.

"No!" Madison yelled, jerking the infant back into her arms before she reached into the hot water.

Manda screamed in Madison's ear.

Madison didn't even wince at the sound. Although she was positive Manda hadn't been burned, she checked her dimpled hands and chubby arms that flailed in the air.

Trembling, Madison sat down in the nearest chair, holding the child to her. If she had been burned, it would have been Madison's fault. Caught in her own misery, she had almost let the baby get hurt. "It's all right. I'm sorry. It's all right."

The cries grew louder and more demanding. Hunger or fear, Madison didn't know. She felt tears prick her own eyes. She couldn't do this.

The doorbell rang. She rushed to the intercom and flicked it on. "Zachary, please let it be you."

"What's the matter?" Zachary's anxious voice came through loud and clear.

She didn't answer, just took off running. Opening the door one-handed, she thrust Manda into his arms with the other.

He caught the baby, his worried gaze going from the crying infant to an equally upset Madison. "What happened?"

"She—she lunged for the bottle in the hot pan of water. I—caught her, but . . ."

Zachary closed the door and stepped inside the wide, tiled foyer. "Why do you think I put her down yesterday? The day after I brought her home she started. She sees a bottle and goes crazy."

"You should have told me!" Madison hit him in the chest with a closed fist. "I thought she did it yesterday because you were late with her feeding."

Understanding it was the aftermath of anxiety and seeing

the residual fear in her eyes, he accepted his punishment. "Sorry. I guess she's feeling more comfortable with us, since she didn't do it in the hospital," he reasoned. "Why don't you hold her while I go get her bottle?"

Madison looked at Manda, quiet now, her lashes spiked with tears. "She's probably afraid of me now."

Zachary heard the hesitancy in Madison's voice and went on instinct. He held Manda out to her. "Let's see."

After a brief moment the baby reached out. Madison's hands closed securely around the infant's waist, then slowly pulled her closer. By the time Madison held Manda against her, the baby was leaning against Madison, her sniffles becoming quieter with each breath she took.

Zachary breathed a sigh of relief and gently urged Madison into the kitchen, then into a carved oval-back upholstered chair at the round pedestal table. Removing the bottle from the water, he tested the milk's temperature before handing it to Madison. Manda lurched, but this time Madison was ready. Taking the bottle, she gave it to Manda, who fastened both hands around it and sucked greedily.

"Better?" Zachary questioned, crouching down in front of Madison.

Madison glanced at him. "Sorry I hit you."

He rubbed his chest and smiled. "Are you really?"

She laughed. "I'm not sure."

Zachary stared up at her, enjoying the smile on her face and the sight of her feeding Manda. She was a beautiful woman. "She'll want her cereal when she finishes. I'll get it ready."

Madison watched him prepare the cereal, then turned back to Manda. Her eyes watched Zachary's every movement. "She's certainly taken to you."

He tossed a careless smile over his shoulder. "I'm an easy guy to like."

Madison considered, then decided he was right. He had an easy, calming way about him. She recalled the day he had asked her about the wallpaper change in what was to be the baby's room. The sympathy and reluctance in his strong face had been evident. He didn't know she had overheard him ask Wes, who had shoved the decision off on her. At that moment she had despised her husband.

"What is it?" Zachary asked, hunkering down in front of her again. Despite Manda's grabbing for the bowl with one hand while she kept the other hand on the bottle, his attention stayed on Madison. "Talking helps."

She couldn't share all her deepest thoughts with him, but perhaps a few wouldn't hurt. "If I hadn't been feeling sorry for myself and thinking of Wes and Manda's mother, I would have been paying better attention to her." She lifted dark eyes to him. "It was my fault she was almost hurt. You may have been wrong to leave her here with me."

Zachary studied the grief etched in her face and wished he could pull her into his arms and comfort her. "None of this is your fault, so don't hang that around your neck. You've got a right to your anger. As far as I know there hasn't been a chance for you to let it out. Until you do, it's going to eat you up inside."

Manda finished off her bottle and reached for the cereal with both hands. Zachary deftly traded the cereal bowl for her. "Burp or you'll have a tummy ache." He casually put Manda over his shoulder and rubbed her back.

Madison's hands fisted. "He's gone. I shouldn't be angry, but I can't help it."

"Don't try," Zachary said.

Manda burped.

"Good girl." Setting her back on Madison's lap, Zachary took the bowl and began to spoon in cereal to a waiting mouth. "If Wes were alive you'd have a chance to tell him off, but he isn't so he left you with no way, plus you have the unexpected responsibility of caring for Manda. Until you accept your anger as normal you're going to be unhappy and tense." He spooned in another bite. "Personally, I'd rather be around a happy woman. Makes life easier. Isn't that right, sweetheart?"

Manda waved her arms and blew cereal at him.

He chuckled and wiped her mouth with the cloth from his shoulder. "See, Manda agrees with me."

"Happiness can be an illusion," Madison said softly, her hands around the child's waist.

"For some. Not for others." He stared at her a long moment before continuing. "Not for my mother and stepfather, and not from what I saw of your parents. They touch. When they talk they lean in, they smile at each other. You can tell the happy couples. They don't have to say a word."

Madison bit her lips, wondering what Zachary had seen when he had looked at her and Wes. Then something in his face told her she didn't have to wonder. "You knew."

"Yes." Their was no need to lie, to evade.

She felt exposed, lacking in some elemental way to keep her husband faithful. She wanted to ask if he and Wes had discussed her; instead she stood. "I better get her bath."

He came easily to his feet, accepting that she was politely tossing him out. "I'll be out in the field all day, but beep if you need me. I plan to check on the farthest sites then work my way back into Dallas."

"Thanks for coming by," Madison said. At least he was trying to help and not just dumping everything in her lap and leaving it up to her to sort it all out.

Zachary's large hand swept over Manda's dark curls as she lay against Madison's chest. "She can be a handful in the morning. She's slippery as an eel during bathtime and likes to splash water."

"That you did tell me."

"See you later, then." He wished he could take the sadness from Madison's face, but only time could do that. Wes had a great deal to answer for. "I'll show myself out. I'm not sure how she'll react to my leaving."

"I'm not sure how I'll react, either," Madison said.

He stared at her a long time, wanting to touch her, reassure her, comfort her. "I'm only a phone call away." Turning, he walked away, each step more difficult than the last.

* * *

Madison and Manda had made it through bath time, but trying to put her flailing arms and legs into her footed coveralls took some effort. Finally, she was dressed. "Now what?" Madison asked.

Light-brown eyes stared watchfully back at her.

"Clueless, too, huh? Well, let's go clean up the kitchen."

In the kitchen, she put Manda in the swing facing outside, but had only gone a few steps when the baby began to whimper. Rushing back, Madison dropped on her knees in front of the swing, her worried gaze quickly running over the unhappy face. "What's the matter?"

Manda squealed and stuck out her arms.

"Don't like being alone, eh?" Picking the baby up, Madison took the swing into the kitchen and put Manda back in, turned on the radio to comfort both of them, then went to the sink.

Occasionally as she cleaned up the kitchen, she glanced at the gibbering baby. Without fail each time she did, she found Manda's light-brown eyes watching her. Uneasiness began to creep over her.

"Don't get used to me. This is only temporary," Madison said, then immediately felt both foolish and mean. This wasn't the baby's fault. Hands clamped on the edge of the sink, Madison's head fell forward.

"Wes, how could you do this to me?"

Her answer was the happy squeal of his baby.

Chapter 11

Zachary checked his cell phone every fifteen minutes to make sure it was working. Manda slept a lot, but when she was up, she wanted attention. There wasn't going to be any way for Madison to avoid seeing her, touching her, talking to her. In a way, that was good because it would force them to be in contact with each other, but it could also lead to problems.

"Zach, if you don't place that tile the glue will dry."

Zachary pressed in the black tile in the shower stall, then reached for another. "You finished in the powder room?"

Kelli Potts folded her arms and leaned against the door jam. Small, delicate, with an impish smile in a pretty, mocha-hued face, she was the head carpenter of this project. "Ten minutes ago. You all right?"

"Just thinking," Zachary said, pressing in another tile.

"If you think any slower, you'll never finish." Coming down beside him, she nudged him aside. "Go take care of whatever it is that's bothering you. Me and the guys know what to do."

"I haven't been much help lately," he said. He believed in doing his best and working alongside his crew.

Kelli picked up another tile. "You will be when you get things settled. It's hard losing a friend. You go check on his wife."

He hadn't told his employees about Manda, but they knew he and Wes had been close and that he had died. Some of them, like Kelli, had worked on Wes and Madison's house. "She's probably fine."

"Then go see for yourself, then come back. This house is not going anywhere."

"I'll be back as soon as I can," Zachary said, knowing Madison's house was a good hour's drive away. Washing up, he headed outside. Getting into his truck, he consoled himself with the knowledge that the sooner he got there and checked on them, the sooner he'd get back.

Madison jerked the door open, ready to give whoever was ringing the doorbell a piece of her mind. She blinked on seeing Zachary. "What are you doing here?"

He hesitated.

"What happened?" she asked anxiously.

"Nothing. I just came to see how things were going," he confessed, wondering why his good idea didn't seem so wonderful now.

Her hand flexed on the doorknob. "I thought you weren't worried about her."

The uncertainly in her face had him scrambling to fully explain. "I'm not worried about her, I just don't want you to feel overwhelmed," he said truthfully. "You've got to be tired. She has a lot of energy and she hates going to sleep."

The corner of Madison's mouth lifted at the understatement. "Another thing you forgot to mention. I finally got her to take a nap after lunch. I put her down about thirty minutes ago." Opening the door wider, she stepped aside. "You took your life in your hands by ringing the doorbell."

"Sorry."

Madison shook her head as he tiptoed in his scuffed workbooks into the house. Quite an accomplishment for a man well over six feet and easily weighing a hundred and ninety pounds. "Would you like some lunch?"

"I can grab a bite on the way back to the site."

"You can just as well eat here." She went to the kitchen.

She didn't want anything, but he probably did. "Where are you working today?"

"Grapevine."

She paused on opening the refrigerator door. "That's over an hour from here."

"I'm used to driving from site to site," he said simply. "I'll just wash up and help."

Before she could stop him, he headed for the half bath near the kitchen. Going to the refrigerator, she gathered the ingredients to fix ham-and-cheese sandwiches, her thoughts on Zachary. She'd never met a man quite like him.

He walked back into the kitchen and took the lettuce out of her hands. "I can do that. Why don't you sit down?"

"I'm not helpless," she said, annoyed. She didn't mind his assistance with Manda, but he wasn't taking over her life.

"You don't have to be for someone to help." He washed the lettuce. "You want heavy or light mayonnaise?"

"Are you always this way?" The question just slipped out, surprising them both.

He frowned. "What way?"

She studied him, realizing he had no idea she was talking about his tendency to help out whenever possible. Then the reason came to her. "You helped your mother, didn't you?"

"Of course." He cut the thick sandwich with one sharp thrust of the knife. Like I said, it was just the two of us for a long time."

There was more to the story—the sudden tension in his body said as much. He knew her secret; she wondered what his was.

Madison wasn't surprised to find Zachary on her doorstep a little after seven that night, or there in the mornings and evenings in the days that followed. Watching him care for Manda without being asked, she came to realize he was a man of his word, a man who took his responsibilities seriously. Not once did he complain or act as if he begrudged being there. His unwavering support comforted her and eased some of her anxiety.

Friday night after they had put Manda to sleep in her crib, he followed Madison down the hall to the foyer. "I can come by tomorrow and keep her if you have some errands to do or just want to get out."

Madison hadn't left the house since the funeral a week ago. She was on hiatus and the station was running reruns of her show. She had no intention of going out, but Zachary didn't have to know that. "I'll call the housekeeper."

Zachary frowned. "The psychologist I spoke with at the hospital said that we should try and limit the number of new people caring for Manda. He says she's probably feeling abandoned. Maybe you should wait a couple of weeks before calling her."

"You failed to mention that as well." She lifted a delicate brow. "Is there anything else about her I should know?"

He shifted uneasily in his chair. For a brief instant his gaze shifted to the baseball cap in his hand. "It's not my intention to keep information from you or to trap you. It's just that I don't always think of it until it comes up."

Madison stared at him. It sounded reasonable, but for a moment she had wondered. "I just don't like being lied to."

"No one does," he replied, this time meeting her gaze. "What time should I come?"

"I wasn't planning on going out," she finally confessed, her hands tightly clasped in her lap.

"Then I'll come around ten." Pushing up from the chair, he went to the front door and opened it. "Good night, Madison."

"Good night, Zachary."

Going down the bricked steps, he stopped and looked back at her. Small and slender, she was framed in the light. Zachary had the urge to walk back, take her in his arms and . . .

"Did you forget to tell me something else?" Madison asked, worried by the strange look on his face.

Fist clenched, he said, “Nope. Get back inside and lock up. I’ll see you in the morning.”

Madison rolled her eyes. Zachary was definitely a throwback to the age where men felt women were helpless and needed protecting.

Opening the door to the truck, he stared pointedly at her. Stepping back, she closed the door. Being around Zachary was certainly going to try her patience—patience that was already thin and frayed. But she had to admit, he also helped.

Saturday morning Zachary arrived exactly at ten with his arms wrapped around two big bags of groceries. After saying good morning, he went to the kitchen and set the paper sacks on the sky-blue tiled counter. “I figured you might be running low on food so I picked up a few things. Hope you don’t mind.”

Madison watched him pull out jars, cans, and boxes of food for Manda. Her eyes widened on seeing him unload yogurt, bagels, milk, and a bite-size-chocolate bag of her favorite candy bar.

Since she personally hated grocery shopping, she knew it had taken time and effort on his part to shop for them, yet he acted as if it was the most natural thing in the world for him to do. Wes would have rather slit an artery than go into a grocery store.

“Thank you.” Pulling her mind away from Wes, she opened the pantry door and began putting away Manda’s food. There was too much for the length of time she planned for Manda to be there, but it would keep. No matter what, she wasn’t staying.

After they finished putting away the groceries, Zachary insisted on putting Manda in the stroller and taking her for a walk around the gated community. There was a children’s park with a duck pond that he wanted to show her. Somehow Madison found herself with them, listening to Zachary talk to Manda as if she understood every word. It only took a moment to realize she did the same thing with Manda when she was alone with the baby.

She slid her hands into the pockets of her white linen slacks as they followed the paved path around a small man-made pond. She'd tried to remain impersonal while caring for Manda, but couldn't quite manage it. She'd find herself talking to Manda, smiling when she thought of her or just holding her because she seemed to need to be held as much as she needed the food.

"Your turn."

"What?" Startled out of her musing, Madison glanced up at Zachary.

"Storytime," he explained, picking Manda up and going to sit on a nearby white wooden bench beneath a willow tree. "Ducks." He pointed as three waddled into the pond, then stared expectantly up at Madison who was still standing.

"Why can't you tell her a story?" she questioned, a bit annoyed.

"Because I've run out of the ones I know." His arm curved around Manda's small body, he patted the bench next to him. "Isn't there a story about three ducks?"

"Pigs," she corrected.

He smiled. "See what I mean?"

Sighing, Madison sat beside him. One story couldn't hurt, and what good was a story without the animation of the storyteller? One story became three. By the time she'd finished "Jack and the Beanstalk," Manda was in her arms grinning up at her.

Madison glanced up at Zachary. He had a strange expression on his face. She knew what he was thinking. But there was no way she was keeping Manda. She stood and placed the infant back in her carriage. "I think it's time we went home."

He didn't say a word, just clamped his large hands around the stroller handle and started back the way they had come. Madison's shoulders slumped. She wondered why his silence made her feel as if she'd disappointed him and why it mattered so much to her if she had.

He stayed most of the day, helping Madison do the laundry, holding Manda on his hip while he vacuumed, and nudging Madison into eating a couple of bites of the steaks he'd grilled. She went to sleep watching him and Manda playing pat-a-cake. When she woke it was dark. She sat up on the leather sofa. Seated across from her in the Barbados chair, Zachary immediately closed the leather-bound book in his hands.

"Have a good nap?" he asked, leaning forward.

She pulled the blanket off her legs. It hadn't been there when she fell asleep. "Yes. Thanks for the throw."

"You're welcome." Zachary stood and walked to the built-in bookshelf near the fireplace to return the biography of Harriet Tubman. He hadn't read one page in the forty-seven minutes he'd held it. His entire attention had been on Madison. At least he could admit his feelings to himself, if not to her.

She simply made his heart pound. She stirred feelings in him he'd never experienced before. He wanted to touch her, hold her, kiss her on the delicate curve of her neck. In sleep, the lines of strain had disappeared from her face and she was at peace. With everything within him he wished he could keep her that way and at the same time he was desperately afraid he wouldn't be able to. Taking a deep breath to gain control of his emotions, he turned.

The soft smile on her face shook him. She had no idea how alluring she was to him or how much he wanted her. He was unsure of when his protectiveness of this one woman had begun to change into something deeper, more intense than it had been before. Perhaps it had started the morning she thrust Manda into his arms and she had been so frightened.

Whenever, he had to get a handle on it. She only wanted his friendship, though at times he knew she wasn't sure she even wanted that. "Manda's been fed, bathed, and is in bed asleep. I'll get out of your way so you can get to bed."

Her lips twitched. "I'm rather surprised I'm not in bed already."

Zachary's breath caught as a vision popped into his head of them together on her wide bed, locked in each other's arms, his mouth on hers, their bodies straining to get closer.

Heat and a burning desire licked through his veins. "You looked so comfortable I didn't want to chance waking you by moving you." *Liar.*

"Thanks." Her face became shadowed. "Sleep is difficult at times."

The need to hold and comfort her was suddenly overwhelming. He started toward her with the full intention of gathering her into his arms, kissing her, showing her that she was desired, wanted. He reached for her.

Her eyes fastened on his and he realized just in time what he had been about to do. Lightly he brushed his thumb across her cheek. He couldn't help himself. "Give yourself time." He stepped back. "Good night." Without a backward glance he left—unaware that Madison had lifted her hand to her cheek, unaware that it was the first time in over a year that a man had touched her with such aching tenderness.

Zachary arrived Sunday afternoon and took them to the Sonic drive-in for ice cream. Manda got it all over herself, Madison, and Zachary and thoroughly enjoyed doing so. It had taken a handful of napkins and Zachary's handkerchief to get her face and hands cleaned. Madison laughed the whole time.

"Sorry, I didn't know she'd get it all over your clothes. Guess we should have brought wet wipes." Zachary chuckled. "I'll pay for the dry-cleaning."

Madison started to tell him not to worry about her blouse, but the sound of the children laughing in the car next to them had her turning in that direction. Two little girls who looked to be no more than three or four years old were playing in the back while a young couple smiled indulgently in the front.

Were they as happy as they seemed or were they pretending, as she and Wes had done? Did they pretend to be faithful to one another, then go off with their lovers as Wes had done? Was he there when she needed him or, like Wes, did the man let the job take priority over his wife and their children?

Anger swirled though Madison. She looked away. Wes hadn't been there for their baby, yet he expected her to care for his baby by another woman.

"Have you contacted a private adoption agency yet?" she asked, her voice tightly controlled and devoid of emotion.

Everything in Zachary went still. "Mad—"

As if aware she wasn't going to like what he had to say, she cut him off. "Yes or no?"

"No."

"Then, please do. I want this over in a couple of weeks." Not wanting to see the disapproval in his face, she gathered up the soiled napkins. She was doing the right thing. She knew she was. "Manda going to live with another family is best. They'll never treat her differently because of who her father was . . . as I might."

"You wouldn't do that."

"You can't be sure of that any more than I am." She began putting the used paper products in the holder their food had come in. "If you're finished, I think we should go back. It's time for Manda's nap."

Zachary didn't say anything, just took the things from her, added his own trash, and got out of the truck to place it in the garbage can. Madison saw the slump of his shoulders, the weary way he walked. She glanced down at Manda. "I'm sorry, Manda. I'm just not sure I can do this right. Zachary is asking too much of me."

As if aware of the seriousness of the situation, the baby simply stared. Madison felt tears prick her eyes. This was the right thing to do. She just wished it didn't make her feel so alone and petty.

Chapter 12

Tuesday morning Gordon glanced at Camille Jacobs's business card, then back at the woman. She was well worth taking a second look. Cool and serene, she still gave off an aura of sexuality that had a man's mind wandering where it shouldn't go. Especially a man his age.

"Thank you for seeing me, Mr. Armstrong."

The voice was low, hushed, the kind that whispered naughty things in a man's ear. He glanced at the card again. Nothing about her went with what he'd expect of a woman working in her profession. The navy-blue suit was prim enough, but the skirt just above the knee showed off a pair of great legs and trim ankles.

"You must be wondering why I'm here."

He was wondering a great deal more than that. "I assume you'll tell me when you're ready."

Camille tilted her head to one side. Gordon Armstrong wasn't what she'd expected. He was younger, for one thing, and much better looking. The gray scattered in his closely cropped black hair gave him a distinguished look, but it was the patience in his brown eyes that was most unexpected. People usually saw her card and either wanted to shove her out the door or know immediately who she was investigating.

"Are you aware that Madison Reed has assumed guardianship of Manda Taylor?"

"And who is Manda Taylor?"

Camille arched a brow. He'd answered her question, but managed to pose one of his own. "The child of the mother killed when Wes Reed stopped to render aid."

"And what does Madison's guardianship of a motherless child have to do with your department?" he asked.

"As the caseworker assigned the case it's my duty to ensure that this guardianship is the best for Manda,"

For the first time the brown eyes went hard. "So you're investigating Madison?"

Another question, and this time it was meant to intimidate. "Acquiring information."

Pinning her with his gaze, Gordon tapped her card on his desk. "You've spoken to Madison, I suppose?"

"Yes."

"When?" The question was sharp and accusing.

"Last Tuesday," she answered, already bracing herself for his reaction.

"Four days after she buried her husband," he flared, his black eyes pinning her to the spot. "What kind of woman are you?"

Camille didn't know how he'd managed to make a statement, accusation, and ask a question all in the same sentence, but he had. "It only takes a moment to inflict pain. It's my duty as a case—"

"And you think Madison would hurt a child?" His temper spiked.

"I don't know Madison Reed well enough to know what to think. That's why I'm here," she answered calmly, despite the growing urge to defend herself.

"Madison is one of those special people who genuinely cares about others. It doesn't matter about race or social standing, wealth, or power, it's the individual. That's what keeps her show at the top and it's not fake. She's for real." He stood. Six feet–plus of muscle and anger. "Good-bye, Ms. Jacobs."

She's been tossed out before and would be again, but it

didn't bother her any less. "I'd like permission to interview the other people who work on the show with her."

"You don't need my permission to do that."

"I do if I want to interview them while they're working. It would allow me to finish my report faster. But if your prefer, I can see them at their homes."

He would have liked to toss her out on her shapely derriere. "I'll let you know tomorrow." He came around the desk and opened the door.

Picking up her bag, she started toward the door. She should have kept going, but something in his gaze wouldn't let her. "I'm not Ms. Reed's enemy."

"You sure aren't her friend, either."

Louis Forbes's office was located in Highland Park, an address in Dallas that signified old money and the socially elite. In this exclusive area people thought nothing of buying a three-million-dollar house, then tearing it down to build a bigger, grander one. The name implied wealth, prestige, the A-list, "arrival" with a capital *A*. Louis Forbes counted himself in that number.

With a growing client list of the top names in the media and entertainment industry, Louis Forbes was accepted because of his connection to the famous people he represented. Rich was good, but rich and famous was even better, and name-dropping never went out of style.

"It's just like Madison to take in the baby even while she's devastated at Wes's death," Louis Forbes said, sitting behind his swirl of glass desk in a two-thousand-dollar tailor-made suit. "Her good heart is what makes her show so popular."

Camille studied Madison Reed's agent and felt as if she were being given a press release. He'd said all the right things, with just the right amount of concern and grief, but the genuine warmth she'd felt when talking with Gordon Armstrong wasn't there.

"Then you'll agree that she's a busy woman and about to get busier," Camille said.

Louis eased back in his expensive leather chair, his grin wide and patronizing. "I'm sure you've heard that Rosie O'Donnell adopted three babies, and Ricki Lake has two kids. Having babies hasn't stopped them. It wouldn't be a problem for me to get the studio to hire a full-time nanny. Babies enhance and round out a woman's life, don't you think?"

Camille could almost see the wheels clicking in his condescending brain. *"Devastated talk-show host takes in motherless infant."* It would make great press. Had that been Madison's intention? Camille hadn't thought so at first. "A nanny can't substitute for the mother."

"No, no," he quickly said, rocking forward in his seat. "I didn't mean that and since you said you've spoken with Madison, you know she's a hands-on kind of person."

Interesting, Camille thought. She hadn't thought that at all. "So you're saying Madison would assume the majority of caring for Manda herself."

His grin came back, quick and full of confidence. "Exactly. Madison would smother the baby with love. Being with Madison is the best place that baby can be. I'll be happy to testify to that in court."

Camille lifted an eyebrow. "Do you have some reason to think this case might go to court?"

Louis almost swallowed his tongue trying to backtrack. "No. No. I simply meant that I'd be willing to swear that Madison has the child's best interest at heart."

I just bet you would, Camille thought. *More press.* "I see. Thank you, Mr. Forbes, you've been very helpful."

The smile came again. "You're welcome. Come back anytime."

Camille reached for her bag on the floor and stood. "Thank you, I just might take you up on that."

Louis waited until he was positive Camille Jacobs had enough time to leave the outer office before he buzzed his secretary. "Call Helen Bass at Channel 7 and tell her I have a scoop for her if I can go live on her *Noon Day* show Friday at the latest or it goes to Freeman at Channel 10. Tell her it's about fellow co-worker Madison Reed."

"Why didn't you tell me?" Gordon demanded the instant Madison answered the door.

"Hello to you too, and tell you what?" Madison greeted, smiling up at Gordon.

He brushed by her, then glanced down the hallway and into the living room. "Where is she?"

The smile slid from her face. Muscles clenched in her stomach. "H-how did you find out?"

"Camille Jacobs," he answered tightly, still annoyed that he had found the muckraker attractive. "She just left my office, but she wants to interview your show's production crew."

"You can't allow her to do that!" Madison said, fear creeping over her.

"There's nothing I can do. I've already spoken to the station lawyers," Gordon said. "The best I could do was put her off until Friday."

Her stomach knotted. She should have realized that the child welfare worker would interview people she knew. She had wanted to keep this quiet; now everyone would know. How long before speculation would begin about the parentage of the child? Did someone know already?

"Madison?" Gordon's hands closed gently around her arms. "Talk to me. Tell me what is going on."

"I—I . . ." She trusted Gordon, but if she hadn't been able to tell him about her failing marriage, she certainly couldn't tell him about Wes's infidelity. "I need to call Zachary."

She went to the nearest phone in the den and picked it up. The silence of the dead line mocked her. Down on her knees, she reached behind the end table for the line to reconnect the phone.

"Madison, what is it?"

Madison watched him watching her and saw the concern in Gordon's eyes. She was acting irrational, but Zachary had to do something. She hadn't bargained on this becoming public knowledge.

Moving her trembling hands aside, Gordon reconnected the phone. But before Madison could dial, he took her hands in his. "So what's the story about your houseguest?"

Madison followed the direction of his gaze to Manda asleep in the playpen. She had finally drifted off after her feeding at noon. They were establishing a routine that now included storytime after lunch and at bedtime.

"Didn't the social worker tell you?" Madison evaded.

By the narrowed look in Gordon's eyes he knew what she was doing. "I'd like to hear it from you."

Think, Madison. "She has no one except an elderly great-aunt in Amarillo." She moistened her dry lips. "We both lost. I—I thought we might help each other."

He studied her a long time. "Are you sure this is a wise decision?"

Her heart thumped. "What do you mean?"

"Come on and sit down and stop looking at me as if I'm the enemy. If the child is what you want, you have my support, but I want you to be sure." Leading her to the nearby couch, he pulled her down beside him. "This is going to sound hard and cruel, but I have to ask. Are you trying to substitute her for the baby you lost?"

Bracing for a question about Manda's paternity, Madison hadn't expected this one. But since Madison had repeatedly asked herself the same thing she had an answer. "No. No child will ever be able to replace the baby I lost. She was irreplaceable."

"Come here." He pulled her to him, his head bent to hers. "I had to ask." He lifted his head and smiled. "Looks like introductions are in order."

Madison looked over to find Manda standing in her playpen, her eyes wide and wary. Madison picked her up, then came back and sat next to Gordon. "This is Manda Taylor."

Gordon reached a single finger toward the baby, but she

shrank against Madison, her thumb going into her mouth. "She doesn't like strangers."

"It's all right. Poor thing," Gordon said, his face thoughtful. "Adrian and Adair were three when Karen died. Both stopped talking and started wetting the bed. It was tough on all of us."

"But you made it through," Madison said, unconsciously rubbing Manda's back in reassurance. "You kept it together. The twins are well adjusted, happy young adults who aren't afraid of tackling the world," she said, referring to Gordon's eighteen-year-olds who were sophomore journalism majors at Howard University in D.C. Both maintained a 4.0 grade-point average.

"I'm proud of them both, but if they get their tongues pierced as they keep threatening to do, you may have two more guests," Gordon said, only half joking.

Feeling more at ease, Madison smiled. "You know you can't wait for them to come home from their internship at the newspaper in Austin."

"After I have them stick out their tongues and make sure they haven't had them pierced, I will," he returned, but he was smiling. "Well, I have to get back." He came to his feet, then threw a glance at the phone. "Let the answering machine do its job and stop unplugging the phone. I came because I couldn't get you on the phone."

She rose, the smile gone from her face. "I just wanted peace and quiet."

Gordon glanced at Manda before speaking. "Take it from a man of experience, with a baby in the house, peace and quiet are a thing of the past."

After a little over a week with her, Madison already knew that. Manda was growing accustomed to the house and to her. She was an active infant who could crawl almost as fast as Madison could walk. Madison decided she much preferred those times to the ones when Manda simply stared at her with those hazel eyes that in turn mocked and lured.

"You all right?" Gordon asked.

"Of course," Madison answered, wincing inwardly at the ease with which she lied, and at the same time pondering what would happen if the truth came out.

"I should hit you again."

Zachary's gaze immediately went to Manda, the key ring clutched in her fist. "What's wrong? What happened?" He didn't wait for an answer; he practically snatched the baby out of Madison's arms and started examining her for himself.

Some of Madison's annoyance vanished when she saw the panic in his eyes. "Manda's fine. It's that caseworker."

"She came back?" Zachary asked, his gaze no less worried as it zipped back up to Madison's face. Since their outing Sunday, she'd become distant. The past two mornings when' he'd stopped by, she hadn't said four words to him.

"She went to the station," Madison said, stepping back, then closing the door behind him. "She's doing a character check on me."

"I'm sorry, Madison. I didn't think of that."

She started toward the den. "Be thankful I can see that or I might just make good on my threat."

There wasn't a doubt in his mind that she had spoken the truth. He'd seen the flare of anger in her eyes. Madison had a compassionate heart, but she didn't like being used. She wasn't going to be happy if she found out he hadn't contacted a private adoption agency. In his opinion there was no need. Despite her reservations, she and Manda were growing closer each day. "You're afraid someone may find out?"

"Yes." She stared out the French doors toward Wes's miniature practice golf course in the back. "I don't think I could take the speculation and gossip now. You have to find her a home."

"There's no reason for people not to accept the reason you've given for taking Manda," Zachary said, coming up beside her. "In fact, I think it would be odd if you didn't want to have some contact with Manda, considering what happened."

Madison turned. "Her eyes are the same color as Wes's."

"Not many people are going to notice, because she shies away from them. Besides, lots of people have eyes that color," he pointed out unnecessarily. "*You* didn't notice their color at first or suspect anything after you saw they were hazel."

Her eyes flashed. "Stupid me."

"You trusted him. You did what a wife is supposed to do."

"Wives are always the last to know," she said bitterly.

"Not always," he said.

Her attention switched back to him. "What's that supposed to mean?"

"The children are the last to know and it hurts them far more than you can imagine and it keeps on hurting."

Zachary's disturbing words stayed with Madison the rest of the evening as he played with Manda and got her ready for bed. Manda was quieter than usual and went to sleep right after eating. Almost immediately afterwards Zachary left.

Suffering was always worse when it touched a child. They had no defenses, no coping skills. Somehow it made her own anger seem trivial. Sitting in bed, the soft glow of the night-light illuminating the crib, Madison's thoughts were chaotic. Was she being petty? Mean-spirited? She hadn't thought so at first.

Reaching for the phone, she dialed.

"Hello?"

She almost hung up when she heard Zachary's deep, distinctive voice.

"Madison?"

She had call blocker so he couldn't tell who she was. All she had to do was hang up. "I grew up thinking I'd have the perfect marriage, like my parents. Have two beautiful children, a boy and a girl, and live happily ever after."

"We all have dreams, Madison, and it's hard when they

don't turn out the way we want. But we can either accept it or keep holding on to something that will eventually destroy us."

"Is that what you think I'm doing?" she questioned.

His sigh came through clearly. "It's not my intention to judge you."

"But you have just the same," she said tightly. "I can hear it in your voice. That's why you left early, isn't it?"

"Manda was asleep."

He didn't say there was no reason for him to stay otherwise, but he might as well have. She was just someone to keep Manda. Her feelings or needs weren't to be considered, just like Wes hadn't considered how his adultery would hurt her. She didn't matter. "I see. Good night." She hung up the phone.

It rang almost immediately.

She picked the receiver up before the second ring came, telling herself she didn't want the noise to wake Manda up. "Yes."

"Madison, give yourself time."

But in the interval, she had to live with the evidence of her husband's betrayal. "Is that what you did with your biological father? Gave it time?" There was a long, telling pause. "I'm sorry, I—"

"No, you have a right to ask," he interrupted, his voice thoughtful. "I'm the one who keeps talking about facing the truth and getting on with your life. To answer your question, I'm not going to lie and say that it didn't rip me open that he didn't care that I existed. I wish he had, but nothing I could do or say will change that. I know that now. Dwelling on it only made me unhappy. I decided years ago that I had more important things to spend my time on."

"Like building homes." Silently she wondered if it was that easy to forgive.

"Yes. Houses and people share a lot in common. Both require care to be at their best."

Madison glanced toward the crib. "She's sleeping quietly."

"I meant you."

The quiet intensity of his words touched her deeply and oddly pricked her at the same time. "I can take care of myself," she blurted, then sighed deeply. "At least I could a long time ago."

"My money is on you that you haven't forgotten. Go to sleep."

"Why don't you come by for breakfast if it's not out of your way?" The invitation just slipped out.

"I'll be there. *If* we're having more than a bagel and yogurt."

She smiled without thinking. "I suppose I might be able to come up with a bit more than that."

"I'll be there, then, thanks. Good night, Madison."

"Good night." Madison took one last look at the crib, cut off the light, then pulled the covers over her shoulder and drifted peacefully off to sleep.

Madison woke up to the ringing of the doorbell. She blinked, then sprang up in bed, her gaze going to the crib. Manda was still curled in a ball asleep under the light comforter. Madison looked at the clock: 7:05. *Zachary.*

Throwing back the covers, she grabbed a robe from the foot of the bed on the way to the door. She was in the hall before unease stopped her and she rushed back in and stared down at the baby. She usually woke up before seven. Why wasn't she awake?

Fear congealed in Madison's stomach. Had the doctors at the hospital missed something in their exam? A co-worker in Chicago had lost a ten-month-old baby to crib death. Madison knew how fragile babies were. Dread clawed its way to her throat.

Manda's face was turned toward the wall and all Madison could see was the top of her curly head. With a trembling hand, she eased back the pink blanket. Her eyes strained to see the almost infinitesimal rise and fall of the baby's chest. But it was there. Weak with relief, Madison reached out and placed a trembling hand over the infant's chest, felt the warmth through her pink footed sleeper. She was all right, but what if she hadn't been?

With a lump in her throat, Madison went to answer the door. Zachary sat on the porch punching data into a handheld organizer. On seeing the misery in her eyes, he hurriedly got to his feet. "Madison, what is it?"

Shaking her head, she stepped back into the foyer.

Closing the door himself, he took her arms. "Talk to me."

"I'm not a bad person," she managed before the tears came. "I don't want anything to happen to her."

"Of course not." His hand swept up and down her back. She fit perfectly. "Don't be so hard on yourself if you make a misstep now and then."

Madison unconsciously snuggled closer to his comforting warmth and his unending strength. "Why are you always so nice to me?"

His broad palmed hand continued to sweep up and down the curve of her back. "Because you deserve it. Now . . ." Stepping back, he tilted her chin with his long finger. His smile was gentle and reassuring. "How can I help?"

She sniffed, using the heel of her hand to brush away tears from her eyes. "You already have."

He handed her a handkerchief. "Here."

"Thanks." She dried her eyes. "I have two of your handkerchiefs already. I'll have a collection if I keep this up."

"I have a drawerful." He glanced down the hall. "If Manda is sleeping late, why don't you go back to bed? I can grab a bite on the way to the first site."

"You're probably itching to see her. Go on. I'll start breakfast."

Zachary went down the hall and into the bedroom. He saw the unmade bed and his thoughts went into an entirely different direction. Rubbing his hand over his face, he looked into the crib at the sleeping child. Much safer than thinking about the woman.

Positive his feelings were under control, he went into the

kitchen. Madison flashed him a smile the moment she saw him. Her hair was tousled, her feet bare, her face free of makeup. She was the most desirable woman he'd ever seen, and if she found out he'd lied to her, she'd hate his guts.

"Don't worry. My cooking isn't that bad," she teased, on seeing the worry in his face. She sat a stack of pancakes on the table.

"I'm not." Taking his seat, he said his blessings and picked up a fork. Instead of eating, he looked at Madison and knew a hunger that no amount of food could satisfy.

He left immediately after breakfast, but all day his thoughts kept straying back to Madison. The next day wasn't any better. He fought the attraction, tried to deny the warmth her smile brought him, chastised himself for admiring the lushness of her breasts, for wanting to taste the sweetness of her mouth. Nothing worked. Each time they were together, the need for her grew.

Looking out the window in his bedroom Thursday night, he felt a loneliness, a restlessness that had become achingly familiar to him. He knew the reason. He just wasn't sure what, if anything, he planned to do about it.

Chapter 13

Gordon considered himself a strong, level-headed man, but when he saw Camille Jacobs waiting for him in the lobby of the station on Friday morning, the sharp slap of lust was totally unexpected and aggravating as hell. He liked nothing about her as a person. But the way she was put together was a different matter altogether. From her long legs to her sleek body encased in a straight black skirt that stopped just below her knees to the way the double-breasted blazer fitted over her high, firm breasts, he liked what he saw and detested himself for it.

He stopped what he considered a safe distance away. "Ms. Jacobs."

"Mr. Armstrong." Her response was just as abrupt and cool as his had been.

His gaze strayed to her mouth painted dark and sassy and looking much too tempting. The frown on his face deepened as he tried to figure out why he couldn't control his growing desire for a woman he disliked.

Neither spoke, simply stared at each other like two opponents squaring off on opposing sides of the arena.

"Do you draw a line in the sand or shall I?" she quipped.

The corner of his mouth tilted upward before he could stop himself. He usually enjoyed a sense of humor in a woman. He didn't want to appreciate anything in Camille Jacobs.

He handed her the sheet of paper he carried. "This is a list of people who work on *The Madison Reed Show*, their title, and general location. All have been advised of your coming."

She tilted her head. "Advised or warned?"

"In your case, it's the same." She had a mole on the corner of her mouth. It wasn't difficult to fantasize about running the tip of his tongue over it, then into her lush, waiting mouth. "I believe you've already met Robert Howard. He'll show you around the studio," he said, indicating the young college student standing directly behind her.

"Yes, his was the first friendly face I've seen."

Gordon's mouth tightened. "If you'll excuse me, I have an appointment."

"I'll be generous and excuse you for both reasons."

He noticed the anger in her brown eyes and clamped down on a sudden need to comfort. "I beg your pardon?"

"That'll be the day." With a curt nod, she walked away.

Gordon's gaze followed, somehow dipping to the enticing sway of her rounded hips. He snarled. There should be some unwritten rule that social workers couldn't have bodies like that.

She stopped and looked back. "You coming?"

He blinked, trying to figure out if her comment was as sexual as he thought it was when the young intern he had assigned to show her around rushed forward. The college student practically tripped over his feet in his eagerness to get to her.

"Yes, Ms. Jacobs, I'm sorry."

Despite the annoyance she felt at Gordon, she smiled at the nervous young man. "No harm done, Robert. I believe Kurt Owens, the set director, is first on the list. If you'll lead, I'll follow."

He nodded eagerly and rushed off. Camille followed and, feeling Gordon's gaze on her again, she added just a dash of sass to her walk, wishing she could look over her shoulder to see his reaction.

Stiff-necked jerk. But he was a good-looking one. And it irritated her to no end that she was bothered by his low opinion of her. But she'd do her job. To do less was unconscionable.

Louis Forbes knew how to work an interview and he had chosen his interviewer well.

Helen Bass wanted what Madison Reed had, and was willing to do whatever it took to get it. Her show was falling in the ratings and there was talk of cancellation or worse—in Helen's competitive opinion—replacement. If she could get a scoop on Madison, it would be a feather in her cap. And if that information was detrimental in some way, so much the better.

The station bigwigs were nervous that Madison might leave at the end of the year. After Wes's death their nervousness had increased. To Helen's disgust, Madison's popularity had grown. She wished Madison would disappear off the face of the earth and, of course, Helen could be *her* replacement. She couldn't see why everyone fell all over themselves for Madison, anyway. Helen knew she was much more attractive and wittier.

The program manager just kept sticking her with lousy guests. Today would be different. For once they agreed, for different reasons of course, to have Louis on live instead of the taped segment of her at a boring literacy read-in with elementary school children. How was *that* going to help ratings?

"It's always tragic when death strikes anyone as talented and young as Wes Reed. He'll be missed and Madison is devastated," Helen said, with just the right amount of sorrow and pity. "I, for one, hope this won't affect her decision to remain in our midst."

Louis sat across from Helen and almost clapped his hands in glee as she gave him his opening. "Madison's future is secure whatever her decision, but that's not her main concern at the moment."

"It isn't?" Helen leaped like a frog on a fly.

"No. It's Manda."

"Manda?" Helen was unable to hide her surprise. "Who's that?"

Louis, against all rules of interview, looked straight into the eyes of the cameras and saw the owner of KGHA in Chicago give him a blank check for Madison. "Manda is the nine-month-old infant who Madison, despite her grief, has assumed guardianship of. Just as Wes Reed gave his life to save the mother, Madison is giving the motherless infant the same selfless love and devotion. The legacy of love continues. Two more braver and compassionate souls never lived."

Helen tried valiantly not to show her anger, and some viewers might not have seen it past their own shock. At the moment she didn't care. Louis, the prick, had set her up. All she could try to do was salvage what was left. "I'm sure the viewers feel the same as I do. We all send our prayers and well wishes out to Madison and Manda. That's all for *Noon Day*. Please join us tomorrow."

With jerky movements Helen unclipped the mike from the lapel of her fuchsia-colored Albert Nipon suit and dragged out the wire. She'd bought a new suit just to be dumped on. She could chew nails.

"Is your mike off?" Louis asked.

Tight-lipped, she considered leaving it on, but something in Louis's eyes had her switching it off. "Yes."

"Work with me on this and when Madison leaves for Chicago, guess who will be my new client who'll take her place?"

Helen's eyes widened. She'd tried for over a year to get Louis to represent her. In certain circles, the agent was just as important as the client.

"I'll be in touch." Taking a cigar out of his silver case, he stuck it in his mouth and walked off, a smirk on his face. Women were such fools.

Helen wore the same smirk. Louis Forbes wasn't the type of man to be generous. There was more going on here than met the eyes. If it involved Madison Reed, Helen was going to make it her business to find out. Louis Forbes wouldn't catch her off guard again.

Angrier than he had been in recent memory, Gordon came out of his office at a fast clip. Co-workers, eternally thankful that he didn't stop to speak with them, hurriedly moved out of his path as he made his way downstairs to the first floor where the set for *Noon Day* was located. He had left his office the instant he'd seen Louis Forbes's smug face. He hadn't expected whatever the weasel had to say to be good. Unfortunately, he'd been right.

Rounding the corner, he saw the agent heading toward the lobby. "Forbes!" The name was like the crack of a rifle.

People turned, saw Gordon's face, then quickly decided they had business elsewhere. Forbes looked over his shoulder, saw Gordon and had the good sense to hasten his steps toward the front door. It didn't do any good. Gordon easily caught up with him, and drew him into a narrow alcove.

"What the hell were you thinking doing an interview on Madison and Manda?"

Louis didn't like the sudden perspiration under his arms any more than he liked Gordon Armstrong. He liked it even less that he was afraid. He had fought hard never to know fear again. "How I handle my clients' affairs is none of your business."

"It is when your client happens to work for me and you use a show at this station to further your own selfish career," Gordon said.

"I've done no such thing," Louis denied, trying to ignore the sweat sliding from his underarms. "What Madison's done for this child is to be commended."

"And it never occurred to you that it would sway public opinion toward her and possibly increase her marketability and thus fatten your bank account?"

Louis managed to look appalled. "What kind of person do you think I am?"

Gordon's eyes narrowed, then he smiled and told Louis exactly what he thought in explicit, crude language.

The agent's eyes bugged. "I don't have to stand here and take this." He tried to push Gordon and found him immovable.

"Hear me good, Louis. Let it alone. Madison has enough to deal with without you making her caring for Manda a publicity stunt." Gordon leaned closer. "The social worker is no fool. You mess this up for Madison and you'll answer to me."

"I can handle the social worker." Louis waved his pudgy hand dismissively.

"You're not only arrogant, you're stupid if you believe that." Gordon stepped aside. "Don't let me see you here again unless you've cleared it with me first."

"You can't keep me out of here," Louis railed.

Gordon crossed his arms. "We both know I can. When it comes to Madison's welfare, whose side do you think the boss will take?"

Doubt flickered in the other man's dark, shifting eyes. "Madison knows I'm working on her behalf."

"You don't even believe that lie yourself. Now get out of my sight."

Louis turned to leave, then abruptly faltered as he saw Camille Jacobs, eyes narrowed and obviously angry, a few feet away. He quickened his steps, nodding, but not making eye contact as he passed.

Gordon had seen angry women before, but none that seemed to seethe. Slowly he walked toward her as if he were approaching a live bomb.

"Thanks," she said.

"For what?" he asked, although he already had a pretty good idea.

"For not thinking I'm as stupid as Mr. Forbes thinks."

"Louis thinks he's superior to everyone." She sidestepped to let two women pass, and moved closer to Gordon. His gaze centered on the little mole, then her enticing mouth again.

Camille found drawing in air difficult and wasn't sure if

she was ready to admit the cause. She stepped back, hoping that would help. It didn't. "Thank you for your cooperation, Mr. Armstrong. I'm finished interviewing."

"So you won't be back?"

"No." She wanted to believe she heard regret in his voice, but she knew better. He wanted her gone. "The people I interviewed had nothing but high marks for Ms. Reed," she said. "No one I spoke with seemed particularly surprised by her helping the child. Ms. Reed has a reputation for helping others in need. Although I'm not particularly pleased with the way the announcement was handled."

Gordon's mouth tightened. "Madison had nothing to do with that!"

"Have you spoken with her to know that for a fact?"

"I don't have to," he snapped. "I know Madison. At the moment she just wants peace and quiet. She won't get it after today. Nothing the media likes better than a tragedy."

"Perhaps it's best she's tested now instead of later?" Camille mused.

"What are you talking about?"

"The media attention and how it affects her care of Manda will now be in the open and tested," she explained. "If it's too much, she can give up the child before either becomes attached to the other."

Gordon's gaze cooled. "For a moment I forgot who I was speaking with. I'm sure you can find your way out. Good-bye."

"Good-bye." Camille walked away, feeling adrift. Not for the first time, she had been judged by a man she found attractive and was found woefully lacking.

A little after one, Madison sat in her office, writing thank-you notes. She'd dreaded the task, but had finally made herself sit down and start. Manda was asleep two doors down in her bedroom and the intercom was on so Madison could hear her when she woke up.

She had yet to get completely over the scare Manda had

given her Tuesday morning, but it had made Madison stop thinking only of herself. She could wallow in self-pity and anger or she could get on with her life. She still wasn't sure if keeping the baby was best for either of them but, while Manda was in her care, Madison planned on doing the best job possible.

Pausing, Madison stared at the small photo of her parents on her desk. Since it appeared Manda would be with her for a while, she'd finally called them that morning and told them the abbreviated version of her assuming temporary guardianship of Manda. Always in her corner, her parents had immediately offered their support. Madison had known they would, just as Dianne had when she called, offering words of advice and horror stories of her rambunctious two at nine months old.

Madison listened, hearing the love and pride in her sister's voice. By the time Madison had finished both phone calls, she was feeling lighter than she had in days. The grief, the anger, the sense of betrayal were still there, but they weren't as sharp.

The phone calls had accomplished something else: it made Madison aware of how good it felt to have family. Manda and her great-aunt were alone. How much worse would Madison feel if she didn't have anyone she could turn to?

Oddly, Zachary's face popped into her mind. Leaning back in her chair she considered the reason. He was pushy. But even as he pushed, he held out a hand to hold and offered a shoulder to lean on. He obviously cared about Manda and seemed to care about Madison. Family was certainly important to him. She could tell when he talked about his mother and stepfather, whom he referred to as "Daddy." Yes, family was important.

So how was Manda's great-aunt doing? Madison mused. Nursing-home reputations varied. Was she being cared for? Did she have friends who visited and made her life brighter? She had to be going through a hard time with losing her niece and not being able to care for the child. She might not have even been able to attend the funeral, either.

Rocking back in the chair, Madison faced another hard fact. She hadn't wanted to think of the great-aunt, other than as a source of information on Manda's mother.

The sad truth was she'd been so busy feeling sorry for herself that she hadn't considered the elderly woman and what the loss had meant to her. Just as she hadn't wanted to consider Manda. Madison hadn't known she could be that rigid or self-righteous. Was that what had sent Wes to another woman?

Her eyes shut and she pushed the thought away. Going down that road again would solve nothing. The reasons didn't matter. The results wouldn't change: the child would still be parentless and in her care. Madison just had to figure out what to do with her, and make a decision as to what she planned to do with her own life from this point on.

The chime of the doorbell coincided with the ringing of the phone. Grateful for once for the interruption, Madison glanced at the caller ID. With a smile on her face she picked up the cordless receiver and rose to answer the intercom. "Hi, Gordon."

"Did you watch Helen's show today?"

Madison tensed. Her hand paused inches from the intercom. The other time Gordon had been abrupt with her, she hadn't liked what he had to say. "No. What happened?"

"Louis was on, discussing your assuming temporary guardianship of Manda."

Her grip on the phone tightened. "I didn't give him permission to do that!"

Gordon *tsk*ed. "Like that would stop Louis."

Madison wrapped her free arm around her waist. "I didn't want this to get out any more than it already had. The station was bad enough."

"I know," he said quietly, then added, "Camille Jacobs was at the station at the time. She heard the entire interview."

It couldn't have been worse. Madison sank to the corner of her desk. "She probably thinks I set the entire thing up. She wasn't very impressed with me the first day we met."

"She has a suspicious mind, but she's finished at the studio and we won't be seeing her again. Everyone gave you high marks."

Madison wasn't surprised. She'd always had a good working relationship with her crew. They'd helped make the show a success as much as she had. She told them that often, then backed up her words with incentives she gave out monthly. "It's a good thing she didn't interview Helen."

"No comment."

Madison made a face. She had expected his reply. Gordon never discussed his employees. The chime of the doorbell came again. "Hold on a minute. Let me see who's at the door."

Madison flicked the intercom for the front door. "Yes?"

"Ms. Reed, it's Camille Jacobs. I'd like to speak with you if it's convenient."

"Just a minute." Madison spoke into the receiver. "I guess you heard who's at the door."

"She didn't waste any time," Gordon said.

"I better go."

"I'm sorry all this has happened, but I've already spoken with the boss about Louis. He won't have free rein of the studio anymore."

"If only that would stop him. He'll cry 'infringement of freedom of speech' and go to another station."

"At least WFTA won't be a part of his sick plan to increase your marketability."

Madison's expression hardened. "I won't stand by and let Manda or me be exploited. I'll take care of Louis."

Gordon chuckled. "Wish I could be there to see that. Call me. 'Bye."

"'Bye."

Hanging up the phone, Madison went to the door. "Ms. Jacobs, I thought you were going to call before coming by."

"This visit wasn't planned," she said. "May I come in?"

That didn't sound good. "Of course. We can talk in the living room. It's closer to the bedroom. Manda is asleep." She closed the door. "Can I get you anything?"

"No, thank you."

In the living room, Madison motioned the social worker to a white sofa piled with fluffy blue and white pillows that matched the curtains and wallpaper in the room, then took a seat in a light-blue side chair trimmed in white. "What is it you want to speak with me about?"

"First, although Mr. Armstrong and you seem to think so, I'm not your enemy. I only want what's best for Manda," Camille answered.

"Then we're on common ground because I want the same thing." She no longer had any doubt about that. She leaned back in the chair. "I suppose you're here about Louis's interview."

"You saw the show?"

"Gordon called."

"He's very protective of you."

Madison eyebrow lifted at the almost wistful tone. "As I am of him. We're friends."

"Yes, of course," Camille said quickly, folding and unfolding her hands. "Do you think I could change my mind and have a glass of water?"

Madison frowned. Camille Jacobs seemed a bit frazzled. Madison wouldn't have thought that possible. "I also have iced tea."

"Water is fine."

Madison went to the kitchen and came back to see the social worker looking around the room. The ivory ceramic compote, the blue-and-white baluster jar, the ribbed box, and books were in the center of the wide coffee table. By the window draped in blue flowers on a white background was Manda's swing. A short distance away was the playpen. A half-empty bottle of water Manda hadn't wanted to finish lay inside. On the side chair matching the one Madison had sat in was one of the teddy bears Zachary had given to Manda. Manda was cuddled up asleep with the other.

Madison had been in here dusting and, as usual, where she went, Manda was nearby. At least Madison had vacuumed up the crumbs from around the playpen. Manda liked whole-wheat crackers.

She continued across the room to Camille. "It looks different from the other day. Manda might be attached to one toy, but the rest of her things make up for them."

Smiling, Camille took the glass. "It looks lived-in. You don't appear bothered by it."

The house had always been too perfect for Madison. She'd actually had very little to do with its decoration. "Trying to keep her things put away would frustrate both of us." Madison leaned back casually on the sofa. "So, what is it you wanted to know?"

"I think you've already answered my questions," Camille said, taking a sip of water. "During my last visit you were nervous, annoyed and angry. Today you're relaxed and apparently finding your way quite nicely."

Madison blinked, then laughed. "We're getting there, but I'm very angry at Louis." Her brown eyes narrowed. "He did not have my permission to go public with information on Manda and he'll certainly hear from me."

"He's already heard from Gor—I mean Mr. Armstrong."

Madison caught the slip and wondered why Camille's nervousness increased. "Wish I could have seen that."

"It was interesting." She sat her glass down on the coaster Madison had given her and stood. "Thanks for seeing me."

Madison came to her feet and to a quick decision. "Would you like to peek in on Manda?"

Camille smiled warmly. "Thank you, I would."

Chapter 14

It was after seven-thirty at night when Zachary pulled up in the parking lot of the Galleria. Work at one of his construction sites had held him up, but he had one quick purchase to make before going to Madison's house.

Opening the glass door of the department store, he headed directly for the toy section. He knew exactly what he wanted. Reaching for the foot-high teddy bear dressed in overalls and a straw hat, he started for the cash register. He'd be glad when Manda was older and he could buy her interactive educational games. Children these days watched too much television.

Growing up, he usually had his head stuck in a book. After his stepfather gave him a tool kit for his ninth birthday, those books then dealt in some way with building and architecture. Looking at the structures that had lasted from one century or one generation to the next, he'd known that he wanted to build homes for families just like his stepfather had built. In his opinion he had the best teacher in the entire world. He'd always be thankful that Jim Holman had come into their lives. He hoped his adopted father felt the same way.

Jim had asked Zachary if it was all right if he adopted him the same night he asked Zachary's mother to marry him. He and his mother had woken Zachary up, then Jim had sat down on Zachary's twin bed and explained what adoption meant. It was more than changing Zachary's last name from Miller to Holman. He'd be Zachary's father; Zachary would be his son.

Zachary hadn't let himself believe, at first. He'd waited too long, wished too hard. But as Jim patiently sat there, his large callused hand stretched out for Zachary to take, the realization sank in. He thought he'd shamed himself and ruined everything when tears formed in his eyes. Jim wouldn't want to adopt a sissy.

Frantically he'd wiped at the tears so he could see Jim's face. What he'd seen would forever remain in his heart and mind. Jim, six feet four, two hundred pounds of rope-hard muscles, was crying too.

"Yes," had burst from Zachary's mouth. Jim had pulled Zachary into his arms. His mother had joined them on his narrow bed. They'd laughed and cried and become a family.

In the years that followed he'd learned that being a family meant more than children having the same last name as the mother or father. A family meant unconditional love and support, discipline when needed, but most of all, the love that was always there. That's what he wanted for Manda, and he planned to do everything within his power to make sure it happened.

"Twenty-eight ninety-eight, sir," the cashier said.

"I always get in the wrong line," said an annoyed female voice behind him.

"Louise, hush," another voice said.

Zachary snapped out of his musing. From the impatient look on the clerk's face, she had asked him for the money more than once. "Sorry." He reached in the back pocket of his jeans for his wallet and handed her two twenties. He was considering apologizing to the woman behind him as well when he heard her mention Madison's name.

"Madison Reed is only assuming custody of that baby as a publicity stunt. Why else would she want a nine-month-old cluttering up her life?" the woman asked snidely. "Some nanny will probably take care of the kid, just like they do for all the other stars."

"Louise, I think she's on the level," the other female voice argued. "You don't watch her show. I do. Madison Reed cares about people."

"What she and her agent care about is ratings. She probably put him up to going on *Noon Day*. He had beady eyes."

"Louise! You've got to trust people more."

"Not after that woman took—"

"Sir, your change." The clerk's face had gone from impatient to annoyed.

Zachary grabbed his money, the teddy bear, and headed for nearest exit.

"You all right?" he asked as soon as Madison opened the door. He'd broken the speed limit getting there.

"You heard." She closed the door after him.

"While I was in line buying this for Manda." He handed her the stuffed animal.

Madison smiled at the teddy bear with the big glassy black eyes as they walked toward the den. "She went down early, but she'll be so excited in the morning when she sees this. I hope you aren't going to buy her a present every week."

"A present or two won't hurt." He studied her face closely. "You seem calm about all this."

"I'm not." The phone rang. She glanced down at the caller ID. "Blocked call."

"I'll get it if you want," he said.

Madison was already shaking her head. "It's probably Wes's parents. Helen's show doesn't reach the Houston area, but they have friends in Dallas and Fort Worth. I'd rather they hear it from me. I called earlier, but the maid said Vanessa was resting. A.J. was expected to arrive home around this time." The troubled expression on Zachary's face wasn't reassuring as she picked up the phone.

"Yes? Hello, A.J. You heard already." She glanced at

Zachary who had come to stand by her. "I'm sorry you had to hear it from someone other than me. Yes, Wes was a hero. No, we don't want his sacrifice to be in vain." Her hand massaged her forehead. "Your fraternity is leading a scholarship drive to be given in Wes's name at his high school. Yes, I think that's a wonderful idea."

She paused, listened. "Please give Vanessa my best when she wakes up. Good-bye."

She felt Zachary's hand on her shoulder. "I couldn't tell them," she said, her fists clenched.

"You did right." His other hand came up to rest on her other shoulder, he turned her to him. "Neither would appreciate knowing about Manda. They're too selfish and self-righteous to love anyone but themselves. Wes was the only person who ever mattered to them and now he's gone."

"How do you know so much about them?"

His fierce expression didn't change, but his hands flexed on her shoulders. "Until my parents moved a couple of years ago to Houston, Wes and I grew up in the same town and went to the same high school."

Her eyes widened in surprise. "He never mentioned that."

Shrugging, he let his hands fall. By sheer force of will he kept his voice light. "We ran in different social circles in high school."

Intuitively she suspected there was more to it than he was telling her. "Then how did you finally meet and become friends?"

"About seven years ago we were both where we shouldn't have been. We had to back each other or get our collective butts kicked," he told her, shaking his head at the memory. "Wes was trying to get a story on the workings of a crack-house and I was trying to get one of my workers out of it and into rehab. The drug dealer didn't like either of us being there."

Fear congealed in the pit of her stomach. Her fingers curled around his arm. "You could have been killed."

"Larry was a good friend. I had to try," he said simply.

"What happened to him?"

Zachary's mouth flattened into a narrow line. "Died six months later from an overdose. He left a wife and two small children."

She saw the pain still etched in his face. "You tried."

"Doesn't help much when I see his wife and children," he said tightly. "He thought he could handle it. Always said there was nothing that could get the best of him."

"Wes and I believed the same thing until we lost our baby," she whispered, her voice shaky.

Without deliberate thought Zachary enfolded her into his arms and rocked her. "Some hurts you never get over, but time helps."

Pain and misery washed across her face. "She would have been so beautiful and smart. I would have loved her so much."

"I know," Zachary said. "For what it's worth, I know."

She leaned into the shelter of his arms and hung on. Her baby hadn't lived, but she had mattered. Madison didn't want people to forget. Zachary hadn't. He shared her regret, her sorrow. She heard it in his voice gone rough, saw it in his dark eyes just before he pulled her into his arms. Somehow he always knew what she needed, then went about seeing that she got it. "Thank you."

At the sound of the doorbell she reluctantly pulled away and brushed the lingering moisture from her eyes. She'd forgotten how comforting it felt to be in a man's arms, to be held and reassured. "That should be Louis. Excuse me."

"I'm going with you."

Madison lifted a delicate brow at the hard expression on his face. Zachary's protective instincts had kicked in again. "That isn't necessary."

"I'm coming," he stated flatly.

Feeling that arguing would have been a waste of time and energy, Madison sighed in resignation. "All right, but only as an observer. Louis has to know that he's dealing with me."

Zachary held up both hands palm out. "I'm just a conscientious observer."

Madison studied him for a moment, then went to answer the door. "Hello, Louis."

"Madison, good to see you," Louis said, coming into the house. He flicked a dismissive glance at Zachary. "I came as soon as I got your message. Ready to talk about a contract with KGHA in Chicago? TriStar Communications doesn't want to be left out of the deal and will work with them. You can have it all."

Closing the door, Madison faced him. "Why did you give an interview disclosing personal information about me today without my authorization?"

The easy smile slid from his face and irritation took its place at the unexpected reprimand. His tossed a cold glance in Zachary's direction. "Perhaps we could talk about it after the workman has left."

"We'll talk now." Madison crossed her arms and pinned him with a look. "Mr. Holman is a friend of mine and I'm waiting."

Louis warily eyed Zachary's threatening stance. "I think it best if we don't discuss our business in front of other people."

Madison shot him a quelling glance. "Strange. You didn't think so today on Helen's show."

"That was different," he told her, dragging a silk handkerchief from his pocket to wipe the moisture from his brow. "What you're doing is an inspiration to people all over the country. It exemplifies your courage, you—"

"Stop blowing smoke, Louis," Madison cut in sharply, unfolding her arms. "You're fooling no one. You did the interview to up the ante of my contact for Chicago and TriStar. I have to trust my agent and know he has my best interest at heart."

"I do. I do," he quickly said, his head bobbing up and down like a crazy jack-in-the-box.

"Your actions today speak otherwise." Her eyes narrowed. "Give another unauthorized interview and you're fired."

His eyes bugged. "You can't be serious?

"I've never been more serious," she said, her voice as sharp and cold as icicles.

"You can't fire me!" More perspiration popped out on his forehead. "I made you."

"No, you didn't, and I haven't fired you . . . yet. But if you say another word about me or Manda without clearing it through me first, you're history. Is that clear?" Her voice was taut with controlled fury

"I was just trying to help," he said, his expression pitiful.

Madison simply stared at him, knowing he was lying.

Louis folded first. "I won't release any information without clearing it with you first."

"I don't plan to have this conversation again." She opened the door. "Good night."

"Good night." Mouth tight, body rigid, he left.

"You handled that well," Zachary said once the door closed.

"Firing him would have raised too much speculation after his announcement today. The best way to handle him is through his pocketbook," Madison explained, walking back into the den. "If I go to the station in Chicago and TriStar gets in the mix as well, it will mean a hefty percentage for him."

He frowned. "You still considering?"

She shoved her hand through her hair. "I don't know. When Wes mentioned it, I was against it, but now . . ." She took a deep breath. "I honestly don't know if a change of scenery would be better. The station has given me an extended leave and we're showing reruns. There's another important rating period in July, but we already have a few shows in the can. I don't have to make any concrete decisions for another couple of months. You eaten yet?"

"No."

"Come on into the kitchen. I made a pot roast." In the kitchen she reached for the oven mitts.

"I'll get that for you." Taking the pot holders, he removed the roast from the oven and set it on the hot plate on the counter. "Smells good."

She opened a cabinet overhead for a plate. "Manda liked the potatoes. She didn't care much for the carrots."

"Is she supposed to have solid food?" Zachary asked with a frown.

Madison sat the plate on the counter and reached for the utensils. "Dianne said it wouldn't hurt her. She also had cheese cubes and whole-wheat crackers today."

"I don't know that much about raising children." Folding his arms, he leaned back against the counter and watched Madison prepare his plate, then she filled a tall glass with iced tea.

"No cousins?" she asked, taking everything to the table.

"My mother was an only child. Daddy's sisters and brothers live in St. Louis." He reached over to pull out her chair when she started to sit down next to him. "You already eaten?"

Taking a seat, she leaned her elbows on the table and linked her fingers. "I wasn't very hungry."

"Humph." Zachary went to the cabinet, removed a plate, flatware, filled another glass with iced tea. Back at the table he transferred half of the food to the plate. "You have to eat."

"I'm not hungry."

He forked a potato wedge and held it out to her mouth. Her head went back and she pressed her lips tight.

He laughed. "Big baby. I bet you're doing a good imitation of Manda when you tried to feed her the carrots. Open up or I'll have to tickle you."

Not sure he was playing, she opened her mouth to take a small bite. "Satisfied?"

"Nope, but I plan to be." He took a bite of meat. "How was your day?"

She slumped back in her chair. "I wrote out thank-you cards, called my parents and sister."

Zachary studied her face again, the shadows beneath her eyes. "Manda run you ragged?"

She glanced around at the bottles on the counter to wash,

the laundry basket full of freshly dried diapers in the den a short distance away. "A bit. I'm thinking about asking Gretchen to come back next week."

He cut a small bit of his roast. "The housework getting too much for you?"

"I—" That was as far as she got before he placed the meat in her mouth. She had no choice but to chew and swallow. "Sneaky."

"Effective. You were saying?"

In spite of herself, she smiled. "The social worker came by today and she commented on the house. Although it was pretty much in the same state it is now, she seemed to approve."

"She should. You're doing a great job. From experience I know taking care of a baby isn't easy, and trying to keep the house straight is a losing battle." He took a bite of food and eyed her, then her plate.

"I can feed myself." She popped a carrot into her mouth. "How about your day?"

"One catastrophe after the other," he said wryly.

"What happened?" she asked, taking a sip of tea, enjoying their time together.

"Mrs. Otis came out to the site, that's what." Zachary pushed back his clean plate. "She wanted to change the installed sink in the powder room. Hardwood floors that were a must last week now have to be replaced with Italian tile in the living room. She simply has to have more closet space. All the time she's changing things, she has two pink poodles yapping at her heels. Her husband is ready to pull his toupee off his head, and the decorator is near tears."

Picturing it, Madison laughed, then took another bite of food. "What do you plan to do?"

"Exactly what I told them. Nothing until they make up their minds as to what they want. We've gone through this a couple of times before." Zachary shook his head. "It's costing them money and me time. I have other customers waiting. I don't like having more than four or five houses going up at the same time. As I told you, I have dependable workers, but I like to keep my hand in things."

"Yet you come by here twice a day to check on Manda when you could be home resting or getting work done," she said, still marveling at all he did.

"I have to pass here anyway," he replied.

She eyes him suspiciously. "Is that the truth?"

"Sure. When I go thirty miles out of my way." Smiling, he got to his feet, taking his plate and hers.

"Go on home. I can get the dishes."

"You worked hard today just like I did. We'll do them together."

She simply looked at him. Wes had never offered to help with the dishes.

"I won't break them." He turned on the water.

"It's not that," she said, squirting soap into the running water.

"Then what is it?"

"Nothing." She grabbed the drying towel. "Do you have the address of Manda's great-aunt?"

His hands unsteady, Zachary dunked the plate in the sink of rinse water, then handed it to her. "I could get it from the lawyer who handled the temporary custody papers."

"I thought I'd write or call." She didn't know why, but she was almost embarrassed by the admission that she hadn't done so before.

"I'd think she'd like that."

"I just wanted her to know that Manda is being cared for." She put up a plate in the cabinet and reached for another.

"You don't have to explain to me." He placed the utensils in the dishwater.

"Yes, I do. I don't want you to think because I'm going to contact the great-aunt that I might change my mind about keeping her."

He stopped washing the meat fork and gazed down at her. "A moment ago she was Manda."

She busied herself with putting up the flatware. "I can finish. You better get home."

"Throwing me out?"

She glanced up expecting to see disapproval or anger. He wore a smile. It still amazed her that he never seemed to think the worst of her. "For your own good."

"And I'm staying for the same reason." Drying his hands with a paper towel, he picked up the roasting pan. "What do you want to put the pot roast in?"

She looked at the stubborn line in his mouth. "I'll get a container.

"How is it that you let Mrs. Otis keep changing her mind?" she asked. He was certainly forceful with her.

"She's a customer. Plus my mother always taught me to respect my elders and, most importantly, I don't have to live with her."

How would he react if he lived with an indecisive woman? Treat her like an angel and always be there for her no matter what, she thought an instant later. He was the type of man a woman would find easy to love and depend on. The dangerous thought popped into Madison's mind before she could stop it. "I'll get that container," she quickly said.

When Madison bent over, Zachary couldn't help but notice the enticing way her slacks cupped her hips. Need clawed at him. All he had to do was reach out and touch. She'd turn to him, her eyes full of shocked desire. He'd take her in his arms, taste her mouth, savor the rich sweetness of it and enjoy the incredible heat.

Wanting her with every off-kilter breath he drew, he quickly turned back to the sink. He had to get a grip. "I think I heard Manda." He was gone before she had a chance to say anything. Deeply troubled, he strode down the hall, hating he had added another lie to the long list, hating that Madison could never be his.

Chapter 15

Saturdays were like any other workday for Zachary. He got up at six or earlier, depending on the location of the construction site, to be there by eight. In the kitchen he gulped down a quick cup of coffee and headed for the front door. A glance at the stainless-steel watch on his wrist confirmed that he'd have enough time to stop at a fast-food restaurant for breakfast. This morning he was going straight to work and would skip going by Madison's house.

Last night had been a warning and he was going to heed it. He was fast coming to realize that he'd gone by as much to check on Madison as on Manda during the past weeks. Madison looked so sad and lost at times. Much the way she had whenever Wes had brought her out to see the progress of the house. He'd wanted to console her then, but hadn't known how. Now he knew exactly how he'd like to take the sadness from her eyes and was even more at a loss.

Locking the front door, he picked up the morning newspaper on the porch, then went down the steps to his truck. He usually only had a chance to glance at the front page and business section. Pulling the plastic covering from the newspaper as he crossed the dew-covered lawn, he considered for the hundredth time just getting Sunday delivery.

Opening the door to the truck, he unfolded the paper and started flipping through the sections. A picture of Madison and Wes jumped out at him. Below was a smaller one of Manda's mother, Bridget.

The muscles in his stomach clenched. His heart pounding, he quickly read the article. It was worse than he'd imagined. He had to get to Madison. Tires squealed as he backed out of the driveway. He hoped Madison hadn't read the newspaper. But even as the thought formed in his mind he realized if she hadn't, he'd have to be the one to tell her.

Madison's hands were trembling. The reaction had started when she saw the photo of Manda's mother. Madison hadn't wanted to let her eyes linger on the face, but she had been unable to stop herself. If the black-and-white picture was current, she had been younger than Madison.

Bridget Taylor stared back at her with a pensive, rather shy look. She was pretty, instead of breathtaking and seductive as Madison had imagined. Unless Manda's mother projected more in person than in the photograph, she was nothing of the femme fatale Madison had imagined her to be. Not for the first time she wondered what had drawn them together, when the illicit relationship that had produced Manda had begun.

"Madison?"

The concern in Zachary's deep voice shook Madison out of her brooding. She began to read the article. With each word, her anger grew.

Zachary laid his hand on her tense shoulder. "I wish I could have prevented this some way."

Madison stared down at the newspaper clutched in her hands. "She's never liked me," she said, speaking of Helen, who was quoted in the article.

"You think your agent put her up to it?"

"He's too greedy to risk me firing him, but all he had to do was point Helen in the right direction. She's made it no secret that she'd like to have my job," Madison answered tightly. "The story is written by her live-in boyfriend, Edward Mayes. The article goes to great length to tell how much effort it takes for a couple in our positions to make the marriage work. Listen to this.

" '*Many famous couples break up because they were apart for long periods of time. But Wes and Madison Reed, known as the perfect couple, somehow managed to remain together despite their frequent periods of separation. Their marriage seemed to thrive while others faltered under the strain. This reporter interviewed several ex-couples who were once as popular as the Reeds. The general public wasn't aware of problems in their marriage until it came out in print. "Fame," said one recently divorced actor, "makes for a cold bedmate." Before his untimely death, Wes Reed had been out of town on assignment eighteen of the last twenty-three days.*' " Madison's voice trembled then firmed.

" '*We're all pulling for Ms. Reed as she struggles with the unexpected tragedy. Once a bright and energetic woman, she has secluded herself from friends and co-workers. We hope that this is a temporary situation and she will return to our midst soon.*' "

Madison balled up the newspaper. "It's an easy stretch for the public to imagine Wes in need of a woman's attention." Stalking into the den, she stuffed the newspaper into the wastebasket. "You know what really peeves me about this?"

"What?"

"The bas—" Madison clamped her lips together and glanced down at Manda playing on the carpeted floor with her teddy bears.

"If you need to go outside and let it out, I'll understand," Zachary said.

The patience in his steady gaze went a long way toward helping to calm her down. In the weeks he'd been there, he'd pushed and prodded, but always, always, he'd supported and believed in her. It was time for her to believe in herself again. "He was right on all counts. But I'm finished hiding." Her chin lifted. "What are your plans for this afternoon?"

"I need to go check on a site in Lewisville," Zachary

said, a slow smile growing. "It will probably take a couple of hours, but after that, I'm all yours."

She might have known. Whenever she needed him, he'd be there. "If you're up for the zoo and lunch on me, I'll look for you around eleven."

"I'm game." Bending, he picked Manda up from the floor. "Why don't we say eleven-thirty? That should give both of you enough time to get ready." He grinned as small hands patted his cheeks. "Then there's a swing set I wanted to get Manda."

"More toys?" Madison tried to sound disapproving, but she ruined it when she smiled.

"This one you both can enjoy. Isn't that right, munchkin?" He held Manda up in the air, and she grinned down at him. Settling the baby back in his arms, he said to Madison, "I won't be surprised if you're not ready when I get back since I'm waiting for *two* ladies to get dressed, but I can always hope." Kissing Manda, he handed her to Madison. He waved at the front door, then he was gone.

Madison rocked the baby in her arms. "It would serve him right if we *weren't* ready."

Manda squealed and grinned up at Madison.

Madison laughed. "Yeah. We'll show him."

"She doesn't have any clothes or shoes."

Zachary didn't know how to take Madison's announcement or the distress in her face. "You didn't see the Foley's sack I brought in?"

Madison waved his words aside. "Those are sleepers. I mean cute little frilly dresses or playclothes. Shoes. She can't go out in her sleepers."

Zachary's gaze went to Manda playing in her playpen. She wore what looked like a one-piece swimsuit, only it had short sleeves. Hadn't she worn something similar to get their ice cream and when they took her out in the carriage? Madison hadn't said anything then.

Madison sighed dramatically. "She's in a bodysuit."

He'd never paid much attention to clothes. All he demanded was that they were clean and mended. A rip or tear wasn't that unusual in his profession, and everyone knew jeans didn't really fit until they gone through the cycle dozens of time. Well, he didn't notice clothes except when it came to Madison. He always paid attention to what she wore.

She'd changed into a light-green sleeveless sweater with some kind of paisley silk wrap skirt. She looked absolutely mouthwatering. His hands itched to loosen that sexy little knot holding the skirt together, slide his hands all the way down, then back up those luscious—

"You don't have a clue, do you?" she asked.

"What?" He jumped, afraid she'd been able to read his mind. Then he realized she was talking about baby clothes. "Uh, if you tell me what she needs, I'll go get it and bring it back."

No fuss, no telling her that he was tired, just the offer to make whatever was wrong right, even if he didn't have the foggiest notion what she was talking about. He probably had no idea how appealing and rare that quality was in a man. Or how attractive he looked in a chambray shirt, jeans that molded his long legs, and cowboy boots. Apparently he dressed for comfort and to suit himself.

She scanned him from head to toe and felt a pleasant tingle of awareness in the pit of her stomach. She blinked. She had just checked the man out! What had gotten into her? She *never* did that. Feeling a betraying heat stain her cheeks, Madison cleared her throat and asked, "Who helped you pick out her clothes?"

He shifted from one eel-skinned boot to the other. "After we checked out of the hospital, I realized she needed things. Since I didn't want to leave her with anybody, I took her with me. She got kinda upset when a strange woman tried to take her so I just got the things hanging on the rack that said 'nine-to-twelve months.' I left as soon as I could. I just pointed at the furniture store and they helped load me up."

Figures, Madison thought. His first priority had been Manda's well-being. "What woman was this?"

He shrugged. "Some shopper. She just said, 'What a cute baby.' You know how Manda is about strangers."

Madison had a feeling that the woman might have had more on her mind than just admiring Manda. "Well, since we'll be shopping together, she'll feel safe." Bending, she picked up Manda. "There's a specialty children's shop near here. That'll be our first stop."

A pained expression on his face, Zachary grabbed the diaper bag. "Maybe I should stay in the truck."

Was there ever a man who didn't dread shopping with a woman? Her father and David certainly did. "We'll see."

Madison almost felt sorry for Zachary. The only way she could get him to accompany her inside was to convince him that she could go through the racks of clothes quicker if both hands were free. He'd wanted to sit in the air-conditioned truck with Manda, but she had told him that she needed Manda with her.

He'd taken his time getting Manda out of her car seat, but she had waited him out. "This shouldn't take long."

The look on Zachary's face said he wasn't so sure, but he opened the half-glass front door of the store and followed her inside, Manda in his arms. His reluctance was glaringly obvious as he trailed behind Madison who moved from rack to rack. She worked hard to keep the smile off her face.

"Excuse me, but aren't you Madison Reed?"

Madison, a pink cotton sundress in her hand, stilled. Her smile faded. She felt Zachary's hand brush her bare arm in reassurance. She turned to see a petite woman in her mid-twenties holding the hand of a dark-haired little boy. "Yes."

The woman moistened her lips, swallowed. "I—I watch your show every chance I get. I just wanted to say I was sorry to hear about your husband." Her pitying gaze went to Manda.

Despite telling herself she was ready for this, Madison felt every muscle in her body tense. "Thank you."

The woman pulled the squirming child closer. "I heard what you're doing and I think it's wonderful. I just wanted you to know." She smiled. "I'll let you finish shopping. Good-bye."

"Good-bye." Madison hung the dress up. She was so tired of all the lies. She wasn't this wonderful paragon of virtue people thought she was. Her marriage had been nothing but a sham. "Maybe we should try this another day."

Zachary reached past Madison and pulled out another garment. "What about this?"

The lavender dress in his hand had rows of lace and net. She grimaced. "No."

"What about this one?"

Madison experienced a flare of irritation. Couldn't he see she wanted to go home? Since the dress was as unsuitable as its predecessor, Madison finally looked up at him. His strong, patient face said it all. *He wasn't letting her run.* She sighed softly. "What would you have done if I said I liked it?"

"Bought it, put it in the back of the truck and let the wind do the rest," he said without missing a beat.

Her lips twitched. "You're incorrigible."

Manda waved her hands as if in agreement.

Zachary pulled a long face as if hurt. "You women always stick together."

"That's right." Madison lifted Manda into her arms and touched her cheek to the infant's. "See that you remember that. Now, let's find Manda a beautiful dress, then shoes." Turning on her heels, she ignored Zachary's tortured groan.

Chapter 16

Gordon couldn't find Madison. Tired of listening to the message on her answering machine, he'd driven over to her house. He felt somewhat better when he saw the morning paper still in its plastic bag on the lawn. At least she hadn't read the underhanded piece.

It was no secret that Helen wanted Madison's position. To further that goal she'd used her boyfriend and Louis's segment to her advantage. His annoyance escalating, he quickly went up the steps and rang the doorbell. He rang it again when there was no answer.

Staring at the door, he finally decided Madison wasn't home. She'd mentioned Zachary the other day, perhaps she was with him. Returning to his car, Gordon slammed the door and started the motor. He didn't have time to look for Madison any longer. He had a speaking engagement in less than an hour.

Camille Jacobs was probably on the phone to Helen now, trying to get an interview. Unlike the rest of the people at the station, Helen's report wouldn't be good, and Camille would use it against Madison. Muckraker!

That woman got to him and it wasn't just because she annoyed him. As much as he tried to tell himself differently, it wasn't working. She was one of the most sensual women he'd ever had the misfortune to meet. She might appear uptight on the surface, but he sensed the passion beneath. Probably a deliberate act on her part. She probably liked confusing a man.

He wasn't going to give her that satisfaction. He'd put her out of his mind.

He had every intention of doing just that until he walked into the monthly meeting of the National Council of Negro Women and saw the person he had been trying so hard to forget. Camille Jacobs.

Had she conjured him up? Camille stared at Gordon Armstrong as he stared at her. From his frosty glare, she knew he wasn't pleased to see her. Despite the unexpected pang of hurt she felt, she lifted her head. He wasn't going to make her feel ashamed for doing her job, but how she wished she hadn't let her mother talk her into attending one of her meetings to help with refreshments. Maybe it wasn't too late to—

"Camille, please come over here. I want you to meet our guest speaker for today, Mr. Armstrong, the producer for *The Madison Reed Show.*"

Caught. Camille considered disregarding her mother's request for all of two seconds, then started toward them. Julia Davis was diminutive in size, but was a terror to those who opposed her. Camille was already skating on thin ice with the formidable lady and she wasn't about to crash through on something as inconsequential as Gordon Armstrong.

"Hello, Mr. Armstrong," she greeted as she stopped in front of him. He wore a sports coat and white shirt. He smelled good and looked better. She was caught between wanting to sniff and bite.

Her mother's gaze whipped between the two. "You know each other?"

"Yes," Camille supplied, leaving it at that. She could see the speculation in her mother's eyes, but knew she was too well-mannered to ask. "I was about to check on the refreshments."

Julia grabbed her daughter's forearm before she could make good her escape. "That can wait. Why don't you introduce Mr. Armstrong around since you two know each other." It was a command, not a question.

"I'm sure Mr. Armstrong would prefer someone else."

"Oh, Camille," Julia said, half embarrassed, half exasperated. "Please, tell me you didn't."

"I can't," Camille said, glaring at Gordon.

"I feel like a man who's come in on the second act of the play," he said with a slight frown.

Julia's smile was apologetic. "I'm sorry, Mr. Armstrong. Please forgive us."

Camille's mouth firmed. "What she means is, forgive *me*."

"Camille, I think I can speak for myself," Julia said, a hint of steel in her voice.

Even at thirty-four, Camille heeded that tone in her mother's voice. "Yes, Mother."

Satisfied, Julia casually curved her arm around her daughter's trim waist. "As I said, since you two know each other, why don't you get Mr. Armstrong some punch, then introduce him to the other members while I make sure everything is ready." She turned to Gordon. "Thank you again for coming. The program should start shortly."

"Thank you, Mrs. Davis," he said. "Julia Davis is your mother?" he asked, once the older woman had walked away.

"Yes."

"Why haven't I ever seen you with your mother at any of the other functions?"

"Would you like a glass of punch before we begin the introductions?"

"I'd rather you answer a question," he said.

She sighed. Her mother was well known and respected in social circles. If something needed to be done, a project pushed through the city council or help with funding, they called Julia Davis. While not wealthy, she had the ear and, if needed, the deep pockets of those who were. "I seldom have time. And to answer your next question, I'm a social worker because there's a need, because I care, and because I'm good at what I do."

He didn't like being that predictable. "Why did it upset you mother that we knew each other?"

"She worries about me doing home visits, but also about interviewing people she might socialize with."

"And her disapproval bothers you?"

There was no sense denying it. "Yes. Punch?"

"Then why do it?"

"Because what I feel doesn't compare to what a helpless child feels when it's abused or abandoned." She turned away. "I see City Councilwoman Blair just arrived. Why don't we go meet her?"

He waited until she faced him. "Why is your last name different?"

Her eyebrow lifted. "I don't think—"

"Why?"

Feeling people watching them she said, "Jacobs is my married name."

"You're married?" The question came out as an accusation.

Heads turned. He asked more questioned than she did. "Divorced," she explained in rising irritation. He was really beginning to get on her last nerve.

"I'd like that drink now," he said casually.

She clenched her teeth. She'd like to pour the entire punch bowl over his head. If the answer hadn't mattered, why had he asked? "Of course."

Gordon closed his hand around her upper arm as she started to walk away. Softness beneath silk. Her head whipped around, surprise and something else shimmering in the depths of her eyes. "Problem?" he asked casually.

"No," she said, but her voice was shaky, her heartbeat unsteady. She quickly looked away.

Liar, he thought, but hadn't he been lying to himself since he'd first met her? He'd done his best not to yield to the strange yearning he experienced each time he saw her. She had the power to hurt a good friend. What's more, he was too old for her. He had recently passed his fifty-seventh birthday.

He extended his hand to Councilwoman Blair, but his gaze kept going back to Camille. She was giving mixed signals again. The dress stopped at midcalf, but the hot-pink color drew him like a magnet. He'd like nothing better than to put his hands at the hem and slide the material up over her long leg and off her body while he feasted on every lush inch of her. Suddenly he realized age or nothing else mattered. He wanted her and there wasn't a darn thing he could do to stop it.

A woman could tell when a man was watching her.

Even though she hadn't caught him, Camille knew Gordon was watching her and she wished he'd quit. Her mother and a couple of her friends were giving her strange looks. The last thing she needed was for them to begin matchmaking.

"We'll finish here, Camille. I'm sure you have something else you'd like to do on a Saturday night," her mother said, looking pointedly at Gordon.

Camille could either protest or run. She kissed her mother on the cheek. "Thanks. I do have plans for tonight."

Julia frowned at her daughter and Camille barely kept from laughing. That would teach her to play matchmaker, not that Gordon wanted her. He was watching her because he didn't like her. "I'll call tomorrow." Untying her apron, she picked up her purse and almost made it to the door.

"Leaving?" Gordon asked, coming up beside her.

"Yes." Why had her voice become breathless?

"I'll walk you to your car," he said, his hand slipping easily around her upper arm.

Although her face was the picture of disinterest, her body began to heat. "That won't be necessary."

"I think it is," he said casually.

Camille didn't have to look over her shoulder to know her

mother and her two closest friends, all of whom had despaired, plotted, and prayed that she'd get married again, were watching her. "Mr. Arm—"

"Gordon."

Her eyes narrowed.

He smiled into her disapproving face. "Come on, let's go outside. If you tell me off in front of your mother, you'll upset her and you don't want to do that." He steered her out the door and toward the parking lot.

"What I don't want is to go anyplace with you," Camille said firmly.

The smile slid from his face. "We both might wish that were the truth, but it isn't."

"We don't like each other."

"That doesn't seem to stop us from wanting each other."

She waited until the butterfly in her stomach settled. "Do you act on all your impulses?" she countered.

He hadn't expected her to admit the attraction between them so readily. Women rarely surprised or intrigued him the way she did. The realization both annoyed and titillated him. "Impulses rarely grow and become sharper."

She glanced away. "Seeing each other on a personal level isn't wise."

"Tell me something I don't know." He stared at her. "I don't like it that you might hurt my friend."

"I understand. Then we end this before it begins."

His other hand came up to draw her closer to him. "I can't do that."

Her breath hitched. "This is a mistake."

"I've made them before." His eyes searched hers. "I want to see you tonight."

Camille felt her resistance slipping and tried again. "If I have to take Manda from Ms. Reed, you're not going to like remembering we went out."

He was gentleman enough not to tell her that he planned to do a lot more with her and *to* her than just take her out. "You aren't going to do that."

Brown eyes went glacial. "You think a date can influence my report?"

"I'll let that insult pass," he said easily. "Where do you live and what time shall I pick you up?"

"You must get tired of tripping over all that self-assurance," she replied flippantly.

Gordon was unfazed. "Scared?"

Camille's chin lifted. "I have plans for tonight."

"With whom?"

"None of your business." She fished her car keys out of her purse and opened the door. "Good-bye, Mr. Armstrong."

His hand closed over hers. "This isn't over."

She felt the heat, the hardness of his body, and was tempted to give in. There was a deep yearning to press closer and see if he could back up the promise in his dark eyes. "It is, for me." She glanced meaningfully at his hand.

After a brief moment, he withdrew his hand and stepped back. Getting in her car, she stuck the key in the ignition with a hand that wasn't quite steady. Looking straight ahead, she pulled off.

Gordon Armstrong was a complication she couldn't afford. He was like none of the men she had ever met. He refused to be put off. If he couldn't get results one way, he tried another. He was tenacious and he made her mouth water. A bad combination for a woman who had finally stopped dreaming of finding the right man.

Dreams meant hope, and when they shattered, you shattered right along with them.

Scared, nothing. She was petrified.

Chapter 17

Manda ended up with seven dresses, three headbands, seven pair of socks, and three pair of shoes. Madison changed her into one of her new dresses in the truck. After putting the headband back on Manda's head four times and having Manda pull it off just as quickly, Madison gave up. "All right. You win." She glanced across the seat at Zachary. "Where do you want to go for lunch?"

"Clint's Barbecue?"

Remembering the ice cream incident, Madison glanced down at Manda in her new yellow-and-white sundress with daisy appliqués. "At least I won't have to worry about you getting barbecue sauce all over your new dress."

"I wouldn't be so sure." Zachary smiled at Manda. "Remember, she likes to eat what you eat."

Reaching into the shopping bag, Madison pulled out Manda's bodysuit she'd worn to the store and ignored Zachary's laughter. "Better prepared than sorry."

After lunch, they went to the zoo. Instead of renting a stroller, they decided Manda would feel better if one or the other held her. They wandered through the bird and small-mammals preserve, but stayed clear of the large animals.

When they left, Zachary drove them to a toy store for Manda's swing set. He insisted on taking the deluxe swing set with him. On the way back, he called two of his employees and asked them to meet him at Madison's house to help set it up. As soon as the last bolt was tightened, he insisted that Madison and Manda have the inaugural swing. Protest was useless.

Madison sat with Manda in her arms in the two-seated swing as Zachary gently put it into motion. Manda's eyes widened, then she squealed with delight. Zachary and the two men watching laughed.

"Thanks, guys. I owe you one," he said to the two men gathering up the tools and folding the cardboard box the swing had come in.

"You certainly helped me put together enough toys for my kids," James said as he picked up the toolbox.

"Same here," Thomas agreed. "See you Monday."

"Good-bye, Mrs. Reed," they said in unison.

"Thank you, and good-bye," Madison said as the men departed through the wooden gate on the side of the house.

Madison stood Manda up. Faces inches apart from each other, the baby squealed with delight, then began to bounce up and down on her sturdy legs while waving her hands. Madison wore a wide smile on her face.

"I wish I had a camera," he said.

"Don't you dare," Madison admonished, her eyes twinkling. "Manda's hands and the wind have done a number on my hair."

"Just makes you look more beautiful," Zachary told her. The words were barely out before he wished he could recall them, especially when Madison's smile faded and she looked away without saying anything. He tried to think of a way to get the conversation started again and came up with nothing. Frustrated, he pushed the swing and cursed his own stupidity.

"I'm sorry if I embarrassed you earlier," Zachary said later when they were inside the house. Madison had been quiet since they'd come in a couple of hours ago. The only time she'd spoken was an hour earlier when Gordon called to check on her. She had assured him that the newspaper article hadn't upset her. Zachary just wished he didn't have the nagging feeling that his clumsy words had. "Madison?"

Madison finally glanced up from the small washcloth she had been folding. "You didn't embarrass me." She sighed and laid the folded cloth on top of the other towels. "The way I look didn't stop Wes from cheating on me, did it?"

"Don't do this to yourself, Madison," Zachary told her.

"Do you think I like doing this, thinking there was some flaw, some inadequacy in me?" With a lost look in her eyes, she made a motion as if to stand.

He caught her wrist. "The flaw was in Wes, not in you."

"I can finish this. You should go home."

She was shutting him out again. There was no way he was going to let that happen. Moving the folded laundry to the other side, he gently placed his hands on her arms and turned her toward him.

"Wes didn't leave you an outlet for your anger. He's not here for you to yell at, to tell him to pack his suitcase and get out of your life. Instead, he's dead and you feel guilty that you're angry at a dead man, a man who should have cherished you, loved you. Perhaps he did, but he also had a child by another woman."

Her face filled with anguish, she tried to pull away. "Please go. I don't want to listen to any more."

His hands tightened. "Then yell, hit, tell me off, stop holding it in."

"No," she choked out. The words she was thinking were too horrible to say; she felt disgust with herself just for thinking them.

"Maybe you're not the woman I thought," he told her bluntly, his face taut.

Her head snapped up. Her eyes went from hurt to rage in a heartbeat. Zachary's words were too close to the ones she had been thinking. *She hadn't been woman enough to keep her husband faithful.*

Zachary never saw the slap coming but if he had he wouldn't have tried to avoid it.

Horror washed across her face. Wrapping her arms around her waist, she rocked forward. "Please. Just go."

He took her by the arms again and turned her toward him. "You've come too far today to give up. You didn't create this problem, but if you don't face it you'll end up hurting yourself more than Wes ever could have." He stared at her ravaged face intently, willing her to understand. "What you feel is natural. If you hold it in you'll never be free."

"I'll never be free anyway," she said in a quiet voice.

"You will if you give yourself permission," he told her. "Hell, I loved Wes, but if he were here I'd beat the hell out of him myself."

The anger in his voice got through where kindness had failed. She finally looked at him.

"Since he's not here, what do you think would get to Wes the most?" he asked speculatively. "What if we took the scissors to his fancy suits or put his wingtips outside and let the sprinkler do a number on them? How about you letting that Franklin guy Wes was always bidding against buy his art collection below cost?" He paused and stared at her. "What could we do that would get to Wes the most?"

"Throw his golf clubs into the water hazard in the backyard," she said softly.

The words were barely out of her mouth before Zachary was moving. "You turn the intercom in your bedroom to the backyard, then we'll go see how far those babies will travel before taking a dunk."

He was halfway down the hall before Madison came out of her daze and followed. She paused in front of Wes's bedroom door, then made herself go in. Zachary was already coming toward her with Wes's bag of custom-made clubs. They had cost over four thousand dollars, and of course he had to have a custom bag to carry them in.

"I don't think you had time to set the intercom." Brushing by her he went into her bedroom, looked at a peacefully sleeping Manda, then switched on the intercom. He was moving down the hall again in seconds. Madison finally caught up with him when he was going out the French doors in the den.

"You're serious?"

He looked back at her. "If it will take that haunted look off your face, I'd toss everything in his room in and if it didn't all fit, there's always the lake in the development."

Her eyes searched his face. He meant it. Whatever it took, he'd do it for her. She couldn't remember anyone caring for her that unselfishly besides her parents and sister. How different their marriage might have been if she and Wes had cared for each other that deeply. They thought they had, but life had taught them differently. It was time she faced that fact.

Then he was moving again. Unsure what she was feeling, Madison followed. The full moon illuminated the backyard, but as they neared the practice area the motion lights Wes had installed so he could putt at night came on.

Zachary stopped at the edge of the kidney-shaped, ten-by fifteen-foot water hazard, and looked at her expectantly. "Which one takes a dunk first?"

"Zachary, they cost a fortune."

"I'll contribute the full amount to a charity." He pulled out a wood iron and grunted. "Never understood why you'd pay good money for a head cover for one of these, then use it to hit a hard ball. Here."

The iron felt cold in her hand. She stared down as light reflected off its shiny surface. Her fingers tightened. This was Wes's symbol of prestige among his chums at the country club. He'd haul them out with pride. She'd heard him brag endlessly about his golfing expertise. If he hadn't become a TV correspondent, he might have turned pro.

A golfer always took care of his clubs, he often said. She'd seen him lovingly wipe a soft cloth across the surface, fuss over them, just look at them and admire their sleek beauty. He'd cared for them, treated them with respect, even loved them while he'd walked over her and her heart every damn day.

Madison gripped the club with both hands and sent it flying. Before the sound of the splash faded, another, and another one followed.

"You lying, stinking *bastard*," she shrilled, grabbing and throwing clubs as fast as she could. "I hate you! You had no right to have an affair, to betray me, to have a baby with another woman! Not once while I was in the hospital or after I came home did you ever say you were sorry or regretted that our baby hadn't lived! You refused to talk about her! How could you have been so cold and unfeeling? You betrayed and hurt me in the worst possible way!"

She grabbed the putter. "You loved these, and not me." *Plunk*. Madison didn't notice tears running down her cheek or that they gleamed in the moonlight. "I trusted you. You hurt me. You bastard, you hurt me so bad."

Tugging the empty bag from Zachary, she heaved it into the water. At the sound of the splash she sank to her knees, her tears flowing freely. "You hurt me. You hurt Manda."

Strong arms closed around her, and pulled her against a hard chest. She inhaled Zachary's scent, felt his strength, his tenderness. "I hate him for doing this to me, for dying and leaving me to take care of his mess. He shouldn't have done that to Manda or to me," she whispered.

The force of her tears shook her body and somehow cleared her mind and lightened her soul. She didn't resist when Zachary pulled her into his arms and sat her on his lap. When she had no more tears, he dried her eyes with his handkerchief. Sniffing, she stared at the smooth surface of the water.

"Wes would have had a fit."

"That he would." Zachary's arms tightened.

She lay for a few moments longer, listening to the steady, reassuring beat of his heart against her cheek, then angled her head up. "Thank you."

His head started to descend, then abruptly stopped. Madison wondered if he had intended to kiss her on the cheek. Suddenly shaky and not quite sure why, she quickly slipped off his lap and tried to stand. Zachary came gracefully to his feet, pulling her upright with him. No matter how many times she saw evidence of his strength and agility, it never ceased to surprise and please her.

She started toward the house on legs that grew steadier with each step. This time it was her who didn't stop until she was inside Wes's room. The king-sized mahogany bed dominated the room with its seven-foot, heavily carved headboard. Platinum arches jutted from the ten-foot four-posters and crisscrossed each other. Wes said it was a bed for a king. There had never been a place for a queen.

"I'd appreciate you helping me pack his clothes," she said, walking farther inside. "There are several charities that could use them. His parents would probably like his personal items. We can start tomorrow, if that's all right with you."

"I'll bring some packing boxes."

Embarrassed by her earlier attack on him, she finally worked up the courage to look him in the face. He smiled down at her. Her fingertips lightly touched his jaw. "I'm sorry about the slap."

"Wes's teeth would still be rattling."

She smiled without thinking. "Meaning yours aren't?"

"I'm made of tougher stuff." Taking her arm, he led her from the room.

"I'm beginning to see that," Madison said, feeling an easing of her spirits she hadn't felt since Wes's accident.

Madison woke up Monday morning determined to get her life back on track. Life went on and, for the time being, her life was tied to Manda's. It wasn't something that she had planned, but the fact remained, Manda was in her care.

Dressing, she checked on the sleeping baby then went to the kitchen to fix her breakfast. Manda didn't like to be kept waiting. Madison recalled Wes had been the same way. He wanted immediate results.

Instead of the jagged pain she usually felt, there was only a slight ache overlaying the grief of his death. Taking the box of baby cereal out of the cabinet, Madison went to get Manda's cereal bowl. Yesterday she and Zachary had packed Wes's things. Without Zachary's reassuring presence she wouldn't have been able to even think of going through Wes's possessions. There was too much anger, too much hurt and grief.

Whenever she faltered, Zachary was there. He'd talked fondly of Wes, the times they'd spent together as friends. She realized how deeply he'd cared about Wes. In Zachary's easy way, he made her remember not just the last devastating minutes with Wes, but what she and Wes had meant to each other before they had lost their baby. It was strange, but comforting.

"Wes was wrong. There's no getting around that fact," Zachary said while they were in the middle of packing Wes's numerous suits into boxes. "But for your own peace of mind and happiness, you have to forgive him and move on by remembering the kind of man he was when you married him. No matter what, don't forget you once loved each other."

She'd cried and used another of Zachary's handkerchiefs. She and Wes *had* loved each other. Their love just hadn't been strong enough to get them past the loss of their child. Now he was gone. And she had to go on.

As Zachary had said, holding bitterness in her heart could hurt her far more than Wes's betrayal. Regardless of what he had done, his last thought had been for Manda, not himself. At the time, she had viewed it as selfish, now she had begun to see it for what it was: his last desperate act to ensure his child's welfare.

Today she was taking another step toward reentering life. After Manda was fed, they were going to Premier Atelier, Neiman Marcus's beauty salon, to get her hair done. Hearing Manda on the intercom, Madison hurried back to the bedroom. The day was going to be wonderful.

* * *

An hour later Madison wasn't so sure about the day anymore. Holding Manda securely in her arms, she contemplated her next move. She looked from Manda's car seat in the back of the Mercedes to Manda. Tears sparkled on her lashes. Madison kissed the baby's cheek in reassurance and held her closer. "Don't worry, sweetie. I'm not putting you back there again by yourself."

"Then what are you going to do, lady?" asked the service-station attendant who had rushed out to help when he'd seen a frantic Madison leap out of the car, then jerk open the back door to take a screaming baby from the car seat. The elderly man scratched his balding head. "You'll get a ticket if she's in the front with you. How are you going to drive with her?"

"Good question." Madison's lips brushed against Manda's forehead. They were less than two blocks from her house. Neiman Marcus was thirty minutes away. "I'm sure I'll come up with a good answer."

Chapter 18

Louis Forbes thought of himself as shrewd, decisive, and smart. It angered him to think he hadn't thought of every angle before he acted. Staring out the window of his third-floor office Monday morning, he surveyed the buildings and homes where the property values ran in the hundreds of thousands per square foot. He liked what he saw, liked being a part of that, liked knowing people with money knew him and sought his favor. He'd come a long way from the tenements of Boston. He'd done well. He planned to do better.

Whipping the cigar out of his mouth, he returned to his desk. He picked up the sheet of paper on which he'd written the latest offer from the television studio in Chicago. Two million dollars plus a penthouse with a maid, car service, a personal masseuse, and membership to the most exclusive spa in the city.

Louis rocked back in his chair. If he pushed, he bet he could get them to throw in a boat she could keep docked at the marina on Lake Michigan. But why should he push for an ungrateful twit? His teeth clamped, mangling the cigar.

Tossing the ruined cigar in the chrome wastebasket, his anger escalated. Threaten him, would she? After all he had done for her. Laying the paper aside, he picked up the newspaper article on Wes and Madison that had run in the Saturday newspaper. This time he allowed the slightest upward tilt of his mouth.

Helen Bass had proved even more effective than he had imagined. He knew she'd run to Edward Mayes with her story. She and the reporter were lovers, and she often fed him tidbits of information. The story was well written, but didn't have enough of the sentimental slant he had wanted. Too factual. Mayes had even given statistics on the number of freeway fatalities associated with vehicle stops.

Louis shuddered. Thank goodness he had emergency car service. Let them risk their butts. Which is exactly what Wes should have done. He'd chosen the wrong time to play the Good Samaritan.

Stupid bastard. His death was senseless. He'd had his life before him. He'd been so pleased with himself. So damn sure that he could get Madison to relocate. He'd messed it all up when he stopped to help some woman with a flat tire.

It was so unlike Wes that Louis wanted to rail at fate for doing this to him. Money lost, in Louis's opinion, was never recouped. He had clients, big clients, but a good agent never rested on his laurels. Why had the fool stopped?

Wes didn't get his hands dirty or do menial labor. He'd been born with a silver spoon in his mouth that had turned to platinum by the time he was eighteen due to his father's car dealerships and shrewd investments in tech stock before it went bust. As far as Louis knew—and he made it his business to know—Wes rented a car with twenty-four-hour emergency maintenance service for that very reason. He didn't like being inconvenienced or to be kept waiting. He wasn't the heroic type or the kind to stop and help a strange woman.

Louis looked at the picture of Madison and Wes. The smiles were there, but he'd been in the business enough to know they'd been having problems. Wes had been out of town a great deal, and when men weren't getting it at home, they got it someplace.

"I wonder . . ." Perhaps he should do a little investigation on Bridget Taylor, the woman Wes had stopped to help. What if she hadn't been a stranger? The sobering thought took root and sprouted. Leaning over, Louis picked up the telephone.

"Dana, get me . . . Never mind." He replaced the phone. He'd take care of this himself.

If his suspicions were right, he'd have the leverage he needed to control Madison. He'd lost a big commission with Wes's death. Louis didn't plan to lose any more money. If he was wrong . . . His gut churned at the thought of what would happen if Madison found out. She'd fire him without a moment's thought of how hard he had worked to get her and Wes their big contracts. And it wouldn't stop there.

Agents were like priests. Their clients told them things they wouldn't dare whisper in the dark. If Madison put the word out that he couldn't be trusted, he'd be ruined. He might very well find himself clientless and back with nothing.

No. He'd have to keep this to himself. The stakes were too high. After all, if you started a brushfire, you better make damn sure you weren't caught in the flames.

Helen came to work Monday morning with a briskness in her step that hadn't been there Friday. She was feeling good. She even condescended to speak to the receptionist and the do-nothing security guard who would probably faint if anyone said boo. Laughing at her own humor, Helen continued to her office near the back of the TV studio.

Inside, the cheerful mood she had carried with her since she'd finished making love with Edward that morning fizzled. Drab and cramped with a tiny window, the ten-by-twelve space was a far stretch from the plush office Madison had on the second floor where all the big guys rested their fat behinds. But her day was coming.

Jerking out the bottom drawer in her desk, she stored her Kate Spade bag, a real one, not a knockoff like some of her girlfriends'. Helen had never liked having second-best. That's why it angered the hell out of her that Madison Reed had her own show. Maybe now the higher-ups would start paying some attention to her.

Pulling back the chair, she sat behind her desk. Edward had done a great job with the story, covered all the angles, including saying Helen had the exclusive with Madison's agent. That should garner her points at the studio. It still rankled that the piece had to be so sappy, but Edward had convinced her that she had to play her cards close to the chest. Be supportive out in the open, while she waited her chance.

After her career took off, she could help him move into TV. With his looks and body, he'd be dynamite. They'd make Wes and Madison look sick. Yeah, she and Edward could be the sweethearts of America. They could have it all.

Lost in thought, Helen barely had time to register the knock on the door before it opened. Her mouth opened to tell the idiot they were supposed to wait for the person to say, *Come in*. The words died in her throat when she saw Gordon. He wasn't smiling.

"Good morning, Gordon."

He closed the door behind him. "I hope you still think that when we're finished talking."

The big breakfast she'd eaten with such gusto suddenly turned on her. "What's the matter?"

Gordon braced his hands on the cluttered desk and leaned toward her. "I want to talk with you about the piece your friend Mayes did on Madison."

Helen swallowed her fear. "You came to congratulate him?"

"Hardly." He straightened to his full height. "I'm only going to say this once. Madison and the baby are off-limits as topics for you or Mayes. We support each other at this station. Not tear people down or create problems for them."

Helen was up before she thought better of it. "Her temporary custody of that baby is public information. Madison is a public figure. It's news."

"For some. Not for this station or for those who work here."

Irate, Helen barely kept herself from kicking the desk. "This can give me more exposure and help ratings for my show."

"Or end it completely." His eyes narrowed. "Do I make myself clear?"

"Yes." She almost choked on the word.

"Good. I have never liked repeating myself." He walked to the door. "Have a good day."

Helen snatched up the Waterford paperweight on her desk. She raised her arm to throw it, but some instinct for self-preservation kicked in. Her fingers uncurled and she dropped the glass oblique onto her desk before sinking into her chair, rage almost choking her.

The entire station treated Madison like a little princess. There probably wasn't a person there who wouldn't jump to her defense, while they barely spoke to Helen. But she didn't need them. And she'd show Gordon he couldn't treat her like a nobody. She'd think of some way to fix him and Madison. She would be more careful this time and keep her name out of it, but they both were going to pay, and pay well.

Gordon didn't like reprimanding his subordinates, but if he had to, he made sure they knew he didn't want a repeat of the infraction that had caused his displeasure. Particularly if the cause was jealousy. Trying to get ahead in the competitive world of television was one thing; stepping on the back of a colleague or anyone else to get there was inexcusable.

Going back to his office, he took the stairs instead of the elevator. He usually did it to keep himself in shape. Today, he had to admit, he did it for an entirely different reason. He needed to work off some of the pent-up energy from sexual frustration, and to prove to himself that he could. Both reasons were tied to Camille Jacobs.

Annoyed with himself *and* Camille, Gordon sat behind his desk and started through the week's schedule. He managed to work only because he had trained himself to multitask. You had to if you wanted to be in management.

He'd worked hard for his position and he liked what he did. He didn't intend to let his personal life interfere in any way with his job. He'd always been able to compartmentalize his life. The only time he hadn't was when his wife had been in the last stages of her cancer, and then, after her death while trying to reassure his children.

Gordon glanced at the picture in the polished wooden frame on his desk. Adrian and Adair with a sign between them that said, ALTHOUGH WE'RE AWAY YOU'LL ALWAYS BE IN OUR THOUGHTS. Gordon smiled and hoped they were thinking of him when the idea of having their tongues pierced came up. Shaking his head, he laid Tuesday's schedule aside and picked up Wednesday's. He had it together.

He kept that thought for the next five minutes before admitting to himself that he was trying so hard to convince himself because he hadn't been able to compartmentalize Camille.

No woman had gotten to him the way she had. He admitted she was beautiful, but there was something else that drew him to her. And if he didn't miss his guess, she felt the same way. She might choose to ignore her feelings or run from them, but he planned to do neither. Nor would he let her.

But she did have one valid point. How would Madison feel if she knew they were seeing each other? Although it wasn't a fact yet, he had no doubt it would happen. He and Camille would be an item. It simply remained to be seen how long Camille could dodge the inevitable.

The corners of his mouth quirked. It had been years since he had tried to lay siege to a woman's affection. He wondered if he was completely out of practice. He'd soon find out. First, he had to make sure their paths crossed again.

He didn't have to think long to figure out that one avenue was her mother. Smiling, Gordon picked up the phone and called Julia Davis. If she was as smart as he thought, and she approved of him seeing her daughter, which he thought she did, he'd have the information he needed without even asking.

Five and a half minutes later Gordon hung up the phone feeling very satisfied. Camille was in Austin at a training meeting, but she would be back Friday for a black-tie fundraiser affair for the Mary McCloud Bethune House at the Anatole Hotel. *Dinner and dancing*, he mused as he leaned back in his chair. He'd better brush up on his dance steps. Camille was not getting away from him.

Madison arrived home later in the day with a growing respect for mothers with small children. She'd obtained permission from the service station to leave her car there, then called the car service she'd used in the past for guests on her show. Manda had gone to sleep in her car seat on the way to the salon, but had awakened just as Madison was being combed out. The baby had taken one look at the strange surroundings and people and let it be known she didn't like it. They'd left immediately.

There had been no more tears since, but the threat of them gave Madison some anxious moments. However, once in the house, the tension in the baby's body ebbed. Madison was finally starting to relax herself when she heard the phone ring.

"Hello," she said, shifting the baby's weight in her arms.

"Mrs. Reed, please," requested a pleasant-sounding male voice.

"Speaking," she said.

"Good morning, Mrs. Reed, this is Don Coggins with the *Atlanta Herald*. I was a great admirer of your husband's work. He was one of the best."

Madison frowned. He could be telling the truth or blowing smoke. Reporters often flattered you to catch you offguard, then went for the jugular. She glanced down at Manda. "Yes. Thank you for the call, but I'm rather busy at the moment."

"With the baby you have custody of, I bet. Her name is Manda, isn't it?

"Yes," Madison answered simply.

"That's wonderful," he said in a conversational tone. "I was thinking about doing a piece on the two of you. I could be there with a photographer tomorrow, if that's convenient. The wonderful way you've channeled your grief into helping Manda is heartwarming. Your courage is commendable."

At the moment Madison felt far from courageous, then she looked into Manda's face. The smile of a moment ago was gone. She had picked up on Madison's distress. She wouldn't like being subjected to the probing stares of strangers, either. "Don't worry, Manda."

"Mrs. Reed?"

"I really have to go. I appreciate your kind words about Wes, but I feel that in Manda's best interests, she should be kept out of the media."

"But your agent Lou—"

"I've stated my wishes, Mr. Coggins. If you admired Wes as much as you say, you'll respect his memory and find another story."

"Others reporters might not be so reasonable," he said, his tone threatening, then it softened to cajoling. "Wouldn't it be best for all concerned if you did an interview and answered all the questions?"

"The questions anyone might ask are of no concern to me. Manda's well-being is. Good-bye, Mr. Coggins. Have a nice day." Madison hung up the phone, considered taking it off the hook, but instead went to her bedroom and turned on the answering machine. The phone rang almost immediately. The caller ID read: OUT OF AREA.

So it has started.

Sitting down on the bed, Madison pulled her cell phone out of her purse, dialed. Her call promptly went into voice mail. Not discouraged, she hung up and tried again. Voice mail. The fourth time he picked up.

"Yeah?" Zachary barked.

Madison jumped. Manda's eyes widened.

He was speaking again almost immediately. "Listen, I'm sorry I snapped at you. There's no excuse, but I was trying to finish an inspection under an old house. How can I help you?"

"I didn't mean to disturb you," Madison finally said.

"Madison, what's the matter?" he asked, walking a short distance from the eagle eye of the elderly woman who owned the three-story house in need of major renovations if it was to be around for another seventy-five years. "Do you need me to come over?"

Once again Zachary had put her needs ahead of his job. No matter how unfair it was for her to compare, she couldn't imagine Wes ever thinking about leaving a project he was working on because she needed him. He hadn't the day she had lost their child.

She'd tried to tell him she was feeling off. She couldn't put her finger on the cause, she had just known something was wrong. He'd patted her on the head and told her not to worry, then left for his interview in New York with a Jamaican drug lord. As was his practice, Wes had turned his cell phone off so he wouldn't be disturbed while doing the interview.

By the time the interview was over and he'd turned the phone back on, five hours had passed and Madison was out of surgery. Wes received an Emmy nomination for his investigative report.

"I'm on my way," Zachary said when she remained silent. "I'm in Forney and it'll take at least forty-five minutes to get there."

"No," she finally managed to say. "I'm—*we're* all right. A reporter called from the *Atlanta Herald*. He got a little pushy, that's all."

"I'd like to push my fist in his face for upsetting you," Zachary said, his voice a low growl.

Madison felt a pleasant flutter in her chest. She'd never had a man who wanted to champion her before. The idea was strange and very appealing. "I took care of it, but it's not going to stop. The calls will keep coming."

"Hmm," he said. "You'll handle them."

She leaned her head against Manda's. "Thanks for the vote of confidence."

"Anytime," he said, with a smile in his voice.

Madison felt her own mouth curve into a smile. "I'd better let you get back to work."

"Sorry about before. You did right to keep on calling. I'd turn off the voice mail, but—"

"You'd spend the day answering the phone instead of getting anything done. I understand. I'm just glad you're there when I need you."

"About time you realized I'm not going anywhere."

Madison felt the weight of his words unfurl softly inside her. "Goodbye." Turning the phone's ringer off, she pulled back the duvet and stretched across the bed with Manda tucked beside her. The baby rubbed her eye with one chubby hand, clutching her teething ring in the other.

"I'm not going to leave you, Manda," Madison whispered. "You're safe. I'm not going to leave you." As soon as the words were out of her mouth, Madison realized she had spoken the truth. There had been enough upheavals in the baby's short life. Madison wouldn't put her through any more. And . . . perhaps they did need each other.

Placing a protective arm around the baby, Madison pulled her even closer, intending to rest just for a moment. Just before she drifted off to sleep she remembered Zachary's last words and smiled.

"I'm not going anywhere."

Chapter 19

When Zachary finally freed himself from two demanding clients it was six-thirty in the evening. He wasn't happy about the lateness of his arrival at Madison's house. After her phone call he'd planned on being there earlier. True, he had competent people working for him, but there were certain responsibilities he couldn't pass on. The owners of homes starting in the high six figures expected the owner of the company to show up if there was a question or concern. In the past he hadn't minded. Now, he had to keep reminding himself that they had a right to his time.

His first sight of Madison had relieved some of the tension nipping at his heels since her call, but not all. She'd explained about having to leave her car and they'd gone to retrieve it.

Returning to the house, at Zachary's suggestion, they listened to the messages on her answering machine. There were ten in all. Two from telemarketers and eight from the print media or TV stations. Madison pushed ERASE and left the machine on.

"You might want to monitor them in case the call is important."

Madison sighed and folded her arms. "I've already decided to do just that. I'd better go check on dinner. It's time for Manda to eat. She had a late lunch so we're a little behind."

"I'll feed her then take her outside to the swing." Holding a babbling Manda, Zachary followed Madison out of the room.

"She'd like that," Madison answered, continuing down the hall.

Watching Madison closely, Zachary followed her back into the kitchen. She seemed preoccupied and it was more than the reporters. He didn't know if that boded bad or good. Rather than try to guess what was on her mind and put his foot in his mouth again, he decided to wait.

And wait he did, through Manda's dinner and her play-time. Instead of joining them as he had hoped, Madison re-mained inside. Returning later with a sleepy Manda, he saw Madison setting the kitchen table. "I didn't mean to keep you from dinner."

She glanced up as she placed a bright red oversized plate on a placemat. "You're not. I hope you'll join me. Meat loaf, cabbage, cornbread. I felt like eating something different."

Comfort food, Zachary thought. "Thanks. I'll put Manda down and come back to help."

"You'll come back and sit down." Madison put the flat-ware on the table, then came across the room to smile at a sleepy Manda. "She's already had her bath and her night-gown is on her bed. Can you handle it?"

"A cinch since she's almost asleep," he said with a grin. Madison smiled back up at him and his heart pounded. Abruptly he turned away. "Be back in a jiffy."

Madison watched him go and wondered about the strange look that had come over his face, then dismissed it. It was probably just her own nervousness. By the time she had put the serving dishes on the table, Zachary had returned. He held the chair out for her, then bowed his head to bless their food. Zachary was definitely old-fashioned in the nicest ways.

"So, why were you under an old house?" she asked, fill-ing his glass with iced tea.

"Thanks." He spread his napkin. "Since I restored the

house I live in, I've started to gain a bit of a reputation. Mrs. Rice's family has lived in the house for three generations. She's eighty-five, and sharp as a tack. Her children and grandchildren have no interest in a house in the country, but she doesn't want it to fall down or be torn down after she's gone. I'm considering buying it and restoring it."

"I love old houses." She piled food high on his plate. "I've always wanted to live in a two-story."

Zachary's brow furrowed as he accepted the plate she handed him. Had Wes known? Probably, Zachary thought. Wes tended to indulge himself rather than others. But that had been the way his parents raised him. They had led him to believe what he wanted far outweighed the needs or desires of others. He'd been taught to equate possessions with love. Caring about Wes would have been impossible if Zachary hadn't known his background.

"Hers is three-story with pinewood floors, a mahogany staircase, and double windows that wrap around the house. Despite the disrepair, the house is structurally sound. I'll take you to see it if she sells it to me."

"I'd like that." She took a sip of her iced tea. "When will you know?"

"She said she'd call this week. Unlike Mrs. Otis, Mrs. Rice can make a decision and stick to it." He took a bite of meatloaf and nodded his head appreciatively. "This is good."

"Thanks."

"That's why I was late. Mrs. Otis now *thinks* she wants rose marble in the guest bath instead of black. Mr. Otis promised to keep her away until the house is finished."

"Do you think he can?" She sprinkled croutons on her green salad.

"He's crazy about her, so I have my doubts." He picked up a cornbread muffin. "She can twist him around her little finger."

"That's the way it should be," Madison said, with only a slight wistfulness in her voice. She caught Zachary's concerned look and rushed on to say, "From what you said, your mother and stepfather are the same way. How did they meet?"

He smiled in remembrance. "A leaky roof brought them together. April showers may bring spring flowers, but it also brings misery to a family with a leaking roof and no money for repair. Mama worked at the university and attended classes there in the evening while I stayed at a center on campus for the children of students."

The bread was forgotten in his large hand. "She'd just finished her sophomore year in college when I was born. It took her three more years to get her degree in English. Another three for her master's. She did it all without help from anyone. By the time she finished she was bogged down in debt from student loans and all the other bills. After she got pregnant with me, her parents wanted nothing to do with her. They didn't change their mind after I was born."

There was no bitterness in his voice. It was as if he was telling someone's else story. Madison couldn't imagine what it would have been like not to have the support of her large, extended family while she was growing up.

She'd always known she was loved and wanted, known that she had people she could turn to. It was only as an adult that foolish pride, then concern about her mother's health had kept her from being truthful about her troubled marriage. But if she had, she knew with certainty that her family would have been there for her.

"Mama had managed to buy a house, and coming home from work one afternoon she saw Jim working on the roof of a house in the neighborhood and stopped to ask if he'd come and give her an estimate." A slow smile kicked up the corners of Zachary's mouth. "To this day she still says that she almost didn't stop because she had no idea how she'd pay for it, but it had rained the night before and we had to set out every pot we had in the house to catch the water. She was desperate."

"So he fixed the roof?"

"More than the roof; he fixed Mama's heart." Pensive,

Zachary stared across the table at Madison. "Her heart was probably just as worn and in need of repair. The man who fathered me was long gone by then. Jim was good for her, for us. His parents were the same way. They accepted us from the first. So did his brothers and sisters." His mouth tightened. "The people who should have loved me didn't."

"Their loss," Madison said, feeling sorry for the little boy wanting to be loved and not understanding why he wasn't.

"Yeah, but growing up I always wondered what was wrong with me. Then in the third grade I found out from an older boy in my school the reason my grandparents wanted nothing to do with me. Why I didn't have a father around like most of the other kids." His face became shadowed.

Without thought, Madison reached across the table and covered his hand with hers. "If you still believe that, you're not the man I've grown to depend on these past weeks."

His head came up. His large hand turned, clasping hers gently. "No. I don't believe it. Being loved by my mother, Jim, and his family helped. Even when I started acting up as a teenager and was angry with everything and everyone, especially Mama and Jim, I knew deep down they loved me."

"Yes, being loved helps." Feeling heat radiating from their clasped hands and a strangeness she didn't understand, Madison pulled her hand free, then took another sip of tea to ease her suddenly dry throat. "I want to discuss Manda with you."

The meat loaf he'd swallowed settled heavily in his stomach. "Yes?"

Madison correctly read the wariness in his black eyes. Funny, she had never noticed how dark they were or how long the thick lashes were. Silently chastising herself for letting her mind wander, she said, "She needs to grow more comfortable with being separated from us. Today is a perfect example. She has to stay in her car seat."

Zachary's shoulders settled against the back of his chair. "Give her time."

Madison shook her head. "I don't think that will help."

She took a deep breath. "I think she needs to be around other children."

He shot forward in his chair. "You want to put her in day care?"

"Day cares are fine, but that's not what I want to propose." Putting her arm on the table, she leaned forward. "I want us to take her to visit the families of your friends, like the ones who came by Saturday to put up the swing," she explained patiently.

The tension seeped from his body. "I don't see that as being a problem."

"Good." Madison picked up her fork. "The sooner we can visit would probably be better. Until she learns that she's not going to be abandoned, I can't take her anyplace by myself."

"You should have called me today."

She waved his words aside. "We managed and I'm not helpless."

"I never thought that." He picked up his glass of iced tea. "I still hate to see you both confined all day. Do you have friends with children who could come over here during the day?"

Madison's gaze flickered to his face, then away. "It's best if she goes out."

He considered her for a long time. He didn't like to keep pushing, but someone had to. "Is that the only reason we're seeing my friends and not yours?"

She sat the glass carefully back down on the table and barely kept from sighing. He saw through her too easily. "I didn't want my close friends to know my marriage was in trouble so I drifted away from them. I have lots of acquaintances and associates, but no close women friends I can talk to, confide in." Her expression saddened.

"Only you can change that."

She looked at him, really looked at him. The patient eyes, the strong jaw, the mobile lips. He was handsome, caring, and dependable. He could probably have his pick of women.

Yet here he was with her as he had been for the past three weeks. It appeared when Zachary took on a responsibility, he didn't so do lightly. "Maybe you should be the host. You have a way of helping people help themselves."

His strong face clouded. He drew back his hand. "Don't pin any medals on me, Madison."

She couldn't tell if he was embarrassed or troubled. She chose to think it was the former. "I will if I want." With a self-satisfied smile on her face, she began to eat.

Later that night Zachary stood at his bedroom window staring out at nothing in particular. His thoughts veered back to Madison, when they had been sitting at the table. She trusted him and was beginning to see him as her friend, not just a friend of Wes's. It was in her eyes, in the unconscious touch of her hand to comfort him.

And he had betrayed her.

The thought, once a small prick to his conscience, had become a jagged plunge that caused him to struggle daily with his decision. He hadn't done it lightly. At the time he had had no choice. He had willingly walked into the storm. The trouble was, he still didn't have a choice.

Madison was stronger, but if she learned the entire truth about Manda she'd shut him out of her life forever. Just the thought of never seeing her again made his gut clench. The emotion was dangerous to both of them, but there didn't appear to be anything he could do to stop how he felt.

Then there was Manda to consider. He'd hoped, prayed for her and Madison to grow closer. That was happening. Tonight when he'd arrived, Madison had been holding Manda and hadn't offered her to Zachary until Manda had reached for him. He hadn't missed the smile on Madison's face when, later sitting in the den, he had put Manda down and she had cruised around the table to Madison, who had immediately praised her, then picked her up and pressed her cheek against Manda's.

The two of them were growing closer, but even that

closeness was a danger to both of them. If the truth came out, it might well tear them apart; then they'd both suffer.

He scrubbed his face. The truth was coming. He could feel it. Waiting. And when it did, he just prayed Manda and Madison wouldn't pay the price for his betrayal.

"We didn't think you were coming this morning."

Zachary gazed down at Madison's smiling face and his breath caught. After thinking about her well into the night, then dreaming about her, seeing her unguarded happiness simply because he had stopped by did strange things to his emotions. His heart beat like a drum against his rib cage.

It had been a long time since he had seen her this carefree and happy. She'd always been beautiful to him, but the haunting sadness she wore like a cloak had filled him with a growing need to make her pain disappear forever. This morning the guileless smile on her honey-colored face stirred the man in him.

Dangerous for both of them.

Reaching out, Madison tugged him inside the house and closed the door. "Manda has been looking around for you all morning. She's already eaten."

Deciding it was safer to look at Manda instead of the tempting woman, Zachary bent to brush his lips across the infant's curly head. He realized his mistake almost instantly. Overlaying the scent of baby powder was the alluring fragrance of Madison's floral perfume, an exotic mix of jasmine and rose. The aroma filled his head with forbidden thoughts and endless possibilities. He straightened abruptly.

Madison's smile slowly faded. "Are you all right?"

"Sure. Come here, munchkin." He held his hands out for Manda. Grinning, she leaped. Catching her closely, he grinned back. "Miss me, huh?"

She patted his cheeks.

Madison stared at them, wondering why she felt a strange fluttering in her stomach. "There's waffles and sausage, if you have time."

"I have time." Zachary followed her into the kitchen, noticing not for the first time the slimness of her body, yet there were curves to entice a man. She wore a green T-shirt and a pair of jeans as faded and well-worn as his own. Her feet were bare.

"Have a seat." Going to the stove, she took out a plate and sat it before him. "I made extra just in case you stopped by."

Settling Manda comfortably on his left knee, his arm around her waist, he bowed his head, said his blessing, then poured syrup over his waffles. "I appreciate it, but you didn't have to bother with breakfast."

"I have to cook anyway." She sat a cup of coffee by his plate, then took a seat across from him, picked up her grapefruit juice, and nodded toward his plate. "Taste all right?"

"Wonderful," Zachary said after swallowing. "You're a great cook."

"Thanks. I haven't done much cooking in a long time," she told him. "There wasn't much point in cooking for myself all the time."

"I know what you mean. I usually grab a bite out if the housekeeper doesn't cook." He sipped his coffee, careful to lean Manda away so she couldn't grab the cup of hot coffee.

"Let me take her." Madison got up and came around the table to pick the baby up.

"She's not any bother. I don't get to hold her very much."

Madison took the seat next to them, twin lines furrowing her brow. "You're here in the morning and in the evenings. That's a lot."

Zachary stopped eating and slowly turned toward her. A heaviness settled in his chest. "I didn't mean to be in the way."

Astonishment widened her eyes. "What are you talking about? I couldn't have made it without you, and I'm selfish enough to want you to continue to come. Manda and I couldn't have made it without you. But it's not fair to you. You must have a life of your own."

The weight lifted. She wasn't throwing him out of her life. "I promised to help."

"And in your book, that's that."

Zachary wasn't sure if she was making a statement or asking a question, but his answer would have been the same. "Yes."

She nodded. "More coffee or waffles?"

"No thanks." Zachary placed the fork on the empty plate, then rose with Manda on his hip to put the plate in the sink. "I better get going. What are you two going to do today?"

Madison stuck her hands in the hip pockets of her jeans, inadvertently pushing out her breasts. Watching Manda, Madison didn't see Zachary gulp. "I thought I'd call the lawyer."

Zachary tensed. His gaze zipped up to her face. "What for?"

"To get Manda's great-aunt's phone number. I want to let her know that Manda is being well cared for. I shouldn't depend on you for things I can do." Madison pulled her hand from her pocket to smooth over Manda's curly black head of hair.

"You had a lot on your mind. I'm sure she'll appreciate hearing from you." He hoped she didn't hear the fear in his voice.

Madison played with the baby's hand. "I thought I'd unearth my camera and take some shots of Manda to send to her."

Zachary's hand reached out to touch a lock of Madison's curly hair. "You don't have an excuse now not to be in them with her. Your hair looks great. I forgot to tell you yesterday. It's almost as soft as Manda's."

Startled, flattered, she froze for all of three seconds. "Th-thank you. Could you give me his phone number?"

"I'll have to call back," he said quickly. He needed to make sure Sam Peters had his story straight. "I'd better get going. The house we're working on is in Cedar Hill." Kissing Manda, he handed her to Madison. "I'll see you both this evening. Don't cook."

Madison followed. They'd discovered that as long as

Madison held her, Manda didn't mind Zachary's leaving. "Why?" she asked as he opened the front door.

"It's a surprise."

Madison couldn't see the intriguing smile on her own facc. Zachary could and it warmed his heart even as he admitted that he was falling in love with a woman who might soon hate his guts.

Chapter 20

Madison's late-afternoon phone call to Velma Taylor was as difficult as she had imagined it would be, but in a different way. Velma Taylor answered the phone herself, her voice wavery and thin, the result of ill health and seventy-six years. It took a few minutes for the woman to adjust her whistling hearing aid and put Madison on the speaker phone for her to understand that Madison was the woman caring for Manda. When Miss Taylor did, her voice thickened, she began to cry softly.

"Bridget was such a good girl. Never did anybody harm. It breaks this old heart of mine up just thinkin' about how she died."

Torn between compassion and anger, Madison's hand on the receiver tightened. "I'm sorry."

"God knows best. I jus' thank you for keepin' Manda. That little bit of sugar was a handful for Bridget, but she loved every minute."

Madison didn't want to hear about the other woman, but realized the older woman probably needed to talk just as much as Madison had. "The nurse at the hospital said Manda was healthy and apparently loved."

"Yes, she was. When the nurse came in and told me what happened to Bridget I lied awake that night and the next worryin' and wonderin' what would happen to her baby, then your lawyer came. I thank God for your kindness. I pray for you and Manda mornin' and night."

A lump formed in Madison's throat. She didn't deserve Velma's prayers, but perhaps prayer, and Zachary, had helped her to stop feeling sorry for herself. "Thank you, Miss Taylor. I thought I'd send you some pictures of Manda."

"Bless you, child, but you better hurry and send 'em. My eyes ain't as sharp as they used to be," she said, her voice growing weary. "Bridget's friend paid for me to come all the way to Dallas to see a specialist and get the surgery for the cataracts, but ain't nothin' they can do about this glaucoma."

"I'm sorry," Madison said, meaning it. She was genuinely glad that Wes had tried to help her. The elderly woman had gone through a lot.

"God's will. I just ask Him to give me the strength to go through each day."

There was no bitterness in her voice, just calm acceptance and unshakable faith. Madison glanced down at Manda, who was in her lap staring up at Madison with a smile on her chubby face, her hazel eyes bright, babbling happily. "I'll have the photos blown up so you can see how beautiful your grandniece is. I've given my name and phone number to the front desk. The nurse said she'd come down later and program it into your phone. If you need anything, please call."

"You've already given me what I need."

Madison was genuinely touched. "Good-bye, Miss Taylor. I'll do my best to get those pictures in the mail in a couple of days."

"Good-bye, child. Kiss that piece of sugar for me and tell her I love her and to be good."

"I will." Madison hung up the phone, then stared at it. Zachary was probably busy. Cedar Hill was forty minutes from her house. She shouldn't worry him. She could probably call Gordon and he'd find a way of getting the film to her and arrange to have it picked up and taken to the lab. She didn't want to call the car service just to take her to get film. Her mind circled back to Zachary.

It didn't take much for Madison to recall the warm approval in Zachary's gaze when he talked about taking her picture with Manda. Although she disagreed with him, she didn't doubt that he'd want to be a part of their photograph session.

Without giving herself time to doubt, she picked up the phone and dialed. Zachary answered on the second ring.

"Zach Holman." His deep voice came through clearly.

"We're fine," she said, aware that his first concern would be their welfare. "Do you think you could pick up two rolls of thirty-five-millimeter film on your way over here tonight? I found the camera, but no film."

"No problem. You going to get in the picture with her?" he asked.

In the background she could hear the sound of hammering and men voices. "I haven't decided yet."

"It's your decision, but I'm hoping you will. I want one for my desk and my wallet."

Madison adjusted the baby in her arms, trying to decide how to take Zachary's last statement.

"You still there?"

"Just thinking."

He chuckled. "Probably about what to wear. This time I know she has clothes, but if you want to go shopping I could come a little early."

"No, that's all right," she said.

"See you later. 'Bye."

"'Bye." Madison hung up the phone. Humming softly, she went to the closet to look for a dress to wear because, just as she was sure that the sun would rise in the morning, she knew without a doubt that Zachary would include her in the photographs.

Seven minutes later Madison was still pushing clothes around in her closet. Manda sat a few feet away with her teething ring in one hand and her teddy bear at her feet. "Nothing looks right."

Hands on her hips, Madison glanced over her shoulder at

Manda's dresses on the bed, then down at Manda. "A closet full of clothes and nothing to wear. Zachary would laugh, but what he doesn't know . . ." Walking over, she picked up the phone on the night stand and dialed Neiman Marcus. "Cindi Foutz, please."

The cheerful voice of Madison's personal shopper came on the line seconds later. "Hi, this is Cindi."

"Hello, Cindi. Madison Reed. I need your help."

Zachary bought three rolls of film and a disposable camera. When Madison answered the door with Manda in her arms, he wished he'd bought more film. She was absolutely beautiful. He tried not to stare or drool. "You look great."

Warmth—she didn't think to question the reason why—curled through her. "Thank you."

Zachary felt himself falling deeper, harder. Taking her arm, they went to the backyard. After a short discussion they decided to pose Manda beneath the leafy branches of the fruitless mulberry and used as a backdrop the seasonal bed of flowers in full bloom.

He'd had a bad moment when Madison glanced toward the water hazard, but when she turned back to Zachary he'd seen acceptance and strength in her face instead of grief or anger. He'd nodded his approval, then set about taking pictures. By the time he and Madison were finished snapping, they had shot all three rolls of film and used up the disposable camera as well.

As Madison had expected, she was in a lot of the pictures. But she'd gotten a couple of shots of him as well.

"We'll drop these off on the way to the surprise. You don't have to change."

The surprise turned out to be a children's restaurant. Storybook characters were servers. The laughter of children was everywhere. The ice cream machine seemed to be the biggest draw as child after child passed with mounds of toppings on a variety of ice cream flavors. Manda took it all in with big eyes.

"How did you find out about this place?" Madison asked over the squeals of children playing in a sea of red and blue balls.

"One of my men had his son's birthday party here." Zachary said from across the table shaped like the branches of a tree.

Madison glanced down at Manda, her ballerina-clothed teddy bear clutched in her arm. "When do you think her birthday is?"

"September twelfth," Zachary said casually, watching her. "The date was on her discharge papers from the hospital."

Madison nodded. After Wes's funeral, she'd counted back nine months to September, then back another nine months to December. Scrutinizing his office calendar yielded nothing. Now she knew. *Manda was born on September twelfth.* Although she couldn't recall Wes's whereabouts in December when Manda was conceived, she had no difficult knowing where he was when she was born. With Madison.

Wes hadn't been there for Manda's mother any more than he'd been there for Madison. The day Manda was born, Madison had received an award for Woman of the Year from the Junior League. He'd been in town the entire weekend, playing the loving husband, the other half of the perfect couple. Lies. All lies. She was so tired of them.

"That means she'll be ten months Saturday," Madison finally said.

Zachary smiled indulgently at Manda. "I guess I'll have to get her an extra-special teddy bear."

"Don't you dare, Zach Holman. I don't want her spoiled," Madison said, getting up with Manda in her arms. The baby's weight and the way she snuggled closer felt good. "How about a game of pinball before we have to leave? The loser buys ice cream."

Zachary, tall and self-assured, stood. The other part of his surprise was working out by itself. He hadn't even had to talk her into playing. Wes had once mentioned Madison played a killer game of pinball. Although she enjoyed playing immensely, he had refused to play against her again. "I hate to beat a woman," Zachary said.

She lifted a delicate brow. "Then you have nothing to worry about since I plan on beating you, and it won't bother me in the least."

Laughing, Zachary curled his arm around her waist, felt the leap of his heart and accepted his fate of loving a woman he shouldn't. He'd even let her win.

Fifteen minutes later, he paid for ice cream. After finishing their banana splits, they slowly walked to the truck. "You were just lucky," he said once they were all buckled in and he was pulling out of the parking lot. He still found it hard to believe she'd beaten his socks off. He'd used all his skills not to embarrass himself. "I demand a rematch."

"Hear that, Manda?" Madison grinned from ear to ear. "Men always have excuses when women beat them. Remember that."

Manda squealed and patted her hands. Madison's answering laughter filled the cab. "That's right. Smart girl."

Zachary listened to her warm, happy laughter and realized it was finally happening. Whether she wanted to admit it or not, she loved Manda. No matter how selfish it was, he wished she cared for him as well.

"We're invited to a cookout tomorrow night around seven."

Zachary had made the announcement Wednesday evening shortly after he'd arrived. Madison started to make excuses, then glanced down at Manda making her way across the floor on all fours while babbling to a bird through the French door. "We'll be ready."

Now they stood on the sidewalk of a middle-class neighborhood of brick homes in Oak Cliff. She was more nervous than she had been for her first interview.

"You both look fine," Zachary said.

Madison's hand stopped straightening Manda's pink playsuit. There were at least ten cars parked on the tree-lined street. "Maybe we should have picked a less social event for Manda's next outing."

"You'll both be all right." He plucked Manda from her arms and held her up in the air. "Isn't that right, munchkin?"

Manda grinned, kicking legs and flapping arms.

He pulled the happy child to his chest. "See? She agrees with me."

"She always agrees with you," Madison said without rancor.

"Because she's smart. You said so yourself." Taking Madison's arm, they continued up the sidewalk. "Claude's monthly fish fries are legendary. Wait until you taste his fried shrimp and crawfish, you'll be glad you came. James and Thomas will be here with their wives and children."

"Won't your men be tired for work in the morning?" she asked as Zachary rang the doorbell.

"We usually break up by ten. Although the kids are out of school, most of the parents like to get home before it's too late. Besides, tomorrow is Friday," he answered just as the door opened. "Hi, Claude, I bought two ladies with me. Madison Reed, and the munchkin is Manda Taylor. This is Claude Hinton, the best carpenter in the state even if he did have the gall to retire on me last year."

Claude's round face widened into a grin. "Pleased to meet you, Ms. Reed. I know you probably get tired of people saying they watch your show, but I watch it every chance I get."

"As a matter of fact, I don't." She held out her hand, liking the friendly man immediately. "Thank you for allowing us to come."

Her hand was swallowed in his skillet-sized hand. "No problem. I like to cook. The more, the better." He closed the door. "Come on outside. I came in for the salad."

"Can I help?" Madison asked, following Claude through the neat home.

"I can always use an extra pair of hands." Opening the refrigerator door, he handed her three bottles of salad dressing, then picked up a huge tossed salad in a clear bowl. "Grab those wooden forks, Zach."

"Got 'em."

They followed Claude into the backyard crowded with people. One by one, they turned to stare at her. Zachary placed the forks on the table, then curved his other hand around Madison's shoulder.

She glanced up at him and the nervousness receded. "I'm all right."

"Never doubted it," Zachary said to her, then spoke to those gathered there. "Most of you probably recognize Madison Reed. She and this little lady, Manda Taylor, are my guests. I'd take it as a personal favor if you didn't let your curiosity run ahead of your common sense and good manners."

Claude chuckled. "I, for one, know which side my bread is buttered on. We can do introductions later. Let's eat."

Madison didn't know what to make of Claude's statement, but as people started for the table she reached for Manda. "Let me have her so you can eat."

"No, I'm fine. You go ahead."

"I haven't worked all day."

"Taking care of Mand—"

"—Is not as hard as what you do. Now, give her to me, you're holding up the line," Madison said, taking matters out of his hands by gathering Manda into her arms.

"He always was hardheaded," said a female voice from directly behind Zachary.

Madison glanced around to see a pixie of a woman in denim jeans and shirt and workboots. Her auburn hair was spiked over her head. She had five earrings in each ear.

"I've noticed that." Madison stepped out of line, then stared at Zachary until he picked up a paper plate.

The woman stuck out her hand. "Kelli Potts, carpenter. I work for Zach."

Madison grasped the hand. It was small, strong and callused. "Have you worked for him long?"

"Seven years." Kelli moved up and took a plate, then proceeded to pile on heaping portions of fried shrimp, cole slaw, and peach cobbler. "The last time I waited for the cobbler I didn't get any."

Madison glanced behind the diminutive woman. There were at least ten men in line along with the five women and several children. "Smart move, I'd say."

"Madison, if you don't mind sharing a plate, I got enough for both of us," Zachary said by her side. "I even got salad."

Madison's lips twitched. "Salad is good for you. You don't want to give Manda any bad ideas about food, do you?"

"I think I'm safe for the moment." Zachary nodded his head toward a card table under a huge maple tree strung with tiny white lights. "Let's grab a seat. Coming, Kelli?"

"Right behind you, boss."

Crossing the lawn, Zachary set the heaping plate on the table, then pulled out the chair beside him for Madison. Taking her seat, she frowned up at him when he sat down without getting Kelli's chair.

The other woman laughed on seeing the expression on Madison face. "I'm just one of the guys after all this time."

"Not to Clarence." Zachary took Manda's bib out of his shirt pocket and snapped it around her neck.

"Mind if I join you?" a young man asked, but he was already pulling out a chair. "Hi, Mrs. Reed. I'm Clarence Hightower."

"Hello." Madison greeted him as the earnest-faced young man dressed similar to Kelli sat down next to her facing Zachary. "Do you work for Zachary also?"

"Sure do. I'm a carpenter apprentice." He smiled at Kelli. "She's my boss."

Kelli started to stand. "I forgot to get a drink."

With the eagerness of a frisky puppy, Clarence was up in a flash. "I'll get it."

"You didn't ask what kind," she said as he started away.

He turned, grinning down at her. "Cream soda."

She wasn't pleased by his answer. "How did you know that?"

"I listen," he said simply.

"Well, tonight I want a light beer." Tucking her head, she dug into her cole slaw.

Frowning, his brows bunched, he said, "Beer gives you a headache."

Kelli's head whipped up and around. "How do you know so much about what I like or dislike or what gives me a headache?" she asked in a voice meant to intimidate and get answers.

Clarence held her gaze without flinching. "A man pays attention to the things that are important to him."

Her lips thinned in aggravation. "Just go get the beer."

"All right, but we're supposed to be at the Henderson place at seven to begin framing their house. With all that hammering, you'll be sorry."

Kelli spread her hands and slowly rose. She only came to the middle of his chest. "You ever heard the saying, 'When I want your opinion I'll beat it out of you'?"

"I think I just have. Light beer coming up."

Making a face, Kelli sat back down in her seat. "The things I have to put up with."

"Why don't you give the kid a break?" Zachary said, handing Manda a piece of whole-wheat bread.

"Because he *is* a kid." Her sharp teeth tore viciously into a shrimp. "He's almost three years younger than I am, has hands like a baby's behind, and is about as naive as they come."

Zachary, about to spear a crawfish, paused. "You know what your problem is, Kelli?"

She smiled at him sweetly. "No, because I don't have any."

"You like him." When she started to sputter, Zachary held up his hand. "I heard my mother and one of her friends talking a while back about a mutual friend who was older than the man she was dating. You know what they said? I'll tell you. They thought it was a good thing. They said he was young and trainable. It irritated my dad and me, but they just might be right."

"Here you are." Clarence set a can of light beer and a cream soda in front of Kelli. Neither had been opened. "Just in case."

Kelli opened the can of beer and turned it up. Setting the can down, she ignored Clarence's scowl and picked up another shrimp.

Madison watched the interchange with growing fascination, wondering if Clarence noticed that although Kelli had put the can to her mouth her throat hadn't moved. She hadn't drunk the beer. She'd just pretended she had to irritate him. From the looks of his hunched shoulders, she had succeeded.

"Eat up, Madison." Zachary nudged his overflowing plate closer. "I don't want them to think I got all this for myself."

"I'm not hun—" she started, but seeing him wave his fork inches from her mouth with a shrimp on it, she picked up her own. The lightly battered butterfly shrimp was fried to perfection and pure heaven on her tongue. "This is delicious."

"Told you," Zachary said. He handed her a fork. "I won't care if you eat all the salad, but I'll race you to see who gets through the shrimp."

Well aware the challenge was designed to get her to eat and that he'd see that she ate by hook or crook, she quickly came to a decision. "I'd bet, but I don't want to hear any excuses if you lose again."

"I won't lose."

Madison simply smiled. Eleven minutes later, Madison was declared the winner after the second helping Clarence had gladly gotten for them. Fifteen to twelve. She smiled at Zachary's stunned expression. "Count your blessings it wasn't smoked salmon. I'd still be eating."

"I'll have to remember that." Standing, Zachary picked up the empty plate and Kelli's can of beer. "I'll toss this for you."

Kelli's eyes widened for a fraction. "Ah, thanks."

Clarence slowly came to his feet. "I'll take your plate if

you're finished." This time the voice was polite, but with none of the guileless happiness of wanting to please that it had held earlier.

Kelli glanced at him, then away. "Thank you."

With both plates, Clarence followed Zachary to the large trash can by the side of the house. His steps didn't have the pep they had earlier, either.

"Don't worry, Zachary won't betray a confidence," Madison said, noticing Kelli's unhappy expression.

"I know." She sounded miserable. She popped the can of cream soda and took a long swallow, then stared at Clarence standing by Zachary and three other people.

Madison adjusted a sleepy Manda in her lap. "Zachary's right, isn't he?"

Kelli's hand closed around the can of soda. She stared at the can a long time before she lifted her unhappy face. "I never dated much, been too busy working." She worked her shoulders. "I thought men appreciated you more if they had to work to get you. I might have pulled it off if my temper hadn't taken over. He just seems so darn sure of himself, so eager." She sighed. "And so young."

Madison felt older than her thirty years. "For some people it's easier to open up than others. It's harder when you've been hurt," she said with feeling. "You can hurt Clarence just as deeply as he can hurt you. Don't waste time, don't play games, and don't lie."

"I may not get a chance," Kelli said, hunching over the table.

"He probably just needs to regroup. He'll be back and when he does, what are you going to do?"

Kelli stared longingly at Clarence, then she turned to Madison. "Train him," she said with an impish smile on her face.

Madison laughed and the women slapped hands in the air.

"Excuse us, Mrs. Reed, but my wife, Eloise, wanted to meet you."

Madison glanced up at a thin-faced woman with James, one of the men who had helped Zachary put up the swing. "Hello, James, nice seeing you again. Eloise. Who's that handsome fellow with you?"

The shy smile on Eloise's face disappeared. Pride and love shone in its place as she turned the chubby toddler in shorts and a T-shirt smeared with catsup in her arms toward Madison. "This is Darrin, our youngest. He's eighteen months."

Madison picked up Manda's hand and waved. "Say hi to Darrin, Manda." Manda leaned against Madison and stuck her finger in her mouth. "She's not used to strangers."

"Pay it no mind," Eloise said. "All mine went through that stage. Now, I can't keep up with them." She glanced around the yard. "That's my two in the Dallas Cowboy T-shirts."

Madison followed her gaze to a group of young boys playing touch football. "They're a handsome pair."

Eloise grinned from ear to ear. "Thank you."

"Would you like to have a seat? Then perhaps Manda could get used to Darrin." Madison asked.

"That sounds like a good idea."

"I'll see you later, Mrs. Reed," James said as his wife pulled out a chair and sat with Darrin a couple of feet from Madison. "I see she has two teeth. The others should be popping in soon. You got something to soothe her gums?"

Madison frowned. "No."

"You should get some medicine tomorrow," Eloise advised. "Nothing worse than a fussy baby when their gums are bothering them."

"I guess I have a lot to learn. Manda will be ten months Saturday," Madison said. Everyone there had probably heard the story by now. "I can always call my sister or buy a book, I guess." Once again she felt what her separation from her close friends had cost her.

Eloise *tsk*ed. "Books are all right for some things, but there's nothing like experience." She waved her arm to another woman. "Beatrice, come over here and bring Little Thomas."

Kelli started to get up.

"You stay put, missy," Eloise ordered. "One of these day you're gonna get married and have a baby and you'll know what to do."

Kelli shot a glance at Clarence, shoulders hunched, a can of soda in his hand, and sat back down. "I might, at that."

Beatrice took a seat with a dark-haired baby that seemed to be a miniature linebacker. She pushed her shoulder-length braids behind her ears. "I couldn't have gone another step."

"How old is he?" Madison asked, in awe of the grinning baby. He reminded her of a tiny sumo wrestler.

"Ten months, twelve days. And before you ask, he weighed ten pounds at birth." She sighed dramatically. "Thank God for C-sections."

"Beatrice, I was just telling Mrs. Reed about teething. You know what a tough time you had a couple of weeks back with Little Thomas."

"Don't remind me," Beatrice said, then leaned over to turn her baby around until they were face-to-face. "If my arms hadn't been so tired from walking the floor with him, I would have pitched him out the door." He squealed in delight as she rubbed her nose to his.

"He certainly seems happy." Madison said.

"Now, this afternoon it was a different story," Beatrice said, letting her son pull up and stand. On his thigh was a Band-Aid.

"Was he hurt?" Madison asked, unconsciously pulling Manda protectively closer to her.

Beatrice shook his head. "Got his shots today. Screamed the office down. I told Thomas, the next time he's taking him."

"He won't do it or either he'll look so pitiful you'll end up taking Little Thomas. James promises every time and not once has he been there to hold one of them down or to see them look at you like you were the one who stuck them with that needle." Eloise shook her head. "Darrin's appointment is coming up next month and I just know I'll have to take him again."

Beatrice gathered Little Thomas closer, then leaned over and whispered to the other women, "I know one sure way to get Thomas to agree to anything, threaten to put him on short ration."

"How long you planning on?" Eloise asked, her voice hushed, her eyes bright with interest.

Beatrice considered, swallowed. "I think I could last two weeks, otherwise I'd tear his clothes off."

Kelli whooped, then slapped the table. "No wonder Thomas comes to work with a grin on his face every day."

"Mother always said take care of your business or some-one else will," Beatrice said emphatically.

"Ain't that the truth." Eloise nodded her head. "Women who turn their back on their husband's needs always act surprised when they cheat. If James strays, it won't be be-cause he's not getting it at home."

"Amen to that," Beatrice said.

The conversation quickly changed from keeping a baby happy to keeping your man happy. It was all Madison could do to remain seated and calm the upheaval in her stomach and keep her hands from shaking.

But as the other women at the cookout drifted over and added their opinions, it became increasingly clear to Madi-son that if they knew she hadn't shared a bed or been inti-mate with her husband in over a year, they'd have little or no sympathy for her.

Chapter 21

"You want to talk about it?"

Madison didn't look up at Zachary when he asked the question. They had already tucked Manda in and were in the foyer on the way to the front door. With anybody else she would have tried to evade the question. She'd learned, with Zachary that didn't work. Still it was worth a try.

Wrapping her slim arms around herself, she stared at the wall decorated with the African art Wes had collected over the years. "I should have packed those."

"Did someone say something tonight at the cookout?"

She didn't have to look at him to know that he watched her closely, that his face was filled with concern. He, a man she barely knew until three weeks ago, would do everything in his power to shield her from the slightest hurt. But he couldn't shield her from herself or life. She studied *Warrior*, the painting of a Zulu chieftain-warrior in full regalia, his nobility stamped in every nuance of his strong features. "You would have made a great warrior."

He glanced at the oil painting, then placed his hands on her shoulders. "Probably, but can you imagine me in a loincloth?"

The words were said playfully, but a picture quickly formed in her mind. Zachary, broad shoulders, his chest hard and gleaming with sleek, conditioned muscles, lean-hipped, eyes fierce. Finally she looked at him, approval and certainty in her eyes. "Yes."

The half smile on Zachary's face froze. Black eyes narrowed. His hands flexed.

Madison felt the change in his body, the ever-so-slight stirring of her own, then his hands were gone. He stepped back.

"What's going on, Madison?"

She almost voiced the thought that had plagued her since the women's conversation at the cookout: *Help me feel less like a failure as a woman. Help me* feel.

The taut way he held his body stopped her. Her arms wrapped tighter around her body as if to keep them from doing the foolish things that kept running through her head. "Nothing."

"I know differently," he said, studying her intently. "I'm not leaving you until I find out what's going on."

"Sometimes the answers aren't what we want to hear."

"You wanted me to kiss you," he said, his voice tense and tightly controlled. "Why?"

"I . . ." She couldn't deny his words, couldn't evade his hard stare. "To see if I could feel anything." He'd feel disgust or pity for her and leave now and it would be her fault.

"Go on."

She wanted to hide, to run away from the words. Then she realized that it was her fear of facing her problems that had helped get her into her present situation. Taking a deep breath, she told him what Beatrice and the other women had said about a wife's duty. Finished, she continued by saying, "You already know it . . . it wasn't like that between Wes and me after I lost our baby. It seems naive now, but I never thought of Wes seeking intimacy elsewhere."

"Because you were faithful, you expected him to be."

She could have let it go at that, but he deserved the truth. She glanced away. "I was faithful because I didn't want intimacy with . . . anyone. It hurt to feel, so I shut my emotions off. I should have seen that he wouldn't feel the same way."

"So you agree with the stereotype that a black man has no loyalty toward one woman? If she can't or won't be intimate with him, he'll go out and get it from another woman?"

The snap in his voice jerked her gaze toward him. She saw anger in his black eyes and instinctively reacted to soothe him. "I didn't mean you."

If anything his expression hardened. "So, I'm the only virtuous black man in the universe."

Madison's own temper was beginning to heat. "You know that's not what I meant."

"No, Madison, I don't."

He'd make her say it. "It's *me*, Zachary. There must be a flaw in me. That's why Wes went to another woman."

"And to test your theory, you thought you'd come on to me," he accused. "Use me in a little experiment?"

Out loud the words sounded ugly and pitiful.

"I could kiss you until you forgot to breathe, but it wouldn't prove a damn thing about why Wes strayed or make you feel like more of a woman," he said, all but snarling. "If it's right, it's not just the man or just the woman. The passion and desire have to come from both." He stepped closer, bringing with him the heat and hardness of his powerful body. "When I kiss a woman, it won't be for an experiment or on a whim. It will be because I feel something for her and I hope she feels something for me. If I'm lucky we'll both forget to breathe."

For a tension-filled moment as she lost herself in the intimacy of his hot gaze, Madison did forget to breathe, a wonderful, frightening first for her. She sucked in air and tried to calm her racing heart. "She'll be a lucky woman."

His expression didn't change. "You think you'll get off that easily?"

"I'm hoping cinnamon biscuits for breakfast in the morning will help?" She smiled cautiously. "That is, if I haven't sent you running for the hills with my poor behavior."

The anger growing inside him faded. He pulled her into his arms without counting the cost to either of them. They both needed this. "Madison, I told you I'm not going anyplace. I blow off steam, then it's over."

Her arms curved around him, holding him almost desperately. "You wouldn't have strayed."

After a long moment, he pushed her from him and answered the only way he could. "I'd like to think I wouldn't have, but I've learned in thirty-five years of living that you never know how you'll react until you're in that position."

Clear eyes stared up at him. "I've never known a man like you."

"That's makes us even. I've never known a woman like you." He brushed the back of his fingers across her cheek. "And in case you don't know it, that's a compliment," he said with a smile.

Madison answering smile was tremulous. She hesitated, then: "The morning of Wes's accident he said he wanted to start over. My feelings for him had changed, but I was afraid of what a divorce might do to our image."

"Don't you think Wes was thinking the same thing?" Zachary asked.

"Yes," she answered without hesitation.

"You both had your reasons for wanting the marriage to go on."

Her voice chilled. "He wouldn't have told me about Manda and her mother, would he?"

His expression didn't change. "I'd like to think he would have."

"I don't." Her hands trembled on Zachary's wide chest, then firmed. She stepped back. "Thank you. I couldn't have gotten through this without you."

"Then I expect a double helping of cinnamon biscuits, but I'll have to take a rain check for tomorrow. I have to be at a site by seven." He started for the door.

"You have to eat breakfast. Is six early enough?" she asked, following him. She had to make up for her inexcusable behavior. He went out of his way for her. It was time she did the same thing for him.

"You don't have to do that." Grasping the doorknob, he glanced over his shoulder. "You get up early enough with Manda."

"And for the last couple of days, I've taken a nap when she has," she told him, not willing to take no for an answer. "I'll expect you at six."

"All right, but toast will be fine."

She shook her head and opened the front door. "You let me worry about the breakfast menu. Good night, and thanks for understanding about the other."

"No problem. Good night." Zachary kept the friendly expression on his face until the door closed and he heard the locks clicks. Then his head fell forward. He felt like howling at the moon. How was he supposed to keep sane when she wanted to experiment and he wanted to lay her down and make endless love to her?

He wanted Madison, wanted to love her as she deserved to be loved. And she had wanted to use him to see if she were desirable when she was *all* that he desired. What irony.

Finally his head came up and he strode to his truck, jerked open the door and got inside. "Wes, I should have kicked your butt when I had the chance." Starting the motor, he pulled out of the circular driveway and headed home. There was no hurry. What he wanted wasn't there. Worse, he knew it never would be.

Computers were wonderful things, Louis Forbes had thought so many times in the past, and he hadn't changed his mind. In the study of his penthouse apartment on Turtle Creek with the commanding view in three directions, he sat in his executive chair, his eyes glued to the twenty-one-inch monitor as he meticulously scrolled through Wes's charges on his credit card.

The information had been ridiculously easy to access. All you needed was the right answers for the file to pop open. Stupid, Louis thought, but that wasn't the computer's fault. That was the programmer's fault. Any close associate probably knew the person's address and mother's maiden name. And how many people innocently put their social-security number down without a moment's worry over who might see the information? All the contracts that came across his desk had the social-security numbers of his clients.

Stupid. Louis reached for the aged scotch on the inlaid blotter of his custom desk and sipped as he continued to scroll. The answer was here. He could feel it. "Wait a minute. Wait a friggin' minute."

He sat the glass down without taking his eyes from the screen and leaned closer, studying the date of the airline ticket to Amarillo, then the others that followed. Oprah had kicked the Texas Cattlemen's Association's collective butts in that city when they had tried to sue her for the drop in their beef sales, but Wes hadn't covered the story. He'd been deep into an inside story on the corruption of politics in New Orleans.

A slow, satisfied smile curved his mouth upward. Bridget Taylor, the woman killed while Wes was trying to change her tire, had been from Amarillo. It might be a coincidence, but Louis had a hunch it wasn't. He'd have to dig deeper, but he was certain of what he'd find and when he did, Madison would dance to his tune.

"Didn't know you had it in you, Wes." Picking up the glass, Louis turned in his chair to the photo of himself, Wes, and Madison in a sterling frame and saluted. "Always thought she was cold." His eyes went hard in an instant. "But if she thinks she's cutting me out of this, she'll find out just how tough I can be."

"I haven't eaten at a table with flowers on it in a long time," Zachary commented as he stared at the table in Madison's kitchen, then at her. "It looks nice. Thank you for going to the trouble."

"Sit down," she gestured, glad she'd decided at the last minute to do the arrangement of ivy and roses. It was nice to be appreciated. "I'll bring everything to the table."

Zachary pulled out a chair and watched as she set the food on the table, then took her seat next to him. He said grace, then served them.

She wrinkled her nose at the large portions of scrambled eggs, hash browns, and grits on her plate. "You're going to leave me no choice but to start my exercise regime if you keep pushing food in my path."

His gaze roamed appreciatively over her in an abstract gold print dress. "Not from where I'm looking."

Her heart thumped. She hadn't imagined it last night. Apparently her emotions weren't as shut off as she thought. Deciding not to worry about it, she smiled and picked up her fork. "Are you going to the house Clarence spoke of last night?"

"Yes. It's a beauty. A two-story Tudor. We were able to preserve most of the mature trees on the wooded lot. The peer-and-beam foundation is finished and we start framing today. It's the second house I've built in the area," he explained.

Madison bit into her pan sausage. "I love trees. One of the lots Wes and I looked at had them, but he liked this one better. He said the right address was more important than trees."

Zachary studied her pensive face, then, satisfied he didn't see any shadows in her eyes, he chose another biscuit. "Very few people I've built for get exactly what they wanted in their lot, and a few have had to scrap an original idea they loved because it went over their budget. Some have regretted where they built."

"You think they will?"

"The trees attracted the Whitfields. That may change when the leaves have to be raked or they blow into one of the two pools they plan."

"I guess I didn't think of that. Just like I didn't think of a lot of other things," she said referring to Wes's infidelity, but without a trace of bitterness in her voice. "It's time I took charge of my life again and do what I can for Manda."

Zachary placed his hand on hers, felt her tense, then relax. "You'll do it."

A tiny shiver raced through her. She attributed it to nerves. Without thought her other hand came up to rest lightly on his. *So strong. So steady.* She could easily learn to depend on him. Too easily. Pulling her hands free, she sat back in her chair. "Thanks again for being there for me while I worked through everything."

He cocked his head to one side. "Did I hear a 'but' in there?"

He read her too easily. "I appreciate your help, but you have a life of your own. I know you don't mind and Manda adores you, but there must be a woman who is getting tired of you spending so much time over here."

"There is no other woman."

For some odd reason, the inflection of his voice, the way his eyes gazed into hers, caused the shiver to deepen. Her throat felt sandpaper-dry. *Easy, Madison.* She forced herself to relax, then said, "You've helped me to stand on my feet, now let me take a step by myself."

His hands clenched. "Your house. Your rules." Picking up his plate, he took it to the sink. His stiff back to her, he said, "Is it all right if I say good-bye to Manda before I leave?"

An impatient hand turned Zachary around. He stared down into eyes that were beginning to simmer with temper. "Don't you dare make me feel bad about this. I have to learn to do this alone."

Then it hit him. "You still think I'm going to bail. Don't you?"

"Wes and I made all kinds of plans. We were supposed to be an unbeatable combination." Her voice wavered, then grew steadier. "But the first hard knock sent us to the mat and we stayed there."

He had to touch her. He placed his hands on her shoulders, felt her tension. "I'm not Wes."

"He made promises too."

"And he let you down, but you gave him the benefit of the doubt. That's all I'm asking. I promise, I'll be here."

She stared up at him wanting to believe. "If you don't want your truck to end up at the bottom of the Trinity River, you'd better."

Laughing, he hugged her to him, felt the softness of her breasts against his chest, inhaled her sweet fragrance. "I'm so proud of you."

"Me too." She hugged him back just as hard.

A sound came over the intercom from Madison's bedroom.

He didn't hesitate. He grabbed her hand and hurried with her toward the bedroom, expecting to hear cries every step. They burst into the room to see Manda sitting in bed watching the door expectantly. Seeing them, she started to pull to her feet with a smile on her face.

Zachary had her in his arms seconds later. "Good morning, munchkin."

"She didn't cry," Madison said, her hand on Manda's thigh.

"Looks like both of my ladies are learning to trust."

"We had a good teacher," she said, taking Manda. "You'd better go or you'll be late."

"'Bye, munchkin, Madison." He considered kissing both, but settled for one. "I'll see myself out."

"We'll walk you to the door," Madison said, following him out.

He opened the door to see a UPS truck pull up behind his truck. "Expecting a delivery?"

"No," she said, then murmured, "Maybe it's something Wes ordered."

Zachary stepped in front of her as the delivery man grabbed a large cardboard box out of the back of the truck and rushed up the walkway. "Good morning."

"Good morning. Package for Mrs. Madison Reed," he said.

Madison saw the Neiman Marcus return address and

relaxed. "Please sign for me, Zachary. Cindi, my personal shopper, must have sent it."

Zachary did as she requested, then picked up the package and brought it back inside. "Where should I put it?"

Madison studied the box. "I'm not sure since I don't know what's in it."

"One way to find out." Zachary went to the kitchen. "Mind if I use one of these?"

"Go ahead," Madison said, then squatted beside him again as he took the paring knife out of the butcher block and ran it along the seam of wrapping tape.

"Sure is packed well." First came the packing paper, then he pulled out a large box with the unmistakable Hermès orange with its chocolate-brown trim and logo.

Madison gasped.

Zachary's worried gaze went to her. "What's the matter? You didn't order it?"

Madison stared at the box. "Y-yes. I ordered it."

Zachary started to put the box back, but slowly Madison's trembling hand reached for it. With reservations he set it in front of her, took Manda, then watched Madison's unsteady hands open the box and pull out the enormous beige velvety bag the size of a pillowcase. The center bore the Hermès horse and carriage.

Zachary started to ask what it was, then decided to wait.

Opening the bag, she pulled out a large roan-colored, hand-crafted leather bag, uncinched the side straps, then opened the nickel closure. Her eyes shut.

The need to comfort overrode caution. His arm circled her shoulders and pulled her to him. "Talk to me."

She leaned against him, unashamed of the tears misting her eyes. "I ordered it the day after I learned I was pregnant."

"And it just got here?" he asked, incredulously.

"It's a Hermès handbag, a Birkin, the Rolls-Royce of purses, ridiculously expensive, but I wanted it for her. I—I knew it was a girl and I'd planned to dress her up like a little princess." His strong arm tightened. "Neiman's doesn't sell them, but through Cindi's connections she was able to order the bag from me." She swallowed, then continued. "Hermès doesn't have a waiting list, it has a dream list. They warned me it might take two or three years, because I wanted it custom-made with bottle and diaper compartments. I didn't care. I wanted a houseful of children so I planned to use it over and over."

"I'm sorry."

"I would have loved her with everything within me," she said, her voice thickening.

He felt his own throat tighten. "I know, Madison."

"Ma-da."

Both adults jerked apart and looked at Manda, their breaths held. She reached toward Madison. "Ma-da."

Laughing, feeling her heart squeeze in her chest, Madison reached for Manda, kissed her on the cheek, then held her tight. "Did I hear what I think I did?"

"She tried to say your name."

"Maybe she was trying to say her name," Madison said, her eyes glued on Manda.

Zachary shook his head. "It was Madison."

"Ma-da," Manda repeated.

"See," he said proudly, grinning broadly.

"Oh my goodness. She did."

"You're always saying how smart she is," Zachary said.

"Yes, she is." Madison pulled the bag over to them. "What do you say we go show the people at the station how chic we are?"

"You're going down there?" Zachary questioned.

"We'll be fine," she assured him. "After last night at the cookout I've had to admit that Manda isn't the only one afraid. Besides, I'd forgotten an iron rule in public relations. Give the press a story before they put their own spin on it."

He frowned. "You're going to give an interview?"

"Yes." She started to get up and he helped her. Going to the refrigerator, she tightened her hold on Manda, opened the door, and took out a bottle. Manda lunged as usual with both hands outstretched.

"I'll get it."

"I've got it." She held the bottle out of both their reach, set it in the sink, and turned on the hot water. "I have it under control. Go to work. Kelli and the rest of your crew are probably wondering what happened to you."

He glanced at the clock. Seven-fifteen. "I've made it a practice never to be late, so I think they'll forgive me this time. Behave, munchkin."

He was halfway out of the kitchen when Madison called. "Dinner will probably be Chinese takeout, so don't worry about me trying to keep food warm or wasting food if you're too tired to stop by."

"I'll bring the wine. See you tonight."

"We'll be waiting."

Wishing it would be with open arms, Zachary let himself out of the house.

Chapter 22

"The TV gods must be smiling on me," Paula Dennis said, excitement ringing in her West Coast–accented voice. "I can't tell you how much I appreciate this exclusive."

"WFTA has been good to me. I wouldn't think of going anyplace else," Madison said. That was true, but she was also aware that she would be able to control the interview more on her territory. Paula was bright and energetic, but she hadn't learned to go for the jugular yet, unlike Helen who would be livid when she learned she had been scooped by another, younger reporter.

"One minute," the assistant said to the cameraman.

Paula took a deep breath, blew it out, then straightened her shoulders.

Madison, hands clasped on her desk, sat miked, calm and ready to go on live television once the newscast came back from commercial. In the carriage, out of camera range, Manda lay asleep in her stroller. Gordon and Traci, Madison's assistant, stood nearby.

Paula took her cue and gazed straight into the eye of the TV camera. "With us today is Madison Reed, popular talk-show host, whose life was touched by tragedy a little over four weeks ago when her award-winning TV journalist husband, Wes Reed at station KKTA in Fort Worth, was fatally injured while attempting to help a female motorist. Ms. Reed's name again became headline news when her agent,

Louis Forbes, reported that she had assumed temporary custody of the motorist's nine-month-old daughter, Manda. Today, we learn why."

She turned to Madison. "Thank you, Ms. Reed, for allowing us this time after the tragic death of your husband."

Madison thought she had been ready for the interview, but still she flinched. Her hands, held loosely atop her desk just seconds ago, clenched. Although Paula's sympathetic expression remained fixed on her face, Madison saw the alarm in her eyes. "I wanted to set the record straight."

"Yes," Paula said, giving Madison a chance to go on.

Madison felt panic clawing at her throat, then the door to her office inched open. Gordon and one of the cameraman's assistant were already trying to shut it. Zachary slipped inside.

The fear receded as quickly as it had came. "Please forgive me."

"That's all right, Ms. Reed. Take your time," Paula said, her shoulders relaxing beneath her tailored red suit.

"Wes's death was senseless, as was that of Bridget Taylor, the young woman he stopped to help. A man who had been arrested twice for drunken driving took their lives, and his own. One heedless act shattered three families. Wes's, Miss Taylor's, and the driver's. I've checked. He left a wife and two small children."

Paula leaned forward. "Have you been in touch with his family?"

"No. I respect their need for privacy and for time to heal. I feel sympathy for the children who wonder why their father isn't coming back home. They can understand no better than Manda Taylor does, the nine-month-old infant strapped securely in the backseat of the car Bridget Taylor was driving. I emphasize that because on my way over to the studio today, I saw too many children who weren't. If her mother had been holding her, if she hadn't been in the backseat . . ." Madison's voice trailed off. She swallowed visibly.

"How is Manda doing?"

A slow smile spread across Madison's face. "Better. We're both getting there. We help each other."

"Could you explain that?"

To the eyes of the people at home, Madison had simply looked away from Paula. People in her office knew she had looked at Zachary. "After Wes's death, I was angry and feeling sorry for myself. You can't do that and take care of an active nine-month-old. Manda helped me to forget myself and my grief, and to think about her. I, at least, knew what had happened. She had no idea of why her mother was not there when she woke up or why she won't be there to sing her a lullaby."

"Some people might say you're being generous, others might question your motives," Paula said.

"That's their problem, not mine. And I don't intend to let it be Manda's." Madison leaned forward, her eyes direct and challenging. "The only other relative Manda has is an elderly great-aunt in a nursing home who understandably can't take care of her. Her great-aunt is the only person I feel I have to answer to. I'm asking my fellow colleagues to leave us in peace and give Manda and me time to heal."

"Thank you, Ms. Reed." Paula faced the camera. "This is Paula Dennis reporting live from the studios of WFTA. Back to you in the newsroom, Mike."

"We're off the air."

Madison was up and around the desk, pulling the mike off as she walked toward Zachary. "How did you get in here?"

He pulled a package of photos from his shirt pocket. "These." They were the pictures they had taken in her backyard.

People crowded around. There were appropriate oohs and aahs.

"Where's the rest?" she asked, when people began to move away. There were none of him and Manda together.

"Didn't turn out, I guess." He smiled innocently into her mutinous face.

"I don't think we've met." All smiles, Paula extended her slim hand. "Paula Dennis."

"Zachary Holman," he said, shaking her hand. "Great interview."

"Thank you." Her interested gaze ran over him in a clearly speculative way. "By any chance are you still available?"

His grin widened. "No, ma'am, I'm afraid not."

"Pity." She faced Madison. "Thanks again, Madison." Then to Zachary. "If your situation ever changes, give me a call."

"Yes, ma'am," Zachary said, a smile still teasing his mobile mouth.

"You seem to have a way with women," Gordon said, extending his hand.

"It's a gift," Zachary said lightly. "Hope I didn't mess up things."

Gordon glanced at a silent Madison, her body rigid, her mouth tight. "A moment ago I would have said no, now I'm not so sure." He turned to the crew. "Let's move it."

"Do you need me to do anything else, Madison?" Traci, her assistant, asked.

"Please call Stanley and have him bring the car around." Looping the Hermès carryall on her arm, she grabbed the handle of the carriage.

"I'll get that." Zachary's hand tried to nudge hers aside.

Hot eyes flashed up at him. "That won't be necessary." She started toward the door.

He easily got in front of her and closed the office door. "What did I do?"

"You lied to me," she accused, her voice shaky.

Fear he didn't want to face, pressed down upon him. "What are you talking about?"

"You told me there wasn't a woman in your life. I'm not so helpless that you have to lie so you can keep hovering over me."

His fear receded. He could breathe normally again. "I

didn't lie to you or to Paula. There are two women in my life and they're right in front of me."

She wouldn't feel ridiculous. She wouldn't. "Where are my other pictures?"

"In the truck." He shifted uncomfortably. "I left them because I didn't want people to get the wrong idea."

That, she understood. She removed her hands from the stroller and opened the door. "I didn't use your name during the interview for the same reason, but almost everything I said I learned from you."

They shared a smile, then side by side they started walking. "You two finished for the day?" he asked.

"I don't want to disturb her naptime, but if she wakes up we might stop by a bookstore."

Zachary glanced down as Manda stirred. "Looks like your next stop is the bookstore."

Madison scooped her up. "Have a nice nap?"

"She sure is a cutie, Ms. Reed," said the security guard as he pushed open the front door for them. "Makes a man want a family of his own." He glanced over his shoulder at Frankie, the receptionist at the front desk, who was staring at him with wide, adoring eyes.

Amen to that, Zachary thought.

The moment the driver of the limo saw them, he popped the trunk then opened the passenger door. At the same time, a car came barreling around the side of the building, tires screeching. Madison, playing with Manda's foot encased in her new white leather shoe, glanced up at the sound and straight into the flash of a camera in the car's open window.

Zachary said one crude expletive, then pulled Madison and Manda into the protective shelter of his arms. Behind him, the security guard ran toward the car. The late-model sedan turned the corner in front of a car and sped away.

"You all right?" Zachary asked anxiously.

"Just mad," Madison said tightly as she stared down the street where the car had disappeared. "There's no telling what outrageous price they'll get when they sell that picture to some sleazy tabloid."

"My daddy always said, 'Don't get mad, get even.'"

She looked up at him and smiled. "I like your daddy's style."

Helen was spitting mad.

It should have worked. It *had* worked. But once again Madison had managed to come out on top.

Teeth gritted, Helen watched photographers from area newspapers, cameramen, and freelancers film footage and take pictures of Madison in the gardens of the studio. Miss High and Mighty had insisted the photos be taken outside. She hadn't wanted the flashbulbs to frighten the brat she held. The newspeople were eating it up and the picture Helen's boyfriend's buddies had taken were now worthless. Worse, that flat-footed security guard had gotten the license plate number. If it was traced back to her, her career at the station was over.

Nothing was going right.

"That's enough." Madison stood, placing the lightweight blanket over Manda's head and turning her away from the cameras. "This is not something I would have chosen, but neither will I have disreputable people profiting from this child's loss. Every time an unauthorized photo is taken of Manda, I will do my best to make sure it's worthless." Turning, she entered the studio through a side door; a hunk of a cowboy Helen had never seen before, as well as Gordon and Traci, followed.

It was then Helen saw the handbag the assistant carried. Her envy and animosity grew. Hermès handbags started at over five thousand dollars. It wasn't fair that one woman had so much. Then there was that gorgeous man who had stood like a guard dog watching the entire photo session as if ready to snatch off the head of anyone who meant Madison or the brat any harm. It was obvious they meant a great deal to him.

Perfect Madison. Men gravitated to her like flies to cow manure. Lips clamped, Helen stalked back inside. She was at her desk before it hit her.

What if there was more to it than friendship? What if Little Miss Perfect was having an affair with him?

Helen didn't have to think too hard to know that she wouldn't consider it a hardship to go a couple of rounds with him herself. Just the easy way he moved that powerfully built body of his made her mouth water. But who was he? There was one way to find out.

At the front desk, she didn't ask the receptionist, just picked up the sign-in book and went down the list of names before the horde of photographers had signed in. Zachary Holman. His name was written in a bold scrawl. Tossing the book back on the desk, she went to her office and sat in front of her computer. In minutes she had Zachary Holman's face on her screen. A few minutes more of searching and she saw Wes and Madison standing in front of their Holman Construction–built home.

Helen now had the connection, but she wasn't sure how to work it to her advantage, only knew that she would. Even if nothing was going on, the right word to the right person, and rumors would start flying. Then people wouldn't think so much of Madison. Maybe Helen would even put in an anonymous call to the social worker.

The idea gaining momentum, Helen leaned back in her seat. She knew just how she'd get back at Madison once and for all. Make damn sure she lost that brat. And when she did, Helen would be there, mike in hand.

"I want you to have a bodyguard."

Madison looked up from straightening the lightweight blanket inside Manda's carriage and into Zachary's very determined eyes, then to the protective way he held Manda, and knew she had to talk fast. "A bodyguard would only give reporters and the paparazzi more reason to hound us."

His lips thinned into a hard line. "But a bodyguard would also keep them from getting too close."

You mean, pound them into the dirt, Madison thought—if the fierce expression on his face was any indication. Without thought she lifted her hand and placed it on his arm. The muscles beneath his denim shirt were taut. "But they'd still take pictures. I'd have a dozen bodyguards if I thought it would keep unscrupulous people away. It won't. What it will do is call more attention to us."

The lines furrowing his forehead deepened. "I'd feel better knowing you have some protection when I'm not with you."

To Zachary, protecting those he cared about was paramount. That was as much a part of him as his gentleness. She couldn't fault him for his desire to keep her and Manda safe. Fact was, it felt nice, but she knew it would cause more problems than it solved.

Feeling she needed help, she glanced over her shoulder to Gordon who had followed them into her office. "Please tell him we're not in any danger."

Gordon slipped his hands into the pockets of his tailored slacks. "She's right. Getting a bodyguard will only make Madison and Manda more noticeable. It will also be seen as a challenge."

"Exactly," Madison agreed. "If I get a bodyguard after the photo shoot, it's going to send a message that regardless of what I said, I'm afraid. And despite what I told the reporters and photographers, I have no intention of subjecting Manda to a photo shoot every other day." She smiled into Manda's happy face. "But you sat through this one like a pro."

"That's because she knew she was safe with you," Zachary said.

"Manda is more resilient than I gave her credit for," she said smoothing a hand over the infant's thick black curly hair. To Madison's delight, Manda hadn't stuck her finger in her mouth or tried to burrow into Madison. She'd looked at the approaching men and women with more curiosity than fear. "Maybe I should return to work soon."

"Anytime you're ready," Gordon said quickly.

"You plan on bringing her with you?" Zachary asked.

Her certainty growing that she was making the right decision, Madison lifted her gaze. "Yes. I think it would be good for both of us. Besides, the more we're seen together, the quicker it will satisfy everyone's curiosity."

"You'll have to use the car service," Zachary reminded her.

"For the time being," she agreed, taking Manda into her arms. "We'll be chauffeured to and from the house, so there will be no need for you to worry about us."

Zachary's dark eyes softened. Reaching out, he brushed a lock of Madison's hair behind her ear. "That might be, but I'll still worry."

Madison's heart gave a hard thump. She glanced away quickly. "Don't." She busied herself putting Manda in the carriage. "Ready to go for a ride?"

The bright smile on Manda's face faded. She lifted both arms. "Ma-da."

Shaking her head, Madison picked her back up. "Guess we'll have to work on separation."

Gordon peered at the baby in surprise. "Did she just try to say your name?"

"She sure did." Madison acknowledged with a grin.

"I'll walk you to the car, Madison." Zachary slung Madison's bag over his shoulder and gripped the handle of the carriage. "Good-bye, Gordon."

"That won't be necessary. I've kept you long enough." She held out her hand patiently for her bag. "Your crew is probably frantic by now."

They probably were, but Zachary wasn't about to admit it. In all the eight years of being his own boss, he'd never missed this much work combined. But he didn't regret it for a second and would gladly do it again. "A few more minutes won't hurt."

"Zachary, I can do this." Her hands closed around the straps of the bag. "Go to work."

He let her have the bag, but one hand remained on the handle of the carriage. "I don't like leaving you."

"We'll be fine."

"All right, but ca—"

"—Call if we need you." She smiled up into his chagrined face. "We'll see you tonight if you can make it."

"I'll do my best." With a final wave he was out the door.

For a long moment Madison stared after him, then at Manda who was also peering at the door Zachary had just gone through. "We'll see him tonight if he can possibly make it. In the meantime, we have to stop at a bookstore."

"I'll get these," Gordon said, taking the bag and the carriage. "Glad to hear you're coming back."

"I think it's time." Madison opened the office door, then followed Gordon into the hallway. "I just hope that social worker understands about the photo session."

"Camille is out of town until this afternoon," Gordon said, his tone filled with an odd mixture of regret and impatience.

Madison came to a dead stop. She lifted a naturally arched brow. "Since when did it become 'Camille' and how do you know she's out of town?"

Gordon didn't even think of evading the answer. "Since I decided she interests me on a personal level."

Madison closely studied his intense expression before replying, "There's going to be a lot of disappointed women when this gets out."

He let out a breath. "Thanks."

Absentmindedly she stroked Manda's back. "You can't tell your heart who to love," she said, her face thoughtful.

Gordon jerked his head around to stare at her. "Who said anything about love? I just plan to see where this leads."

Madison laughed softly at the panic in his voice. " 'There are none as blind,' et cetera, et cetera, et cetera."

"Strange. I was thinking the same thing about you."

She spun around to face him. "What are you talking about?"

"Zachary Holman," he answered.

Madison swallowed, trying to relieve the sudden dryness in her throat. "You were there at the hospital when we met again. He was a friend of Wes's," she said, trying to forget how Zachary's presence had calmed and centered her during the interview.

"Seems like more to me."

She sputtered. "Wh-what do you mean?"

"He certainly seems to care for you and Manda," Gordon explained, watching her closely. "I'd say he was your friend as well and that you're lucky to have him."

Knowing she'd overreacted, Madison continued through the front lobby. "I couldn't have gotten through this without him."

"I'm glad he was there for you." Gordon pushed open the front glass door. Her driver immediately started toward them.

"I'll take those, sir," the uniformed man said politely. "I'll put your bag in the backseat, Ms. Reed."

"Thanks, Stanley." Crossing to the limo, she slipped into the backseat with Manda, then put her in her car seat. "I'll be in Monday around ten, if that's all right."

One arm propped on the top of the door, Gordon leaned down into the car. "Whatever works for you."

"I appreciate that," she said, fastening her seat belt. "Goodbye."

"One more thing." He leaned closer, his eyes piercing. "You and I both know that life isn't promised. Don't waste time denying what is right in front of you or wondering about what other people think. If love comes along, snatch it with both hands. You deserve happiness without conditions."

Before she could respond, he stepped back and closed the door. Through the tinted window Madison saw him walking back to the station. She knew he had been talking about her and Zachary. *That's ridiculous,* she thought as the driver pulled away from the curve smoothly. They were just friends.

Chapter 23

Madison had expected to receive a lot of calls in response to the live interview, but she had underestimated the sheer number. Although her number wasn't listed, the media, she knew, had a way of finding things out.

After listening to the messages on the answering machine, she had some calls of her own to make. The first one was to her parents. Seconds into the conversation, they wanted to know when they were going to get a picture and see Manda for themselves. Madison promised to scan one into the computer and send it that afternoon. Her father wouldn't touch a computer with a ten-foot pole, but her mother loved her "little toy," as she called it.

Dianne was next. Madison wasn't aware she was bragging about how smart Manda was until her sister called her on it. "I think I heard you mention a few times already that she said your name," Dianne said with a laugh. "I can't wait to see her."

"She's going to charm all of you."

Not the least bit ashamed, Madison hung up a little while later. "You are my smart girl," she said to Manda who was lying on the bed surrounded by her teddy bears, the teething ring in her mouth, drooling. Madison took a soft washcloth and gently wiped her mouth, then phoned Manda's great-aunt.

The elderly woman's voice brightened considerably when

Madison identified herself. She'd received the pictures. One of the eleven-by-fourteens of Manda was hanging on the wall her bed faced so she could see it every time she looked up.

Glad she had arranged to have several of the pictures of Manda enlarged and shipped directly to Velma, Madison explained about the reason for the photo session and the possibility that the media might try to contact her for an interview. Velma said a couple of people had already called, but as soon as she understood what they wanted she had hung up the phone.

"I wouldn't have talked to them even if that lawyer you sent to have me sign those paper hadn't warned me that it might happen. Said it might be best if I didn't talk with them."

"I hate that they bothered you."

"Ain't your fault some people got nothin' better to do than harass other people," she said. "This ain't none of their business. Probably twist everythin' I said around anyway."

Unfortunately, Madison knew she was right. After talking a few more minutes, Madison hung up. There was one last call she had to make. It wasn't lost on her that she had put it off to last because it had always been a strain to talk with Wes's parents and it had gotten worse since his death.

Madison glanced down just as Manda crawled into her lap. Madison wasn't sure how to tell them about Manda, but she definitely didn't agree with Zachary that they should not be told. They deserved to know they had a grandchild. She just wasn't sure if the knowledge would comfort them or cause more pain.

Gathering the infant to her, she dialed her in-laws' home phone number. As expected, the maid answered. Vanessa once bragged that she had never answered her own phone and wouldn't know how to make her bed or do her hair if her life depended on it. "May I please speak with Vanessa?"

"I'm sorry, but Mrs. Reed isn't feeling up to talking to anyone now," Betty said.

"Is A.J. there?"

"No, ma'am. He's playing golf at the country club. Is there a message, Mrs. Reed?"

Like father, like son. While Vanessa was prostrate with grief, A.J. was playing golf with his buddies. He had a cell phone, but he would have turned it off before they teed off. Again like father, like son. "Please ask A.J. to call me when he comes in. It's very important."

"Yes, ma'am."

"Thank you, Betty. Good-bye." As soon as she put the phone down it rang again. A reporter, she was sure of it. Standing, Madison picked up Manda and the storybook on the bedside table and continued out of the room.

Madison was going to be worth a mint.

His teeth clamped around his Havana cigar, Louis Forbes watched the short film clip of Madison and Manda on CNN. Madison had acted like a mother bear with the kid. She'd looked unflinchingly at the camera when she said she'd do whatever it took to keep Manda safe and happy. Even as cynical as he was, he didn't doubt she meant every word.

He could have kissed her. Her worth had just climbed higher.

Bursting with pleasure over the way things were unfolding, Louis rocked back on his handmade Italian loafers. The president of KGHA in Chicago had called personally to commend Louis for setting up the interview and on the way Madison had handled herself. Louis had seen no reason to correct him.

Louis had received other calls. The magazines were expected, but the book publisher had his mouth salivating. He bet he could get them to seven figures easy. MADD's call didn't count . . . unless they wanted pay Madison to act as a spokesperson.

Everyone wanted Madison and when he finished collecting his file on Wes and the kid's mother, she'd do exactly what Louis told her to do.

* * *

"These pictures are worthless," snarled Edward Mayes, slinging the five-by-seven color glossies of Madison and Manda across the already cluttered living room of Helen's apartment. "At least those two inept jerks I hired had the sense to switch license plates on their car."

"Take it easy, baby," Helen soothed, running her French-manicured nails up the hard, muscled chest Edward worked an hour each day to maintain. "We can still work this to our advantage."

Sharp black eyes fastened on the lush mauve-painted lips inches from his. Roughly grabbing her hips, he ground his arousal against the junction of her thighs, and had the satisfaction of seeing her wince. Women didn't appreciate it if it wasn't a little rough. "Keep talking."

"I think there's something going on between Madison and the man who was with her today at the station. If we can get compromising pictures of them, they'd be worth even more than those of her and that brat she seems so fond of."

His hands inched up her shirt. "And you'd be one step closer to getting her job."

"And you'd be there with me." Helen's practiced fingers began unfastening his shirt.

"I'd better be," he warned just before his finger speared deep inside her. He found her wet and hot. Moments later he took her on the floor, thinking about how well he controlled her with sex.

With her legs wrapped around him, her eyes closed, Helen thought of Zachary.

Gordon saw Camille the moment she entered the Grand Ballroom at the Anatole Hotel Friday night. His first thought was relief that she was alone, the second was pure lust. She wore a floor-length strapless white gown that hugged her lush breasts then flowed seductively over the enticing curves of her body. He had waited six long days to see her again. He saw no reason to wait another minute. He moved through the jovial crowd with practiced ease.

He knew the instant she saw him. Her big, chocolate-brown eyes went wide. Her breathing accelerated, causing the creamy swell of her breasts to rise and fall with beckoning madness. He actually felt his tongue tingle in anticipation.

"Welcome home, Camille."

"Mr. Armstrong," she greeted coolly.

He grinned. "Back to that, are we?"

Her mouth tightened. "If you'll excuse me, people are waiting for me."

"Of course." He took her arm and ignored her hard glare. "I told your mother I'd bring you to our table as soon as you arrived."

Her head whipped around. "You're sitting with us?"

"I'm always willing to give any help I can to worthwhile causes," he answered, steering her around a group of people.

"I don't remember you being on the list," she said, glancing up at him.

"All that matters is that I'm here now," he said. His tone carried a wealth of meaning.

Camille felt her entire body quiver at the softly spoken words. She quickly glanced away. She thought she had gotten over whatever it was that sent her mind and body into a spin when she was near Gordon. She'd been wrong. Worse, he realized it and wasn't going to let her ignore him or the humming sensuality between them.

"There you are, Camille. I'm glad you made it," her mother said from her place at a round, white linen–draped table. A beautiful fresh-cut flower arrangement was centered on top. Two seats where empty.

"Hello, Mother." Camille took her mother's offered hands, kissed her cheek. Both were soft and often caused a person to think Julia Davis was as soft on the inside as she was on the outside. A fatal mistake. She was tenacious when it came to those she loved or one of her causes.

Straightening, Camille was afraid she had just become both. Then she greeted the other people at the table. All were her mother's contemporaries. Camille hadn't had time to sell the tickets to the charity affair and had asked her mother to do it for her. She had given her a list of names. Gordon Armstrong wasn't one of them.

"Who's missing?" she asked pointedly. Her mother didn't even blink.

"No one now that you are here," she said, gesturing to the seat beside her. "Now, tell us all about your conference."

Camille took the chair Gordon pulled out for her, determined to ignore him, until his hand brushed against her bare arm, accidentally or on purpose. The results were the same. Once again she was aware of him, of how close their bodies were.

She launched into an explanation of the conference she had attended. As expected, the eyes of a few of the people at the table glazed over. Gordon wasn't one of them. He had asked intelligent, thought-provoking questions over their dinner.

"How do you answer to the critics that say you act too slow in some cases or too harshly in others?"

Because he seemed sincere, she answered honestly. "There might be similarities in cases, but each case is different, with its own unique set of circumstances, and each caseworker brings to it his or her background and knowledge. There is uniformity in some decisions, but not all. We're not perfect, but we're all we have."

"There's a high burnout rate and turnover." He sipped his wine. "How long have you been a caseworker?"

Her fork poised over the grilled chicken which had stayed under the heat-light hours too long. "Five years."

His eyes narrowed. "Ever think of taking a job that wasn't as emotionally draining or dangerous?"

Camille didn't have to look at her mother to know who he had gotten the last part of the question from. "How much more emotionally draining or dangerous is it for a child to live with fear of emotional, physical, or sexual abuse on a daily basis? Do you have children?"

"Yes," he answered, his wine forgotten.

"You ever physically discipline them?" she asked.

"Camille, please pass the rolls," her mother asked, nudging her daughter in the side.

Camille passed the rolls and ignored the elbow. Her entire attention was on Gordon.

"If they needed it, yes." He wasn't backing down, if that was what she expected. He was aware some books said don't physically discipline a child, but it hadn't hurt him when he was growing up.

"Until they bled or you left marks or they needed major medical care?"

"Camille!" her mother admonished.

Anger flared in Gordon's eyes. "What kind of man do you think I am?"

"I'll take that as a no," she said calmly. "Your children are the fortunate ones. You discipline, but you do it with love, not with a need to inflict pain or out of misplaced anger or because of your own insecurities." She touched his arm as if to apologize. "I've seen children who aren't so blessed."

She placed her napkin beside her plate and glanced around the table. Eyes that were friendly when she sat down were now cautious or antagonistic. "If you'll excuse me. After being away from home for five days I need to go unpack and get ready to hit the road again on Sunday."

She scooted her chair back. The men stood. "I'll call you tomorrow, Mother."

"You certainly will," Julia said with a frown of disapproval.

Camille started from the room. A few feet later she realized Gordon was behind her. She sighed inwardly. She supposed her outspokenness had run off another man. He probably wanted to tell her off for embarrassing him, for even thinking a man in his position would harm his child. She had too many files in her office that said abuse ran across economic, social, racial, and religious lines to believe it couldn't happen.

Outside in the towering atrium lined with flags of nations, she braced herself and turned. "You wanted to say something?"

"What time shall I pick you up tomorrow night for dinner?"

She blinked. "What?"

"Dinner. What time?"

She studied him looking for a trace of the anger she'd felt earlier. She couldn't see any. "You aren't angry?"

"That you'd insinuate in front of total strangers that I might beat my kids? You were just making a point," he said.

She saw it then, the angry glint in his dark eyes. "I didn't mean—"

"Yes, you did," he told her, stepping closer. "Were you that desperate to send me packing?"

"I simply wanted you to understand why I do what I do. It's not a job to do until I get a better one. It's what I do. My mother refuses to believe that."

"She worries about you."

"Because of one incident."

His eyes went glacial as his hands circled her upper arms. "What happened?"

She didn't even think of not answering. "A man I opened a case on broke into my apartment. I managed to lock myself in the bathroom with the cell phone. It's a procedure that abused women are taught."

"Where is he now?"

"Where he can't hurt me," she answered. She touched the rigid line of Gordon's jaw. "I'm all right."

He stared at her a long time. "Now. What about then?"

"I was so shaken I had to take off work for two weeks. I jumped at everything that moved," she confessed. "I know mother is afraid for me, but I have to live my own life, my own way."

"Yet you went back."

"Children go back to their abusers day after day," she said. "It may be the only way out for some of them. If they have that much courage, how can I do less?"

He kissed her, a gentle touching of lips that was as tender as it was fleeting. "It's going to be interesting getting to know you better."

Her body went into hyperdrive. She desperately tried to gather her scattered thoughts. "I—I still don't think that's a good idea."

"One date. We'll see what happens and go from there." His thumb stroked her bare arm.

Her breath trembled out over her lips. Lips that she wanted on his again. From the hot way he looked at her, he did too.

"Please. I want to see you."

His mouth hovered over hers. Their breaths mingled. Her nipples peaked.

"Eight," she said shakily.

"You won't regret it." He brushed his lips across hers again, then stepped back.

For a moment, Camille considered dragging him back and fastening her mouth on his, then his words reached though the sensuous haze. "I told you about your arrogance."

He smiled. "So you have. Come on, I'll see you to your car, then home."

She frowned. "I can get home by myself."

"Humor me."

She opened her mouth to tell him that wasn't necessary, but his next words stopped her.

"If you insist on trying to dissuade me, I might have to kiss you until you forget to argue. I won't mind, but you might."

"I wouldn't be so sure about that," she told him.

She had the pleasure of seeing his eyes go dark with passion and need before she blithely strolled off. Tomorrow night was going to be very, very interesting.

It was after nine. He wasn't coming.

Lifting the sheer curtain from the elongated window by the front door, Madison stared at the empty driveway illuminated by two gaslights at the beginning of the drive, then beyond to the street in front of her house. A truck passed, but it wasn't the one she wanted to see. Letting the curtain fall, she slowly went to the kitchen and began gathering up the plates.

She didn't know why she felt so sad and restless. Just this morning she had tried to push Zachary out of their lives, telling him he had a life of his own. Now that he wasn't around, she ached a little inside. Shaking her head at the odd feeling, she put up the plates, closed the cabinet door, then finished clearing the table.

It wasn't as if she hadn't seen him today, she tried to tell herself. He'd even called to make sure she reached home without any more incidents. He had warned her before they hung up that he might not be able to come over tonight. She'd hoped he would.

She wanted to tell him she'd received Manda's medical record from her pediatrician in Amarillo. Manda was as healthy as the nurse at Children's Medical Center had said.

Pulling containers from beneath the cabinet, Madison put the Chinese takeout away, cut off the light, and started toward the bedroom. She glanced at the double front door and saw a beam of light arc across the sheer curtains.

Anticipation surging through her, she raced to the door and opened it just as Zachary stepped out of the truck. Without thought she was off the steps in an instant. Her arms closed around him. The loneliness vanished. "I didn't think you were coming."

He hesitated, then he pulled her closer. "I know it's late."

"It's never too late." Stepping back, she grinned up at him. "After all my talk this morning, I missed you."

"I'm glad," he told her, brushing her hair behind her ear. "I've been putting out fires all evening."

"You can tell me all about it over dinner." She looped her arm through his. "I just put the food away. You can look in on Manda while I heat it up."

As they went inside, neither noticed the car parked down the street or the camera clicking away.

At Zachary's suggestion they sat side by side and ate out of the containers. Their chopsticks crisscrossed without a moment's hesitation while they told each other about their days. He seemed as disappointed as she felt when he said he wouldn't be able to stop by in the morning, but he said he'd be there that evening.

It was only after Zachary had left, when Madison was standing in front of her mirror in her bathroom putting cold cream on her face, that she noticed the brightness in her eyes, the little smile on her face.

Her hand paused. She inched closer to the mirror.

The woman staring back at her was happy. The shadows that had been in her eyes and beneath them were gone.

It didn't seem possible that this was the same miserable, angry woman that had stared back at her four weeks ago. She didn't have to think hard to know the reason.

Zachary.

Reaching for a tissue, she wiped off the excess cream, then brushed her teeth. Cutting off the light in the bathroom, she checked on Manda, then flipped off the overhead light. A unicorn nightlight showed the way to her bed. Smiling, she crawled beneath the covers.

Zachary again.

As she drifted off to sleep, she didn't think it odd that she still had a smile on her face and that her last thoughts were of Zachary.

Chapter 24

Zachary was out of bed at five and arrived at his latest building site in Grapevine at six-ten. Unlocking the front door, he went straight to the kitchen, strapped on his kneepads, and began laying tile on the floor. He whistled as he worked. He had plans for this evening and he didn't plan to be late.

By the time his crew arrived at eight, he'd finished tiling the kitchen and two of the three baths. His shirt was soaked with perspiration, and he wore a grin. "About time you guys arrived."

Kelli, her tool belt strapped to her narrow waist, smiled down at him. "You're raring to go today. Got a hot date tonight, boss?"

"I might," he said.

"Since I might have one, too, if a certain fellow plays his cards right, let's get this show on the road." Stepping around Zachary, she went to the garage to get the cabinet door they had stained the day before.

Zachary was closing the adhesive when he saw the unhappy look on Clarence's face. "She meant you."

"She did?" Clarence asked, grinning broadly.

"She did, and if you hurt her I'll pound you into the dirt."

"Me too."

"That goes for all of us."

Clarence stared at the glaring men he'd called friends for

the past two months. He spoke from his heart. "All I want to do is love her."

Zachary could certainly empathize with him. "Well, don't stand there looking pitiful. She's the one you need to tell, but keep your mind on your job. If you mess up, she'll chew your butt out and you'll be home alone tonight," Zachary warned.

"I won't. Thanks." He hurried to the garage.

"Come on, James. Let's get that sink installed."

"Right behind you, boss. With all this love talk, I might take the hen out tonight myself," he said, following Zachary down the wide hall.

"If Eloise hears you call her a hen, you'll be taking yourself to the hospital tonight," one of the crew said. Laughter followed them down the hall.

"I thought she had enough teddy bears," Zachary said, feeling more nervous by the second. He'd arrived a little after six that evening. Madison had waited to have dinner with him. Afterwards they'd gone outside to the swing, then returned to the den. "But I saw those and . . ." He shrugged.

Madison glanced up from the two gold bracelets delicately etched with hearts and ivy in the jewelry box from Tiffany's. There was only one location in the city. "I suppose you were in the neighborhood?"

"Had to pass right by the Galleria to get here."

She glanced down at the heavy gold bracelets. "I don't know what to say."

"There's nothing to say." He lifted the largest bracelet and clamped it around her wrist. "Manda will have to wait until she's a little older to wear hers."

"Looks like she wants hers now," Madison said as Manda wrestled the bracelet from the case, then promptly stuck it into her mouth. "I think she's teething."

Zachary ran his large hand over the baby's head. "I heard Thomas say his son nearly drove them crazy when he was teething. Do you think we should call the doctor?"

"I already have." Madison removed the bracelet, then rubbed her index finger against Manda's gums. She clamped her little hands around Madison's hand. "The nurse said giving her something cold to drink or chew on would help the gum irritation. Acetaminophen if nothing else works.

Zachary continued to brush Manda's head, careful to keep a safe distance from Madison's breast covered by a bright yellow knit top. "Thomas said he rubbed whiskey on Little Thomas's gums and his wife almost kicked him out of the house."

Madison's shocked gaze flew up to him. "Alcohol is a poison to babies!"

"Thomas loves his son," Zachary said in the defense of his friend. "He said his mother had given it to him and it hadn't hurt him any."

"Humph." Madison went back to rubbing Manda's gums. "If he rubbed whiskey on his baby's gums, I wouldn't be so sure the alcohol *he* absorbed as a baby didn't pickle his brain."

"Same thing his wife told him," Zachary said with a laugh as he wiped the drool from Manda's chin with a diaper. "You want me to go to the drugstore and get that medicine in case you need it?"

"Please." Getting up, Madison went to the kitchen and handed him a sheet of paper. "I tried to go to the store, but she wasn't ready. I didn't even get the car out of the garage."

Seeing Manda crinkling up her face to cry, Zachary gave her his finger. She clamped down immediately. He winced. "Sharp teeth."

"Very. The nurse said they sell rubber teething rings, but I don't know if the drugstore up the street will have any," she said.

"I'll find one." He leaned over until he and Manda were eye-to-eye. "When I get back you can chew on my finger all you like." Instead of her usual smile, she simply stared. Straightening, he stuffed the list into his shirt pocket. "I'll be back as soon as I can."

Madison followed him to the front door, but as he opened it they and the couple coming up the walk froze. Zachary turned back to her. "Need me to stay?"

She smiled in reassurance. "We'll be fine."

Zachary passed the Reeds with a curt nod of his baseball cap-covered head. They didn't move until the truck's engine turned over.

Her mouth pursed in disapproval, Vanessa walked gracefully up the walkway. "I'm not sure I approve of the company you're keeping, Madison."

"Won't you come inside?" Ignoring Vanessa's remark, Madison stepped back inside the foyer. Neither of Wes's parents even glanced at Manda as they entered the house. Closing the door behind them, Madison went to the den and took a seat on the leather couch.

For a long moment, she didn't think they were going to sit down. Vanessa's shoulders were stiff in her stylish suit, her hands clamped tightly on her small Fendi bag. A.J. had yet to remove his pearl-gray Stetson. His gaze leaped from Madison to Vanessa. He took his cue from his wife in social situations. He had the money, but Vanessa had the class. He was as aware as Madison was that Vanessa preferred sitting in the living room she had decorated with carte blanche approval from Wes. Picking out furniture and drapes hadn't seemed important six weeks after Madison lost her baby.

Madison leaned back and crossed her legs.

Vanessa noted the movement with disapproving eyes. With ill-concealed grace, she finally took a seat on one of the matching leather chairs, her back stiff. A.J. removed his hat and took the chair next to his wife.

"What was he doing here?" Vanessa asked, her voice terse.

"Just visiting. Why? What do you have against Zachary?" Madison asked.

"I'm not ready to see another man make himself so comfortable in my son's home."

Madison's eyes narrowed. Feeling Manda move restlessly

in her arms, she forced herself not to take offense at her mother-in-law's words. "Zachary and Wes were good friends, and he's been a friend to me. He's welcome in this house."

"You wouldn't have this home if it wasn't for my son," Vanessa snapped.

Madison swallowed the retort that leaped to her tongue. It was mostly her money, not Wes's, that had paid for the lot and the house. "I can understand you're distraught over Wes's death, but we've all got to let go and move on."

" 'Move on'!" Vanessa repeated in disbelief and rage. "How dare you turn your back on Wes's memory! How can you forget what a brilliant—"

"Vanessa," A.J. said, cutting off his wife and earning a sharp look for his trouble. "We don't want to forget why we came." His gaze finally settled on Manda. "My boy was a hero. He gave his life for that little girl's mother and made sure she was cared for. People have called from all over the country to tell us how proud of Wes they are after seeing her on television. Money is pouring in for his scholarship fund."

Madison understood then. This wasn't a visit to comfort; it was to pay homage to their son's memory.

Vanessa's hazel eyes misted. "Why did it have to be him? Why was my son the only caring man to stop and help that woman?"

"That was the kind of man my son was," A.J. said, his head bowed. "He died a hero."

"He died helping his mistress change a flat tire. Manda is his child." The instant the words were out, Madison regretted them. She honestly didn't know if she had told them because they deserved the truth or if she'd wanted to put an end to the glowing adulation of Wes. "I'm sorry. I shouldn't have told you that way."

Vanessa's mouth gaped. She shot to her feet. "That's a vicious lie! My son wasn't that kind of man."

Manda stilled, then turned to burrow into the curve of Madison's arms. Madison's arms tightened, her words comforted and reassured. "It's all right, Manda, I'm here."

To Vanessa she said, "I apologize again for telling you so abruptly, and I can understand your being upset, but please keep your voice down. Loud noises upset Mand—"

"That child is not Wes's," Vanessa said, cutting her off.

"Van—"

"No. I don't want to hear another lie about my son!" Vanessa's eyes shone with tears and anger. "You're just jealous of him. He told us about your wanting to hold him back. Your refusal to move to Chicago because then he'd make more money and have more prestige with the CNN affiliate. He reached below his level to marry you. I tried to tell him. He should have divorced you long ago."

She paused only for a breath. "You just want an excuse to keep that baby because of the one you lost. You won't destroy my son's reputation to do it. I won't let you." Snatching up her purse, she stormed out of the house.

Stunned at the venom and the accusations, Madison sat there for a long moment, holding a trembling Manda to her.

A.J. didn't move, he simply stared at Manda.

"She's your grandchild, A.J.," Madison managed to say despite the hurt she felt. Had Wes really told his parents such hateful lies about her? She swallowed. "I wouldn't make up something like this."

His face drawn and haggard, A.J. put on his hat and started from the room.

Madison came to her feet and followed. "She's Wes's child. A part of your son is still alive. Just look at her eyes."

He didn't even pause. The front door closed with an audible click.

Madison held Manda closer as if to shield her from being unwanted, then she thought of the way she had reacted when Zachary had tried to get her to accept Manda's parentage.

"They just need time, the way I did." She just wished she believed that's all it was.

Zachary had tried to hurry back to the house, but the instant Madison opened the door and he saw the anguish in her face it was apparent that he hadn't been fast enough. "What did they say to you?"

"It's what I said to them." She bit her lower lip. "I told them Wes was Manda's father."

Zachary shifted the bags to one hand. He curved the other around her shoulder and led her back into the kitchen. "I didn't think they'd take it very well."

Madison took a carton of yogurt out of the refrigerator and sat with Manda at the kitchen table. "They reminded me of the way I'd reacted when I found out about Manda."

"I highly doubt that," he said, shredding the clear wrapping on a circular-shaped rubber teething ring. "I'm sure they're worried about what this will do to the public's perfect image of Wes." He shook his head in disgust. "Forget them." Holding the teething ring beneath the running hot water, he nodded toward the yogurt Madison was feeding Manda. "You starting to give her yogurt?"

"The nurse suggested it," she said, her voice distracted.

He frowned and cut off the water. He didn't like the way Madison sounded. And as soon as Manda was feeling better and asleep for the night, he and Madison were going to have a serious conversation.

Camille chose her dress with care. Antoine's was a very exclusive restaurant. She'd been there dozens of time, but tonight was different. She knew it was because of the man sitting across from her.

Gordon's salt-and-pepper hair gleamed in the soft glow of the crystal chandelier. His black suit fit his elegant build perfectly. She didn't need the pinot noir to make her feel light-headed, Gordon had already accomplished that.

"Tell me about your ex-husband."

The mellow feeling evaporated. Camille set her wineglass down.

"That bad?"

She simply stared at him.

"My wife and I were married five years when she was

diagnosed with uterine cancer. Six months later she was gone. We had twins, Adrian and Adair, a boy and girl. They're college sophomores and doing a summer internship at a newspaper in Austin."

"You and your wife were probably very happy."

"We were."

"Congratulations," she said, appalled at the tinge of bitterness in her voice. "I'm sorry. Maybe this was a mistake."

"We've already discussed that." Gordon cut into his bloodred prime rib. "Do you like to dance?"

"Do you always shift topics so quickly?" she asked.

"When necessary." He nodded toward her barely touched fillet of sole. "Not to your liking? I'll get the waiter."

She picked up her fork when he started to lift his hand. "Don't even think it. Howard would have a conniption fit if he heard you."

"The chef?"

"And owner." She took a bite, savored. "Delicious." She looked up to see Gordon watching her. Her breath snagged.

"I'm looking forward to finding out for myself before the night is over just how delicious."

He wasn't talking about food. The heat in his black eyes told her as much. "I think we've also discussed that self-assurance of yours."

"A black man who doesn't have self-assurance won't get very far in the corporate world," he told her.

He had her there. "Was the climb bumpy?"

"You jumped on that one, didn't you?" he replied. At her innocent look, he smiled. "From day one. I come from a family of seven children." His smile broadened at the astonishment in her eyes. "That many in a family teaches you early how to stick up for yourself. Daddy left after I was born. Mama worked hard to get us through high school. Two of us made it through college. Mama cried through the entire ceremony."

"It must be wonderful, knowing you haven't disappointed your parents." Wistfulness entered her voice.

He reached out and placed his hand on top of hers. "I think you may be judging your mother too harshly. It's obvious to anyone who sees the two of you together for five seconds that she loves you."

"Love and pride are two different things." She pulled her hand back. "I'd like to leave now."

Gordon felt her putting up a wall. He wasn't about to let that happen. He'd give her space for now, but later . . . "Certainly." He signaled their waiter.

Camille's thoughts were chaotic as Gordon drove her home. He was doing what she asked. Why wasn't she happy about it? Silly question—and one she knew the answer to. She wanted to be with him. Somehow she wanted him to care enough not to let her walk away. She rubbed her head.

"Headache?"

"No." She moistened her lips.

Gordon turned into the drive of her gated complex, stopped at the manned gatehouse, then drove on. Soon he'd be at her house and out of her life. She just wished she could be as happy about it as she had thought she would be.

Parking the Infiniti, Gordon came around, opened Camille's door, and lightly took her arm. For once she found her key immediately and opened her door. This was it, she thought, and turned. "Thanks fo—"

His mouth descended on hers. The shock of his lips, then the pleasure, zipped through her. Her arms went around his neck, pulling him closer, sinking into the kiss and into him. She wasn't aware of him backing her into her condo, of him closing the door.

When he lifted his head, their labored breathing was harsh in the room lit only by a gracefully curved iron lamp on the end table. "Did you think I'd let you walk away from me?"

"I—"

Sharp teeth nipped her lip, then suckled. Camille's insides quivered. "Did you?" he repeated.

Her dazed eyes focused on him. "I—I guess I hoped not."

His lips took hers again, hot and demanding, drawing her into him, taking her deep, faster than a kiss had ever done before. She had no will nor did she want any. She simply followed where he and the pleasure led.

His hands framed her face and waited until her thick lashes lifted. "I want you, but I'm willing to wait. It's not just a night that I want. Do you understand?"

With her body clamoring for his hands and mouth, it was difficult to concentrate. She hadn't known she could want like this. She tried to kiss him and he pulled his head back.

"I want more."

The haze cleared. She stared at him. "More?"

"I've never been a hit-and-run kind of guy. Since Karen died, there have been few women in my life."

She backed up. Swallowed. The butterflies in her stomach turned to lead. "I—I think you better define 'more.' "

Gordon saw the panic in her face and made a quick adjustment in what he had been about to say. "I'm rather old-fashioned. I believe in one woman, one man, at one time."

Her eyes snapped. "You think I sleep around?"

"If I thought that, I wouldn't be standing here," he said. "Why do you always believe that I think the worst about you?" Something flickered in her eyes. His voice gentled. "Is that what he thought?"

Evading his hand, she turned on another lamp. Bright light flooded the room done almost entirely in white with splashes of red and yellow in the side chair and pillows. A mustard pot of sunflowers and a bowl of apples and pears in a metal centerpiece sat on the wooden coffee table. "You'd better go."

"Not if the entire Dallas Police Department's SWAT team came." He went to stand in front of her. "Talk to me."

She folded her arms. "Why should I?"

"Because, in spite of everything we have going against us, there's a connection between us."

Her chin lifted. "Hormones."

His hands gently closed around her upper arm. He felt her tremble, heard her breath hitch. "How many 'hormonal' feelings like this have you felt in the last year?"

She wanted to lie, considered, then felt the erratic thump of her heart. "None."

The tension building in him eased. "I see you and I forget you're probably twenty years younger than I am." His eyes narrowed. "How old are you, anyway?"

Since it was the first time she had seen Gordon the slightest bit exasperated, she enjoyed the moment. "Thirty-four."

He groaned. "Make that twenty-three years."

She chuckled. Something she hadn't done with a man in a long time. Gordon might irritate, but he interested her as few men had. Plus, there was no denying the sexual pull between them. "Then maybe we won't have to worry about other things."

"Wanna bet?"

The sharp glitter in his eyes had her body quivering. The only thing she'd bet was that he didn't take Viagra.

"So how do you feel about dating an older man?"

She answered honestly. "I don't think of you as older when I look at you." She wrinkled her mouth. "You certainly don't kiss like one."

His teeth flashed in a satisfied grin. He braced his hands on her hips. "That's because you inspire me."

His words curled through her like mulled wine. "You're rather inspiring, yourself."

"Why don't we inspire each other?" His mouth took hers again, this time gentle and slow, as if they had all the time in the world to sample the taste and textures of each other. His hands moved down to her hips, softly kneading as his mouth played and savored her, learning what she liked and what excited her.

"Can I see you tomorrow night?"

"I'm leaving tomorrow for a conference in Houston for four days," she said, her disappointment obvious.

His fingers massaged the small of her back. "What time do you leave and get back?"

"My plane leaves from Love Field at one tomorrow afternoon and I arrive back Wednesday at six P.M." Her fingertips stroked his chest through his cotton shirt. They itched to touch bare skin.

"How about I take you, then pick you up, and then we can have a late dinner?" His mind was already formulating the dinner and what would happen afterwards.

Camille read his thoughts as accurately as if had spoken the words out loud. "Pick me up at eleven-thirty."

"How about ten, and we can have champagne brunch at Antares?" Now that he knew what he wanted, he wanted to see her every possible chance he got.

Her body melted against the hard line of his body a bit more. "I'd like that." Her replay came out a bit breathless.

"I'll see you at ten." After another soul-stirring kiss Gordon made himself release her and walk to the door. "Good night, Camille."

"Good night, Gordon, and thanks for a wonderful evening."

"The pleasure was all mine, I assure you."

Camille blushed, something she thought she had outgrown, and was very pleased to find she hadn't. The knowing grin on Gordon's face pleased her even more. Locking the door, she went to her room to start packing.

"Zachary, it's after one," Madison whispered. "You should go home."

"Not until I'm sure she's down for the night," he whispered back as he stared down at Manda asleep in her crib. The room lay in soft shadows. The only light in the room came from the unicorn nightlight. "You grab some sleep. I'll watch her."

Madison sighed. Stubborn, wonderful man. She didn't know what she would have done over the past hours without him. She understood a little of what Little Thomas's mother was talking about. After a while a sixteen-pound baby made your arms ache. But when she neared that point, Zachary was there to take Manda, to sing to her in an off-key voice she hadn't seemed to mind, to read to her from her new books. He was a man a woman could count on.

"Since you're too big to toss out, at least go sit in the love seat and prop your feet on the hassock."

"I'm fine," he said without looking up.

"Zachary, she's all right. She's not running a fever. She took her bottle and she hasn't moved in thirty minutes."

"We thought that the last time."

He had her there. He had been about to leave around eleven when Manda woke up in her crib and let them know she wasn't happy about this teething business. "And they call mothers overprotective," she muttered.

He finally looked up. She couldn't see his eyes clearly, but she heard the concern in his voice. "I just don't want her to wake up thinking that she's all alone."

His sincerity touched her. She rested her hand on his tense shoulder. "She has us, her great-aunt, and my family. She has people who care," she said. "She'd have her grandparents if I'd handled things better. They may not ever accept her."

Pulling her hand away, she went to take a seat on the love seat near the French doors. She picked up a pillow that echoed the rose wallpaper and the drapes on the half-canopy bed and hugged it to her chest.

Zachary didn't care about the hurt feelings of A.J. or Vanessa. He did care about Madison's. Adjusting the thermal blanket on Manda, he took a seat beside Madison, taking care that their bodies didn't touch. "Tell me what happened."

Gathering the pillow closer, she did, and ended by saying, "I'm still not sure if I told them because I wanted to show them that Wes wasn't the perfect man they thought or to let them know Manda was their grandchild."

"Would it be so bad if you did want to show Wes up?"

Her dark head whipped around. "That would be mean."

"So you were mean." Callused hands settled on her hunched shoulders and turned her toward him. "You're human."

She was silent for a long while. There was something that had been nagging her. "Did . . . Did Wes ever say to you that I tried to hold him back? That I was jealous?"

He seriously considered lying. After all, what was one more lie, especially when the truth would hurt. He couldn't. She had been lied to enough. "You made more money than Wes, had more popularity. For a man like Wes, who had always been at the top, it was hard to take at times."

"So his mother told the truth," she said in a choked whisper.

His callused fingers flexed on her bare arm. "Wes was never a patient person. He never had to be. What he wanted, his parents got him. His charms and intelligence got the rest. He admired you, was proud of your accomplishments, but was anxious to make his own mark, be recognized for his own accomplishments."

"She mentioned divorce. Did he say he wanted to divorce me? Was he going to marry Manda's mother?"

"He never mentioned divorce, Madison. He might not have liked standing in your shadow, but his popularity was linked to yours."

Feeling foolish and gullible, she glanced away. "So he used both of us to get what he wanted and I let him." Her voice was tinged with weariness.

Zachary saw her slumped shoulders and did what he had wanted to do since he'd arrived; he pulled her into his arms. "It's over, Madison."

She leaned closer into the shelter of his embrace, listened to the comforting beat of his heart. "A.J. said his fraternity is establishing a scholarship at Wes's high school."

"Wes told me a lot of times that he wished he'd see more black faces in journalism."

It hit her all at once. She twisted until she could stare up into Zachary's face. "You were behind his fraternity starting the scholarship fund, weren't you?"

"Doesn't matter who started it, just that it gets done."

Simple answer from a complex man. Wes's parents disliked Zachary intensely. He didn't seem particularly fond of them, either. Yet he had gone to great measures to ensure that neither Wes nor his dream would be forgotten. She settled back against his wide chest, snuggling to get more comfortable. "I'll contact his boss and mine. I'm sure they'd like to contribute and get the word out."

His hand rubbed up and down her arm. "Like I said, you're quite a woman."

She yawned and placed her feet on the hassock.

"Go to sleep," he murmured into her hair.

"If you're staying up, then so am I." She yawned again. "How was work today?"

Her breath heated his skin where his shirt was open. "Fine."

She angled her head up to ask him another question and discovered their lips were a sigh apart. They froze. Their breaths mingled. A sweet yearning coursed through her. Without thought she moved closer. Their lips met with the gossamer touch of butterfly wings. The kiss gradually deepened by slow, aching degrees. Their tongues stroked, feasted, mated.

Pleasure curled through her, tempting her, luring her. She wanted to get closer. No, she *had* to. She twisted her body more fully toward his, her leg shifting . . . and froze. His hard arousal pulsed against her thigh. Her eyes popped open. She scrambled to her feet.

"I—I'm sorry . . . I didn't—You'll be more comfortable by yourself." Shaken, embarrassed, Madison hurried to the bathroom. Closing the door, she leaned against it. Her breathing was erratic, her heart thumped wildly in her chest. She pressed trembling fingers against her moist, kiss-swollen lips and all she could think of was that she'd never felt more alive or more frightened in her life.

What was she doing? What must he think of her? Going to the sink she splashed cold water on her face. It did nothing to cool the fires in her blood. She was deeply attracted to Zachary. Wanted him. But how could she, so soon after her husband's death? And just what kind of woman did that make her?

Zachary sat on the side of the love seat, his fists clenched. He wanted Madison like hell burning. It took all his control not to kick the bathroom door down and take her. She'd been so sweet, so responsive. He hadn't dared let himself hope. And she had run from him. His head fell forward in regret and despair. He hadn't wanted that.

He should have known what might happen if she got too close. The last thing he wanted was for her to be wary of him.

The door finally opened. The light was out in the bathroom. He could only make out the faint outline of her body as she moved across the room and climbed into bed. She didn't say anything and he didn't know what he could say. All he knew was that their relationship had changed, and not for the better.

Chapter 25

Zachary hadn't expected to get much sleep and he hadn't. He was too conscious of Madison several feet away, the whisper of bedcovers as she tossed restlessly during the night. He was awake when the first orange-yellow streak of gold lit the day. When Manda finally roused, he was there to lift her out of the crib by the time she had pulled her knees under her.

She grinned at him, showing off a shining new tooth in her bottom gum. At least one of his ladies wasn't upset with him. "Good morning, munchkin."

She patted his cheeks.

"Glad to see you're feeling better. Let's get you changed and go get breakfast. We'll let Madison sleep."

"I'm awake." Her hair mussed, her clothes rumpled from sleeping in them, she slipped out of bed, her expression cautious.

Zachary's gut clenched. He had put that look in her eyes. "I'm sorry about last night. I didn't mean for that to happen."

She glanced away. "It's forgotten." Crossing the room, she stopped an arm's length away and reached out for Manda. "'Morning, sweetheart."

The sinking sensation in his gut became worse when he handed the baby to Madison and noticed that she no longer wore her bracelet from Tiffany's. "I'll go start breakfast."

"That won't be necessary." Her gaze bounced to him, then away. "We can manage."

He decided not to press the issue. "I'll stop by later today."

"I'll be pretty busy working on scripts for the next season."

She was pushing him away. His fault. "I'll see you Monday, or will you be busy then?"

"I expect I'll become busier, but you can always come by to see Manda or pick her up."

For a long time he studied her. "Are you scared of me, or yourself?"

"Very few things scare me." Clasping Manda tightly, she went to the changing table, keeping her back to him, hoping he didn't see that her hands were trembling. "I'd see you out, but I need to change Manda."

"All right, Madison. Have it your way for the time being. You know how to reach me." He clenched his jaw.

"Good-bye, Zachary."

"Not by a long shot," he warned.

Madison stiffened. When she looked up he was gone, and she had never felt more miserable or more alone in her life.

Gordon knew it might happen, but he hadn't expected it to happen so soon. Forty minutes after they had left the brunch at Antares, he was still smoldering.

"You aren't going to forget it, are you?" Camille asked, sitting beside him in the passenger waiting area of Southwest Airlines.

Gordon folded his arms. "I doubt if the shoe were on the other foot, you'd be so glib about it."

Camille knew a man's ego was as fragile as a woman's. "He apologized and, after the dressing-down you gave him, I don't think he'll jump to conclusions like that again."

The muscle in Gordon's jaw jerked. He could still hear the maître d's words.

"Would you like a table for you and your daughter, sir?"

He'd never been so embarrassed in his life. He'd looked forward to seeing Camille again, felt young, until the careless words of the maître d' at Antares had brought him crashing back to reality.

"I'm twenty-three years older than you are," he muttered.

"The age difference didn't bother you last night," she said with an impish smile.

"We both know why," he said, aware of the crowded waiting area.

Camille leaned closer, by accident or by design letting him feel the softness of her breast and catch a whiff of her perfume. "Has something changed I don't know about?"

Gordon went from annoyed to lusting in an instant. "If we weren't here, I'd answer that for you."

Laughing, Camille stood and reached for her roll-on luggage. She'd been right, seeing Gordon was going to be fun. No attachments, no broken hearts when they said good-bye. "I'll have to take a rain check. They just called my flight."

Gordon came to his feet with a disgruntled look on his face. "You think I'm being foolish?"

She stuck her tongue in her cheek. "You really expect me to answer that and then get on a plane?"

"No."

"Good." Leaning over, she brushed her lips across his cheek. "See you Wednesday night." Then she was merging with the other passengers.

Gordon waved good-bye as she went though the door to board. His hands deep in his pocket, he went to his car. He hadn't told Camille the entire reason the man's words bothered him. His age was part of it, but it tied in directly with his ability to keep her satisfied in bed and out.

He hadn't had sexual relations in over two years, but he hadn't worried about his performance in bed . . . until the maître d's blunder. What if he couldn't satisfy her? How embarrassing would that be for both of them? Then, too, he tended to be a homebody. Women Camille's age wanted to go out, party, do things, meet people. If he wasn't working or at some speaking engagement, he was at home. The twins referred to him as "the only walking, breathing fossil."

Unlocking his car, he got in and backed out. He'd let his desire for Camille cloud his usual practical judgment. He had to think this through before she returned and he humiliated himself.

Monday morning Zachary was the first person to work at seven-ten. By seven fifty-five all of his crew was there except Kelli and Clarence. The men were colorful and descriptive as to the reason the two were late.

At eight-thirteen Kelli whirled her aged truck into the ungraded front yard of the 5,500-square-foot house and came to a dusty stop. Slamming out of the truck, she passed him at a fast clip. Words of apology flowed from her mouth. Seconds later Clarence's dented Buick came to a stop beside Kelli's truck. He was just as apologetic as he tried to strap on his tool belt and run at the same time.

It didn't take much imagination to realize why they were late or why they arrived directly behind each other, especially since they lived in different cities and had the slumberous satisfied look of being well loved in their eyes.

Zachary picked up the sanding pads from the back of his truck and went inside. The chances of him ever putting that look in Madison's eyes were slim to none. At least until he came clean with her. But if she thought she was going to keep him out of her life, she was wrong.

He caught his men nudging each other as Kelli and Clarence walked through their work area, but no one said anything to either of them. They admired and respected Kelli. They also knew she had a devious mind and would think of an ingenious way to pay them back, which placed Clarence off-limits as well.

However, an hour later problems arose between the couple. "I'm perfectly capable of getting off a ladder by myself," Kelli snapped when Clarence tried to help her down the last three rungs.

"I was—"

"—Being an ass," she finished. Neither seemed to notice men making themselves scarce. "I've been doing this before you got here and will still be doing it after you're gone. I don't need you."

Clarence's head snapped back as if she had slapped him. The wounded look on his face said he'd have much preferred the slap to the words. Silently he turned and walked away with his head hanging, his big feet dragging.

Kelli reached for him, her lower lip tucked between her teeth. Shaking her head, she went back to work.

Witnessing the incident made Zachary think of Madison. Women wanted their independence. Men felt the need to protect. It was a fine line to walk.

Hadn't he called a friend of his who owned a takeout deli downtown near her TV station and ordered Madison's lunch? As upset with him as she was, she might toss it. He hoped not. He had no doubt she'd take care of Manda, but what about herself? He'd pushed himself into her life with half-truths and promises. She'd accepted his help, but occasionally she wanted to go it alone. He admired her for her strength as much as he loved her, and it could all blow up in his face.

"I don't know what to do, boss." Clarence wore a bleak expression, his hands pushed deep into the pockets of his worn denims.

Zachary cut off the sander and lifted his goggles. He could empathize with him. "Go tell Kelli I want you to work with me today."

Clarence hesitated. "We're supposed to hang the cabinets in the master bathroom."

"I'm still the boss around here. Besides, I think it's time you learned that you might never understand a woman. All you can do is love them."

"But is that enough?" he asked, his thin shoulders slumped.

"If you do it the right way, it is."

Clarence whipped his hands out of his pockets, hope shining in his eyes. "I'll go tell her."

Zachary went back to sanding the cabinet. Sometimes all you had was your love. Nobody ever said it would be easy.

Madison went to work Monday morning with none of the enthusiasm she had anticipated before The Incident, as she preferred to think of the kiss. Getting out of the limo with Manda, she had to make herself keep walking. Perhaps keeping busy would help. Thinking about it certainly hadn't. Nor had Zachary coming over Sunday to take Manda to the park. Her awareness of him was driving her crazy and giving her one of her famous headaches.

Greeting the receptionist and the security guard, Madison continued to her office. Inside, she was glad to see that at least the playpen and daybed she'd ordered were there, the electrical outlets covered, the cords to her draperies and blinds out of reach, the spot empty where her philodendron once thrived. The big-leaf ivy was on top of her file cabinet. Whenever Manda was on the floor she liked to investigate, and had eyes like an eagle.

"Thank you, Traci, everything looks perfect," she said to her assistant, then sat behind her desk with Manda still in her arms. Her desk looked bare without the computer, printer, and all their hanging cords. They were now housed in a console against the wall.

"Mr. Bills said to tell you he'd vacuumed the carpet in your office twice. There isn't anything that Manda might pick up and put in her mouth," Traci said, her pad in her hands. "He'd said he'd come by later to see if there was anything else you needed."

"I can't think of a thing." Handing Manda the teething ring, Madison flipped though her day planner. "Let's start to work on lining up the guests for the programs for the sweeps in September. Let's take them week by week. Any problems with the first show?"

Traci hesitated. She hugged her steno pad to her chest.

"Yes?"

"The first one is 'Couples in the Public Eye.' You still want to do that one, or push it back farther in the season?"

Madison had forgotten about that show. The president of the station had wanted this one. He was well aware that the public loved to take a peek into the private lives of celebrities. He'd suggested Wes come on the show with her. It would have been the first time that they would have shared live airtime. It had been promoted that way. Without asking, she knew the ads had been pulled.

"It's all right, Traci," Madison said. "If all the couples are confirmed, we'll do it as scheduled. Check and double-check to make sure we have any special requests for their hotel room or for the guest lounge of the studio."

"You're so brave," Traci said with open admiration.

If you only knew, Madison thought. "What's the next show?"

Gordon loved his job. He'd loved it when things came together and the station was alive with activity as it was today. Peeking into Madison's office, he waved as she glanced up from talking with the segment producer. Frowning, he continued to his office. Her smile was there, but it didn't have the sparkle it had the other day. Manda, he noted, was asleep in her Port-a-crib.

Continuing to his office, he thought of his twins. At that age Adrian would have tried to climb over the side with Adair following close behind. He couldn't believe they'd be nineteen in a couple of months.

His steps slowed. His hand rubbed over the back of his neck. He was dating a woman sixteen years older than his kids. Entering his office, he seriously considered seeing if he could still do a hundred push-ups. He went to his desk instead. He'd probably have a coronary and where would that leave him?

But wasn't sex just as strenuous?

For a man who never worried, he had certainly developed

a bad case. Picking up his gold fountain pen, he flipped it end over end, then glanced at the framed picture of the twins. He'd taught them to go after what they wanted. To at least get in the game, play fair, but play to win with no regrets if you had given it your all. No excuses. No time-outs.

Tossing the fountain pen on the desk, he positioned himself on the floor for his push-ups. Better to find out now than with Camille.

Zachary hadn't known what to expect from Madison when he went to her house Monday after work, but it certainly hadn't been Gretchen answering the door. "Yes?" the maid inquired politely.

"Zachary Holman. Is Madison at home?"

"Yes, sir. Come in. I'll tell her you're here."

She didn't ask him to sit down, so he didn't. He felt like a lowly servant, hat in hand, coming to see the mistress of the house. He didn't like it.

The door to Madison's office opened down the hallway and she came out carrying Manda. "Good evening, Zachary. I have some paperwork to do, but Manda is all yours." Face expressionless, she held Manda out to him. "You're welcome to stay here or take her out."

"We'll go outside to the swing."

Irritation swept across her face for the briefest moment. "Gretchen is here if you need anything." She wiggled Manda's bare foot. "Have fun. Thanks for lunch today, but it won't be necessary in the future."

"Whatever you say." She couldn't have made it much clearer that she didn't want him in her life.

"Good-bye." Turning, she went back down the hall and into her office.

"Ma-da," Manda cried, looking in the direction Madison had gone.

"Looks like we're on our own." Carrying Manda, Zachary went into the backyard.

* * *

Madison told herself not to, but somehow she found herself in the living room peeking though the sheers at Manda and Zachary. She desperately wished he hadn't stayed around to tempt her. Despite everything she had tried to convince herself of, she wanted to be out there, to have him hold her, kiss her mindless again, and—

She let the curtain fall and she went back to her office. She couldn't, wouldn't, think about him that way. It wasn't proper.

Besides, she was obviously not very astute in picking men and knowing their feelings. She'd forgiven Wes, but she had no intention of being duped again.

Sitting at her desk, she picked up the sheet of paper listing the possible topics of shows. No man would ever interfere with her life again. She wouldn't let it happen.

Gordon was waiting for Camille Wednesday night when she disembarked from the plane. Seeing her, he was glad he had been putting stress on his heart. She wore a red sundress in a lightweight material that shifted and flowed over her body and stopped at least five inches above her knees. She had impossibly long legs and he immediately thought of them wrapped tightly around his waist. On her feet were four-inch red sandals with a wisp of a strap across the toes and one just above her ankles. By the time she reached him, his breathing was hard and he was harder.

"You trying to give me a coronary?" he asked, taking the handle of her roll-on.

She flashed a grin, then linked her arm through his. "Thank you. And no, I have plans for you."

"Goodness, Camille," he said, groaning.

She laughed a throaty sound, one meant for lovers. "How was your week?"

"Hectic." Because he hadn't been able to get his mind off her. "Yours seems to have been good."

"Learned a lot, and it was great seeing old friends," she told him as they made their way outside. "The main thrust, as it always is is finding ways to decrease paperwork, increase public awareness, and getting people to report possible abuse." All playfulness left her voice.

"If there is anything I or the station can do, let me know." Opening the car door, he placed her suitcase in the backseat. He turned back and she was in his arms, her greedy mouth on his.

Gordon thought if he did have a coronary, he'd die a happy man, and quickly took the kiss deeper. She was with him all the way.

"Not that I'm complaining, but what was that for?"

"For caring." Her fingers tenderly rubbed the back of his neck. "So many people don't." She stepped back, her playful smile flashing as she opened her door and slipped inside. "I had an early lunch and the peanuts they served on the flight didn't cut it. Do you think you could feed a girl?"

"I know the perfect place."

Chapter 26

Camille hadn't been surprised when Gordon pulled into the garage of a magnificent, traditional house. The house had a cozy feel despite the twenty-five-foot ceilings in the living room. Gold, oyster, and chocolate colors effortlessly tied one room to the other. "You have a beautiful home."

"Thanks. We moved in about three years ago. An electrical fire caused extensive damage to the old place and I decided it was a good time as any to move."

Sipping her wine, she glanced around the stainless-steel kitchen. "You did it in grand style."

"We enjoy it."

She slipped off the stool in front of the island and came to peer over his shoulder at the pot he was stirring. She inhaled appreciatively. "I hope that tastes as good as it smells."

"It does." He held out the wooden spoon filled with bits of chicken, Polish sausage, corn, and okra to her. "One of Mama's specialties. You throw everything but the kitchen sink in here."

Gingerly she tasted. Spicy and delicious. "More."

"I'm going to give you all you can handle."

Camille sucked in her breath. Anticipation zipped through her. "I hope you can back that up."

"Only one way to find out." He cut off the fire. "How hungry are you?"

Her fingers wobbled on the stem of the glass. "I suppose

if my mind was occupied with other things, I could wait for a little while."

"Let's see how long." He pulled her into his arms, his mouth crashing down on hers. She was ready, sinking into him and the kiss. Heat and need shot through them both.

His hands drew the thin straps of the dress over her arm, past the lush swell of her breasts to the delicate lace strapless bra. A little black bow sat naughtily in the center. He pressed his lip to the swell, felt her tremble. When the dress wouldn't come down any farther, he gathered the material in both hands and pulled it over her head, letting it fall heedlessly to the floor.

He sucked in his breath as he let his eyes roam the length of her. Past the lush breasts to the narrow waist, the scrap of lace that lovingly cupped her womanhood, the graceful curve of legs. "You're beautiful."

Before she could answer, his mouth was on hers again, hotter, more demanding. Her fingers trembled as much as her body did as she tried to unbutton his shirt. The room titled crazily and she grabbed him around the neck. She realized he had picked her up.

Minutes later she felt the softness of his bed beneath her, the hardness of Gordon above her. Vaguely she registered the skylight over the bed. Her bra slipped off. His hot mouth greedily sucked her nipple. She moaned, then arched as his hand slipped inside her panties and found the tiny nub, gently flicking.

The twin pleasures had her whimpering, her hands fisted on the bed linen. "G-Gordon."

"I'm going to make a feast of you."

His tongue laved one breast, then the other, then started a downward path and didn't stop until he found the essence of her. She couldn't stop the scream that tore from her throat, nor the one that came later when he was inside her and they were both spinning out of control.

Gordon's breath wheezed in and out of his lungs so hard, he sounded as if he had emphysema, but since Camille was lying beside him in all her naked splendor, her breathing only slightly less labored, he grinned.

He hadn't died on her.

"Pleased with yourself, aren't you?"

Since she had a satisfied look on her face, he figured he could be truthful. "Very. I didn't conk out on you."

Her eyes widened in distress. She scrambled to sit up. "You have heart problems?"

He took the trembling hand from his chest and kissed it. "Age problems?"

Her other hand slipped between his legs and felt his manhood leap in response, then begin to harden as she measured the length of him. "I think that worry can be eliminated."

"Why don't we make sure?" Quickly grabbing another condom, he sheathed himself then pulled her down on top of him. He watched her eyes close in pleasure as he slipped inside her, then open as she rode him for all he was worth.

A tray between them, Camille in Gordon's short terrycloth robe, Gordon in his slacks, they finished off a bowl of goulash and breadsticks. "You could spend the night, you know."

Camille's hand paused as she picked up her wine. "I don't spend the night with men."

He hadn't thought it would be easy, and tried not to lose his temper at the thought of her being with another man. "Your things are already here."

She sat her glass down with a sharp *clink* and came off the bed. His oversized robe slipped off her shoulder. "Don't spoil it, Gordon. I come and go as I please."

The abrupt tone had him reassessing the situation. He rose from the bed and stood in front of her. "Who made you so scared of commitment?"

Her kiss-softened lips firmed. "Thanks for dinner. I can get a cab home."

His hands on her arms stopped her as she started past him. He ignored the sharp glint in her eyes. "I want to know you better. I'm not probing to be nosy. I care. If I step on a sensitive area, tell me to back off."

"Back off," she said immediately.

"Not if we intend for this to work," he said softly.

Her eyes went from anger to wary in an instant. "We're just enjoying each other."

It was more than that to him, felt it was more to her as well, but instinctively knew if he pushed he'd lose. He kissed her bare shoulder, pulled his robe back up, then picked up the tray. "I'll take care of this while you get dressed."

She wanted to keep it simple. They could enjoy each other's bodies without invading each other's souls. Once you opened up, the other person could hurt you. She'd learned that painful lesson the hard way; she just couldn't reconcile that knowledge with the patient demand in Gordon's eyes. She shoved her hands into the pockets of the robe. "My husband and I married out of lust. We didn't know it at the time, but as our jobs demanded more of us, we quickly learned. He wanted me there for him and I couldn't be.

"When the lust faded there was nothing left. We each blamed the other for the marriage falling apart. Our parents were old friends and they kept pressuring us to work it out." Impatiently she dragged one hand out of the pocket and shoved it through her hair. "When my apartment was broken into, we were still married. He wasn't there, but he walked after that."

Gordon put the tray back on the bed, and went to her. "So you don't trust lust or love?"

"I don't want any emotional entanglements. If you can't agree to that, we should end it right now."

His finger touched the base of her throat where her pulse beat erratically, felt her swallow. Easiest wasn't always the best. He went back and picked up the tray. "You free tomorrow night for a movie?"

"Yes," she answered, confused.

"Good. We'll decide on the movie on the way to your place," he said as he carried the tray from the room.

Camille tugged the tie on Gordon's robe loose and reached for her panties. It was going to be all right. He wasn't going to demand more of her than she could give. She wasn't going to go through those feelings of inadequacy and of being a failure again for anyone.

"Madison, there's a Ms. Jacobs to see you," Traci said.

Madison's grip on the phone tightened. Automatically she glanced around the office. The baby furniture was pushed against the back wall. Manda was asleep in her crib, the blanket Madison's mother had crocheted for her was tucked around her little shoulders. "Please have her come in." Hanging up the phone, she stepped around her desk.

Camille entered with a smile. She wore a long lavender one-button jacket over a crisp white blouse and lavender mid-calf skirt. She extended her slim hand. "I went by your house and your maid said you had returned to work. Thank you for seeing me."

"Did I have a choice?" Madison said, slipping her hand into the pockets of her navy pinstriped trousers.

Camille tilted her head to one side. "I remember us as getting along better the last time we met."

"That came out badly." A lot of things had come out badly since The Incident. Madison waved the social worker to the chair in front of her desk. "I'm just a little nervous on how you'll react to my bringing Manda to the office."

Instead of taking the seat, Camille walked over to the crib. "How is Manda adjusting?"

"Beautifully." Hands on the crib, Madison stared down at the sleeping child. Her mouth softened. "This is the second week. I come in around ten each day after she's had her bath and playtime. She has her afternoon nap and feeding as usual. Occasionally in the evenings she wants to wait and eat with Zachary."

"Mr. Holman is still assisting you?

Madison felt her heart give a quick and familiar thump in her chest. "Yes."

Camille placed her hand on the rail of the crib. "That must be a big help since you've returned to work."

"I can take care of Manda by myself." Aware her tone had become defensive and that she was handling the interview all wrong, she strove for control. She'd known that kiss would lead to trouble. "How was your trip?"

Camille stiffened. "How did you know I had gone out of town?"

"Gordon mentioned it."

Camille drew her straight shoulders back farther. "I hope you realize my dating Mr. Armstrong has no bearing on this case."

Madison's eyes narrowed. The woman didn't trust anyone. "Why should it? You've already gotten a statement from Gordon."

"Yes, I have," Camille said, her body losing its rigidness. "If everything continues to go well, I plan to close the case by the end of next month."

"Why the delay?" Madison questioned, uneasiness creeping over her.

"To ensure that this placement is best for Manda," Camille answered calmly.

Madison didn't believe her. "Or to try and find an excuse to take her from me?"

Camille's eyes widened at the accusation. "That is not my intention."

"You could have fooled me." Brisk, agitated steps carried Madison behind her desk. "If there is nothing else, Manda should wake up soon and I want to finish the paperwork on my desk before she does."

"Would you like to hear what my report of today will say?" As if aware she wouldn't get an answer, Camille continued. "It will say that you have done an excellent job in caring for Manda. Your office is cluttered with things she needs to make her life, not yours, easier. It's obvious you've taken safety precautions to bring her here. Although you have a maid and could easily hire a nanny, you continue to care for her yourself."

Madison sat down heavily in her chair. "I was ready to pull your hair out by the roots."

"So I gathered," Camille said, seemingly not the least bit disturbed by the threat. "I can tell you care for Manda. But it could have been different. Would you want me to be less diligent?"

"No."

Satisfied, Camille nodded. "Then if I promise to stay out of your way, I'd like to wait until Manda is awake."

Madison's eyes cooled. "You almost had me fooled. You never give up, do you?"

"The report wouldn't be complete otherwise."

"And, of course, trying to catch people off-guard is just part of your job." Madison retorted.

A shadow moved across Camille's face. "I want what's best for Manda."

"So you say. Forgive me if I'm not particularly fond of how you gather your information." Rising, Madison picked up Manda, who had awakened and was grinning. "By all means, get the information you need for your report. Manda and I have storytime after lunch—just the two of us. I'm sure you'll understand if I don't ask you to stay."

Tossed out again, Camille thought, shoving the strap of her purse over her shoulder. She wasn't going to let it bother her. So what if she'd hoped she and Madison could be friends? She knew better. She was the enemy. Untrusted. Unwanted.

"Camille?"

Camille didn't want to turn around, but she wasn't given a choice when Gordon stepped in front of her. After a week of hot and heavy sex that showed no sign of abating, the sight of him gave her a sharp punch, quickly followed by a strong desire to rip his clothes off. "Hello, Gordon."

He was surprised by her frigid tone. The last time he'd

spoken to her she'd been draped in nothing but moonlight and a thin sheen of perspiration from their lovemaking. "Were you coming to see me?"

"I just left Ms. Reed's office. If you'll excuse me, I have another appointment."

He took her arm and steered her into an empty conference room. "So what happened between you and Madison?"

"That's confidential."

He said one very explicit word. He whirled away, then back and kept coming until his body was aligned with hers, her hips pressed against the edge of the oval conference table. "Madison loves Manda. Surely you can see that."

Her eyes went wide at the implications of his words. He might make love to her, but he didn't trust her or her judgment. "Get away from me."

The misery in her voice pulled at him. "Camille." At the moment there was nothing he wanted more than take her in his arms, but he knew from the moisture shining in her eyes he'd have a fight on his hands. "Please talk to me."

"I'm not defending myself to you or anyone else ever again." Shoving him aside, she left.

Gordon didn't even hesitate. He headed to Madison's office. If he couldn't get answers from one place, he'd try another. He passed Madison's assistant with a brief nod, then knocked on her door. There was no answer.

He glanced at Traci. "Is she in there?"

"Yes, sir, but she's probably reading Manda a story and she doesn't like to be disturbed," Traci answered, apprehension in her voice.

Any other time he might adhere to her wishes, but not after seeing the sheen of tears in Camille's eyes. He knocked again. "Madison?"

"Enter at your own risk," she called out, her voice steely.

"I think I'll take lunch now." Traci quickly grabbed her purse and left.

Gordon was made of tougher stuff. He opened the door.

Madison was in the rocking chair with Manda in her lap, and an oversized picture book in her hands.

"What happened between you and Camille?"

Madison kept rocking. "I don't like your taste in lady friends."

That much was obvious. "She cares deeply about the children in her caseload."

"That's your opinion."

He stared down at Madison, the tight set of her lips, the misery in her eyes. "She left here almost in tears. That doesn't sound like a woman who doesn't care."

"Tears are the oldest weapon in the book to soften up a man," Madison said.

Gordon squatted down and placed his hands on the arms of the rocker to stop its motion. "Then what's the reason for yours?"

She shook her head. "I don't want to talk about it and if you push I might say something we both will regret."

"You want me to call Zachary?"

Her eyes widened in alarm. "Zachary?"

Gordon couldn't tell where her wariness was coming from. "He left his number yesterday when he delivered the rocking chair."

"You said it was a gift."

Gordon frowned. "It was a gift. From Zachary."

She came to her feet, causing him to stand and step back. Going to the double window, she stared out.

"Did something happen between you two?"

"No," she snapped, then took a deep, calming breath. "I've got the guests for the shows almost lined up. You want to go over it tomorrow?"

"In other words, mind my own business."

"Please." Her voice wavered.

Gordon sighed. "I'm calling for your car and sending you home. You're not going to get much more done today."

"I'll be in tomorrow."

He started to tell her not to bother, then realized it might be best for her to come back after a good cry. "See you to-morrow, then." Leaving her office, he stopped at Traci's desk and called the car service. He knew the number by heart. The station used the same service for all their executives and guests. For his next call he waited until he was in his office with the door closed. The phone was answered on the second ring.

"Zachary Holman."

"Zachary, it's Gordon."

"Are Madison and Manda all right?" he questioned sharply.

"Manda seems fine. I'm not so sure about Madison," Gordon said, sitting on the edge of the desk.

"Why? What's the matter?" Zachary asked anxiously.

"I was hoping you could tell me," Gordon said. "She's hasn't been the same since she came back to work from the weekend."

There was a brief moment of silence before Zachary, his tone guarded, said, "Maybe she's just having trouble getting back into the routine."

Gordon tapped his gold pen on his desk. "It's more than that. Camille was here and both of them ended their meeting upset."

"What happened? Did she upset Madison?" Zachary's voice took on a hard edge.

Gordon had to make himself not take offense. The pen in his hand stilled. "I don't know who did what. Neither is talking."

His tone strained, Zachary said, "I can't help you."

"I thought you cared about her."

"Sometimes that's not enough," Zachary said quietly.

Gordon thought about Camille. "Don't I know it."

"Just take care of her."

"I'll do my best." Gordon hung up the phone, no closer to learning what was going on now than he had been thirty minutes ago. Once he had been the best investigative reporter in the business. He was definitely losing his touch.

Picking up the phone again, he dialed Camille's cell number, then her work number, and got her answering machine or voice mail each time. She could be busy, but he had a bad feeling that their relationship had just hit another bumpy patch.

Chapter 27

Helen couldn't believe her good fortune. She could have jumped with glee when she saw Madison, head down, coming down the hall toward her. She wasn't smiling and playing with the brat as she usually was. If the scuttlebutt around the station was true, Madison wasn't too happy these days . . . except with the kid. That wouldn't be for long, though. Helen planned to see to that.

For more nights than she'd cared to remember, she and Edward had sat outside Madison's home, and for what? One lousy picture of her hugging the carpenter. They probably were going at it hot and heavy after they went inside. The cowardly Edward hadn't wanted to sneak around to the back to try and get another shot, but Helen wasn't giving up. She'd go back by herself if necessary.

Since she had gone to Madison's house after the funeral, the guards at the gate remembered her and always let her in. No way she wasn't going to see this through. She wanted Madison's job and she was getting it.

"Leaving early, Madison?" Helen asked sweetly.

Madison's head came up and she stared straight into Helen's smirking face. Of all the people she could have run into while she was upset, Madison couldn't think of a worse one. "Yes."

Madison knew her shaky voice had betrayed her when Helen's smirk grew.

"Getting settled back in all right?"

"Yes. If you'll excuse me, Gordon called the car service and the driver is probably waiting," Madison said, clutching Manda to her.

The smirk vanished. "I can't even get the station to pay for a lousy refrigerator in my office and you have a driver at your beck and call."

Madison had no intention of pointing out that it was in her contract or that she hadn't used the service before Manda or that Helen was only two doors down from the lounge. "Excuse me."

"Cute kid." Helen reached toward Manda.

Manda burrowed against Madison at the same time Madison stepped back. The hatred that flashed across Helen's face had Madison wanting to step back farther. "She's shy. Good-bye, Helen." Madison hurried to the front door, her skin prickling with unease.

After a glance at the readout on her pager, Camille ignored the vibration of her beeper. She had nothing to say to Gordon. And if he thought he was getting her into bed tonight or any other night, he was very much mistaken.

Leaving the courthouse, she slipped into her car just as the meter clicked off. The case she was slated to testify in had been canceled. The defendant's lawyer had said he hadn't had enough time to prepare his client's case. Six months was more than enough, but by getting a contingency, the bruises on his wife's face would be less noticeable. Thank goodness the children were in foster care. The wife, however, kept going back.

Camille's temper kicked up a notch when she thought of the woman's battered face in the emergency room last night, of her sticking to her pitiful story that she had tripped in the dark. An imbecile could tell that was a lie. All the time her husband, who outweighed her by seventy-five pounds, watched her with cold eyes that promised retribution if she didn't lie to keep his sorry butt out of jail.

And people wondered why she didn't give, why she pushed.

Turning up the air-conditioning to full-blast, she drove down the side street then made a U-turn onto Commerce, heading for her office on Central Expressway. She was too keyed-up and too angry to do a home visit. There was always paperwork at her office.

Downtown traffic snarled. Pedestrians jaywalked. City buses pulled in front of cars with only the briefest signal. Everything was normal. Sighing, she glanced over and saw a sign on the specialty-store glass window that caused her to perk up. LAST CALL.

Clicking on her signal, she ignored the blast of the car horn behind her until she could pull into the far left lane and the store's parking lot. She considered it a stroke of good fortune when the attendant put up a LOT FULL sign behind her car. Finally, something was going right in her day.

Madison couldn't shut her mind off. The more she tried, the more Zachary's face intruded. In the backseat next to her Manda sat quietly in her car seat with one tiny arm circling the neck of her teddy bear as the limo crept through the heavy downtown traffic toward Central Expressway.

Her silence added to Madison's worries.

Manda was usually a whirlwind of action and loved to try to talk. Today had been different. Intuitively she had picked up on Madison's growing discontent. It made no difference if Madison smiled or not, Manda seemed to know if her heart was in it.

She had to snap out of it. But how? Looking out the window, she saw the LAST CALL sign and considered the possibilities. It had been a long time since she had indulged in a frantic search through racks or on tables for the deal of a lifetime. With her six-figure salary she had the money to buy what she wanted, but her time was at a premium; that was why she had Cindi. But if she went home now, what would she do?

Think of Zachary and mope.

Leaning over, she hit the intercom. "Stanley, pull over."

Madison knew exactly where she wanted to shop first. Ladies' Shoes, located on the first floor. Manolo Blahnik wouldn't be on sale, but it wouldn't hurt to look at the latest style of the most coveted shoe of women today.

As expected, the area was a beehive of activity, LAST CALL sales at Neiman Marcus always were. Salespersons rushed to and fro with boxes of shoes, women sat in comfortable leather chairs or waited at the pickup area for shoes already purchased during the presale. Madison hefted Manda in her arms.

She'd left her bag and the carriage in the limo because she'd known how congested the area would be. Her platinum card tucked in the pocket of her double-breasted navy blazer was all she needed. She kissed Manda on the cheek.

"First lesson in shopping. Shoes can make or break an outfit and, despite what some people say, a black, white, or bone shoe does not go with everything."

Madison picked up a mauve, hand-crafted shoe with narrow stripes of leather over the toe and around the ankle. "Now, this is a shoe." Sexy. That was the only word for the Manolo Blahnik. Seven hundred ninety-five dollars and worth every penny . . . if a woman wanted to impress the right man or indulge herself. Since Madison wanted to do neither, she replaced the shoe on the elongated rosewood table and headed for the sales rack. She might have money, but she had enough of her mother in her to keep an eye out for a bargain.

While Madison was looking, Manda promptly pulled a shoe from the upright rack. By the time Madison had that one out of her hand and back on the rack, she had grabbed another. This time Madison stepped out of the aisle of shoes. "Mustn't touch, sweetheart."

Not wanting to give Manda another chance to get any

shoes, but just as reluctant not to place the shoe back where it belonged, Madison tried to figure out what to do.

"I'll put it back for you."

Madison turned toward the softly spoken voice, words of thanks forming on her tongue until she saw the social worker. She hesitated, then held out the shoe. "Thank you."

Taking the shoe, Camille replaced it on the rack and walked around to the other side. Madison could go upstairs to the children's department as she'd planned, or she could do something else her mother had taught her. "Ms. Jacobs, can I please speak with you?"

Camille stared at the Ferragamo slingback pump in her hand a moment longer, then put the pewter-colored shoe back. "What about?"

The woman wasn't going to make this easy for Madison and she couldn't blame her. "My behavior in my office earlier. Perhaps we can find a seat by the espresso bar."

"All right."

Madison made her way to the cozy area tucked between the escalator and the cases of rich and exclusive chocolates. Sitting on the three-foot-high stool, she pushed the napkin holder out of Manda's reach. The baby promptly began slapping her hand against the smooth surface of the small round table. "She likes to pretend she's a drummer," Madison said indulgently.

"Children should be allowed to express themselves."

Madison almost sighed. The words were stiff and formal. "I overreacted in my office and I apologize. It wasn't your fault, but you took the fall out. I don't want you to write in your report that I'm difficult."

"Are you apologizing so you'll look better in my report?"

"I'm apologizing because I was wrong," she told her, her voice barely short of snapping. Her eyes closed. "Sorry."

"You want to talk about it?" Camille asked softly.

Zachary's name almost tumbled out of her mouth. "No."

Shrewd eyes measured her. "Would it have anything to do with Mr. Holman?"

Madison straightened with a desperate look on her face. She barely kept from spluttering. "Why do you say that?"

Camille pulled the chain strap of the Prada bag from her shoulder and placed the lavender quilted leather bag on the round table. "Perhaps because when I mentioned his name earlier you got the same shell-shocked look you have in your eyes now."

"He's just a friend," Madison said, and felt her face heat. A kiss from a friend did not make your body burn with heat and desire.

Camille folded her hands and placed them beside her bag. "People who were in a happy marriage are far more likely to enter into a relationship quicker after losing a partner than those who were unhappy."

"I have no intention of entering into a relationship with Zachary or anyone else," Madison told her, her irritation growing. "Why do you insist on thinking there is something between Zachary and me?"

"Perhaps because I look at you and see me. Perhaps because I know what it is to have mixed feelings about a man and not know what to do about them," Camille told her.

"Gordon," Madison guessed.

Camille's sigh was long-suffering. "For the first time in years I've met a man I could really care about, but he could also hurt me."

Madison shifted Manda on her leg. "Gordon's my friend and boss. Why would you tell me something like that?"

"If I expect you to trust me, I have to be honest with you." She brushed her hair behind her ear. "Besides, talking helps and I was hoping that we could be friends."

Madison wanted to talk with someone. But there were secrets she couldn't share with Manda's caseworker. "Is that possible given the circumstances?"

"We could try," Camille suggested, her willingness obvious by the burgeoning smile on her face.

Madison realized the decision was hers. Wasn't it about time she took the next step in taking control of her life again?

And that meant friends. "So, I gather you're upset with Gordon."

Camille's pleasant expression vanished. "I met him after I left your office, and he immediately assumed the worse of me."

"I'm sorry. That's my fault," Madison said, trying to help Gordon out. He obviously cared about Camille. "I treated you badly—"

Camille interrupted with her upraised hand. "No matter what, he should have known I would never treat a client unfairly. I was doing just fine before he pushed his way into my life. Why do men always make life so complicated?"

"Why do we let them?" Madison asked with a twist of her lips.

"Touché."

"Can I get you ladies anything?" asked the smiling young waiter as he came up to their table.

Camille propped her elbows on the table and rested her chin on her folded hands. "What do you have that's super-high in calories, and decadent? Preferably with chocolate and strawberries."

His smile broadened. "Chocolate supreme. A double chocolate brownie topped with freshly made ice cream, slivers of chocolate, and strawberries."

"I'll have that."

"Make that two. Bring the baby a bowl of vanilla yogurt," Madison said. The women looked at each other and smiled. The next best thing to shopping when it came to getting over your blues was indulging yourself with mounds of calories.

In less than a minute their orders were sitting before them. The two-inch-thick brownie was at least five inches across and piled nearly as high with toppings. Manda reached with both hands for the strawberry on top that was as big as her fist. Madison deftly moved the dessert aside and gave the baby yogurt instead.

"Very well done," Camille said, taking a bite and moaning

in pleasure. "Good stuff. Push her bowl over and I'll help feed her. That way you'll get a chance to eat."

Madison gave Manda another bite. "Thanks, but I'm not sure if she'll let you feed her."

"As long as you're holding her, it shouldn't be a problem." Camille held her hand out. "You or Mr. Holman won't be able to be with her all the time."

Madison handed the other woman the spoon. Manda looked at Camille, then back at Madison. "It's all right, sweetheart. I'm not going anyplace."

Manda inched forward and opened her mouth wide to receive the yogurt. Both women grinned as the baby smacked her lips. Between the two of them they managed to eat and feed Manda. Madison didn't know if it was the chocolate high that loosened her tongue or brain freeze from the ice cream that made her say, "Zachary bothers me. I mean, he doesn't bother me . . . you know what I mean."

Camille licked her spoon elegantly. "You're preaching to the choir."

Madison scrunched up her nose. "It's so annoying. Why did things have to change? There's enough going on in my life right now." She wiped Manda's sticky hands.

"Life seldom takes a full schedule or being inconvenienced into consideration," Camille said philosophically. "I'm breaking my date with Gordon tonight, but if I know him, he'll be banging on my door anyway. That's one man who can't take no, and I'm not all that sure how long I'll be able to keep saying no if he gets too close."

Madison knew exactly what she meant. Hadn't she been hiding from Zachary because she was too scared to find out where their attraction might lead? "Zachary can be pushy, too. He's coming over tonight." She grimaced, then straightened, a small grin curving her mouth. "You know, I think we should forget about them for one night and do something for ourselves."

Camille pushed her empty dish aside. "I'm listening."

* * *

Louis almost had the information he needed. Calling and trying to speak to Velma Taylor certainly hadn't worked. She'd refused to talk to him. Now the old bat wouldn't even take his calls. That grated on Louis most of all. Everyone took his calls. He'd even tried using other names and disguising his voice, but the results were the same. She'd hang up on him. He'd have to go in person and catch her offguard. He had his story ready.

Annoyed, he stood and began to pace. The damn president of the Chicago station was breathing down his neck for a decision. If Madison wasn't going to sign, they needed to start looking for someone else. Louis had felt like going though the phone and giving the bastard a hard kick to the balls. The prick had promised they'd hold off on a decision. It might be a scare tactic, but he wasn't taking any chances. He wasn't losing out on the money.

Just this week a manufacturer of baby furniture had called to inquire about Manda doing commercials for them. With all the baby stuff out there, the kid might be worth almost as much as Madison. Too much money was involved for Madison to mess this up for him.

"Southwest Airline Flight 102 for Amarillo is now ready to board."

Louis picked up his briefcase and watched passengers rush to the three boarding sections. His displeasure inched up a knot. The damn airline didn't even have first class or seating assignments. He wasn't used to waiting and hadn't flown coach in fifteen years. And just as bad was the ban on smoking in the entire airport. For all his inconveniences someone was going to pay a high price.

He'd considered hiring someone, but he'd known too many occasions when confidentiality was tossed aside for the right price. He had to get the information himself. Passengers jostled him trying to board the aircraft. His aggravation turned to anger. With all he had to endure, the old lady better not give him any guff. He wanted proof that Wes was the kid's father, then he was going to nail Madison to the wall.

Louis walked out of Amarillo International Airport at 7:50 P.M. and hailed a cab. He had exactly one hour to get what he needed and get back for his 8:50 flight back to Dallas. The last one of the night. There was no way he was staying in this hick town overnight.

Puffing on his cigar, he got into the backseat of the cab and gave the address of the nursing home. His fake beard itched, but he didn't dare scratch it. He wanted to do nothing that would attract attention. He was just another Westerner going to visit a relative. He'd dressed the part in denim, boots, and straw hat. He'd thought of everything.

Zachary thought he was prepared for anything when he arrived at Madison's house that night, but quickly found he was wrong when she met him at the door with a cordial greeting, acting as if she didn't have a care in the world. Passing Manda to him, she politely informed him she was going to a movie with a girlfriend. A few minutes later, she went out the door with a wave.

Despite it being intrusive and nosy, he went to the window just in time to see her get inside a late-model Lexus. He recognized the driver as Camille Jacobs. Seems they had patched up their problems. Too bad he and Madison couldn't do the same.

Gordon's fingers and knuckles were sore from ringing the unanswered doorbell and rapping on Camille's door. She either wasn't going to answer or she wasn't in. Either way, it peeved him. It was almost eight. They had a seven-thirty date to go to the ballpark for a Rangers baseball game. Even if she'd left a message on his answering machine at home and called his office to cancel, wasn't there an unwritten rule that you weren't supposed to cancel without giving the other person at least eight hours notice?

Hands deep in his pocket, grumbling every step of the way, Gordon went to his car. If he was dateless, someone was giving him an explanation. Madison might be calm enough by now to tell him what happened at the station with Camille. At least he'd have something to go on if she ever talked to him again.

He arrived at Madison's house twenty-one minutes later. "What do you mean, they went to a movie?"

"Just that." Zachary leaned back on the leather seat in the den. "They're doing fine without us."

Gordon said one explicit word under his breath, then glanced guiltily around the room.

"She's asleep," Zachary said, picking up a deck of cards from the coffee table. "You want to play a game until they get back?"

Unknotting his tie, Gordon pulled off his jacket and took a seat. "Deal."

Louis paid the cab with rumpled five and tens, and waited on his chance. The nursing home was a single-story nondescript beige building. Adjusting his hat, he went inside. Thanks to his inquiry about placing his grandmother there with her "good friend" Velma Taylor, he knew the layout and where the Taylor woman's room was located.

In less than a minute, he stood in front of Velma Taylor's door. Checking the hall, he entered. The only light in the room came from the eighteen-inch color TV in the far corner of the room. A small woman lay in bed with her eyes closed, her eyeglasses askew on her face. Louis wasn't a man to lose an opportunity. Silently he crept to the nightstand and inched open the drawer. He pounced on the worn Bible, then slung it back. Manda's birth was recorded there, but the space for the father's name was blank.

Finding nothing about Manda or her mother besides

pictures and some worthless old Mother's Day and birthday cards they'd sent, he went to the double dresser which proved just as futile. Frustrated, he shoved the drawer back more forcefully than he had intended.

"Wh-what?"

By the time Velma had sat up and righted her glasses, Louis was beside the bed, smiling and charming. "How do you do, Miss Taylor. I'm sorry to disturb you. My name is Henry Allen, attorney-at-law. Madison Reed sent me because she wanted you to hear this in person." He forced sadness to his face. "I have some unfortunate news for you. Manda is critically ill and it's imperative that we learn the identity of the father to help her get well."

What little color in the woman's face drained away. "My Bridget's baby is sick? Oh Lord. Oh Lord."

Louis nodded gravely. "There's a problem with her blood. If you'll just tell me the name of the father, we'll contact him."

Tears streamed down the woman's thin cheeks. "Oh Lord. Oh Lord. Not the baby. Not the baby too."

The wailing and all the crying was beginning to grate on his nerves. "We need the name."

"The Bible says He won't put more on us than we can bear." Her sobs grew louder, more desolate.

Louis gritted his teeth. "Stop crying and tell me the name of the damn kid's father."

Velma jumped at the crudeness of the language and the angry tone.

"The name!" he snapped when she continued to stare at him with her mouth agape. "I don't have all night. Don't you want to save the kid?"

Velma's tears stopped as quickly as they had started. Leaning toward Louis, she squinted to get a better look at his face. "Where's the other lawyer?"

"He's sick," Louis put in smoothly, trying to hide his escalating anger. He'd thought she'd be so upset about the kid being ill that she'd tell him what he wanted immediately. "He sent me in his place. Ms. Reed needs to know the name of the baby's father so she can contact him and help the baby."

"You're lyin'. If anythin' hadda happened to Manda, Miss Reed woulda called. You're lyin' and I'm gonna call the nurse." Velma leaned toward the call button, but before she could reach it a sharp pain sliced though her. She gasped and clutched her chest with both hands.

Louis's eyes widened as the old woman slumped back against the pillows, her face pale, her breathing rapid and shallow. Spit dried in his mouth. Damn! She was having a heart attack! He couldn't get out the door fast enough.

Chapter 28

The movie was a melodrama where the hero died in the heroine's arms after saving her life. Disgusted with an ending that left another woman lonely and miserable, Camille and Madison walked out before the credits started to roll.

"That's Gordon's car," Madison said as Camille pulled into her driveway. "What are you going to do?"

"Stay away from him until I'm completely over him," she said without hesitation as she came to a stop.

Madison's hand paused on the door handle. "As men go, he's one of thc best."

Camille drew in a shaky breath. "I know. That's why this is so hard. If he were a user, I wouldn't waste a second of my time thinking about him. He cooks for me, gives marvelous foot rubs, and when he kisses me I just come undone."

She and Camille might be developing a friendship, but Madison wasn't ready to share her kiss with Zachary just yet. The front door of the house opened. Zachary and Gordon stood framed in the light, then Gordon moved off the porch. "Looks like Gordon has other ideas," Madison said.

"Oh my," she said with rising panic in her voice. "'Night, Madison."

"Good night." Madison hurriedly got out. The door had barely closed before Camille backed up and took off down the street.

"Camille," Gordon yelled, running a few steps after her

fleeing car. When she didn't stop he turned to Madison, his handsome face fierce. "You knew I wanted to talk with her. Why didn't you stay in the car?"

Madison's chin lifted. "Because she didn't want to talk with you and neither do I at the moment." Passing him, she went up the walkway to the door where Zachary waited. "Thanks for keeping Manda. Good night." She closed the door with him on the outside.

Zachary marched up to Gordon. "See what you caused."

"I wanted to talk with Camille, and Madison knew it," Gordon said, peeved with both women.

"Well, I wanted to spend some time with Madison, and you knew it," Zachary shot back.

"Damn!"

Zachary's eyes narrowed. "You're gonna have to watch your language around Manda."

Gordon studied Zachary's tense features closely. "You think you'll be around to chastise me if I don't?"

"Count on it," he answered with complete assurance.

"Then you're not giving up?" Gordon asked, already having guessed the answer.

"Not in this lifetime." Zachary started toward his truck.

Gordon fell into step beside him. "You know it won't be easy."

Zachary opened the door to his truck. "Most things worthwhile aren't."

Gordon activated the locks on his car. "See you around."

"Like I said, count on it."

Madison had dreamed of Zachary—a dream so erotic that, even awake, it caused her cheeks to heat, her body to yearn. She vividly remembered how he'd slowly undressed her, his lips and hands everywhere. She'd trembled beneath his touch. There had been no hesitation, no worries, only the two of them, uninhibited and needy. His mouth had been hot and avid on her breasts, her stomach. He'd savored and lingered.

Frantic with need, she had whimpered for him to come into her and, when he had, she'd come apart in his arms.

Standing in front of the vanity mirror, Madison's nipples pouted beneath her sheer, ivory-colored camisole, in memory and anticipation, but this time there was no greedy mouth to take the turgid nipple and gently suckle. No slow hand to knead and stroke and drive her wild with longing.

"Stop it, Madison," she chastised herself. If she expected to get over whatever it was, she had to stop thinking about him. With jerky movements she pulled on her blouse and trousers.

The phone on the nightstand rang. She threw it a nasty look. Whoever the reporter was, he or she was very enterprising to call before seven A.M. She slipped the gold hoop through her pierced ear lobe as the answering machine clicked on.

"Ms. Reed, this is Harriet Gamble, the head nurse at Green Oaks Convalescent Center in Amarillo. I have some bad news for you."

Madison snatched up the receiver. "What is it?"

"Is this Ms. Reed?" the woman asked.

"Yes, I'm Ms. Reed. Is there a problem with Ms. Taylor?"

"She having some chest pains and some difficulty breathing. I thought it best she be taken to the hospital and checked out. Her doctor is meeting her there. The ambulance just left. You asked us to notify you if we had any concerns."

Not again, Madison thought. "Yes. Thank you. How . . . how bad is it? Do you think it's her heart?"

"I'm sorry, but nurses don't diagnose. But it might be best if you could come," the nurse said. "She's been taken to Amarillo General."

Madison glanced at Manda in the crib. How much more would be taken from her? "I'll have to make travel arrangements, but I'll be there as soon as possible. Thank you for calling."

"You're welcome. Velma is a favorite here. I've never seen her as upset as she was this morning. She seemed worried about Manda—is she all right?"

"Yes," Madison answered, looking again toward the crib.

"That's good news. She worried herself sick about who would take care of the baby until your lawyer arrived," the nurse said. "She showed off the pictures you sent to everyone. She's a wonderful woman. We're all praying for her."

"Thank you." Hanging up the phone, Madison walked to the crib and picked up Manda and hugged her. "I'm so sorry, sweetheart."

Zachary knew exactly what he wanted to say, had rehearsed it several times on his way to Madison's house that morning. However, when she yanked open the door, her eyes frantic, he forgot all about his speech saying she had kicked him out last night before he had gotten his cap. "What's the matter?"

"It's Velma Taylor. The nurse called this morning. She had trouble breathing, and chest pains. She was taken by ambulance to the hospital. I called, but I can't get any information. I thought you were my driver coming to take me to the airport." Biting her lip, she scanned the empty driveway.

"I'll take you. Where's Manda?" Stepping inside, he closed the door.

"In her playpen." Madison went into the den and picked the baby up. "You don't have to bother. Stanley should be here shortly."

Zachary didn't plan to argue. He simply stuck the Birkin under his arm, picked up the carriage and suitcase, then headed for his truck. "What time is your plane?"

"Zacha—"

He turned and stared down at her. "Let me help you, Madison. Please. I don't want you to go by yourself."

Madison stared back at him. Relief she didn't want to feel, swept through her. She nodded. "We have the nine A.M. flight out of Love Field."

He didn't have to glance at his watch to know it was 7:45. "With morning rush-hour traffic it'll take at least forty-five minutes to reach Love Field."

"It can't be helped," she said, following him out to his

truck. "I didn't get the call until almost seven and I had to pack and call the station. The next flight isn't until after twelve and I wanted to get there as quickly as possible."

He put the things in the truck's club cab before facing her. "Madison, I'm not criticizing. You got a lot accomplished in a short period of time. Let's get the rest and head for the airport."

"I think I have everything. I've never done this before, but I didn't want to leave her with anyone."

She looked so frenzied he wanted to take her in his arms to reassure her, but now wasn't the time. He reached for Manda. She gave a delighted laugh and came willingly. "Go make a final check of the house and we'll leave."

"I'll be right back."

Zachary pulled out his cell phone. He had a few calls to make.

They arrived at Love Field at 8:49. They sprinted all the way to their gate. Passengers were already lined up at the door, waiting to be the first to board, to grab the best unassigned seating.

Out of breath, Madison dug in the Birkin for her wallet. "I'm flying ticketless." She barely glanced at the questions taped on the counter asking if the passenger had been approached by anyone to take a package or if they had left their bags unattended. "No and no."

Used to passengers answering the questions before being asked, the young ticket agent smiled and gave Madison a blue boarding pass. "Is the baby flying with you?"

"Yes," she answered, trying to catch her breath and watching the growing number of people gathered around the entrance door to board the plane.

Frowning, he typed more information into the computer. "I don't see that you purchased another seat. You'll have to hold her and leave her car seat outside the gate. We'll make sure it and the carriage arrives safely. The preboarding area for passengers with small children is to the right."

Madison pulled out a credit card. It was safer for infants to travel on airplanes in their car seats. "Then I need to buy her a seat."

"Sorry. We don't sell tickets at this counter and you don't have time to go purchase one."

"She has a seat." Zachary stepped up and placed his driver's license on the counter. "I have two seats for us. The answers are no and no."

"You're going with us?" she asked.

"Did you think I wouldn't?"

"Here you go." The agent placed the boarding passes on the counter. "You better hurry if you want to have a few minutes to get on board and get settled."

"Thanks." Grabbing Madison's arm, Zachary went through the preboarding area and down the ramp. Leaving the carriage outside the door of the plane, they took the first three seats: "More leg room." Storing Madison's carry-ons, he helped her install the car seat between them.

"What about your company?" she asked, reaching for her seat belt.

"They can handle things until we can get back."

Eyes wide, her hands paused. "You plan to stay with us the entire time?"

His gaze held hers. "Where else would I stay?"

Madison busied herself with her seat belt, her mind recalling the dream all too clearly. Her body heated, her blood pulsed. Why couldn't her driver have arrived ten minutes early instead of ten minutes late?

"Camille, I thought you'd like to know that Madison had to go out of town unexpectedly. Manda's great-aunt is ill. She took Manda with her. Good-bye."

Gordon hung up the phone in his office at the TV station, propped his elbows on his desk and linked his fingers. He'd never heard Madison sound as rattled as she had that morning. She'd insisted she didn't need anyone to go with her.

Not knowing what the situation might be in Amarillo, Gordon didn't agree. He'd immediately thought to call Zachary, but he'd left Zach's business card at his office. He hadn't thought he'd need it away from work.

The only recourse Gordon had been able to think of was to call the car service and delay the driver and hope that causing her to be held up an hour wasn't the wrong thing to do. He was almost at the station when the dispatcher had called to let him know that Madison had canceled the car. Mr. Holman was taking her to the airport.

The ringing of his private line dragged him back to the present. He glanced at the readout and unlinked his hands. Camille Jacobs. She'd call for her clients, but wouldn't give the man she had been sleeping with for the past week the same courtesy.

While he admired her professionalism and work ethic, the way she had shoved him out of her life angered the hell out of him. But he'd be damned if he'd let her know it . . . at least not yet. "Gordon Armstrong speaking."

"Gordon, thank you for calling. Did Madison know the extent of Ms. Taylor's illness?" Camille asked, her voice filled with concern.

Now she called him by his first name. "All the nurse could tell Madison was that Manda's great aunt had had trouble breathing, and chest pains. She was taken to an area hospital for evaluation."

"Did Madison go by herself?"

Gordon wished he could see her face when he answered. "Zachary went with her."

"I see."

He leaned back in his chair. Camille used that phrase when she was puzzled. He intended to give her something else to rack her pretty little brain over. "I hate to run, but I have another appointment."

"Oh, I didn't mean to keep you."

He'd caught her by surprise that time. She actually sounded

flustered. Welcome to the club. "No problem. By the way, I wanted you to know that I regret interfering at the studio between you and Madison. Rest assured it won't happen again. Good-bye."

"G-good-bye."

Gordon hung up the phone, pleased that he'd been able to slip in his apology. Last night, standing under the spray of cold water, he'd decided he'd handled the situation all wrong. She had a right to be upset with him. Camille went to bat for her kids with her heart and soul. Judging her had been wrong and totally out of line. In any relationship there had to be trust. He'd let his apology sink in, then he'd hit her with phase two.

Louis woke up with a hangover. Half a bottle of aged scotch sat on his nightstand. It had been full last night. Sitting on the side of the bed, he rested his head in his hands. *What if the old woman died and Madison found out?* He didn't have to think long to know that his hide, not hers, would be the one nailed to the wall. He might even face prosecution. Sweat beaded on his forehead and in his armpits.

Louis grabbed the bottle. His hands shook so hard the neck of the bottle tap-danced against the squat glass. Disgusted with his own fear and lack of control, he slammed both down, then came unsteadily to his feet, swiping his trembling hand over his face as he did so.

He had to think. He was smart. There was nothing to connect him to Velma Taylor. He'd paid cash for the ticket. It would take an act of Congress to get the flight manifest. He'd taken off the beard in an airport bathroom, then put it in his briefcase before he went to the ticket counter. He was in the clear. All he had to do was stay calm. He could still come out on top, exactly where he deserved to be.

Thank God for Zachary, Madison thought. He'd made the difficult trip flawless.

He stopped the rental truck at an airport toll booth and dug in his pocket for change. "After we see how Miss Taylor is doing, we'll check in to a hotel so Manda can eat and have her nap."

Madison's mind went where it shouldn't go again—she and Zachary wrapped together in sizzling passion. Her breath tangled in her throat. Aroused and flustered, she stared straight ahead and mumbled, "I forgot to get the address of the hospital."

Zachary pulled off. "I'll find it."

Madison's first glimpse of Amarillo General Hospital brought back painful memories of Wes's death. But this time she mourned rather than cursed him, and thanked God that she had moved beyond the pain and started to heal.

"You all right?" Zachary asked as he cut off the motor.

She was glad that in this she could be truthful. "Yes."

Without a word, he unstrapped Manda, picked her up, then came around the truck. She thought he'd take her arm. He curved his arm around her shoulder. Giving in to her own need, she didn't pull away.

Velma Taylor lay quietly in her bed. Her mocha-colored face was heavily lined, her eyes closed. The end of a single plait of gray hair stopped just below her thin shoulder.

"Are you sure she's going to be all right?" Madison asked, remembering all too well what had happened to Wes. At least Miss Taylor's condition wasn't critical.

Greg Wood, the male RN assigned to Velma, smiled in practiced reassurance. "Her heart attack was a mild one, and there was no damage to any major vessels. She'll be out of here by tomorrow and back in the nursing home. She's on mild sedation so she can rest." He leaned over and closed his hand over Velma's. "Miss Taylor, you have visitors all the way from Dallas to see you. Miss Taylor?"

Velma Taylor's eyelashes fluttered, then lifted. Her eyes were slightly opaque. "What'd you say?"

"Visitors," the nurse repeated, stepping back. "You can stay for a little while. The doctor doesn't want her to overexert herself."

Madison stepped closer to the bed as the nurse moved aside. "Miss Taylor, it's Madison Reed. I've bought Manda with me."

"Manda? Bridget's baby?" she asked, trying to lift her head from the pillow.

"Yes. That's right." Madison gently laid her hand on the woman's frail shoulder. "Please, just rest. We'll be back later when you're more awake and we can visit and you can see Manda. She's just fine."

Tears formed in the woman's eyes. "Wish I could see Bridget, but she's gone. She's gone."

"But Manda is here." Hoping, praying that Manda remembered her aunt, and that the machines didn't frighten her, Madison lifted a silent Manda from Zachary and placed her small hand on the woman's. "Manda's here. That's her hand you feel on yours."

"My baby's baby is here. Lord, how I prayed she was safe. Thank you." Her eyes drifted closed.

For a long time, Madison stared down at the older woman, then pulled Manda to her.

Driving away from the hospital, Zachary could no longer put off the inevitable. "Do you want to get a room where there's a refrigerator and a stove for Manda's food?"

"Y-yes. I—I guess so."

Zachary heard the nervousness in Madison's voice and wished he could reassure her that he wasn't going to make a move on her. He couldn't. He wanted her mouth on his, burning and frenzied, more than he wanted his next breath. But she was going through too much for him to add to her troubles. She might be worried about Velma Taylor now, but sooner or later her thoughts would turn to Manda's mother and Wes. He wished he knew how she'd handle the situation.

"I told the nurse I'd call and let him know where we're

staying. They'll call us when Miss Taylor is awake and feeling like having visitors," Zachary said. "We might as well stop at a store and get everything we need now."

"That sounds fine."

Zachary flexed his fingers on the steering wheel. If she were any more stiff or formal, she'd break. His fault. Spotting a Super K up ahead, he pulled into the parking lot of the store. It was going to be a long day.

It took three tries to find a hotel suite with two bedrooms and the amenities they wanted. Madison didn't say anything after the first time Zachary came back to the truck and told her why he hadn't gotten them a room. Although she wasn't particularly looking forward to being in such close proximity to Zachary, she wouldn't be able to watch Manda every moment by herself.

"This all right?"

"It's fine." Madison walked farther into the two-bedroom suite. The sofa was covered in a soft floral print with matching draperies. Each bedroom had a double bed. She estimated there would be just enough room in the second bedroom to squeeze in the crib for Manda that housekeeping had promised to deliver later.

He placed the Birkin on the bed. "I'll bring everything in. You and Manda take a nap."

She wrinkled her nose. "I think I'm a little old for a nap. Besides, it's just a little after one."

He stopped on going out the door. "You said you sometimes lay down when she did."

The man never forgot a thing. "That was before I started back to work."

"The way Manda's rubbing her eyes, she's about to go out. It wouldn't hurt for you to stretch out beside her."

"What are you going to do?"

He went to the bedroom door. "Don't worry about me."

She did. "You didn't buy anything for yourself at the store except a baseball cap."

"No need. I keep a change of clothes in the truck. It's in the small duffel I brought in. I never know if I have to visit a client, so I stay prepared."

She remembered the bag. She just hoped a pair of pajamas were inside. "Thank you for coming. I don't know how we would have gotten along without you."

"My pleasure." Then he was gone.

"My pleasure." Madison pulled a diaper out of the bag to change Manda, but her thoughts were on Zachary.

Chapter 29

The call from the hospital came a little after four that afternoon. They found Velma sitting up in bed in a pretty blue gown, her hair in a coronet on her head, but her eyes remained opaque. "Fighting glaucoma and cataract. Doctor can't do anything with this high blood pressure. Now, after this, I guess I won't never see any better."

Sitting by the bed with Manda in her lap, Madison placed her hand on Velma's. "Would you like to see another specialist? Cost is no problem."

"Bless you, child. That's awfully sweet and generous of you, but like I said, Bridget's friend already sent me." She shook her head. "No sense wastin' good money."

Manda squealed.

Velma turned toward the sound, her smile growing. "Does this old heart good to hear her so happy. Wish I could see her better." Her face clouded. "That hateful man said she was ill."

"What man?" Zachary asked, nearing the bed. He'd hung back to let the women visit.

"He came to my room last night. A noise woke me up and he was standing over my bed. Said he was a lawyer and that Miss Reed sent him. He said Manda was deathly ill," she told them. "I believed him at first, until he started yelling and talking mean. That other lawyer you sent was soft-spoken and he kept asking me if I was all right. If I needed anything."

"Most likely he was a reporter or was paid by some tabloid. I'd hoped they wouldn't bother you," Madison said, regretting the incident.

"Some people just don't have any home training. After I guessed he was lying I reached for the call button." Her hand rubbed her chest. The heart monitor spiked, then settled. "The pain hit and he left."

"He didn't try to get you any help?" Madison asked, angrier than she had been in a long time. Zachary touched her rigid shoulder.

"No. He just left. I managed to take one of my nitro tablets. The pain eased up and I felt better for a while, but I just couldn't stop worryin'. Guess my heart couldn't take it." Her frail hand reached out to touch Manda's curly head. "I know I should have called you, but part of me was afraid he was tellin' the truth."

"That's understandable," Zachary said. "The reporter is at fault, not you. Was there anything you remember about him that might help identity him?"

"No." Miss Taylor sighed in regret. "I was just too upset."

"I'll look into it anyway. Maybe someone saw something."

"Would you like us to have your room changed or do you want to go to another facility?" Madison asked.

Velma's small chin jutted. "Ain't nobody running me from here. This is close to my church and my friends. I won't be fooled next time. What he wanted to know, I couldn't tell him anyhow."

"What was that?" Madison asked, keeping Manda entertained by patting her hands together.

"Who Manda's daddy was."

Madison stilled. Fear knotted her stomach. The reporter might just have been digging for information or he might suspect the connection between Wes and Manda.

Velma's quiet voice was filled with sadness when she continued. "Bridget never said much about him. I raised her to be a good girl. She went to college, got that teaching degree. Never had a moment's trouble out of her. She was so happy when she found out about the baby. Thought he'd marry her. He never did."

Madison didn't want to hear about Wes and his mistress. Unconsciously she started to rise. Zachary's hand on her shoulder calmed and steadied her. She eased back in her seat.

"My baby loved that man," Velma said softly. "I guess I should have known it wouldn't work out like she wanted, but I kept hoping and praying. My baby was a good girl. She deserved to be happy. Now she won't ever be."

Zachary watched Madison and could do nothing about the pain he saw etched in her face. His free hand clenched into a tight fist.

Velma wiped her eyes with the tissue in her hand. "I hoped you'd come so I could tell you in person, make you understand so you'd tell Manda when she got older, help her understand that her mother wasn't no fast woman. She went to church, sang in the choir, but just like her mother she fell in love with the wrong man. Like her mother, she left a child behind. You believe me, don't you?"

"I believe you," Madison said, her eyes stinging with unshed tears.

Velma nodded her gray head. "I thank God for you every night. Because of you I won't have to worry about Manda. I can tell by your voice you love her. You're gonna to be a good mother to her."

Madison swallowed before she spoke. "I'll do my best."

Nodding again, Velma drew her hand back and placed it on top of the pristine white sheet. "I know you will, child. I know, but I gotta ask one more thing of you."

"Yes, ma'am."

"I want you to go by the house and get a few things that belonged to Bridget and me. I want Manda to have keepsakes. There's a photo album, and baby things. Augusta Johnson, the neighbor on the right-hand side, will have the key. She takes care of things since I'm in here. I know it's a lot to ask, but it would make me rest better knowin' Manda had some of her mother's things."

"Don't worry," Madison reassured the elderly woman. "We'll go over there when we leave here."

Velma settled deeper into the bedding. "You take whatever you see. I ain't goin' back there no more. No sense waitin' until I'm gone."

Madison wanted to deny the woman's words, but seeing Velma's frail body, Madison realized she had accepted her fate. She had to be as strong. "Yes, ma'am."

"You just go see Augusta. She'll let you in."

The neat frame house had beds of begonias on either side of the walkway, and a large hanging fern basket on the wooden porch. Nothing about the house gave the appearance that no one lived there. By the time Zachary pulled up in front of the one-car carport, a light-skinned, full-figured woman with short blonde hair had come out of the brick house on the passenger's side.

"Can I help you?" she asked as soon as Madison stepped out of the truck onto the freshly cut grass.

"I'm Madison Re—"

"Reed," the woman finished in an excited rush. Her eyes rounded and she came off the porch and crossed the cropped lawn. "I'll be! I can't believe I'm talking to Madison Reed."

"Are you Augusta Johnson?"

"The one and only," she said with a gap-toothed grin. "Velma must have sent you. How's she doing? Me and some of the ladies of the church plan to go by there when they get off work. I retired last year. Taught Home Ec thirty years."

Madison wasn't sure which question or statement to answer first. "She's resting well. Miss Taylor said you'd have the key. She wanted us to get some of Manda's belongings."

Her eyes zeroed in on Manda in Zachary's arms. "My, she's grown." Grinning, she reached for the baby. It didn't seem to bother her when Manda didn't come. "You haven't forgotten Augusta, have you?"

The key ring finally came out of Manda's mouth and she reached for the woman, who enveloped her into her arms, then gave her a loud smacking kiss on her cheek. Manda grinned.

"Best sugar in the whole world."

Madison felt a jab of possession. "You must have spent a lot of time with her."

"Kept her while Bridget worked. My husband is retired too. He's off fishing," Augusta related. "She didn't want Manda in a day-care center. I kept her on the days when Bridget had to work or wanted to spend the day sitting with Velma." Her eyes saddened. "She was a good girl. The church was packed for her home-going. The Lord must have needed a special angel."

Madison thought, *What kind of "good girl" sleeps with a married man?* Then she looked at Zachary and thought of his mother. Men didn't always tell the truth. Zachary's father certainly hadn't. Had Wes lied to Bridget?

"Don't I know you?" Augusta asked with a frown, staring at Zachary.

"I would have remembered meeting you, I'm sure." He held out his hand. "Zachary Holman."

Her hand was almost as wide as his. "Pleased to meet you," she said, still studying him closely. "I'm usually pretty good with faces."

"Velma said you'd let us in," Zachary said, pulling the bib of his cap down over his face. "I'd like to get started. We flew in so we'll have to ship back whatever Madison decides to take."

Augusta handed Manda back to Zachary, then dug in the deep pocket of her flowered apron. "Got the key right here. I was just over here watering her flowers."

"The house and yard are so well kept," Madison commented, walking up on the steps.

"My nephew takes care of both our yards." Augusta

glanced at the freshly cut lawn, then followed Madison. "Hers is not that big. She used to love to just sit on the porch. Every time we visit she always asks about her flowers. She mentioned a couple of weeks ago that she wanted to send some things to Manda, but she wasn't sure they'd be welcomed."

Augusta stuck the key into the lock, then glanced over her shoulder at Madison. "Guess seeing you changed her mind. The Lord will bless you for that. She loved Manda, but Bridget was her heart. Manda was Bridget's. Wasn't nothing she wouldn't do for her. Too bad she let some no-account man get her into trouble. After Bridget was killed, Velma worried she'd let Bridget down by not caring for Manda. If she sent you over here, that means she's not worried anymore."

Madison entered the house. The first thing she saw was a large color picture of Manda and her mother. Madison's steps faltered. The sharp slap of betrayal hit her without warning. She couldn't do this. "I—" Her eyes shut.

"Take Manda and wait in the truck," Zachary said, seeing the pain etched in Madison's face.

"Where's my brain?" Full of regret and apology, Augusta slapped her palm against her forehead. "You're still grieving, yourself. You just go on over to the house. I left the door open. Make yourself at home. I'll help this young man pack."

Madison didn't argue. "Thank you." Taking Manda, she quickly left.

Augusta turned to Zachary. "Let's start with Bridget's room first."

Without hesitation Zachary walked into the first bedroom to the left, then came to an abrupt stop. Too late, he realized his mistake. Augusta stood in the doorway, her eyes narrowed.

"How did you know which room was Bridget's?"

"A lucky guess," he said. "I stopped by the store and picked up a couple of shipping boxes. I'll get them out of th truck." Zachary strode from the room, feeling Augusta's gaze on him, hoping she believed the lie he'd just told.

Madison hadn't said ten words since they'd left Velma Taylor's house, not even during dinner later at the restaurant. He knew she liked Italian food and thought that might cheer her up. It hadn't.

At least they weren't going to see Augusta again and he didn't have to worry that she'd remember him. He'd taken a chance on returning to Amarillo, but he hadn't had a choice. There was no way he would have let Madison come by herself. But he wasn't able to tell if his presence made things worse or better for her.

Sitting on the sofa, he stared at her closed bedroom door. It was only a little past eight, but she had said good night shortly after she had put Manda to bed thirty minutes earlier. He was unsure if she was upset about all the talk about Bridget or if she was simply uncomfortable being around him.

There was nothing he could do about either, unless she opened up to him. Reaching over, he cut off the light and sat in the dark.

He wasn't getting much sleep whether he was in the bed or on the sofa. Too many unsettling thoughts were running around in his head.

He had to find a way to tell her the truth or at least the part he felt she could handle. He was almost out of the door now; if he confessed everything to her, he didn't doubt for a second she'd kick him out of her life completely.

Camille had a miserable day. Even when things went right, she had a difficult time finding enjoyment in them. The reason kept flashing through her mind: Gordon didn't want to see her anymore.

There'd been no more phone calls, he hadn't beeped her, hadn't tried to contact her in any way. She'd gotten what she wanted and she was miserable.

The remote in hand, she channel-surfed, then clicked the television off. Uncurling from the sofa, she started for the bedroom just as the doorbell rang. A ripple of excitement rushed through her. *It couldn't be him.*

Even as she told herself it wasn't Gordon, she rushed across the room, smoothing her hair back as she went. Her fingers fumbled as she slid the chain back, flicked the lock, then opened the door. "Gordon!" His name burst from her mouth in a breathless rush.

"Hello, Camille," Gordon greeted, his voice as cool as his gaze. "I hope you don't mind my dropping by without calling, but I wanted to discuss an idea I had for your kids. Those in your caseload, rather."

As much as she cared about her children, she couldn't quite stop the twinge of disappointment. "Of course, come on in."

Briefcase in hand, Gordon took a seat on the white sofa. "Mind if I move this flower arrangement?"

Still standing, she picked up the pitcher of sunflowers and sat them on the far corner of the coffee table. "Would you like something to drink?"

"No thanks. I won't be here that long." Setting the leather case on the table he opened it, then looked up expectantly at her. "Could you sit over here? I'd like to show you something."

Camille sat and clasped her hands, then hooked her foot behind her lower leg. Perhaps that way she wouldn't be tempted to touch him, her body wouldn't remember his.

He handed her several sheets of paper. "It occurred to me that many of your children might think no one cares about them and I started thinking about what I could do to help them realize they were wrong. So I made some phone calls."

"These are pledge cards from athletes," she said, flipping through the papers.

"Money, time, personal appearances. They're at your disposal to use for visits or for personal appearances to help raise funds. This way you can utilize them the best way you want. I figured you'd know the agencies that could utilize the pledges most effectively." He reached in his coat pocket and pulled out a check. "The kids wouldn't want to see me, but this will help buy school supplies or whatever. I also asked the guys to work on their wives and girlfriends to volunteer."

Stunned, she looked from the check back to Gordon. "I don't know what to say."

He clicked the case closed, then stood. "There's nothing to say. You have a heavy load in more ways than one. Hopefully this will help."

She came to her feet with the papers clutched in her hands. "It will. In so many ways."

"Good. Good night." He started for the door.

"Is . . . Is that all you wanted to say?" she asked before she could stop herself.

He stopped and turned, his face expressionless. "I can't think of anything else."

Misery almost buckled her knees. Her eyes shut. It was over.

"Was there something *you* wanted to say?"

Her eyes flashed open. What she saw in his eyes caused her heart to beat, her pulse to pound: naked desire. "Don't go."

In seconds she was in his arms, his lips on hers. "You were going to leave me," she accused.

His head lifted. "If you felt a tenth of the misery I felt last night, I'm not sorry. You know why? Because then you'll have a fair idea of how much you mean to me."

Her knees shook. "Gordon."

"I'll say it again. I want all of you, not just your body."

Even as Camille's mind shied away from such a commitment, her body strained to get closer. Her lips brushed across his. "Can't we just enjoy each other?"

His arms unfolded from around her body. "That's not my way. I've never done anything by halves and I don't plan to start now."

Camille felt like screaming. "Why does it have to be your way or no way?"

"Probably because I'm a selfish bastard or because I love you. Take your pick."

Camille's eyes widened; she staggered back until the back of her legs came up against the couch. Her heart raced. She plopped down. "You—you shouldn't joke like that."

"Do I look like I'm joking?"

He didn't. His eyes were fierce, determined. She put her face in her hands. "I don't want this."

"You're lying." Her head came up at the accusation. "You're scared spit-less, but you care for me, too."

She surged upward. "Caring isn't loving. You have to have more to make it work. I know."

"You got it wrong with your husband and now you're afraid to try again."

"You're damn right." She shook her head fiercely. "I won't go through that again. The accusations. The arguments. I won't apologize for what I do or who I am."

He took a step closer. "I said I was wrong. Why can't you get over it?"

"Because it's the same thing my ex-husband said at first, but he changed his mind soon enough when trouble came." Camille drew in a shaky breath. "I—I didn't tell you everything. When Duncan, the man who broke into our apartment, got out of jail, he kidnapped his two girls, ages seven and five. There was a tragic traffic accident. Duncan and the youngest daughter, Laurie, were killed instantly. Paula was paralyzed from the neck down. Everyone felt sorry for the family. Someone had to bear the brunt of the tragedy and it fell on me, the case investigator."

Gordon kept silent with an effort.

"Everyone, including my husband, friends, and family, began acting differently toward me. A few told me that perhaps I had been too diligent, perhaps I should have left the children in the home. Gloria, Duncan's wife, was the most vocal and bitter of all. Although she had instigated the investigation of sexual abuse of her daughters by her husband, she said she hadn't meant it the way it came out. I had taken her words out of context.

"She blamed the department for her husband and child's death, the lifetime of misery the other child would endure. Newspapers had a field day at my expense. My ex wanted a future in politics. I became a liability instead of an asset. He filed for divorce. I left D.C. and came back to Dallas. Mother accepted me because she knew I needed a refuge, but deep down I think she feels it was my fault."

"It wasn't." He went to her.

She bit her lower lip. "Sometimes I think maybe they were right."

His hands circled her upper forearms. "No. Don't do that to yourself. You weren't to blame."

She lifted pain-filled eyes to his. "You weren't there."

"I didn't have to be. You care too much not to be sure. If there was the slightest doubt in your mind, you had to act. To do otherwise would have been negligent. If anything, you care too much. That's why you were upset the other day leaving Madison's office. You feel too much."

He understood her better than anyone. "You could hurt me."

"You could hurt *me*. But what we feel for each other far outweighs the risk." He brushed his lips across her mouth.

She quivered. "That's not fair."

His hands swept under her blouse and closed over her breasts. "Should I stop?"

She stared into his steady eyes and saw what she had thought impossible. Unconditional love. Scary as hell, but so was the alternative. Her hands went to his belt. "You do and you're a dead man."

Madison watched the sun push back the night. She doubted if she'd slept more than a couple of hours. Dressed, she opened the door to the bedroom and stared at the reason. Zachary lay sprawled on the sofa, one arm behind his head, the other on his bare, muscular chest. His jeans were unsnapped. His gaze captured hers and she felt breathless, lightheaded. Needy.

"Good morning." He came to a sitting position with the elegance of a giant cat. "You're up early."

She moistened her dry lips. "So are you."

He pulled his shirt off the arm of the couch, but made no move to put it on. "You want me to go get you breakfast?"

They'd purchased Manda food, but had decided they didn't want to bother with cooking and cleaning up for themselves. "I just want some juice." Dragging her gaze away from his hand lazily rubbing his flat stomach, she hurried to the kitchen.

She sensed him behind her before she heard him. Her skin prickled. Trying to ignore him and her body's reaction to him, she opened the refrigerator for the carton of juice. She turned. He stood in front of her with a plastic cup. Helplessly her gaze traveled over his wide chest and broad shoulders, then lifted unerringly to his mouth. She wanted—

Spinning around, she struggled for composure. Opening the refrigerator, she put the juice away with a hand that trembled. "I've decided I don't want any." Giving him a wide berth, she went back to her room and closed the door. She didn't come out again until Manda was awake and ready for her breakfast. Madison wasn't taking any more chances of being alone with Zachary until whatever it was that caused her to act so strongly toward him was under control.

They planned to take the last flight out of Amarillo Friday night. Velma had been transferred back to the nursing home that afternoon. While Madison and Manda visited, Zachary had taken the boxes Augusta had helped him pack and shipped them to Madison's house.

When he'd arrived back at the nursing home, he visited the administrator to express his displeasure that a stranger had been able to walk into Miss Taylor's room. He was assured that this was an unusual occurrence, that they wanted their residents and staff to feel safe, that's why they had surveillance cameras in each entrance and in the parking lot.

"How soon before I can view the disc?" Zachary asked.

Picking up the phone, the administrator called the security firm. "Wednesday by the latest. They have to run through all of it, then find the section you need," he answered, hanging up the phone. "I'll see that the police receive a copy."

"You have Ms. Reed's address. I'd consider it a big favor if you could send her a copy," Zachary requested. "Maybe she can identify the man."

"I'll take care of it."

Shaking the man's hand, Zachary left and located Madison, Manda, and Miss Taylor in the lounge. Velma had wanted to show off Manda and introduce her guardian. Manda had taken all the strange faces and attention in stride. Madison signed autograph after autograph with a smile. The only time she'd tensed up was when she looked at him. He took a seat in the back of the room. His time was coming. She wasn't going to be able to avoid him when they reached her house. He planned to make sure of that.

Tense, and bone-tired, Madison unlocked the front door to her house a little after eleven that night. Zachary stepped around her and continued down the hall with Manda. She'd been asleep since they'd left the nursing home.

Her nerves stretched almost to the breaking point, Madison closed the door and started for the bedroom. She met Zachary on the way.

"I'll bring the rest of your things."

"Thank you." In the bedroom, she undressed Manda, washed her face and hands, then put her in a fresh gown. Zachary had come in while she was changing Manda, but he had gone back out. She was glad he had. She wished he'd leave. She was too aware of him.

When she could think of nothing else to keep her from facing him, she wiped her sweaty palms on her slacks and went to the den. He was sitting on the sofa, his arm on the back of the seat, his gaze tracking her every movement.

Her stomach felt jittery. "Thank you, Zachary. I—"

"Sit down, Madison."

"What?" He'd never used that sharp tone with her before.

His arm came off the back of the chair. "I said sit down."

Her brow lifted. "I won't be talked—"

"It's about Wes."

She shoved her hand through her hair. "I don't want to talk about it tonight."

His gaze locked on her and he came to his feet. "Too bad, but I've waited long enough to tell you."

If he wanted a fight, he had come to the right place. "What could possibly be so important that it can't wait until tomorrow?"

"Wes was my half-brother."

Chapter 30

Madison sank in the nearest seat. "Your half-brother? But that . . . that would mean . . ."

"A.J. Reed is my father."

"Your father?" Madison was aware that she was parroting, but she wasn't able to help herself. "Your mother . . ."

His mouth flattered into a hard line. "My mother loved the bastard. She believed every lie he told her, but he married Vanessa. Vanessa's family had social connections if little money. She had more to offer than the daughter of a laborer."

"D-did Wes know?"

"He knew. We bloodied each other's noses over it more than once." He paced away than back. "I found out who my father was when I was in the tenth grade. Seeing Wes in his new Corvette while I walked, his expensive clothes, his big house, put me in a rage. I took it upon myself to tell him after school when I caught him alone. We fought like two wild dogs.

"I came home bloody and angry at the world, at what I thought I had been deprived of. I told my mama how I felt, and hurt her. For the first time my stepfather looked at me with something other than pride."

"You were hurting." She defended him. Years later he continued to hurt. "They understood."

"It doesn't excuse how I acted." He walked to the French

doors and stared out at the night. "I took it upon myself to introduce myself to A.J. You know what he said?"

Madison's stomach knotted. "Please, don't."

"He said he had a lot of bastards, but he only had one son."

Nausea rose in her throat. Fury propelled her across the room. "You make a hundred A.J. Reeds. Don't you dare let his stupidity cause you to feel less."

He almost smiled. "I don't. Through the years I learned I got the best of the deal." He brushed her hair back from her face. "I only envied Wes one thing."

Her breath caught.

His hands came to rest gently on her shoulders to keep her from retreating. "He was my brother and I loved him, and I mourn him, but I can't stop thinking about you."

A odd mixture of fear and anticipation swept through her. "You shouldn't—talk that way."

His smile was heartbreakingly sad. "You might as well tell me to stop breathing."

"We can't do this," she told him, her body trembling.

"Too late. Much too late." With infinite tenderness he pulled her into his arms, his head lowering until their mouths met, their breaths mingled, their hearts touched.

She couldn't seem to think clearly. Everything seemed centered on the kiss. She'd never been kissed as if she was all that a man desired, as if she was all that mattered to him, as if all his attention was focused on pleasing her.

His hand slipped beneath her blouse to close over her breast. Her breath caught, then snagged as his thumb and finger closed around her nipple. She moaned his name. "Z-Zachary."

His hot mouth took the place of his hand. He suckled. With a little whimper, Madison's knees buckled. Lifting her in his arms, he lowered her to the sofa then came down on top of her, his mouth taking hers again.

She wanted to feel his skin. She had to. Impatiently she unbuttoned his shirt and shoved the fabric aside. She sighed in pleasure as she ran her hands across his muscular flesh. "You feel so good."

He nipped her bottom lip. "Not as good as you feel or taste."

She licked his nipple like a hungry cat licking cream. He groaned, then made short work of the rest of her clothes, then his own. He took care of protecting her, then came back to her. His questing fingers found her hot and wet.

"I love you, Madison," he told her as he entered.

She tried to speak, but words wouldn't come. She'd never felt such exquisite sensations, never wanted to give as she did now. She wrapped her legs around his waist, her arms around his neck, and gave herself to him body and soul. He gave back, again and again.

"Come with me."

She was helpless not to. The husky, whispered words in her ear lured her. His moans of pleasure doubled hers. His muscled hardness fascinated her. His big body pressed against her felt deliciously decadent. His callused hands sent spirals of heat racing through her.

"You're all that I desire."

He pleased her, undid her, made her feel reborn. "Zachary."

His hands gripped her hips, his powerful body surged into her moist heat again and again. The pleasure mounted. All Madison could do was hold on and follow.

Instinctively she wrapped her legs around him, caught the rhythm, let the sensations sweep her up, then she was falling. With a hoarse shout of gratification, he followed.

Madison roused to feel to the hardness and warmth of Zachary's body next to hers. Resistance didn't enter her mind as he rolled on top of her and entered her. His eyes watched desire sweep through her, over her. The loving was slower, but just as passionate. Madison felt her body tighten, then she went over, secure in Zachary's arms.

She lost count of the number of times they loved each

other. If he was insatiable, then she was more so. It was as if she were in a thirsty wasteland and Zachary was her rain.

The next time she awoke it was morning and she was in her bed alone. Sitting up, the sheet dropped from over her bare breasts. The crib was empty. A glance at the bedside clock told her why. Eight-thirty.

Grabbing a robe from the closet, she felt the weight of the gold bracelet from Tiffany's on her arm. Zachary had put it back on last night. It was the only thing she had worn during the night. Thoroughly pleased with herself and him, she slipped on the robe and went to find Zachary and Manda.

They were in the den. Zachary's back was propped against the sofa, his knees raised to support Manda's back as he clasped her hands and played pat-a-cake. Love filled her heart for both of them.

He glanced up and smiled. "Good morning, beautiful."

Smiling, she knelt on the floor by them. Her hair was a wreck. She had no makeup on, but he thought she was beautiful. With Zachary, she felt beautiful. She kissed them both. "Good morning."

"Ma-da." Manda crawled from one to the other.

Zachary's arm curved around them. "We tried to let you sleep. You must be tired."

With an impish smile on her face, she looked up at him. "I wonder why?" She grinned when he blushed.

"Later I'm going to have to make you pay for that." He kissed her, then stood and helped her to her feet. "Now I have to go to work."

Disappointment slumped her shoulders, but she managed a smile. "You have time for breakfast?"

"Manda and I had a bowl of cooked cereal. Is it all right if I take a shower here? That will save time."

"If Manda was asleep, I'd scrub your back," she teased, enjoying herself immensely.

His eyes darkened. "I'm going to remember that."

"I'm counting on it."

* * *

Staring down at Gordon asleep in his bed, Camille brushed her finger tenderly across his cheek. He smiled. Trembling, she folded her hands on her lap. She'd done it now. She'd fallen in love. There was no escape. She loved him irrevocably, hopelessly. Slipping from the bed, she put on Gordon's short robe that was becoming hers, and headed for the kitchen. The moment called for breakfast in bed.

Her lips twitched at the thought. She hated to cook, but couldn't wait to make Gordon's breakfast. He'd be so surprised. For the past two days they'd been together, he'd done the cooking if they were at home. They'd quickly discovered they preferred being at home and together, than being out.

In the kitchen, she began opening cabinets trying to decide what to prepare. There was a rosebush in the back by the arbor. She'd put a rose on his tray. She'd get him the morning paper. After breakfast they'd make slow, lazy love.

"You're not the maid."

"Or the cleaning lady."

Camille whirled. Adrian and Adair. There was no doubt in her mind, even if the good-looking duo didn't look like their father or Camille hadn't seen the many photographs of them in his office and throughout the house. "I—" What could she say?

Adrian pulled his backpack from his shoulder and laid it on the butcher block in the center of the kitchen. *"Habla español?"*

"Parlez-vous français?"

"Sprechen sie Deutsch?"

Adair placed her oversized bag beside her brother's. "There are too many African dialects to run through. So . . ." In sign language she asked Camille her name.

"That's enough, showoffs."

Camille almost slumped in relief at seeing Gordon. Apparently his children were as precocious and brassy as they came. Just like their father. "Uh, if you'll excuse me."

Gordon caught her by the arm as she began backing out of the kitchen. "Camille Jacobs, my children, Adrian and Adair."

Adrian bowed from the waist.

Adair curtsied.

Camille blinked. "H-Hello."

"We might as well get this over with. Let me see them," Gordon said to his children. Neither twin moved. "Now."

Sharing a long-suffering look, they went to their father and stuck out their tongues.

Gordon relaxed. He never knew what to expect from his independent children whose IQs were in the mid-140s. "I would have hated to kick you out of the house."

"Ms. Jacobs, do you feel people have a right to express themselves?" Adrian asked.

Camille would have had to be a dummy not to know she had just been handed a ticking time bomb. "I—"

"That's an unfair question," Gordon interrupted.

Adair lifted a naturally arched brow. "Are you one of those women who lets a man speak for her?"

"No," Camille answered without hesitation.

"Excellent." Adair grinned triumphantly. "Your answer, please."

"It depends on the form of expression and, of course, the age of the one expressing him- or herself," Camille answered. "Too often young people bow to peer pressure and do things they would never think of doing otherwise. Then there are those who aren't expressing themselves, they're rebelling. Unless a person is mature and self-sufficient, I think all life-altering decisions should have parental approval."

Gordon laughed and hugged her to him. "Couldn't have said it better. There'll be no more talk about piercing your tongues. Go put your things away and I'll start breakfast."

Grabbing their belongings, the twins started from the room. Camille figured it was a great time to make her escape. "I'll say good-bye now. It was nice meeting you."

Gordon caught her arm again. "Why are you leaving? We'd planned to spend the day together."

"Gordon." Camille flushed and glanced toward the twins.

"I told them about us. That's why they came home."

Camille absorbed the information, then hit Gordon in the chest with the flat of her hand. "You knew they were coming and you didn't tell me. You let them walk in here and find me in a robe?"

"I didn't plan on oversleeping." She flushed again, but he wasn't finished. "I didn't tell you because I knew you'd make up an excuse to leave."

"What have I told you about your arrogance?" she asked, her voice rising.

"So sue me. I love you!" he said, his voice just as loud.

The fight went out of her. "I told you to stop saying that."

"I love you. You might as well get used to hearing it because I'm not going to stop saying it. I've loved you since you drove away from me at the meeting of the National Council of Negro Women." He gently but firmly pulled her into his arms. "I'm not about to stop. I know I'm older than you."

"Your age never mattered," she told him softly. "You're a wonderful, caring man."

"You won't mind marrying me, then?"

Her mouth gaped. She gulped. "Marry you?"

"I told you I wanted it all. Say yes and make me the happiest man alive."

Camille couldn't keep from looking at his children. Adrian had his arm slung across Adair's shoulder. They were smiling. "You don't mind?"

"After Mom died, Dad put his life on hold for us."

"We never had to trip over women or vie for his attention."

"If you make him happy, that's all that matters."

"Not *all*. What's your dress and shoe size?" Adair asked, her eyes sparkling with humor. "I promise to only borrow in an emergency."

"Say yes and put me out of my misery." Gordon pleaded. "You know I love you."

She looked into his steady gaze and knew he'd love her for a lifetime . . . just as she would love him. "I do love you."

Grinning, he pulled her closer. "I know. You're almost there."

Arrogant, impossible man, she thought. He'd never settle for less than total commitment. And neither would she. Instead of fear, she felt a peace she'd never known before. Her face lit with joy. "Yes, I'll marry you."

"Hallelujah!" Gordon shouted just before his lips took hers.

The twins erupted with laughter and applause. "Way to go, Dad."

Zachary watched Clarence pull up in his truck at the work site, then go around to the passenger side and open the door for Kelli. Giving him her hand, she stepped down onto the ground. Exchanging frequent, longing looks, they walked into the house together. Apparently they had been able to work through their problems. A man wanting to protect and cherish the woman he loved didn't mean that he thought any less of her.

Going inside, Zachary checked the blueprints against the structure of the house. If you wanted the structure to stand, it had to begin with a solid foundation. Relationships required a solid foundation, too. Different materials could be used for the foundation of a house, but in a relationship, for it to last, it always required complete honesty and trust.

To his regret, he still hadn't been able to be completely honest with Madison. He had reasons, good reasons, but he wasn't sure if Madison would agree. If she found out he'd lied to her about Manda's mother, everything would crumble down on top of him.

Madison greeted Zachary with a kiss that vividly reminded him of the passion they'd shared. When he finally lifted his head, his breathing was ragged. He handed her a single, long-stemmed pink rose which earned him another kiss.

Trying to ignore the growing ache in the center of her

body, Madison reluctantly pulled away and asked him to light the gas grill. Gordon and Camille were coming over. Gordon's twins were in town, but they'd probably zip in and out.

Zachary did as instructed, enjoying the smile on Madison's face, Manda on her hip as she finished setting the table. A man could get used to coming home to a happy family. That's what he wanted. He just hoped he'd have the opportunity.

Gordon and Camille arrived shortly after seven. As expected, the twins stayed only long enough to be cordial, then were gone. Madison didn't see the two-carat diamond engagement ring on Camille's finger until she was playing with Manda.

"Oh, my goodness!" she cried, hugging Camille, then Gordon. "I knew it!"

Zachary slapped a proud Gordon on the back. "Still waters run deep, I see."

Gordon took it in his stride. "When a man sees a woman he can't live without, he better grab her and hold on with both hands."

Zachary stared longingly at Madison. "I couldn't agree more."

That night when Manda was asleep, Zachary made good on his promise to pay Madison back for her teasing. She thoroughly enjoyed every moment in the shower, on the floor, in the bed.

"Zachary, your home is simply gorgeous," Madison said, her voice full of warmth and appreciation.

Inordinately pleased, Zachary watched Madison stroll through the dining room, her slim fingers lightly grazing the Duncan Phyfe table that seated twelve, the buffet, the restored mahogany mantle of the stone fireplace. He'd woken with her in his arms that morning and wanted her to see his house. Since it was Sunday and they were both off, he saw no reason not to bring her. They had already been upstairs.

"There are a lot of rooms still empty," he admitted, crossing the hardwood flooring to her.

"Finding the right furniture takes time," she said, her voice thoughtful. "You've chosen well."

"Thank you. Your approval means a lot."

She stopped admiring the three-step crown molding and sent him a saucy grin. "I approve of you a lot. If Manda wasn't due to wake up from her nap about now, we could go back upstairs to that big bed of yours and I'd show you."

He groaned. "Now I won't be able to sleep in there tonight."

Something flickered in her eyes. "You're not staying with us tonight?"

His hand circled her neck and drew her to him. His eyes were intense as he stared down at her. "More than anything I want to. I just don't want to crowd you."

"You aren't."

He pulled her to him, felt the slight trembling in her body. Desire or uncertainty, he wasn't sure. "I can't imagine not wanting to be near you, holding you, loving you. Never forget that." The smile that slowly blossomed on her face made his chest tight.

"I won't."

His head started to descend.

"Ma-da. Ma-da."

Their foreheads touched briefly, then hand in hand they walked across the hall to the living room. Manda, on several blankets, surrounded by bed pillows, grinned up at them.

Zachary scooped the baby up from her makeshift bed on the floor. "We're going to have to work on your timing, munchkin."

She squealed in delight.

Madison laughed and kissed them both.

The day had been wonderful, Zachary thought as he went down the hall toward Madison's bedroom. After they left his house, they'd gone to the aquarium, out to dinner, then visited with James and his family. It was dark when they finally arrived back at Madison's house. His plan was working out perfectly.

"I want to show you something when you finish," Zachary said, entering her bedroom.

A wicked gleam in her eyes, Madison glanced up from tucking Manda in her crib. "And I can't wait to see it."

Zachary's lips twitched. Shaking his head, he hauled Madison into his arms and kissed her. "I love that mouth of yours. Now, come on." His arm around her waist, they started down the hall.

"I'm partial to your mouth as well," she said, brushing a kiss across his chin.

"Stop trying to distract me."

"I will if I want," Madison said, loving the freedom to tease and love Zachary as the mood struck. It continued to amaze her how much she wanted him. She'd been desolate when she'd thought he wouldn't be spending the night. It had made her almost giddy with pleasure to hear him admit how much he wanted her.

She was looking at him and considering the quickest way to get him undressed when they entered the den. She reached for the buttons of his shirt.

"I told you to behave yourself." He cut the light out, placed his hands on her shoulders, then firmly turned her.

She gasped. Her hands palmed her face. A fire glowed in the fireplace. Directly in front was a blanket and several throw pillows from the sofa. Light reflected off the silver ice bucket, the neck of a wine bottle, and two wineglasses within arms reach. Soft music drifted from somewhere unseen.

"Zach, it's wonderful. Absolutely wonderful."

"You're sure? I got the idea when we made Manda's bed on the floor at my place."

She turned to him, her eyes misting. "It's charming and impossibly romantic."

He looked sheepishly proud. "I turned the zone air-conditioning down in here and I didn't add many logs to the fire, so you shouldn't get too hot."

"I'm hot already." She began releasing shirt buttons. "I think you have a way of cooling me down, though."

"What about the wine?" he asked, his hands braced on her waist.

"It can wait. I can't." Her hands splayed on his bare, muscled flesh. She bit.

He shuddered. "Me neither." Quickly he picked her up, placed her on the blanket in front of the fireplace, then came down beside her. "So many times in the past I've wanted to give to you, just to see you smile, to laugh." His fingers brushed across her cheek, felt her tremble. This time he knew it was with desire.

"If I gave you the world it still wouldn't be enough. You give me so much just by being you."

Tears misted in her eyes. One hand covered his on her cheek, the other palmed his cheek. "Zach, I feel the same way. I never knew I could be this happy, this free to love a man who loves me for me."

A moment of unease rippled through him. "Always remember I love you."

"How can I forget?"

The answer almost caused him to moan in despair. She deserved the truth, but he was afraid of losing her. He couldn't bear that.

Determined to banish the dark thought and show her how much he loved her, his hot, greedy mouth took hers in a shattering kiss. His hands stroked, kneaded, excited. As he felt the world slipping away, he prayed he'd always have her with him. She deserved to know the truth. Tomorrow. He'd tell her tomorrow, he thought as he forgot about everything but the woman in his arms.

Chapter 31

Sitting in her office Monday morning, Madison felt as if she could conquer the world. She couldn't keep the silly grin off her face and didn't try. The office staff munched on the danishes she'd ordered for them and speculated among themselves what had caused the change in Madison. She knew they were discussing her and she searched her heart and conscience to see how she felt about it, only to discover she wasn't concerned.

She wanted Zachary in her and Manda's life, and that was all that mattered. She was happier than she had been in years. She'd loved Wes, but somehow her love for Zachary was deeper, more solid. With Wes, she'd felt on occasion that she had to prove herself or measure up. With Zachary, all she had to be was herself. That was liberating and exhilarating.

"Madison, Gordon asked to see you immediately in his office," Traci said.

Madison glanced at Manda playing with one of the many toys the people in the station had given her. "Did he say what it was about?"

"No. He just said he wanted to see you immediately," Traci answered.

Rising, Madison went to the playpen and crouched down. "You did beautifully at the nursing home and yesterday at the restaurant, let's see about today." Her hand rubbed affectionately across Manda's head. "Traci will be here. Be Madison and Zachary's big girl."

Standing, Madison headed for Gordon's office. His secretary waved her in. Opening the door, she paused on seeing Helen, arms folded, her face tight and angry, sitting across from him. "Did you want to see me?" Madison asked with a frown of puzzlement. He knew she and Helen kept out of each other's way whenever possible.

"Yes, come in and take a seat." Gordon, his face impassive, sat behind his desk.

Unsure of what was going on, she perched on the edge of the chair beside Helen. Madison didn't have long to wait for her answer.

"*Noon Day*'s ratings are slipping. If they don't improve, it'll have to be taken off the air."

"I don't see why you have to have her in here to tell me that," Helen flared, snatching her arms apart.

"That's for me to decide," Gordon said calmly.

Helen refolded her arms, crossed her legs and started slinging her foot.

"I don't want the show to die," he continued. "There are too few black hosts already. If *Noon Day* goes down the tube, it'll reflect badly not only on the station, but on a black host."

"What can I do?" Madison asked. She didn't particularly like Helen, but she didn't want her show canceled.

Gordon placed his arms on his desk. "I want you to coach Helen."

"What!"

"What!"

Both women came to their feet.

"Madison, you're the best I have. I wouldn't ask if it wasn't important." His attention turned to Helen. "You'll listen and work your butt off or you'll find yourself without a job."

Shock swept across her face. "You'd fire me?"

"Your contract is up in two months. It would not be renewed."

"The bigwigs will listen to you." She planted her hands on his desk and stared across at him. "You can make them keep me on."

"I won't carry deadweight. The ratings climb or you're out."

"You bastard!" she yelled, pounding her fist on his desk. "You can't do this to me. I've worked too hard. You won't get away with this."

"I'll help if you want," Madison said, trying to help the angry woman. She'd be lucky if Gordon didn't fire her on the spot. He didn't take insubordination from anyone.

"I have some time in the morning."

Helen turned her venom on Madison. "I don't need your help! I'm as good as you. Better! They think you're such a saint. I know better. Your husband hasn't been dead six weeks and you're screwing around with that carpenter. Wait until the public finds out. They'll crucify you. I'll see to that. I've got the pictures to prove—" Her diatribe stopped abruptly.

"You've been spying on me?" Madison asked in stunned disbelief.

Helen gulped and remained silent.

"Answer me!" Madison shouted, advancing on the other woman.

"I—I was just mouthing off," Helen finally said. "If Gordon wants us to work together, I'm willing. I'll be in my office."

"Stay where you are, Helen." Gordon came around the desk. "If you hope to salvage your career at this or any other station, I advise you to start talking and it had better be the truth."

Helen correctly read the anger in Gordon's face and decided it was everyone for themselves. "It wasn't my idea, it was Edward's."

Hours later, Madison was still trembling. "She ruined her career and Edward's with her jealousy. In Gordon's office, they were both pointing the finger at the other. The station is not going to renew her contract. Edward freelances, but the *Morning News* doesn't want any more of his work. He's ruined his credibility."

"Don't think about it," Zachary said, stroking her arm as she lay beside him in bed. "She's out of your life. If either of them ever discusses you, what's left of their career is over."

"I know Helen and I were never close, but to find out a person you've worked with is capable of that kind of deceit is frightening."

Zachary's arms tightened. Was his duplicity any different? He'd said to himself he would tell her today. He tried to convince himself that he hadn't because she had enough to deal with now. That was a lie. He was afraid of losing her. But if she somehow found out before he told her, he stood a good chance of losing her anyway. Not wanting to think of that unbearable consequence, he kissed her, shutting everything out for the both of them except each other.

Good news travels fast. Bad news travels faster.

Helen's hasty departure from the station was considered good news; Gordon's engagement was bad news for every single woman and some not-so-single women who had tried to get his attention. It was difficult to tell which of the two was happiest as Gordon proudly introduced Camille to the people in the office. Those who weren't quite sure how to react to the engagement of an executive to the social worker who was investigating Madison quickly found out when Madison took the engaged couple to lunch at the Mansion on Turtle Creek.

Madison arrived home Tuesday afternoon just as a UPS truck delivered the boxes from Miss Taylor's house. She had them put in the hall. She'd decide later where to store them. As the deliveryman was walking down the walk, Louis drove up.

"Have you decided if you're going to take the Chicago offer?" Louis asked when they were seated in the den. "The president of the station called again today."

"I've decided to stay here." *With Zachary*, she thought.

Incredulous, Louis's eyes bugged. He jerked the unlit cigar out of his mouth. "You can't do that! They're willing to pay a fortune for you!"

"It's not the money." Madison tucked her bare foot under her. "I don't want to leave the area. Besides, I don't want to uproot Manda."

Louis barely kept from cursing. "This is the opportunity of a lifetime! Think what you could do with the extra money. I could even get Manda endorsements or modeling contracts."

Madison uncurled her foot and leaned forward. Her eyes were cold and as hard as her clipped voice. "Listen, Louis, and listen good. Under no circumstances do I want you to seek or entertain conversation regarding Manda doing *anything*. Do I make myself clear?"

"Sure, Madison. Whatever you say." He stuck his cigar in his mouth. "But Wes would have wanted you to take the job."

She came to her feet. A queen staring down her nose at her subject. "I'm doing what *I* want."

Louis wanted to slap that superior look from her face. "I never heard anything about Manda's father. You know who he is?"

Madison couldn't stop the startled expression that came over her face. "No."

"Since you have her somebody will want to make a buck or two with the information. Sooner or later it will come out." He stood, enjoying the panic in her face. "Things like that never stay hidden for long." He left wearing a nasty little smile. *That fixed the haughty bitch.*

Opening the door to his silver Jaguar, he slid inside. Half a block away he punched in a phone number. If he couldn't get money out of Madison one way, he'd get it another.

"National Enquirer," answered the chirpy voice.

"Let me talk to the editor. I've got something for him."

* * *

Madison's nagging headache had started with Louis's visit and became worse when Gretchen showed Wes's parents and the well-dressed man with them into the den just before the housekeeper left for the day. Madison recognized the man immediately. He was Thomas Quail, the Reeds' lawyer. He'd tried unsuccessfully to get Madison to sign a prenup when she married Wes. There was only one reason she could think of for him to be here with them.

"I don't want nor do I intend to claim any of Wes's assets that were not in both of our names," Madison said after they were seated.

Quail's smile was patronizing. "That might be hard to do since his father's name is on those assets."

"Then what do you want?" There was no sense pretending this was a social visit.

Once again it was Quail who spoke. "We've come to ask you attend the ceremony for the establishment of the scholarship fund in Wes's name this Saturday at his high school in Sugarland."

"If Zachary attends, I'll be there."

Vanessa's head snapped back. "I don't want him there!"

"It was through Zachary's instigation that the scholarship fund was begun," Madison told them.

Distaste curled Vanessa's mouth. "One good deed doesn't erase his behavior in the past. I can't stand to be in the same room with him."

"What about you, A.J.? How do you feel about your son?"

Both parents gasped. "That's a lie!" A.J. said, flushing and shooting worried looks at his wife.

"That's a libelous accusation, Madison," the lawyer told her.

She wasn't about to back down. "The truth is not libel. Despite our differences, I didn't say that to embarrass either of you, but I think Zachary has been ostracized from your family long enough."

"*You* think!" Vanessa came to her feet. "Who do you

think you are? You're just a little nobody my son picked up. He made you what you are. Don't you forget it."

For once Madison didn't feel anger, just pity for a woman so filled with hate. "You're Manda's grandparents. You can see her when you want, but I won't cut Zachary out of my life to please you."

"You're sleeping with him, aren't you?"

Madison stood. "Perhaps you should leave."

"You soiled my son's memory with that bastard," Vanessa raged.

"Blame A.J. for his parentage, not Zachary."

Furious, Vanessa turned to the lawyer. "Tell her so we can leave."

"Tell me what?" The nape of Madison's neck prickled with unease.

"After careful deliberation, my clients have decided to adopt Manda Taylor."

Madison's world reeled. "No!"

"That's not for you to decide," he continued. "Miss Taylor only granted you temporary, not permanent, custody."

"She will. I just visited her this weekend," she told them, fear streaking through her.

"She's an old woman, frail, her faculties in question." Quail smiled his greasy smile. "A judge would see that and overrule her."

Madison understood immediately. "You'd pay a judge off or get one of your friends to sit on the case."

The smile slid away. "I'd watch what I say or you'll find yourself being sued."

Madison ached to hold Manda, but she was too upset. "I won't let you take my baby."

"You killed my son's baby," Vanessa raged, her face filled with hatred. "If you had stayed at home like a decent woman our grandchild would be alive."

"Get out of my house!" Madison said, trembling.

"You won't be allowed to raise that child. I promise you that." Grabbing her purse, Vanessa left.

Madison looked at A.J. "Why? Why are you doing this?"

He didn't answer, just walked from the room.

"I'm flying to Amarillo tomorrow," the lawyer told her. "Don't bother packing her things. The Reeds want nothing from you."

Tears streaming down her cheek, Madison went to the crib and picked Manda up. Her baby. They were going to take her baby.

It took Zachary over thirty minutes to get Madison calmed down enough to tell him what had happened. Enraged, he'd called Gordon and asked him to find Camille and come sit with Madison.

"Don't worry. They are not taking Manda."

Madison couldn't seem to stop the tears. She couldn't stand the thought of Manda not being in her life. "She ceased being Wes's child by his mistress, she's mine now. I can't lose her. I love her too much."

"You're not," Zachary said emphatically.

Hope stirred in her eyes. "Their lawyer is going to Amarillo tomorrow."

"You have to trust me. I'll be back as soon as I can." Kissing her, he opened the door. "I'll take care of everything."

"Where are you going?"

"To settle a long overdue debt."

Two hours later Zachary stood on the walkway and stared up at the Reeds' imposing white mansion. The antebellum house sat on three acres of prime land. Three hundred feet from the back door a snappy speedboat was docked. To the left and around the house was a five-car garage. Every bay was filled. A.J. sold Mercedes and Cadillacs in his dealerships and he had the top of the line of each, but he also had a Bentley. Vanessa preferred to be chauffeured around in the Rolls.

And, as the old saying went, neither would spit on Zachary if he were on fire.

His large hands clenched and unclenched. He'd lived with that knowledge since he was sixteen. It had eaten at his soul, his pride. Until this moment he'd thought he had dealt with the hurt their rejection and hatred had caused. Now, standing in the twilight, looking at the house where he would never be welcomed, he realized he hadn't.

He'd hidden behind indifference. Lord, help him, he'd even hidden behind his caring for Wes. He'd used Wes to get back at A.J. and Vanessa, to rub it in their faces that they couldn't shut him out of their lives. He'd been a fool. He just thanked God that he'd come to genuinely care for his brother. The bond between them had proved stronger than the hate.

He'd stood in this very spot years ago, his heart aching because his biological father hadn't wanted him. Now he didn't care. He was finally free. And he'd be damned if they'd ruin Madison and Manda's life as they'd ruined Wes's, tried to ruin his.

Going up the steps, he rapped the brass lion's head on the door. An attractive black woman in a gray maid's uniform answered the door. "Yes, sir?"

"The Reeds at home?" He'd track them down if he had to.

"Yes, sir, but they aren't receiving guests. If you'll—"

Zachary brushed past her. "They'll see me. A.J. where are you?" he called out as he passed through the two-story entryway.

"Sir, you can't come in here!" the maid cried, her rubber-soled shoes slapping against the hardwood floor as she ran behind Zachary as he shoved open one door after the other.

"What the hell—" A.J. came out of the sitting room and abruptly stopped to stare at Zachary.

"Unless you want the maid to hear what I have to say, you'll tell her to find something else to do," Zachary said.

A.J.'s mouth tightened angrily, but he said, "I'll take care of this."

The maid looked uneasily at Zachary, then said, "Yes, sir."

"Wise decision." Zachary entered the room A.J. had come out of. "Evening, Vanessa."

Loathing flashed in her eyes. She surged from the silk sofa. "How dare you enter my house! Get out!"

"Believe me, I don't want to be here any more than either of you want me here, but you've gone too far this time," Zachary said flatly. "To think I was stupid enough to envy Wes."

"Don't you say his name!" Vanessa ordered, tossing the needlework in her hand aside.

"I'll say whatever I want to." Zachary's gaze went cold and hard. "You spoiled him, gave him things instead of your time. He grew up thinking he could have anything he wanted, that everyone should treat him the same way. He never learned how to compromise, to give instead of take."

"My son was the best. He deserved the best," A.J. insisted.

Zachary shook his head in disgust. "Did you hear what you said? What you both said? Wes was always *my* son to you he was never *our* son. You both tugged at him to love one more than the other. You won't get the chance to ruin Manda's life."

"I'm calling the police." Vanessa picked up the old-fashioned white phone on the ornate desk.

"Call them, and then I'll have to tell them who my father is. How Wes and I were born an hour apart. Is that what you want your friends at the country club whispering about? I can tell you it isn't a good feeling when you walk into a room and people stop talking. I know."

Her hand trembling, Vanessa replaced the phone. "Get out!"

"I plan to." He pulled an envelope from his pocket and removed a sheet of paper from inside. "My lawyer drew this up. Your signature on here will mean that you give up now and in the future any rights to seek custody of Manda. You accept Madison as her legal guardian."

"I won't sign it!" A.J. shouted. "She's all of Wes we have left."

Zachary's narrowed gaze swung back to A.J. "How long have you known?"

A.J. went to the bar, poured himself two fingers of scotch, then tossed it down. "Wes came down after she was born. He wanted us to know we had a grandchild." He tossed down another drink. "She was just some teacher. He couldn't ruin his career and his social standing by acknowledging the baby."

Zachary had heard it all before. People didn't matter in A.J. and Vanessa's opinion, money and social standing did. "What changed your mind about accepting her now?"

"The house gets lonely and she's all of Wes that's left," A.J. answered, his shoulders slumped, his face lined. He'd aged since Wes's death. Vanessa's face also showed lines of strain and grief. However, instead of clinging to each other, they chose to inflict pain on Madison.

Zachary didn't doubt the house was lonely. It couldn't be otherwise with two cold people living there. But he also wouldn't put it past Vanessa to want to get back at Madison because she was living and Wes was dead. She wasn't going to use Manda to do it.

"I promised Wes I'd take care of Manda and I intend to keep my promise," Zachary said, his voice edged with steel. "Manda won't be sacrificed to ward off your loneliness or to hurt Madison. Now sign the paper or the *Sugarland Gazette* will have a shocking front headline in the morning."

He'd done it.

Madison had sent Gordon and Camille home after Zachary called. Luckily, there were flights to Dallas from Houston every hour and there wasn't a cloud in the sky. Too keyed-up to sleep, she decided to put the boxes from the Taylors' house away. Picking one up, she glanced at *Warrior*, the picture of a majestic and fierce Zulu, and thought of Zachary. He certainly had been a warrior for Manda and her. Suddenly she was glad she had kept Wes's art collection. She was keeping *Warrior* and saving the rest for Manda.

Smiling, she continued down the hall to Wes's bedroom where she was storing the boxes. She was carrying the last one when it slipped, spilling the contents.

Squatting, she reached to pick up a book that had fallen open. The name on the page jumped out at her. *Wes*. Her body began to tremble. Slowly she picked up the bound leather volume and looked at the front page. *Bridget Taylor. My Journal.* The words were written in neat, precise script. Madison's breath caught, then trembled out. The decent thing to do would be to put it back in the box, but the lure was too strong.

Madison sat on the floor and started to read.

Chapter 32

Through the pages, Madison discovered a shy, sensitive woman who dreamed of finding the right man, a woman who hurt when she didn't have a date for the prom, a woman who lost her virginity her freshman year in college to a callous boy who later bragged of his conquest. Bridget had been hurt, but she hadn't given up on love.

One day I'll find a man to love me, a man who won't leave me like my mother and my father did. I'll find my own special love. I know he's out there. He has to be.

Bridget had met Wes at the San Antonio conference of the National Association of Black Journalists. One of her high-school honors English students had won first prize for best newspaper story and she had gone as his chaperone. Wes had presented the award. Her words were glowing and awestruck in describing him.

Wes Reed is even more handsome and charismatic in person than on television. My heart was heating so fast and loud when he was talking to me after the awards ceremony I was afraid he could hear it. He's charming and intelligent. I thought I'd faint, I was so excited. He's married. I know it's wrong, but I just can't stop thinking about him.

Madison turned the page.

I can't believe it! He asked me to dinner tonight. I accepted. One of the other chaperones is going to watch my student. I'm going to buy a new dress because I want to look pretty for him.

I had a wonderful time. It was the best night of my life. He took me to my first five-star restaurant. The maître d' and all the waiters acted like we were royalty. I knew it was because of Wes. We had an expensive bottle of champagne. He said the bubbles sparkled like my eyes. He told me I was pretty and smart. It was as if I had waited all my life for him. We came back to my hotel room. He kissed me and I just melted. I couldn't stop. It was too wonderful.

Madison skipped over the intimate details. But at last she knew the answer to another question.

Bridget had known Wes was married. Distraught, she had gone home to Amarillo without hopes of seeing him again. Then she'd found out she was pregnant. The pages clearly showed her panic, her fear of telling Wes, then her hope that he would eventually marry her, her near-depression when he would not.

I know I've disappointed Aunt Velma, but I already love this baby I'm carrying just as I love the father. He didn't trick me or promise me anything. It wasn't his fault that he thought I was on the pill. I could have stopped him when I saw he didn't have protection. I didn't. I just wanted him to love me.

I just got off the phone with Wes. He begged me not to have an abortion. His wife lost a baby. He said she still grieves. I told him no matter what I'm having the baby and I'll love it. I want our baby. I believe Wes does too. It'll help make up for the one he lost. He also still grieves. I can hear it in his voice.

Madison's hands clenched the diary. Could she really believe Wes had grieved for their child? Was it possible? All this time she'd thought their baby hadn't mattered to him. She'd been mistaken. Why couldn't they have grieved together? Opening the book again, she continued to read.

I'm in labor. I called Wes, but he can't come although he promised me he'd be with me. I'm afraid, but he said he's sending his best friend. He's already booked a flight from Dallas.

"You weren't able to keep your promise to either of us," Madison whispered. There was no bitterness in her voice, just acceptance that Wes had shirked his responsibilities to both of them. He was charming . . . and weak.

Madison turned the page to see which one of his cronies he'd sent in his place. She expected to see the name of one of his golfing buddies. She blinked. That couldn't be right. Hands trembling, she held the book closer and reread the entry.

Zachary is here, but it won't make up for Wes not being with me. I miss him so much.

Zachary. A crippling pain swept through Madison

Zachary had stayed with Bridget, coached her during her long labor, taken her and Manda home from the hospital. In the months that followed, he'd returned at least once a month to see that they were all right. He'd been the one to pay for Miss Taylor's eye examination, the one to help Bridget find a nursing facility for the elderly woman, the one to install central air when their window unit stopped working.

He'd been the one Bridget called when she needed help.

He'd known all along. He'd lied to her.

Betrayal. Madison closed her eyes, but was unable to keep them closed or stop from reading.

The last notation was of Bridget coming to Dallas to visit

Wes. Bridget had accepted that Wes would never leave his wife and marry her. But she was going to do her best to see that her daughter knew her father.

Simmering with anger, Madison was waiting for Zachary when he arrived late that night. He had played her for a fool. Just as Wes had. More so because, as much as she had once loved Wes, she loved Zachary more.

She stepped back when he reached for her, angrily shoving a bulging duffel bag against his chest. "Take your things and get out."

Clearly stunned, he let the bag drop to the floor. "Madison, what's the matter?"

Her hand trembling, she shoved the book at Zachary.

"What's that?" he asked.

"What's that?" she retorted. "Bridget's journal, that's what! I know. I know everything. All about Wes and Bridget. All about you being there for Manda's birth, the trips to Amarillo. The deceit. The lies."

"Oh no," he groaned. "Madison, please let me explain."

She evaded the hands reaching for her. "You knew everything and you never told me! You're as big a liar as he was!"

"I love you," he pleaded, his face pinched, his body trembling, his world turn upside down.

She laughed raggedly. "You don't know what love is. Get out and don't come back."

"I didn't tell you for this very reason," he tried to explain. "Please understand. I knew how you'd react. I know I waited too long and I'm sorry, but please listen to me."

"I've listened to enough lies." Stepping around him, she opened the door wider. "Leave and don't come back. This time I will call the police."

He didn't move. "Wes was my brother. Manda was my niece. I couldn't turn my back on either of them. Then he was gone and Manda needed you." His voice softened. "You needed each other. You would have never let either of us stay if you'd known, then I fell in love with you and was scared of losing you."

"You don't know what love it," she said, her voice shaking. "Love means being honest, trusting, sharing. Things you know nothing about!"

"Pl—"

"No! No more. I'll never forgive you," she said, tears streaming down her cheek. "*You knew!* You knew everything and you never told me!"

"Please try to understand why I did what I did. Please believe I love you," he said, his face ravaged with anguish and remorse.

Madison shook her head. The ache inside was so devastating she couldn't speak for the pain.

"Talk to me," Zachary begged. "Don't do the same thing to me you did to Wes. Don't shut me out."

She gasped. "How dare you!"

"I dare because I love you and I'll be damned if I'll let you get away. Did you ever think if you had reached out to Wes things might have been different? By your own admission you shut your emotions down because you didn't want to feel. You shut him out. You didn't share your grief. You gave up on your marriage, on him."

"He didn't want to talk about the baby," she said, her voice trembling with remembered grief and anger.

"Because he thought men weren't supposed to show their emotions." Zachary leaned his face closer to hers. "You're slicing me apart, Madison. I hurt. Don't shut me out. Don't do this to me. To us. Fight, hit, scream, whatever it takes, but please don't shut me out. Talk!"

"You hurt me!" she blurted, hating the scalding tears that streamed down her cheek, wanting to hate him just as much. She couldn't. "I've been unbelievably stupid to let two men, two brothers, lie to me, and I swallowed every word."

He grabbed her and held on when she tried to twist free. "You know I love you!"

Miserable, she shook her head. "I don't know anything anymore."

His hands fell, away from her. "You're tired. Go to bed."

"I don't want to go to bed!" she retorted, swiping a hand across her wet cheeks.

Zachary held out his handkerchief. "What do you want to do?"

She sniffed again, but she had fire in her eyes when she answered. "Drive your truck into the Trinity River."

He handed her his keys. "I'll get Manda. Lord knows how we'll get back."

Her hand clamped around the key ring. "You'd let me, wouldn't you?"

He stared down at her with unwavering love. "Haven't you learned I'd do anything for you?"

Once, she believed that was true. Now she wasn't sure what she thought or felt. Exhausted, she brushed the last lingering tear away, pushed the keys back into his hands, tried and failed to ignore the pleasure that raced though her at the brief touch. "Just go."

"I won't let you push me out of your life. I'm not losing you. I'm coming back in the morning and we're going to talk."

He stared at her, daring her to refuse. Madison said nothing.

"Believe me, this isn't over." Taking an envelope from his pocket, he held it out to her. "Here, you'll need this for Manda."

Too tired to respond, she simply took it from his hand.

Turning away, he left, closing the door softly behind him.

Madison stared at the closed door. Bridget had taken two men from her. First Wes, then Zachary.

Fighting more tears, she turned and saw the duffel bag on the floor. She picked it up and buried her tear-streaked face against the rough fabric. How could he have betrayed her when she loved him so much?

"Oh my god," she moaned. She lifted her head abruptly. Had she told him? Surely she had. She recalled all the times he'd told her he loved her, but try as she might, she couldn't remember her telling him.

Not once.

She told herself she should be glad. At least her pride wasn't totally shattered. But then she remembered how giving Zachary had been. How eager to give her what she needed, what she wanted. Her hands on the bag clenched. The envelope crackled. She stared at it, wondering if she should just toss it. She didn't want anything from him. She didn't need him. She could take care of Manda by herself. Couldn't she?

Sniffling she dropped the duffel bag, then opened the envelope and pulled out a legal document. Her hands began to tremble.

A.J. and Vanessa had signed over any claims to Manda. They agreed that the baby should remain in Madison's custody and care. The names of two witnesses were at the bottom. Betty Spears, the maid, and Zachary Holman.

Even as she rejoiced that she wasn't going to lose Manda, Madison thought of the one person who had made it possible. *Zachary.* She had no doubt that she would have lost Manda if he hadn't intervened.

Once again, he had moved heaven and earth to take care of them.

Madison's hand tunneled through her hair. Was Zachary right? Would things have been different if she had pulled herself out of her own pain and misery and anger at Wes long enough to reach out to him? Would he have turned to her? Would they have helped each other to heal?

Fresh tears formed on her lashes. She had no way of knowing. She *did* know that she hadn't tried very hard. Zachary *was* right. She had enclosed herself in her grief and hurt to the exclusion of everything and everyone. She'd pushed Wes out of her life just as she had pushed Zachary away.

But she wouldn't be a fool again. She jerked the front door open, desperate to stop Zachary before he drove away, and gasped when she saw him hunched over on the steps, his head in his hands.

He surged to his feet and whirled to face her; hope and love shining in his dark eyes. "Madison."

"Don't go," she pleaded. "Please don't leave me. I love you."

His eyes widened. In one step he was inside the house, kicking the door shut behind him. His arms closed tightly around her. "Say it again, please."

Laughter spilled from her lips. "I love you. I love you."

His mouth covered hers in a kiss that left both of them trembling. "I love you so much. I never meant to hurt you or betray your trust."

"I finally figured that out. To you loving means forever." Her smile faded. "You were right about my shutting Wes out. It takes two to make a marriage work. I stopped trying." Her finger stroked his strong jaw. "You wouldn't stand for me doing that for too long. Your not leaving proved that."

"I couldn't make myself leave." He kissed her palm. "I had a better example than Wes about how a marriage should work." His head rested against hers. "I realized something tonight about myself as well. Deep down I hadn't gotten over A.J. turning his back on me until I stood in front of his house and thought about how much he and Vanessa had hurt you. For me, that was the end of it."

"Then we're both free of the past," she said. "But, if you ever lie to me again . . ."

He kissed her quickly. "Never," he vowed.

"And you're going to marry me?"

He didn't hesitate. "Tomorrow, if you want to fly to Vegas."

She rubbed her cheek against his chest. "People will talk, you know."

His thumb made lazy circles on her arm. "I don't care. Do you?"

She searched her heart and listened to the comforting beat of his. "No. But the last couple of days have taught me that secrets never stay buried. Louis was even hinting at the identity of Manda's father."

"What do you want to do?"

She lifted her head. "Talk with Miss Taylor in the morning and, if she agrees, call a news conference. First, we're going to wake my parents and sister. Introductions and explanation are long overdue."

Fifteen minutes later, Madison hung up the phone in the den, still a bit stunned. Her parents had suspected her marriage was in trouble. They'd waited and worried for her to come to them. With Zachary's arm around her, she'd tried to explain about her pride and fear for her mother's health, but was brought up short when her mother asked, "When Manda is older how will you feel if you know she's having problems, but she won't open up for you to help her?"

Madison hadn't had to think long. "Miserable. A failure as a mother." She'd blinked back tears. "Mama, I'm so sorry."

"You're forgiven since you're giving us another grandbaby to spoil, *and* a son-in-law."

"A yummy one at that," Dianne chimed in on the three-way.

Madison had smiled through her tears. "I love you."

They'd chatted a few minutes more, then she'd hung up with a promise to call the next day to discuss wedding plans. "Your parents are next."

Zachary's mother cried when he told her he was getting married. Any doubts that Madison might have had that his mother and father would dislike her because she'd been married to Wes quickly faded. They were happy for them both and they were coming for the weekend.

"Now that that's taken care of, how about we take care of each other?" Zachary slipped off her robe and pulled Madison down on the couch.

His zipper rasped as she tugged. "An excellent idea."

* * *

After discussing her plans for a news conference with Gordon the next morning, he persuaded her to use the *Noon Day* time slot. They could use the first fifteen minutes to expound on the need for volunteers, donations, and programs to help children in abusive situations. The last fifteen would be Madison's. It was Zachary's idea to use the tape of the man in Miss Taylor's room which had arrived that morning to illustrate what lengths unscrupulous people went to to uncover information.

"Counting. Five. Four. Three. Two. One."

"This is Madison Reed, back for a special segment of *Noon Day*. Be sure and tune in tomorrow for the new host, Paula Dennis." She switched to camera three. "What I'm about to tell you is very personal, but I feel it's necessary if I am to live a life without fear. If Manda, the baby who I'm adopting, will live without fear. Because of my so-called popularity, people may be tempted to use any means necessary to ferret out information, no matter who they hurt." Camera one zoomed in for a close-up of her face, composed and determined.

"What you're about to see is the tape of a man who went into the room of Manda's great-aunt to get information about her father. Roll tape."

The camera picked up Louis Forbes when he got out of the cab, tracked him as he entered the building and lost him when he entered Velma Taylor's room. It picked him back up when he came out, his eyes wide and frightened, two minutes and thirty-eight seconds later.

Madison's hands clenched. She wished they were around Louis's neck. With difficulty she controlled her anger. Louis would get his. She'd made sure of it.

"The man you just saw was my agent. My ex-agent. When he left Miss Taylor's room she was having chest pains and was later diagnosed as having had a heart attack. He did nothing to help. What he did was unconsionable. He snuck into her room to find out the identity of Manda's father. He jeopardized a life for profit. To stop him and any other unethical person from any further harassment of Miss Taylor, myself, or Manda, I'll give the name of Manda's father."

Briefly, she paused, and gazed unblinkingly into the eye of the camera: "Wes Reed."

Standing off-camera, Gordon had to glare at the camera crew for them to be quiet. "The public thought Wes and I had a perfect marriage. It obviously wasn't. He fell in love with a bright, intelligent woman who died before her time. Unknown to the public, my co-workers, or our closest friends, Wes and I were about to file for divorce. He had taken a position in Chicago, and I was being courted for one there as well."

She paused briefly. A little more and she'd be finished. "Without the slightest hesitation or regret, I will decline the position and remain in the Metroplex."

Gordon pumped his fist.

"There are two special reasons for my decision. One is Manda; and the other one I'd like you to meet." Madison stood and beckoned. Zachary walked onto the set, a smiling Manda in his arms.

"This is Zachary Holman, a man of incomparable measure, the man I love and plan to marry." She leaned into him as his arm circled her waist. "It has taken me time to figure it out, but I know who holds my tomorrow. Talk, speculate, whisper. It matters not. *This* is what matters."

Lifting her head, she kissed him as their arms circled each other. "Love is all that matters."

"Fade to black," Gordon said, his grin huge and ecstatic. The cameras stopped rolling.

His arm still around Madison, Zachary walked off the set counting his blessings. The police would handle Louis. No one messed with Zachary's family. He had more happiness than he ever thought possible. It was only going to get better. He also knew who held his tomorrows and they were in his arms.

Epilogue

As Madison predicted, people talked, speculated, whispered, but true to her word, she didn't let it bother her because the people who supported and loved her far outweighed the people who didn't. Besides, she was too happy preparing for her wedding, moving into Zachary's house, finding a balance between caring for her new family and work, and renewing old friendships.

One worry she didn't have was finding an agent. She had been inundated with requests. Those numbers climbed once it became known that TriStar still wanted to take *The Madison Reed Show* into national syndication and if she wanted to stay in Dallas, that was fine with them.

Madison thought it couldn't get any better than the day she married Zachary. She was bursting with joy. She and Zachary spent the next two days in the honeymoon suite of the Mansion with a DO NOT DISTURB sign on the door. She already knew Zachary was an inventive and attentive lover, but he outdid himself.

As expected, when they arrived home, Manda had made out like a bandit with new toys and clothes. On outings she had picked up more loot. Her two sets of doting grandparents who had stayed with her had spoiled her rotten. She was a charmer and a heartbreaker-in-the-making.

It couldn't get any better, or so Madison had thought until

she held a screaming Zachary Lowell Holman, Jr. in her arms. Tears streamed down her cheek as she counted and recounted fingers and toes, checked him thoroughly and decided he was the most perfect, the most precious baby in the entire world. His father was just as awed, and didn't feel the least ashamed of his own tears or the fact that his hand was unsteady as he cut the umbilical cord.

As soon as Madison was back in her room, friends and co-workers streamed in. Three-and-a-half-year-old Manda was scooped up by her father and sat on the side of the bed to see her new brother.

"Daddy, how long before he can play with me?" she asked.

"Not for a little while, munchkin," Zachary said. "But you still have me."

She giggled as he swept her up in his arms and gave her a smacking kiss. Her Tiffany bracelet dangled on her wrist. "I love you, Daddy."

"I love you, too." With his daughter in his arms, Zachary reached for Madison's hand, then stared down at his sleeping son with pride and a heart bursting with love. "He's so incredibly small."

"Six pounds three ounces is just right, from my point of view. He can get big *afterwards*," Madison said with a smile.

"Men," Camille said, and frowned at Gordon. "If this one weighs an ounce over seven pounds you're in trouble."

Grinning, Gordon curved his arms around her bulging stomach. "It was probably a fluke that Jeremy weighed eight and a half pounds," he said referring to their fifteen-month-old son.

"Chastity weighed six pounds," Clarence announced proudly, as if he'd personally seen to the weight of his nine-month-old daughter.

"And we'd better get going to pick her up from the sitter," Kelli said; then, to Madison, "He's beautiful."

"Thank you," Madison said, gazing adoringly back at her son, tears misted in her eyes. He was absolutely perfect.

Immediately Zachary was by her side. "What's the matter?"

She blinked back tears. "I'm just happy. I have everything I've ever wanted."

Gently he brushed his lips across hers. "That makes both of us."

The door opened. Madison's parents, her sister, and Zachary's parents, who had gone to pick them up at the airport, entered. They rushed across the room. Hugs were given, Zachary Junior and Manda praised.

Through it all, Zachary's and Madison's gazes touched again and again. Life couldn't be better.

Or could it? There was always tomorrow.

Letter to Readers

Dear Readers:

I want to thank you for the wonderful support of *The Turning Point.* It meant so much to me as did your concern about my vision. I'm doing well. As for your inquiries about Rafe and Kristen, if all goes well their book should be finished by the time you read this letter. We'll have to wait and see if Nicole will get her own story.

I Know Who Holds Tomorrow is a different kind of book, but one that I feel will touch your heart just as much. What would you give for fame and fortune? Many people think if they just had enough money, if they could just make it to the top, all their problems would be solved. Perhaps, but as Madison Reed learns, money and prestige can't bring happiness. In fact, they can be more binding than liberating.

I hope *I Know Who Holds Tomorrow* made you think of the healing power of love, of how important family is, how you should never take people you care about for granted. *Tomorrow isn't promised and hugs are free.*

Have a wonderful, blessed life,
Francis Ray
www.francisray.com
e-mail:francisray@aol.com

Reader Discussion Questions

1. A lot has been said and published about the disintegration of the family. What do you think are the most important elements in staying happily married? Sexual compatibility? Financial success? Education? What?

2. Madison and Wes both had busy, high-profile careers and were often apart. Can a marriage survive if the couple spends a great deal of time away from each other? How?

3. In researching *I Know Who Holds Tomorrow*, I interviewed a lot of women to ask if, given the same circumstances Madison faced, they would take Manda. The majority said yes. Some even related they'd grown up in a blended family. Others emphatically said no way. What is your opinion? Why?

4. Zachary helped Wes because he loved him, and because he was his half-brother. Are there occasions when family members ask too much? Was this one of those times? Initially what would you have done in Zachary's place?

5. How do you feel about older men/younger women, and younger men/older woman being in a relationship? Can it work? Do you immediately rule out a person because of age?

6. People often show the side of them that is most flattering. Do your friends really know the real "you" or do they only see what you want them to see?

7. Who holds your tomorrows? Why?

Read on for an excerpt from Francis Ray's

When Morning Comes

Chapter 1

Sabrina Thomas clutched the leather-bound notebook to her chest and tried not to be impatient as the elevator in the south tower of Texas Hospital near downtown Dallas stopped once again on its climb to the eighteenth and top floor. But it was difficult.

Dr. Cade Mathis, the bane of her existence, would reach Mrs. Ward's room first and then there'd be hell to pay. Sabrina jabbed the button to close the doors as soon as the last person stepped onto the already crowded elevator. Evenings were always busy at the hospital with the staggered change of shifts and people dropping by to visit after work. Usually she didn't mind the crowd, but today wasn't usual.

Dr. Mathis wasn't going to be happy with Mrs. Ward's decision to postpone her surgery, and he wouldn't be shy about voicing his opinion.

The elevator finally stopped on the eighteenth floor. As soon as there was enough space to allow her to slip through the doors, Sabrina stepped off the elevator, excusing herself as she brushed by people trying to get on. Hurrying down the hall, she almost groaned on seeing Dr. Mathis's tall, imposing figure. At six foot three, he moved with a smooth, unhurried grace as he entered Mrs. Ward's room.

Sabrina increased her frantic pace.

Cade Mathis might be the best neurosurgeon in the country, but unfortunately, too often he had the disposition of a warthog in heat. And no one, at least as far as Sabrina knew, questioned him or went against his medical dictates. The hospital's board had gone all out to woo him from the Mayo Clinic. Housewife Ann Ward, in her mid-twenties, and her loving blue-collar worker husband a few years older, wouldn't stand a snowball's chance in hell of standing up against him.

No one on the staff even tried. As patient advocate for Texas Hospital, it was Sabrina's job to try. Her eyes narrowed. She'd do more than try.

Two steps from the door she heard Dr. Mathis's clipped, precise voice that could be as lethal and as cutting as the scalpel he wielded so skillfully. She didn't waste time knocking, she just went in. What she saw confirmed her fears.

Ann, in a patient's gown, was sitting up in bed. Her husband's work-worn hands clutched hers as he hovered over her as if to protect her from Dr. Mathis. Unfortunately, it would do no good. Dr. Mathis was a law unto himself and listened to no one, but that wouldn't stop Sabrina.

"Hello, Mr. and Mrs. Ward," Sabrina greeted. "Dr. Mathis."

The Wards' frantic gazes swung to Sabrina, clearly begging her to intervene. Dr. Mathis, hands on his lean hips, didn't even glance in her direction. Clearly he thought her insignificant. Tough. "Is there a problem?"

Ann nodded, swallowed a couple of times before she could get the words out. "I-I just told Dr. Mathis I want to postpone my surgery like I mentioned to you yesterday."

Finally Dr. Mathis's gaze, cold and cutting, swung to Sabrina. Since she'd been subjected to his disapproval before, she didn't cower as most of the staff did. Her first responsibility was to the patient. A fact that had put her at odds with her last supervisor, and the reason she had made the difficult decision to transfer from a Texas Hospital affiliate in Houston to Dallas six months ago.

"You knew about this yesterday?" he accused.

"Yes," she admitted, aware that her chin had jutted.

"And did she tell you why?" he asked, his tone no less cutting.

"Her daughter's birthday party is Saturday, the day after her surgery and she doesn't want to miss it," Sabrina answered.

Dr. Mathis's midnight black eyes narrowed, then turned to his patient. "You have a tumor in the brain. Every second we wait to go in is a second too long."

"I feel fine," Mrs. Ward said, seeming to draw strength from her husband, who now had his arm around her shoulders. "The medicine you're giving me is helping the headaches and my other symptoms. Clarissa, my little girl, wants me there with her Saturday. I've missed so much because I was sick for so long and could hardly get out of bed, let alone play or take care of her. I can't disappoint her."

"If you don't have the surgery, you might not live to see her have another birthday," Dr. Mathis told her.

Ann's lips began to tremble, tears flowed freely from her big hazel eyes. She burrowed into the arms of her husband and sobbed. Her husband looked scared and angry.

"Dr. Mathis—" Sabrina began, only to be cut off.

"The next time one of my patients makes a critical decision, I'd advise you to tell me and not wait for the patient to call me less than sixteen hours before the surgery," he said to her, then strode from the room.

Sabrina considered throwing the notebook at his retreating back, then wisely went to Ann to try to console her.

"What kind of doctor talks to a patient like that?" Mr. Ward asked, his body trembling as much as his voice. "Don't listen to him, honey. You'll be there to dance at Clarissa's wedding. Isn't that right, Sabrina?"

Two pairs of eyes, begging for reassurance, fixed on her face. "I hope you'll invite me," Sabrina told them. She'd made it a practice never to lie to patients. They had to trust her. She just hoped the evasive answer was enough.

"Let me talk to Dr. Mathis, and I'll be right back." Sabrina left the room and went straight to the charting area for doctors behind the nurses' desk. Dr. Mathis was there, his broad shoulders rigid, his mouth set in a tight line. The charge nurse, standing beside the secretary, kept throwing troubled glances at him. When Dr. Mathis was unhappy, heads rolled. Two other nurses decided they could finish charting elsewhere and moved their carts away. Sabrina didn't hesitate.

"Mrs. Ward was frightened enough without you adding to it."

Dr. Mathis finished making his notation on a chart in quick, slashing motions before looking up. He stared at her as if she were some icky bug that had dared cross his path. The look angered her just as much as the annoying unsteady pulse. He might have the manners of a warthog, but he was as gorgeous as forbidden sin.

"It's critical that Mrs. Ward have surgery sooner rather than later."

Sabrina trusted his knowledge. It was his professionalism that set her teeth on edge. "You could have told her differently."

Dr. Mathis slowly stood, towering over her five feet four inches, his unblinking black gaze locked on hers. "She's playing Russian roulette for a birthday party that can just as easily be postponed. The surgery can't."

"She—"

"Is dying, Ms. Thomas. Enough time has been wasted already. Patients are too emotional. They don't always think clearly. I thought it was your job to help, not make matters worse," he said.

Her temper spiked at his accusing tone. Knowing she shouldn't didn't stop her from stepping into his space. "Making things worse is *your* specialty, Dr. Mathis." She spat out the last word as if distasteful. Clutching the notebook, she spun to see two other doctors there. Disapproval was clearly visible on their shocked faces.

Sabrina cursed inwardly. In the short two years Dr. Mathis had been at Texas his reputation as a top neurosurgeon had grown. He was revered as much as he was feared. No matter what Drs. Mims and Carter might personally think of Dr. Mathis, doctors stuck together against the lesser mortals on the hospital staff. Doctors were never reprimanded—and certainly not in public.

And before now, she'd had a good relationship with both doctors. Her rash actions might have endangered that relationship. Even the charge nurse frowned at Sabrina.

One thing life had taught her early was not to falter over what couldn't be changed. Head high, Sabrina walked from the nursing station aware that the efficiency of the hospital grapevine would have their conversation all over the hospital in a matter of hours.

She didn't have time to think about it. Right now, a family needed her help. But how? She loved her job as patient advocate, but it wasn't an easy one. Often there were hard choices to make. Her job was to ensure that patients had the information needed for them to make the best possible decisions.

She knew firsthand how important that was. If someone hadn't been there to speak for her when she was too young to speak for herself, she wouldn't be alive today.

Stopping in front of Mrs. Ward's door, Sabrina took a calming breath. The patient's decision had been based on emotions, but reasoning—not anger—was needed to help her decide if her decision was the best one. She opened the door and wasn't surprised to see Mr. Ward still holding his softly crying wife in his arms. He glanced up.

In his gaze she saw helplessness, fear with a good dose of anger. "He had no right to upset Ann like that. I'm reporting him to the medical association."

Sabrina let the door swing closed. "Dr. Mathis is brusque, but he's also the best neurosurgeon in the state, possibly the country. He was at the Mayo Clinic for three years before coming to Texas two years ago. Patients come from all over the country to see him."

"That doesn't give him the right to scare my wife," Mr. Ward said, clutching his wife closer.

Sabrina knew he was doing his best to hide his fear. "Despite Mrs. Ward doing better, Dr. Mathis believes it's in

Mrs. Ward's best interest to have the surgery tomorrow as scheduled." Sabrina stopped at the foot of the hospital bed.

Mrs. Ward lifted her tearstained face from her husband's chest. "What do you think?"

Sabrina had been asked her opinion many times in her job and always answered truthfully. "Dr. Mathis might not have the best bedside manner, but few neurosurgeons have his skill in the operating room. He was sought by some very prestigious hospitals. Texas is fortunate to have a man of his gifts and accomplishments."

"He's rude," her husband snapped, clearly not wanting to let go of his anger.

"And gifted, as I said. He diagnosed your wife's condition when no one else had been able to," Sabrina reminded them gently. Grudgingly she had to give Mathis points for not pointing that out to her during their conversations. She'd never heard of him bragging. His accomplishments spoke for him.

Mrs. Ward glanced at her husband, then tucked her head. "The surgery has risks. He told us that. I just wanted to be there for Clarissa's birthday—in case—" Her voice broke, trailed off. Her husband pulled her closer.

Sabrina went to the bedside. "I might not have any children, but I understand why you made the emotional decision. Dr. Mathis made his decision based on your test results."

"If you needed a neurosurgeon, would you use Dr. Mathis?" Mrs. Ward asked, staring at Sabrina intently.

Sabrina didn't even have to think. "He'd be at the top of my very short list."

Mrs. Ward looked at her husband, then spoke to Sabrina. "Thank you. If you don't mind I'd like to talk to my husband alone."

"Of course. If you need anything else, just have me paged. Good-bye." Sabrina left the room, hoping that she had helped, annoyed with herself that she hadn't handled things better with Dr. Mathis, and even more annoyed with him.

* * *

Sabrina Thomas annoyed the hell out of him, Cade thought as he went through the hospital's double exit doors and headed for his car. He paid no attention to the hot blast of June air that enveloped him. He might not have been in Texas for long, but he was used to the stifling heat. What he wasn't used to was being questioned.

His mouth tight, he activated the locks on the black Lamborghini. No one at Texas Hospital, not even the chief of staff, had questioned Cade in the years he'd been associated with the hospital. Doctors from all over the country sought his advice. He was respected, feared, revered. He knew he was maligned—but never to his face.

Except by Sabrina Thomas.

Yanking open the door, he slid inside and started the engine. His mind still on Sabrina, he backed out of the space and headed for the exit gate. At first he'd thought she was on a power trip until he'd seen her more than once holding a less than clean child while talking to a patient or family member or buying food from the vending machine for patient family members. Dirty bedpans didn't even faze her. She didn't appear to mind doing menial things for patients or working late to push departments and agencies to help a family in need.

Sabrina Thomas cared about her patients. But she had to understand that patients didn't look at their medical conditions logically. Unfortunately, neither did she, which made for a bad combination, especially since he preferred a calm, nonconfrontational life at work and at home. His life had been too chaotic and uncertain growing up not to crave peace. He wasn't going to get that when they had the same patient.

The ringing phone interrupted his thoughts. He pushed ACCEPT on the wood grain control panel. "Dr. Mathis."

"Dr. Mathis, you have a call from Mrs. Ward. She says it's urgent," came the cool, efficient voice of his office manager, Iris, through his radio. "Your three late appointments just signed in."

He stopped at a red light. "Please tell them I'm on the way and put them in a room. I'll be there in less than five minutes." Some of his patients had difficulty getting off work so he had late appointments one day a week. "Put Mrs. Ward through."

"Dr. Mathis?" came the tentative voice. By all rights she shouldn't be alive. He'd stopped believing in a higher power for himself long ago, but he realized that for others there was such a thing.

He was different. He ruled his destiny, not some unseen force.

"Yes, Mrs. Ward." She sounded shaky. "Are you feeling all right?" As much as he disagreed with her decision, she was still his patient and deserved his best. He never wanted to give less.

He'd gone into medicine to show a man he hated that he wasn't worthless as he'd been told all of his life. Yet, somehow along the way he'd learned he could make a difference in people's lives, and perhaps make up for the fact that no one had been there to make a difference in his.

"Yes. I-I . . ."

"Mrs. Ward, I have patients waiting at my office."

"If it's not too late, I want to have the surgery in the morning as scheduled."

Frowning, he pulled through the light. "I haven't taken you off the schedule so there shouldn't be a problem. What changed your mind?"

"Sabrina."

Surprised, he turned into the underground parking lot of his office building. "Ms. Thomas?"

"She said if she needed a neurosurgeon, you would be at the top of her very short list."

Stunned—a rare occasion for him—Cade was momentarily at a loss for words, an even rarer occasion. He'd had the impression that Sabrina Thomas didn't think too highly of him. He hadn't minded. Usually, he couldn't care less what people thought of him. Never had. Had always thought he never would. "I'll see you in the morning. Good-bye."

"Good-bye."

Cade disconnected the call, pulled into his reserved parking spot, and got out of his car. He had patients to see and then he was going to track down Sabrina Thomas. They were going to figure out a way to work together without all the friction.

Which meant she wouldn't interfere with his patients' care and he would have his calm, quiet life back, just the way it was before she'd come into it.